The Battle for Dole Acre

Ian Marchant is from Newhaven in East Sussex, and was born in the same week that Elvis joined the army. Before writing books, he worked as a bookmaker's clerk, and in second-hand bookshops. He still occasionally gets bookings as a singer and stripper. An economic migrant, he currently lives in London, where he works as an antiquarian bookseller on the Charing Cross Road. His previous book is called *In Southern Waters*.

Also by Ian Marchant
In Southern Waters

The Battle for Dole Acre

a masque

Ian Marchant

Weidenfeld & Nicolson
LONDON

First published in Great Britain in 2001 by
Weidenfeld & Nicolson

Copyright © Ian Marchant 2001

The right of Ian Marchant to be identified as the
author of this work has been asserted by him in accordance
with the Copyright, Designs and Patents Act of 1988.

A CIP catalogue record for this book
is available from the British Library.

ISBN 0575 072067

Typeset by Deltatype Limited, Birkenhead, Merseyside

Printed by Clays Ltd, St Ives Plc

Weidenfeld & Nicolson

The Orion Publishing Group Ltd
Orion House
5 Upper Saint Martin's Lane
London WC2H 9EA

And so we came to Pancester, as vulgarly called Panster, once a good old town of great antiquity, but now a much decay'd port for vessels of no great burthen which lies, as it were, in its own ruins. Here's no manufacture, yet good company may still be found, though much reduced of late.

But I must not quit Pancester till I give some account of the fairs and queer festivals antiently executed there . . .

Daniel Defoe, *A Tour through the
Whole island of Great Britain*, 1724

With thanks to Ian Dicken and the Lancaster Musicians' Co-op, Stephen Grew and Kathryn Fahy, Jeff Woodman and Satori, Chrissie and Ben Gladwin, George and Adrienne Green, Cheeky and Ginger, Chas Ambler and dear Sir Gideon Vein, ECWM and Adam, Jill and Nell, Annette Green and David Smith, Mike and Sue and The Yorkshire House Quiz Team, Emi Manby and Monique Roffey. Without you crazy kids, this would have been a much shorter book.

Dramatis Personae

Terry Whittaker, a chef
Alex Whittaker, a retired tube train driver
Juliana Blezzard, a council official
Dr Q Sandahl, a museum director
Paolo 'Taffy' Gabatini, a record shop proprietor
Dawn Gabatini, a housewife
Gwyneth Gabatini, a restaurant manager
Nicolo 'Papa Nico' Gabatini, a retired café proprietor
Sally Gould, a social worker
Edmund, a tramp
Oliver Halton, a second-hand bookseller
Dexter Halton, a local councillor
Dolly Halton, a pensioner
Mrs Jocelyn Innes, a donkey sanctuary owner and antiquarian
Neil Winterburn, an archaeologist
Steve Medlicott, a builder
Sandra Medlicott, a hippy chick
Sydney Montague-Forrester, a nurseryman
Ursula Armistead, Aolderwoman and JP
Penny Lester, an interior designer
Emma and Gemma Robbins, schoolgirls
Trevor Mallinson, a businessman and chair of Pancester City
   Council Planning Committee
Professor Enoch Daggers, a naturalist
Brian Carless, a solicitor
Ash, a travelling metal-worker
Phil the Painter, Ronnie of the Pink Bus, Tony the Tunneller,
   travellers
Timmy Rubenstein, a television presenter
Zahid Ali, a newsagent
Frank Welford, a dairyman

Ted Blezzard, a shopkeeper
Francesca Salt, a food writer
Martha Buck, a cook
Dennis Alvey, a kitchen porter
Sir Kenelm de Courtney, a landowner
Donald McCracken, a police inspector
Christopher Turner, a museum director
Dame Margot Prosser, a Member of Parliament

and countless hippies, ravers, chefs, waiters, council officials, secretaries, receptionists, musicians, museum officials, archaeologists, television producers, cameramen, tourists, Gabatinis, animal rights activists, telephone helpline workers, innocent bystanders, antiquarians, policemen, bailiffs, stage heavies, Alarumists, plummeteers, ring-divers, nick-hangers, clanghandlers and ringlers. By kind permission of the Mayor and Corporation of Pancester.

For Madeleine Weymouth and Saleel Nurbhai

Elver Day

As Whittaker was well aware, as aware as you or I, throwing a large tin of pineapple chunks at your boss's head is no way to get on in business. Throwing anything at your boss's head is probably ill-advised, but tins hurt, and Whittaker was not really surprised when Ron Walton, owner of Rococo, the painfully modish mega-restaurant in Islington where Whittaker was head chef, rose from the kitchen floor, blood pouring from the wound on his forehead and said, 'You can take your Michelin stars and bugger off, Terry, don't you think?'

So that was that.

Whittaker had always thought of himself as the most even-tempered of the super-chefs, and he was almost as shocked by his tin-hurling as Walton. All Ron had done, after all, was to describe Terry's Wild Boar Liver Pâté as 'nice'. Terry's staff were shocked too. They all loved him, loved him for his uncomplicated amiability, his quiet professionalism, his openness and vulnerability. They called him 'Cuggles'.

As he sat in his flat that evening trying to think it through, Terry Whittaker suspected that life was conspiring to tell him that things were wrong. It was a warning signal, that tin-throwing fit. All was not well, Terry decided.

For one thing, he was bored, bored witless by London and the overheated world of London restaurants, bored by his occasional appearances on daytime television, bored by the series of recipes

1

he had been preparing for the *Independent on Sunday* showcasing new English cooking, bored bored bored.

And stressed. Stressed? Not many. Not only was he trying to keep his career running on track from success to success, the restaurant buzzing with happening hipsters night after night and the critics and pundits raving, but he was having to do it in the teeth of raging, rampant insomnia. He got home from work at two in the morning, and tried to sleep, his pulses ticking like Geppetto's shop. He chased sleep, laid traps for it, lay in wait for it, and just as it came he was jerked awake, every morning at around seven, as his father phoned him from the hospice.

'I loves ya, boy.' His father's voice, hard and commonplace, made Whittaker ashamed: ashamed of his father's lack of class, ashamed of his own snobbish sensibilities.

'Yeah.'

'I loves ya, you soft wanker. You all right? I didn't phone at a bad time, boy?'

'Yes, Dad. You did.'

'Why? Did I catch you on the job? Eh? Did I catch you on the vinegar strokes? Are you getting yours?'

'No, it's just that, like I say every morning, I work as a chef, very late, and this is early for me, and I'm finding it hard to sleep and could you please phone a bit later. About midday.'

'It's not early for me. I've been up all night. Thinking. And pissing. And coughing. I'm dying. I might be dead by midday.'

'Yes, Dad.'

'And what are you doing about it? Fuck all. My rich son, what does he do for his dying dad? Fuck all. That's why you can't get shagged, 'cos you're a cruel heartless fucker. Even if you are on the telly. On the telly, and can't get shagged? You're pathetic.'

'Well, Dad, it's been nice chatting. Is there anything you want me to bring you this afternoon?'

'You? What can you bring me that I want? Can you bring me health? Course you can't. Bring my sweets.'

'I always do.'

'I know. I loves ya, boy.'

'See you later, Dad.'

'If I'm not dead.'

'Sure.'

Terry usually managed to fall asleep again, but on the morning of the tin-throwing he had found it impossible. His pulses were banging too insistently. He got up, made himself coffee, and showered. The radio played 'Pretty Vacant' while he was dressing, and Whittaker thrashed with unusual savagery at his air-guitar, his fleshy white thighs wobbling at him in the mirror.

The song finished, and Whittaker put on his trousers while Wogan introduced the traffic report.

My father is dying, and I'm listening to Radio Two. I'm middle-aged.

He sat at his computer, and stared at the recipe for Lancashire Cheese Tartlets he was working on for the paper.

And stared. And stared.

On his way to work that morning, he had bought his father's sweets, and had stopped by to visit the old man in the fanatically expensive St John's Wood hospice which Whittaker was paying for. He was asleep, and Terry sat for an hour in his room, watching his lined grey face, listening to his snorting breath, smelling the decay from his father's lungs, his bones, his colon, before heading for Rococo and the fateful tin. That was one reason Terry was stressed, he guessed. No sleep.

And he was lonely. He shook his head in painful realisation of how lonely he was. His dad was right. He was pathetic. He tried not to think of it.

But that was why he had attacked poor old Ronnie, no question. He was bored, he was wound up to breaking point by stress, and he was so lonely that thinking about it made him want to curl up in a corner and sob. He wanted out, and he hadn't had the courage to face it. Well, now he *was* out, and it was going to have to be faced.

But what to do?

He was going to take a holiday. He hadn't had one for three years, years in which he'd worked his spreading arse off to get those two Michelin stars for Rococo, those glowing reviews. That was it. A holiday. He must get away.

He flicked through Teletext to see what trips were on offer, and speared a piece of pear from the tin on the arm of his chair with a fork. Strange how he still liked tinned fruit more than anything, after all those years of cooking sophisticated dishes for the well-heeled. The pineapple chunks, which he had been on the verge of opening when provoked, were to have been his lunch.

Terry slowly worked through the pears as he studied the availability of flights. There was one in the morning for Bali, and he pictured himself lying on a golden beach, gamelans tinkling soothingly, while he ate tinned durians, scented like a lavatory door. Then again, there was another for San Francisco, and Terry thought of sea-frets ghosting around the Golden Gate, cable cars winding up into the sunshine, and succulent California prunes in a thick, dark syrup. Or there was Ibiza – long nights of inappropriate E-fuelled partying and sexual adventuring, followed by languid days eating stewed apricots in the pellucid Mediterranean air. Nothing seemed quite to fit the bill. He dropped the empty pear tin on to the pile next to his chair, clicked off the TV, and ran himself a bath.

The water was displaced higher up the tub with each passing year, as Whittaker got fatter and fatter. When he started as a chef he had been like a French bean – now he was just broad. His face, once described as looking like a cross between the young Peter Purves and a middle-period Donald Sinden, now looked Churchillian in the shaving mirror. If he squinted down at his ever-growing little tits, pert and expectant like a pubescent girl's, it looked as though he was wearing a fur bikini. He rubbed his nipples with a bar of Neal's Yard soap and considered which of the various flights he might take.

No, thought Terry as he lay back in the warm water, no, none of the above. All he would do was pack a bag, get into the car, and drive off somewhere. He had always specialised in British cuisine – well, now was his chance to take off and find out something about his own country. A Londoner by birth and upbringing, the time had come to get out of town and up into the hills, to explore strange new dishes, to seek out new ingredients and new flavours, to boldly go where no chef had been before. It would be the equivalent of the Australian's walkabout, except he would be in his new Subaru Impreza, rather than on foot, and would stay in four-star hotels instead of improvised bush bivouacs. He would go where his juices led him. It would be fun. After a couple of weeks, he'd come back, and see what he wanted to do then. There was no great rush. He emptied the bath, got into bed and fell easily into sleep. He dreamed of man-eating pineapples.

When his father phoned in the morning, Terry told him he was going away on holiday.

'A shagging trip, is it? Will you get your bell-end polished? Where you going? Hamburg? Bangkok?'

'No, Dad. Just a driving holiday.'

'Wish I could go on holiday. It would be nice to go on holiday, instead of dying.'

'Yes, Dad. You'll be all right. The sisters say you're good for another six months yet.' Probably, he muttered under his breath.

'Fuck off then. Fuck off and leave me here to die.'

'Sure. I've fixed it so the sisters bring you your sweets. See you in a couple of weeks.' Terry hung up.

As he packed a bag, he thought he might phone Francesca one last time. To say what? Let's give it another try? I still love you? He had done it a hundred times before, and still she stayed with her husband and children. One more call might do the trick, or it might be the one to trigger a restraining order, forbidding him from contacting her. Face it, that was over too, a year ago now. A good thing, probably, thought Whittaker. Children need a mother. It's time to be noble. God only knows I've tried everything else.

He locked the door of his flat, and pointed his infra-red key at the car, which hummed and clicked into expensive life. A full-on lad-spec Impreza, and he'd never been further than Whitstable in the three months he'd had it. He'd been too busy, and still in bits over Francesca's return home. The two things were related, he suspected, if he was looking for reasons for losing it with Ron

Walton. It was time to get over them both, love and work, and time to start again. So he put his bag into the boot, started up the car, turned into Warwick Avenue, round the back streets of Paddington and on to the Westway, up the M40 and was gone.

He didn't drive fast, not as fast as the car was capable. He was out of practice, and cautious by nature. Before Oxford, he got off the crowded motorway, and stopped at a famous old inn in Thame for some lunch, a fairly creditable steak and ale pie, and then moved on again, always heading west and slightly to the north, always skirting around the big cities. By late afternoon, he had arrived in Ludlow. He parked the car, and walked around the little town. It was late February, cold but halogen-bright, and the setting sun sparkled on the river. This is nice, thought Terry. I'm a long way away from London here. What lovely architecture. He booked himself into the Feathers Inn for the night, and looked around for dinner. Every other building was occupied by restaurants, brasseries, trattorias, tapas bars, cafés, fast-food joints and pubs. Three of them seemed to have Michelin stars. He was reading the menu in the window of one of these, when a short lively woman wearing chef's whites came bustling out.

'Terry Whittaker! Cuggles! As I live and breathe! Come in, you fat old bastard, and tell me what's been happening in Rococo!'

'Hello, Ali,' said Whittaker. 'What are you doing here?'

'I live here. This is my place, didn't you know?'

'No, I'm sorry. I thought I hadn't seen you for a bit.'

'I suppose I should feel complimented that you thought about me at all. Come in, come in. Dinner on the house.'

Whittaker sat in the kitchen, eating Ali's mucked-about, over-fussy, post-River Café neo-Italian cooking, while she pumped him for information. He told her that he had left Rococo, and was looking around for something new.

'You should come here. Everyone else has. There are more Michelin stars per square mile in south Shropshire than anywhere else in Britain. It was you who earned them for Ronald Walton, everyone knows that. You'll soon get more. Got mine just this year. You'd love it! All your friends are here. Alan

Gregory has the Old Watermill, and Frank Kettle has just opened a post-imperialist Anglo-Indian. The *Guardian* have already given him an 8. It's just like being in London, except you can park. And the rents! My God, you wouldn't believe how low they are.'

'I don't know, Ali. I don't know if I really want my own place. I might. I might not. Besides, aren't there enough restaurants in Ludlow?'

'You can't have enough, not here. Look at this place – packed every night. People are coming here from all over the country. Stay a few days. Have a look round. Think about it. Christ, if the worst comes to the worst, you can come and work with me. How's Francesca?'

'Gone back to her husband. A year ago. It doesn't seem like home without her, really, Ali.'

'Poor old Cugs. I loved Francesca. Everyone did. Only food writer worth reading.'

Terry got up very early in the morning, so early that he was forced to go without his Full English in the hotel, and took the back way out of town, hoping Ali wouldn't be too offended. London was what he wanted to escape, not re-create. He headed north now, up the Welsh border and towards Chester. It was still only nine when he arrived in the old city; he bought a road atlas from a newsagent, and sat in a greasy spoon, eating his missed breakfast. Looking at the maps, he saw that it would be the easiest thing in the world to get on to the M6 and hit Scotland. He'd never been. If he wound the car up a little, he could be in Dumfries by lunchtime, and then see where he wanted to go from there. The Scottish Islands, maybe. You couldn't get much further away from it all than that.

A rather distinguished gentleman in his fifties, a solicitor, or an architect perhaps, sat reading *The Times* and looking over at Whittaker. He cleared his throat.

'Excuse me,' he said, 'I hope you don't mind me asking, but aren't you Terence Whittaker, the chef? I think I saw you on *Junior Masterchef.* Your fellow judge was Timmy Rubenstein, the comedy actor and *Time Gang* presenter. I like him, too. "I've got a wizard wheeze," that's him, isn't it? The girl from Norwich won it.'

Terry smiled and admitted it was true.

'Well, then, I'd like to say thank you. My wife and I had dinner in Rococo last year, after we'd been to see *Phantom* for our anniversary, and, my God, your Arbroath Smokie Kedgeree will stay with me for a long time.'

'Bit indigestible?' asked Terry.

'No, no, it was superb. And the breast of ptarmigan in balsamic vinegar! Marvellous. Worth every penny.'

Terry thanked the man, and wondered if there was anywhere he could escape the past. He stopped at Asda on the outskirts of town, bought himself some tins of fruit and an opener, and made for the motorway. It was, Whittaker imagined, foot-down time.

Four hours later, his fruit eaten, the syrup slurped, the empty tins rolling around the passenger's footwell, and sitting in the mother of all tailbacks somewhere north of Preston, Whittaker sensed that he would probably not make Dumfries by nightfall now, after all. This was no fun. He hadn't realised that it wasn't just London that was gridlocked, it was the whole motorway network too. For the first hour or so of creeping along, he had amused himself by ringing the numbers on the back of wagons from his mobile phone.

'Well driven? Phone 0800 782642 and let us know!'

A woman with a slight West Country accent answered.

'Hello? Truckers' Helpline. Can I help you?'

'Yes, hello, I'm sitting in a traffic jam behind one of your vehicles, registration S for sugar 9er3er6er T for tortilla R for risotto E for extra virgin olive oil, and I'd just like to say that, as far as I can tell, it is being very well driven. A thoroughly professional job.'

'Oh . . . er . . . thank you.'

'No, thank you. You're offering a very valuable service.'

The woman sobbed. 'No one's ever said that to me before.'

'Well, I'm glad to be the bringer of good news.'

'You're very kind . . . I didn't catch your name?'

'Terry. Whittaker.'

'Well, thank you, Mr Whittaker.'

'My pleasure. Goodbye.'

'Goodbye, sir.'

This had kept him amused for a while, so long as his tinned fruit lasted, but now he was going frantic with boredom, and to make the situation worse, the sun of the early morning had been obscured by a freezing February fog. The traffic inched through the icy vapour, which clung to the cars and made their windscreens opaque. He resolved to take the next junction, and see where he was. It didn't matter too much if he didn't make Scotland today. Nothing much mattered at all. The traffic crept for another five miles or so, and still there was no way off the motorway.

When the junction eventually came up, it was one of those funny little ones that you never see anyone use, right out in the middle of nowhere. The signpost said Pancester and Laikley.

I've never heard of either of them, thought Whittaker, as he took the sliproad. Funny how you can live on a little island your whole life, and never hear of places. At the top of the slip there was a brown heritage sign, pointing westward into the fog: 'Historic City of Pancester. 17 miles.'

'Might as well,' said Whittaker aloud, and followed the sign.

Even through the freezing fog, Whittaker could make out that he was in flat country, the fields drained by dykes skimmed with cat-ice. After a few miles, he flashed through a large but undistinguished village called Blackhampton, and then, for almost ten miles more, there was nothing at all, just more flat fields and stagnant ditches. The mist-wreathed road carried hardly any traffic, except that twice Whittaker passed two ghostly empty coaches, coming away from wherever it was that he was heading.

Suddenly, as he came around a sharp corner, the fog in front of him seemed to stir and lift as a light salty breeze trembled the twig tips of pollarded willows along the field margins. The late afternoon sun lanced the gloom and he could see where he was. The flat fields were now divided by what looked like tidal creeks, and rising in front of him from out of the marshy country, a mile or so away, there was a walled stone city on a rocky hill, crowned by a huge castle, glowing orange as the sun dipped towards the horizon, which shimmered with the promise of the sea. Far away to the north scintillated high snow-topped mountains. It was the most beautiful place that Terry Whittaker had ever seen. It would be nice to report that Whittaker heard angelic voices going 'Aaaah' too, but he would insist on listening to Radio Two while he drove, so he had to make do with 'Calling Occupants of Interplanetary Craft' by The Carpenters instead. Strangely appropriate, thought Whittaker. This was another world. He would park up and find somewhere to stay for a night or two. He passed the sign which read 'Pancester Welcomes Careful Drivers. Twinned with Brigadoon and Tilling', and entered the one-way system.

That's some one-way system, as visitors to Pancester will no doubt remember. The signposts offered Whittaker two options: 'Through Traffic' and 'City Centre'. Naively, he followed the City Centre arrows, which just took him right round the walls. The sun seemed to have brought out other drivers, and Whittaker felt that he was in a race. Cars whizzed around the orbital road; Whittaker became involved in trying to beat a disgusting old Maestro van, once white but now with a maroon bonnet and one green door, and forgot that he was supposed to be looking for somewhere to park. Whittaker had the better vehicle, the van had the better driver, and they were neck and neck on the twin-laned road. They crossed a sluggish estuarine river on a modern bridge; Terry was staring out the van driver, and so failed to notice the signs saying 'Parking' pointing up through a gate in the walls and into the city proper.

As Whittaker and his rival came round to the side of the city which was hidden from view on first arrival, he could see that there was a fair amount of building that was not inside the walls – the railway station and a large, over-full coach-parking facility, some waterside warehouses tastefully and obviously fairly recently converted into a four-star hotel and conference centre, a couple of sports grounds, some thirties semis with an arcade of shops: a newsagent, a car spares place, a fish-and-chip shop – and behind them all a large council estate and a small industrial area. Next to some scrubby meadowland beside the river, a graceful medieval stone bridge arched over a loop of the river and up through yet another gate into Pancester. A sign said 'Pack Bridge, Pedestrians Only'. The road divided, with a sign pointing to 'Laikley, 3 miles', and Whittaker's rival peeled off, giving him a grin and the thumbs-up as the Maestro disappeared, leaving Terry to finish the circuit of the city on his own. He came back to where he had come in; the signs said 'Blackhampton 11, M6 17'.

He started again, somewhat more assiduously, and this time spotted the way through the walls. He drove through the ancient gate and into a warren of steep, narrow streets, shop-front lights shining on the smooth pavements, pedestrians (many of them, judging from their fluorescent fleeces and dangling photographic equipment, clearly tourists) spilling out into the roadway. The car crawled through the throng, and Whittaker found it difficult to concentrate on the undoubted beauty of the honey-coloured buildings and the uniquely unspoiled character of the city, as he tried to follow the parking signs. They took him up past the huge castle and its attendant church, round the ramparts, and down into more streets packed with pedestrians, until the signs finally spat him out again on to the ring road, through the gate by which he had come in.

This place could do with a new car park, thought Whittaker, as he pulled up in front of the converted warehouses outside the city proper, but at least those fruitless circuits of the city had solved the problem of where to stay. He locked the car, took his bag from the boot and entered the lobby of the new hotel.

Framed reproductions of 'Spy' cartoons showing famous gentleman golfers of the nineteenth century lined the walls. A pegboard informed visitors that the North-West Regional Meeting of the British Dental Association was being held in the Charter Room. Sales reps from central casting sat around in the lobby sipping lager and talking shop with their sharp-faced wives in chairs which looked inviting, but which Whittaker knew from long experience would be just slightly too narrow for his comfort.

A Muzak version of 'Why Does It Always Rain On Me?' piped inoffensively from hidden speakers. A cheerful and pretty automaton greeted him from behind the reception desk. Her on/off button indicated that she was called Stacy.

'Good afternoon, sir. Welcome to the Panster Riverside Hotel. How can I help you?'

'Yes, hello. I'd like a single room for the night, please.'

A look of synthetic concern crossed her make-up. 'I'm very much afraid that we don't have any single rooms at present. The city is full of visitors for the ceremony, not to mention the dentists.'

'Oh, well, a double will be fine.'

'I'm afraid that we don't have any doubles, or twins either. We do have a large family room, or the Lady Abigail Courtney Suite, if that would be of service. It is rather expensive . . .' she said coyly, looking up at Terry from lowered eyes.

'How much?'

'Lady Abigail Courtney? That's ninety pounds a night, I'm afraid, but it does include the continental breakfast, use of a sitting room, and full en suite facilities, obviously.'

Ninety pounds a night? Expensive? A carafe of house white at Rococo was ninety pounds. Money, if I may be so vulgar, was the least of Terry's concerns.

'Could I take it for two nights?'

'Of course, sir. A pleasure to have you stay with us. If you could just sign here? And here? Will you be requiring a morning paper . . .' she extended her neck with a faint hum of servos, '. . . Mr Whittaker?'

'Yes please, Stacy. Could I have the *Christian Science Monitor* and the *Morning Star*?'

The creature smiled again. She had been on a course, 'Recognising and responding to jokes in a hotel environment'.

'Certainly, sir. I'll call the boy for your bags . . .'

'No need.'

Terry took the keys, and made his way to the top floor. The last of the westering sun shone through the picture windows. He looked out at the city, high on its rocky hill beside the brown slow-moving river, and smiled at it. He showered and changed before setting out to explore.

On his way back through reception, the android called, 'Is this your first time in Panster, sir?'

'Yes. Did you say Panster? I thought it was called Pancester.'

'Yes, sir, it's spelt Pancester, but pronounced Panster. Would sir like a brochure map?'

'Yes, thank you. And did you say something about a ceremony?'

'Oh, yes, sir. It's Elver Day. If you cross the river by the Pack Bridge, through the West Gate, and up West Street, you'll find the ceremony on the Guildhall steps, at about eight. Enjoy the spectacle, sir.'

The brochure map was called *Pancester – Where History Lives*. On the cover was a picture of a plump, rubicund man, dressed in a red frock-coat and a black topper, standing on the city walls, sounding a great silver horn shaped like that of a ram. Whittaker opened the map and walked along the riverside ring road. He came to the unkempt meadowland he had passed earlier. There was a hand-painted sign by the gateway into the large field. It said 'Dole Acre Donkey Sanctuary. Please Feed The Donkeys. Mrs Jocelyn Innes, Custodian.'

Whittaker liked donkeys, and he always felt they liked him. Two of them were standing by the gate, and he leaned across and scratched one between the ears.

'Hello, old donk. I haven't got anything for you, I'm afraid.'

The donkey nuzzled his hand, and Whittaker resolved never to serve mortadella sausage again.

He took his leave of the old animals, and crossed into the city by the beautiful old bridge he had seen earlier.

It was five-thirty and already dark, but the streets still teemed with life. Walking up the road that both Stacy and the map called West Street, Terry was forced off the York stone pavements into the cobbled gutter by the sheer press of numbers. The mullioned windows of the tall and elegant stone houses lit the way, as did the illuminated shop fronts and open doors of the crowded pubs. Here and there hot-dog carts did great business, one of them displaying an enigmatic sign written in marker pen on cardboard – 'No Elvers until after the ceremony.' The tourists made up a fair percentage of the crowd, but there were also large numbers of people dressed more conservatively, without cameras and camcorders, many of the men sporting Denis Compton hairdos, and many of the women with beehives. They looked very much like Khazak peasants, Terry thought – bad suits worn with migrainous Christmas jumpers, dresses and coats even the Queen would think twice about wearing. These Whittaker judged to be locals. He stopped a couple, and asked why there were so many people in the street.

'Visitor?' said the man suspiciously. 'Visitors should visit the Tourist Information Office.'

'Which is situated in the Castle Gatehouse,' said his female companion. They moved on, laughing to one another.

'Oh, thanks!' shouted Whittaker at their retreating backs. They did not respond. He turned to *Pancester – Where History Lives* for guidance. It said:

> Pancester is renowned for the survival of many of its ancient traditions, ceremonies and rituals, including Wally Oop, Elver Day, the Pancester Dole, Burning the Midsummer Ring, Apple Plummeting, Eastering, and Hanging Nick. Visitors requiring more information should visit the Tourist Information Office, which is situated in the Castle Gatehouse, where they can also buy tickets for the National Museum of Crime and Punishment and the Lady Abigail Courtney Museum and Art Gallery. We hope you enjoy your stay.

Both the map and Terry's earlier experience of looking for a parking space showed that the Castle, now revealed by the brochure as the National Museum of Crime and Punishment, was right at the top of the town. He passed into the large square in front of the Guildhall, where a small brazier full of logs behind a roped-off area on the steps waited for ignition. Opposite the Guildhall were two black and white half-timbered buildings, the first Whittaker had seen in the stone-built city: one a huge and beautifully preserved coaching inn, called Ye Blacke Bull, the other a large, brightly lit and clearly very busy café, De'Ath's. Heading up towards the castle, and passing more shops and pubs, Whittaker became uncomfortable. There was something missing, something not quite right. Whittaker realised that all the shops were small, family-run concerns, and that not one of the pubs was themed. The biggest shop he passed was a department store called Courtney's. But where were Debenhams, BHS, Marks and Sparks, the Irish and Australian concept bars; where were all of the usual bland franchised businesses which stripped high streets across the country of their individuality? Not here. He stopped another local.

'Excuse me . . .'

'Visitor?' said the man.

'Yes. I wonder if you could tell me the . . .'

'Visitors should visit the Tourist Information Office . . .'

'Yes, which is situated in the Castle Gatehouse, yes, but could you possibly direct me to McDonald's, please?'

The man stared hard at Whittaker.

'Macdonald's? You need shoes repairing? He'll be closed by now.'

'Er . . . no, I mean McDonald's, the burger place.'

'There's one in Laikley, I believe,' said the man, with a superior smile. 'If you require more information . . .'

'Yes, thank you, I'm on my way there now.' The man walked off. No McDonald's. This wasn't just another world, it was a whole new galaxy. Whittaker reached the castle, and walked around the walls, looking for the Gatehouse.

He found it, adorned with a huge coat of arms, and a sign saying, 'Welcome to the National Museum of Crime and Punishment', and in smaller writing, 'Abandon hope all ye who enter in', and in tiny writing, 'Director, Dr Q Sandahl'. In the Gatehouse, under the sign, was the Tourist Information Office, just as advertised.

It was like the usual run of Tourist Information Offices, with one major difference, in Whittaker's view, which was that Francesca was standing behind the counter helping an elderly American couple to book a hotel room. Why was she here, he wondered in shock, instead of reading a bedtime story to her spoiled brats, Satan and Beelzebub, or whatever they were called? Why wasn't she having dinner with the untalented misanthropic flabby-minded pasty-faced mummy's boy she'd preferred to Whittaker? Had she come looking for him, and somehow accidentally got a job in a Tourist Information Office?

Of course, it wasn't really Francesca, Whittaker saw after a moment's open-mouthed incredulity. In fact, where Francesca was short, plump and bouncy, this woman was tall, slim and elegant; where Francesca was dark, this woman was strawberry-blonde and grey-eyed; and where Francesca was full-mouthed with a strong jaw, it would be fair to say that this thin-lipped woman's weakest point was a slightly receding chin and a hint of over-bite, an impression that her teeth were perhaps slightly too large for her mouth. But there was something – or maybe, Whittaker thought, an absence of something – which they had in common, crucially so. Or how could he have mistaken this unknown woman for his mistress of three years? Yes, that was it. An absence. Both Francesca, and this . . . this . . . vision of glory, this goddess, lacked an awareness of how sexy they really were. It was something in the way they carried themselves. They didn't know why men followed them around like slavering dogs. They were also both completely indifferent to Whittaker too, for different reasons. This was not going to deter Terry. Indifference from women convinced Whittaker that they were crazy about him and spurred him on to greater and greater heights of fevered devotion. Actually, active hostility encouraged him even more, as we shall see.

Whittaker looked around him while Francesca Two dealt with the old couple. He picked up a few books, and turned the pages, watching her as her hands flickered over the keyboard of her computer. There were several colourful guides to Pancester, and a rather less well-produced pamphlet called *Laikley, Crazy Golf Capital of England*, which showed photographs of a muddy beach, a ratty zoo, and several crazy golf courses. He considered *Bygone Pancester in Old Photographs*, but as he leafed through it, and saw pictures of the Pack Bridge, the Guildhall, De'Ath's café and the castle, all of which looked completely unchanged, he couldn't quite see the point. But the ceremonies interested him, so he choose a facsimile book called *An Account of the Antiquarian Customs and Curious Survivals of Pancester* by the Reverend Clement Dadd, originally published in 1907, and took it over to the counter, where She, The Only Girl Whittaker Had Ever Really Loved, had just finished with her Americans.

'Can I help you, sir?' she asked, looking up at Whittaker. Her eyes, bright as bullets, seemed to drill into Whittaker's flesh. She knew everything about him, Whittaker realised; everything he had ever felt and everything he had ever desired was all laid bare before her gaze. He found that he suddenly had a painful and potentially embarrassing erection.

'Are you married?' said Whittaker dreamily.

'Sorry?' said the woman.

'No! Hahahaha! Are you married?! Hahaha. No, what I mean is . . . hello,' said Whittaker.

The woman raised her eyebrows, and a frisson of pleasure ran up Terry's spine.

'Ohh, my God, I mean . . . that is . . . I wonder if you can help me . . .' He looked at the name button pinned to her dress. 'Juliana. What a lovely name. Juliana. Anyway, Juliana, I'm a visitor, and whenever I ask anyone for directions, all they do is send me here. To see you. So here I am, seeing you.' He gulped, and tried to be cool.

'Well, where do you want to go?' said Juliana.

'Well, Juliana . . .' He leant forward again. 'Blezzard. Oh, that's not *as* nice, is it? Blezzard? Well, Juliana, I don't really want to go anywhere in particular, but what I would like to know is why are all these people here? It's so crowded. It's like Piccadilly Circus.' His attempt at cool was not succeeding, he felt.

'Are you not here for Elver Day, sir?'

'Don't call me sir. I can't bear it. Terry. Whittaker. No. Never heard of it. I'm not really here for anything. I'm just . . . you know . . . passing through.'

'Passing through? On your way from where to where?' said Juliana with some bitterness.

'Oh, you know, heading on the highway, looking for adventure. Footloose and fancy free. Single.' Whittaker raised his eyebrows and laughed. Ms Blezzard frowned and did not.

'Well, Mr Whittaker, Elver Day is when the City Alarumist, who is this gentleman here,' she said, indicating the red-coated man on the cover of *Pancester – Where History Lives*, 'gets paid by the Mayor and Aoldermen of Pancester for his exertions on the Ramstheng with a silver bowl full of freshly netted elvers from the Athon, which he then cooks on a brazier on the Guildhall steps. To celebrate this, all the children under eleven march in torchlight procession through the streets, culminating in a feast inside the hall itself. A feast of elvers, of course. After the ceremony, elvers are available in the pubs and from street vendors for those unfortunates without a ticket for the Guildhall.'

Whittaker was entranced by her voice. It was one of those Northern voices, most often found in Lancashire and Cumbria, where the 'R' is rolled at the back of the throat, as if the speaker is gargling with saliva. Perhaps you remember the old Hovis advert? The one with the brass band, and the old geezer going on about 'rrreal brrread'? Like that. Whittaker's own voice, what you might call a kind of Received Estuary, or default generic Southern English, sounded in his ears pale and anaemic by contrast.

'I see,' said Whittaker. 'Pretty obvious really. Is that horn the Ramstheng?'

'Yes, sir. The Alarumist sounds the Alarum with it every morning on the city walls. At six. In the morning.' She winced.

'How marvellous,' said Whittaker.

'Lots of people think so, yes. That's why all the tourists come. For the ceremonies. We're the seventh most popular tourist destination in the UK.'

'Well, I never knew that.'

'Oh, yes ... London, Stratford, Edinburgh, York, Bath, the Lake District, Pancester.'

'I never knew that.'

'No. So you said.'

'And are you going down to see the ceremony, Juliana?'

'I'm afraid I'm allergic to elvers, sir. Will you be wanting the book?'

'Yes please.'

She took the details from Terry's AMEX card, put the book in a 'Pancester – An Older, Better England' plastic carrier bag, and hustled him out of the door, while he tried, and failed, to think of a legitimate way to ask for her phone number.

'Thank you for calling, you fat-arsed blob of slime,' she said as he stood in the doorway, opening and closing his mouth like an impotent goldfish.

'Sorry?' said Whittaker.

'I said, have an interesting time at the ceremony. Good night, Mr Whittaker.'

She slammed the door shut, put up the 'Closed' sign, and drew down the blind.

'Good night . . . Juliana,' said Whittaker to the door. He turned down the hill to look for dinner, his heart full of undying love.

He looked around for a chi-chi little eatery where he would feel at home, but could find none. There only seemed to be pubs and De'Ath's, and De'Ath's was packed, so he fought his way into the crowded dining room of Ye Blacke Bull.

He managed to attract the attention of one of the surly waiting staff, and asked him for the menu.

'We don't have a menu. It's Brown Windsor Soup, baked cod, and treacle tart or cheese. £4.95.'

'Good God. Are you kidding?'

'Take it or leave it.'

'Well . . . I'll take it, I guess.'

The soup was cold and smelt of diesel, the fish was lukewarm and gelatinous, the vegetables villainously overcooked and the treacle tart hard as the waiter's eyes. Whittaker was charmed. He hadn't had a meal so bad since he was a teenager in the seventies. The service set new low standards. He paid his bill, taking care to leave an ironically large tip, and wandered out into the square to find a good place from which to watch the ceremony.

The square in front of the Guildhall teemed with life, both visitor and local. The vapour of their breath hung in the freezing night air. By standing on the steps of Ye Blacke Bull, Whittaker found he could see right across the square to where the Alarumist in his red frock-coat stood holding the gleaming Ramstheng next to the newly lit brazier. The Guildhall steps were covered with children, all holding unlit torches. The Alarumist raised the Ramstheng to his lips and blew one long blaring, braying note whose ancient tones rattled the windows around the square. The crowd fell silent as the Mayor, leading the Aoldermen, emerged from the hall, carrying a large silver dish. They all wore red robes and large black hats with feathers in them, the Mayor's dyed yellow and the Aoldermen's green. The Alarumist bowed to the Mayor, who bowed in return. The Mayor then turned to the crowd and shouted something – Terry was too far away to hear what. The mayor turned again and presented the dish to the Alarumist, who bowed once more, and shouted something else. There was a ragged cheer from those at the front who could hear what was going on. Then Terry watched as the Alarumist poured what looked like water out of the silver dish into a bucket, which he placed on top of the brazier. This was the cue for the children to start singing, and to come forward to light their torches from the brazier. There were at least a hundred children giving voice, but still Terry could only make out one or two words – 'Elvers' and 'Athon', nothing more. Their torches lit, they processed down the hill, still singing, while the Mayor and the Aoldermen watched as the Alarumist tipped the contents of the bucket, cooked now and no longer transparent, back into the silver dish. He began to eat his wage of elvers with a gold fork. More cheering started, and many of the crowd set off to follow the children round the town. Terry noticed he was standing next to the American couple from the Tourist Information Office. The woman smiled at him with expensive orthodontics while her husband sucked the scene into his camcorder.

'Wasn't that the cutest thing you've ever seen?' she said.

'I had a chinchilla called Barry when I was a kid. He was very cute indeed. Big floppy ears. But this came close.'

'Does the fat man in the red coat really eat the elvers, do you think?'

'They're very nice. I had them once at a hotel in Bath.'

'Really? Do you think I should try some?'

'Oh, yes. You'll probably never get another chance. I recommend them.'

'Really? You hear that, Zbigniew? This guy says we should try the elvers.'

'Well, they can't be worse than dinner. Jesus, I've never had anything like it.'

'Where did you go?'

'That place there. Deaths. I should have known from the name.'

'It's strange,' said the woman. 'This place is fulla tourists, but there don't really seem to be any facilities.'

'Somebody should do something,' said Zbigniew. 'Anyone who opened a decent place would clean up.'

Whittaker smiled a goodbye and started down the hill, pausing at one of the hot-dog carts to buy a paper cone full of steaming hot, freshly cooked elvers.

'Do you serve elvers all year round?' he asked the vendor.

'No, sir, just this one week when they runs up the river. I wish I could, they sell like hot cakes.'

'Why not sell hot cakes the rest of the year?' suggested Whittaker helpfully.

'No, I only sells hot cakes for Hanging Nick,' said the man, with a puzzled look.

Whittaker carried on down the hill, eating his elvers. They were superb, a little like whitebait, but with a faint aftertaste of seaweed. These would be nice seared in bacon fat, he thought, with a little puréed fennel.

On the Pack Bridge, the children were throwing their torches into the river and calling:

'Here be the torches to light the way,
Elvers come back another day.'

Whittaker watched the extinguished torches swirl in the

outgoing tide for a moment, before walking back along the river to his hotel.

The robot had gone off duty, to be replaced by a cadaverous night porter whose badge said 'Hi, I'm Dennis. How can I help you?'

'Hello, Dennis,' said Terry. 'Can I have the keys to the Lady Abigail Courtney Suite, please?'

'Nice Elver ceremony, sir?' said Dennis, as he handed them over. 'Not like it was in my day, of course.'

'I'm sure nothing is, Dennis. Good night.'

'You're right enough there. Good night, sir.'

Back in his sitting room, Whittaker drew the curtains and turned on the TV. He flipped through the channels, and couldn't find anything to arouse his interest. He wondered about taking advantage of the free five minutes of the adult channel, but wasn't in the mood. He hardly ever was these days. He clicked the TV off and reopened the curtains, to look at his view of the old city glowing on its hill. He rubbed his belly, and wished he had a nice tin of something fruity.

But still, he just couldn't stop smiling. Zbigniew had a point.

'I could clean up,' he said aloud to the world outside his window. 'I could bloody well clean up.'

An Account of the Antiquarian Customs and Curious Survivals of Pancester

The dining room of the Pancester Riverside was full of visitors for breakfast. Whittaker didn't fancy the continental; he contented himself with some grapefruit segments, and set off to explore the city with the Reverend Clement Dadd's book for company. The tide was out, and extinguished torches from the night before were washed up on the mudflats. Terry had remembered to pick up some apples from the restaurant, and he stopped by the gateway to the Dole Acre to feed them to the grizzled old donkeys. Over the Pack Bridge and inside the city walls, more torches lay discarded in the cobbled gutters, along with abandoned elver cones. A fat old tramp dressed in a greasy duffel coat, with a mouldy pipe sticking out from his full and filthy grey beard, was picking up the cones and scooping the remains of cold elvers from them into an old Courtney's carrier bag. He looked up and grinned through blackened teeth at Whittaker as he passed. Terry smiled back and made his way up through the town and into De'Ath's, where he ordered a pot of coffee and a plate of toast. He took out his book, and started to read.

As he read *An Account of the Antiquarian Customs and Curious Survivals of Pancester*, Terry learned of the origin of Elver Day and of the various functions of the Alarumist; and of how Sir Alexander Honeyball, the greatest of Pancester's mayors and the architect of the city's eighteenth-century renaissance, had courted controversy by replacing the ancient practice of having the Alarumist sound the curfew on a set of ancient handbells, known as the Clangers, with a modern, and somewhat more melodious carillon, which can still be heard, even today, each evening at nine. He read of the founding of the Pancester Dole by Sir Kenelm de Courtney in 1503, whereby pensioners from the city's two almshouses collect a dole of bread each morning in the parish church, in return for prayers for the soul of their benefactor. He learned that the Dole was paid for by the rent of a piece of land just outside the city walls, called Dole Acre. He remembered the donkey sanctuary, and wondered how much rent it brought the city. It couldn't be much. He read of Wally Oop, the great medieval street football game which engulfs the city each Candlemas; of how the city is divided into two perpetually warring factions for the game, the Ringlers and the Clanghandlers, and of how every able-bodied man is expected to take part in what is really little more than a vast and bruising street fight. And he read, with quickening pulse, of the courtship rituals of Pancester; of the Eastering, when the women of Pancester sleep out for the night and light candles on the Dole Acre, the unmarried in order that they might dream of their husband-to-be, their married sisters in order that they might fall pregnant; and of Apple Plummeting, the potentially lethal practice of girls throwing apples from the Pack Bridge into the Athon for their lovers to dive after; and of how, if the boys caught the apples, the girls would bake them into elaborate pastry cases, known as plummettys.

As he read, Whittaker couldn't help noticing that each of the practices had a feast or a dish of some kind attached to it. All these buggers do is eat, thought Whittaker. There's a whole traditional cuisine just waiting to be marketed. Elvers, traditional breads, hog roasts, puddings, the lot. This place needs a first-class modern restaurant dedicated to reinventing regional dishes for a sophisticated twenty-first-century clientele. This place needs me.

I'll tell Juliana. He had dreamed of her all night. Just thinking her name sent a quiver through Terry's body. Those eyes. She knows everything already, deep inside. She knows, just as well as I do, that we're meant to be together. I must find her.

He put the Reverend Dadd's book into his pocket, paid his bill, and hurried up to the Tourist Information Office. Juliana wasn't there, Whittaker quickly realised as he entered the office.

'Where's Juliana?' asked Whittaker of the very attractive but not the love-of-his-life woman behind the counter.

'Do you mean Ms Blezzard, sir? Ms Blezzard is the Chief Tourism Officer, and not likely to be staffing the desk, sir.'

'She was here last night.' From his pocket came the sound of a mobile phone. The screen showed that it was his father.

'Hello, Dad.' Terry grinned apologetically at the assistant, who turned to her computer.

'Didn't catch you at a bad moment, boy? Didn't catch you about to make a pearly deposit over the thighs of a dusky maiden?'

'How are you, Dad?'

'Still fucking dying, what do you fucking think? When are you coming home?'

'Um . . . not sure, Dad.'

'Where are you?'

'Er . . . Pancester.'

'Pancester? Is that on the Central Line?'

'No, I'm not in London, Dad. You remember. I'm on holiday in the north of England.'

'If you cared, you'd come home.'

'I . . . well, yeah, maybe you're right, Dad. If I did, then I would. The sisters giving you your sweets?'

'They steal my money. My fucking pension I've worked all my life for, and those old bitches steal it.'

'Good. Well, Dad, it's always a pleasure to talk. I'll give you a bell in a few days.'

'I'll be dead in a few . . .' Whittaker cut off his father, and turned off the phone.

'Sorry about that,' he said to the Tourist Office assistant, who looked up from her computer screen, 'but as I said, Ms Blezzard was here last night.'

'We were a little short-handed yesterday, sir. Is there anything I can help you with?'

'Yes. Where can I find her?'

'I believe she's in meetings all day, sir. Her office is in the City Hall, if you'd care to make an appointment for another day?'

'No thank you.'

Whittaker left the office, and continued his exploration of the city. He'd keep the idea of coming here to open a decent restaurant as a surprise for her. Imagine how pleased she'd be, Whittaker thought.

He decided to save the National Museum of Crime and Punishment for another day, but he did visit the Lady Abigail Courtney Museum and Art Gallery, where he saw the Clangers and the Charter of 1503 which established the Pancester Dole. He stared at some fine portraits of Sir Kenelm de Courtney and Sir Alexander Honeyball. He saw a display of wax apple plummettys, and was amazed by the intricate basket-like pastry cases.

One of them, drop of crème fraîche, eleven quid, thought Whittaker.

He learned that Lady Abigail, who had died in 1952, had spent a great part of her personal fortune on restoration work in the city, not just on the museum, but also on the Pack Bridge, which had been in danger of falling into the Athon. The museum had been renamed in her honour after her death. There was a portrait of her too. She was very thin, with a pointed nose and a sharp chin, and was dressed in tweeds. A toy poodle sat on her lap.

He visited St Gilbert's, the fine old parish church which stood next to the castle. He marvelled at the Anglo-Saxon foundations and apse, the Norman porch, the Early English nave, the Perpendicular steeple, clerestory and Lady Chapel, the exquisite carved reredos, and the unusual piscina. He also visited the Roman Catholic cathedral, the Holy English Martyrs, down by the Great Gate, but it was Victorian Gothic, the most modern building inside the city walls, and not to his taste. He visited the Banqueting Room in the Guildhall, and wondered at the array of silver billhooks that hung from the ceiling, one presented to the city by each of its mayors since 1493. He was hungry.

He didn't fancy De'Ath's or Ye Blacke Bull, so he walked through the labyrinthine streets, looking for somewhere at least bearable that he hadn't tried. Out of one corner of the Guildhall Square he saw an archway, with a sign saying Shy Street. He passed under the arch, and found himself in a small street which opened out into a little square, and which led down to the walkway around the city walls. There were several shops and a café. He looked in the window of a second-hand bookshop called Heavily Foxed. The door tinkled as he went in, but the shop was empty, although Whittaker could have sworn that he saw a figure scuttling through into the back as he entered.

Whittaker looked around at the shelves. All the Pancester favourites were represented: Warwick Deeping, Jeffrey Farnol, Howard Spring, Edgar Wallace, *Green Dolphin Country* by Elizabeth Goudge; but there were also works by great thinkers (such as *Reflections* by C. E. M. Joad and Colin Wilson's radical *The Outsider*), and the great travel writers (*In Search of England* by H. V. Morton, and *The Lake Country* by Arthur Mee). There was history (*Corn Law Reform in Maidstone, 1835–1846* by Prof. Qu Ziang Lee), religion (*It's Very Blue Here – more voices of Doris Stokes*), ethnography (*Betel Chewing amongst the Pava-Pavas of East New Guinea* by Bishop Edwin Blastover), architecture (*Bus Stops of Huntingdonshire* by E. W. Pugh), art (*Bulgarian Watercolourists of the Nineteenth Century* by Crispin Tolby) and science (*Pass School Certificate Physics* by J. C. W. Hemmery). Yet, despite this pantheon of literary giants, Heavily Foxed clearly lay largely undisturbed from one week to the next, the stale air smelling slightly of urine.

Whittaker called, and called again. The dust hung heavy in the room.

'Hello!' bellowed Whittaker one last time, and a man's head popped out from round the corner of the door to the back room, eyebrows raised in query. It was the most handsome head that Terry had ever seen. It looked as though it was the head-child of Clint Eastwood and Audrey Hepburn. It was a head which would have been remarkable in Hollywood, and which in Pancester made Whittaker strangely flustered. The body might have been good too, but Whittaker couldn't see it, as it stayed hidden in the back room.

Whittaker said, 'Oh . . . hello. I'm . . . sorry to disturb you. It's just that, I was wondering if, by any chance, you had any books of local recipes, anything of that sort.'

The head shook, and disappeared again.

'Thanks!' shouted Whittaker as he left. 'Sorry to disturb you!'

Now Whittaker stood outside the bookshop, and turned his attention to the café next door. It was brown. The paintwork was brown. The windows were brown with nicotine and tar. A brown sign above the window announced that it was called 'The 4i's Coffee Bar'. There were steps down into the basement where there was clearly a small shop of some kind. Another more colourful sign announced it as 'The Rock Cave, Pancester's Top Pop Platter Stop!'

Whittaker went inside the coffee bar. It was brown. Yellowing signed photographs of Vince Eager and Terry Dene hung from brown walls. A young woman, almost orange with fake tan, stood at the brown counter, a fly-blown glass display cabinet full of sweets beside an ancient boiler and an antediluvian cash register. Whittaker ordered coffee and a bacon sandwich. The coffee was largely froth, and was served in a shallow glass cup.

Authentic, thought Terry. Sound thumped through the floor from the Rock Cave.

The bacon sandwich, when it came, was rather good. The only other customer, a youth of eighteen or so who was dressed like a teddy boy, chatted to the waitress.

It was a long room, three tables wide by seven long, with the counter at the back, and the kitchen behind. Well proportioned, Whittaker thought. Easy to work. Fifty, sixty seats maybe if you took out these old tables. Through the unwashed windows at the front, Whittaker noticed again that it opened on to the courtyard.

You could put tables out there in good weather, thought Whittaker. He settled down to read some more selections from Dadd's *Account*.

This time, he read of the medieval Pancester Mummers' Play, which is produced every Plough Monday by the losers at Wally

Oop, largely unchanged from at least the late fifteenth century; and of the fire festivals: Burning the Midsummer Ring and Hanging Nick, with its traditional Nick cakes. But his concentration kept wandering, and he found himself watching passers-by through the grubby windows of the café. Everyone walks much slower here than in London, thought Whittaker, locals and tourists alike. And everyone looks much less worried, somehow. And people know one another. He watched as, time and again, people would stop and talk to one another. OK, so the locals might not be wholly welcoming to the tourists at first, but there's a rhythm in Pancester that's relaxed and easygoing. No wonder visitors flock here, thought Whittaker. This city is a cash cow, waiting to be milked.

He went back to the counter, to order some more coffee-scented froth, and, with a lurch in his stomach, realised that there was a handwritten notice stuck inside the display cabinet, almost obscured by grime.

It read:

'Business for Sale. Apply within.'

'Excuse me,' said Whittaker, 'but is this business really for sale?'

'Aye,' said the waitress.

'Is it really? Is it? Look . . . are you the owner?'

'Noh.'

'Well, who is?'

'Taffy.'

'And where can I find Taffy? Is he here?'

'Noh. He's downstairs.'

'In the Rock Cave?'

'Aye.'

'Thank you for all your help.'

Whittaker looked around him again, and then stood outside the coffee bar, looking at the building. Georgian, Whittaker thought. He smiled, and walked down the steps into the Rock Cave.

The basement room was built to the same proportions as the café upstairs. It had a low ceiling, and Whittaker had to duck as he came through the door. The room was lined with hundreds of second-hand records and CDs, and the walls were covered with more signed photos: 'All the best, Taffy, Helen Shapiro', 'Taff, don't stop the rock, Billy Fury'. Eddie Cochran's 'Twenty Flight Rock' was playing over crackling loudspeakers. An odd-looking man, of medium height, dressed, like the boy upstairs, in a drape coat and drainpipe jeans, was behind the counter at the back.

'Can I 'elp you, bach, or are you just browsing?' he said cheerfully, in a strange accent which he clearly felt was Welsh.

'I'm looking for Taffy. I'm sorry, I don't know the surname.'

'Gabatini. Taffy Gabatini, that's me. What can I do you for?' He stood up, and Whittaker realised that he had been kneeling behind the counter. He was actually almost seven foot tall, and he had to twist his head and stoop his upper body as he reached down to shake Terry's hand.

Now Taffy Gabatini had seen better days. In 1957, Taffy had discovered a hairstyle which he felt suited him; and who is to say he was wrong? A District Attorney, as they still call it in parts of Pancester, was the great haircut sensation of its age. The twenty-one-year-old Taffy, fresh from two years' National Service as a cook at RAF Valley, his head stuffed full of Cliff Richard and Joe Brown and The Bruvvers and Wee Willie Harris, had left the Air Force to work as a barman in the Butlin's on Barry Island, and by a strange twist of fate, had ended up playing the drums for the camp rock and roll band, Bill Zee Bubble and The Helltones. Clearly, in 1957, if you were working class, ex-RAF *and* a drummer in a holiday-camp rock and roll band to boot, a DA was pretty much de rigueur, if not actually compulsory. When the season finished, and Taffy came back to his parents' café in Pancester with his newly acquired Welsh accent and his DA, the *Pancester Mail* (known as the *Mail* in Pancester, where the *Mail* is known as the *London Mail*) had sent its teen correspondent, Dawn Etherington, along to 'do' Taff (or Paolo, as he was then called) for the 'What's Hot' column. So struck was she by Taff's hair that she almost instantaneously fell pregnant with twins, Dai and Bethan, earning herself the envy of every teenage girl in town.

Over forty years later, no one envied Dawn Gabatini any more, and she felt that the time had come for a new look for Taff. The DA, she had to admit, no longer did it for her in the same kind of way. Perhaps this could be attributed to the undoubted fact that of all the great innovations in men's barbering of the post-war era, the DA is the least able to withstand the ravages of male pattern baldness. Hair resources have to be marshalled from right across the whole surface of the scalp in order to muster the wherewithal for a quiff at the front; any remaining hairs must be viciously trained with industrial-strength Brylcreem to produce the famous Duck's Arse effect; little or nothing remains for the top or sides. This was Taff's fate, and if he hadn't lost most of his hair, then the scarring to his head caused by his prodigious height wouldn't have been so obvious.

Taff bumped into stuff, inevitably, and it showed. His poor head was covered in scars like the surface of Mars. His eyes were horrifyingly close together in some lights, and insanely far apart in others. His nose and ears were good, so far as they went, but critics pointed out that there was perhaps a little too much of both. In 1957 Dawn the soon-to-be Mrs Gabatini had found Taff's slightly protruding milk-white teeth sweet; now they were just sticky-out, and yellow and brown and silver. His Italianate chin was still his best feature, everyone agreed, attractively cleft like Kirk Douglas's, yet firmly self-assertive like Jimmy Hill's. He stooped, of course, which made him cough, and the coughing brought on his knees. He suffered from housemaid's knee, from kneeling in the Rock Cave all day.

And for three years, since his father had retired from running the café upstairs and had gone to live in the Hospital of St Homobonus, he had dreamed that one day some idiot like Terry Whittaker would come through the door, attracted by the notice upstairs, and make him an offer he couldn't refuse. So when Whittaker told him that he had seen the notice, and could Taffy tell him more, his face lit up like Christmas in Las Vegas.

'Boy bach . . .'

'Terry. Whittaker. Call me Terry.'

'Call me Taffy. Boy bach, once I show you round, I won't be

able to get rid of you. You'll be smitten. If you're looking for a business opportunity in Pancester, you'll not find a better, I guarantee. Now, I'm looking to sell the whole building. You get this place, and the café upstairs ... come and have a look. Ow.' He had banged his head on the door of the Rock Cave. Whittaker waited while he rubbed his head and locked up.

'Now you've been into the café, obviously. You've seen its potential. A nice area, too. What do you have in mind?'

'A restaurant.'

'A restaurant, is it? Ideal! This place would make an ideal restaurant! It's almost like a restaurant already! Come into the kitchen. Barry,' said Taffy to the Ted who was still leaning on the counter, 'look after the Cave for me for 'alf an 'our or so, will you?' He threw the keys at the lad, who caught them, blew a kiss at the waitress and sauntered out.

A fat woman in her late forties with despairing eyes and a greasy pinafore sat in an armchair in the kitchen, watching TV.

'Martha! This is Martha Buck, the cook. Martha, this is Mr Whittaker, who wants to buy the 4i's and turn it into a restaurant.'

'Hello,' said Martha dully, her eyes glued to the set.

'Hello, Martha. That was a nice bacon sandwich you did me earlier. And I'm just looking, you know, Taffy.'

'Nice big old kitchen, though, isn't it?'

It was. Lit by a skylight, which showed up a superficial tattiness in the large room, Whittaker nonetheless liked it at once. He did some sums in his head as he worked out how much he'd have to invest to bring it up to his standard. Anything too much over 250K for the building, and he'd have to look at a mortgage, which he didn't fancy. Twenty grand should see both the kitchen and the dining area completely modernised. Call it 275 to be safe. Not bad. Can find that all right. Whittaker's heart started to beat a little faster.

'There's a flat upstairs too. Come and see the flat.'

Taffy opened a door in the back of the kitchen and revealed a staircase which led up into the flat above the café. It was huge and dusty, and lit by large sash windows.

'Grew up here, I did. My parents' place, till my mam died, and my dad went into St Homobonus' a few years back. Four bedrooms. My youngest, Gwyneth, had it till she went to work in London. All right, isn't it?'

Whittaker had to agree. There was an electric fire in the sitting-room fireplace. Whittaker imagined it taken out, a real fire blazing in the Georgian hearth, and a smiling Juliana, her belly heavy with Whittaker's child, knitting as he came home at closing time. The bedrooms were just right. One, overlooking the small yard at the back, Whittaker earmarked as the nursery. A few grand spent up here, and you had the perfect family home.

'Shall we go and have a drink, boy?' said Taff.

'I'd like that,' said Whittaker.

They went downstairs, and out into Shy Street.

'Why's it called Shy Street, Taff?' asked Whittaker.

'Ah, now. It used to be called Bum Alley. But the ladies, you know, didn't like it. So the Victorians changed it. It's still Bum Alley to the locals, of course.'

'Why don't you live in the flat?'

'No, too gloomy for me. Never did like it. I live in a lovely great big council house on the estate with my lovely great big wife. Been there since the sixties, we 'ave. Raised five kids.'

Taffy navigated them through narrow streets and passages. Every other passer-by hailed Taff.

'Everyone knows you, Taffy.'

'Course they do. Born and bred here. Lived and worked here all my life, 'cept for when I was in Wales.'

'So what will you do if you sell the Rock Cave?'

'Ah. Thought it all out, I have. You didn't by any chance notice the bookshop next door to me?'

'I did, yes. There was a very beautiful man who didn't speak.'

Taffy laughed. 'Oliver Halton. Chased by all the ladies of Pancester. My best mate. He don't speak to no one, even me, least not often. Well, old Olly's business isn't going too great, to be honest, so we thought we might go in together, share his shop, do it up a bit. He'd keep the flat above the shop, though look. We thought we might get some new stock in, do new records, and graphic novels, books about oppressed Indians and things like that. Twelve-inch singles for DJs. We'd sew up the whole youth slash alternative market in Pancester.'

'Is there a youth slash alternative market in Pancester?'

'I don't know, reely. Bound to be. Anyway, if I 'ad a partner, I'd be able to spend more time with my band, The Knightwatchmen. Barry, the lad in the café, he's the bass player. Here we are.' They had arrived at the Holly Bush, Taffy's local. The walls were lined with grainy photographs from Wally Oop, the faces of the players crumpled with effort, as the two sides locked in mortal combat.

'Are you a Clanghandler or a Ringler, Taff?'

'Clanghandler, I am. Everyone here is. This is the Clanghandler pub. Two pints please, Sue.'

'How did you do this year?'

'Lost. As bloody usual.'

They took their beers and sat down.

'Well now, Terry. Tell me honest. What do you think?'

'Taff, to be honest, I like it. I'd have to have a survey done, have a word with my accountant. But I like it. How much were you thinking?'

Taffy's palms were sweating.

'Well now, Terry. It's a very well-established business. A lot of goodwill. And that's a roomy old flat. Let it out, you could. So what with one thing and another, and prices being what they are, and what with me having to move next door, I thought ...' he paused, his throat constricted with tension, '... forty thousand pounds!'

Whittaker spat beer over the table.

'Forty thousand pounds!' he gasped.

'All right, thirty-seven. But not a penny less.'

Whittaker smiled.

'Taff. Taffy, my son. If forty is what you want, forty is what you'll get. I'll write you a cheque.'

'Whoa, hold on, Mr Whittaker. What about the survey? Your accountant?'

'No, I'm sure it will be fine. You were right, I'm smitten. Who should I make it out to?'

'Me,' said Taffy weakly. 'Paolo Gabatini.'

'There you go, Taff,' said Whittaker, handing over the cheque. 'A pleasure doing business with you.'

'And with you, Terry. And with you. By Christ, we're in for some exciting times! Welcome to Pancester! Welcome indeed! And here's to . . . what's your restaurant going to be called?'

'I like the 4i's.'

'So . . . to the 4i's!'

'The 4i's!'

So Whittaker had a place of his own, after all, without really stopping to think. At least it was a long way away from his dad, from Francesca, from London.

And all he needed now to complete his happiness was the love of a good woman.

Juliana, he felt sure, was one lucky lady.

Car Parking in the New Millennium

Juliana Blezzard didn't believe in luck. She had rationality on her side. As she walked to work on the morning of Whittaker's tour of Pancester, she thought through her plan again. It was perfect. This would be the one, the stroke of genius that would take her away from Pancester for ever. God, she hated Pancester. The bellowing of the Ramstheng woke her every morning, and sent her straight to the bathroom to vomit. The sun-warmed stone of the city walls felt like the skin of decomposing toads under her slim hand. On arrival in her tiny cupboard of an office, she struggled to control a panic attack as she read through her file one last time. Her secretary buzzed.

'Juliana. It's five past ten. Time for the planning meeting.'

'Thank you, Gaynor.'

She straightened her skirt, pursed her lips in the mirror, and walked down the corridor of City Hall to the committee room.

She was, as she had intended, last in to the meeting. The planning committee had nine members, eight men and one woman, Aolderwoman Ursula Armistead. Pancester has long been under the control of the Pancester Independents, and eight of the committee, including the chairman, Trevor Mallinson, were PIs. But the opposition, the Independent Pancester Independents, were also represented in the person of Dexter Halton, twin brother of the beautiful Oliver, whom we have already glimpsed, peeping out from the back room of his bookshop, Heavily Foxed.

Juliana was sleeping with Trevor Mallinson, and expected no

political opposition, except perhaps from Aolderman Halton. But she had worked in Pancester Tourism long enough to know the motto of the Pancester City Council: *Every public action which is not customary, either is wrong, or, if it is right, a dangerous precedent. It follows that nothing ever should be done for the first time.* Juliana was well aware that centuries of inaction would not be easily overcome.

Juliana was presenting her scheme with the help of the traffic superintendent, Nigel Morris, and the city architect, Polly Seagrave, both of whom were present at the meeting, but it was her baby, her own wee newborn thing, and she had been chosen to head up the project. If this was the success she hoped, she'd be applying for a job in Stratford or Bath – London even. She smiled around the room, and shook off her nerves as she stepped up to her overhead projector.

'Good morning, ladies and gentlemen, and thank you for taking the time to listen to our presentation. I hope you've all received your copy of our detailed plan, *Car Parking in the New Millennium*? Yes? I hope you've all had a chance to study it. It has been produced jointly by the traffic department, the city architect, and the Tourism Office, so you can see that it has the unanimous support of the professionals employed to advise the Council. My intention this morning is to run over the main points of the plan, and then to answer any questions you may have.

'As you are well aware, tourism is the largest employer in the Pancester area. Year on year, since 1995, our visitation rate has grown by an average of 17 per cent. Almost half a million visitors came to Pancester last year, and figures this year are already indicating that we are set for yet another increase. Over 50 per cent of our visitors come by coach, and a further 15 per cent by rail. This still means that over 175,000 people visit Pancester each year by car, and it is here that we are encountering grave problems.

'In a recent study conducted for the Tourism Office by MORI, when asked "What factors would deter you from re-visiting Pancester?" an overwhelming 68 per cent of those visitors who came by car gave difficulty in parking as their first choice. Of the current facilities, the short-stay car park by the National Museum of Crime and Punishment is woefully badly signed, and too small by some 500 spaces on an average Festival day, whilst the long-stay car park next to the station is unpaved and too far from the city centre for elderly visitors to walk in comfort – and as I'm sure you're aware, the average age of motor-borne visitors to Pancester is fifty-four. You will see from the report that the traffic department is increasingly concerned that illegal parking within the city walls is the main factor in congestion. That the time has come to commit to a new car-parking facility is beyond dispute. The question therefore arises – where is the new car park to be?

'Three solutions have been explored in some depth. Firstly, the erection of a new multi-storey car park on the site of the current short-stay car park by the museum. A sympathetic construction in local stone was envisaged, and the city architect is satisfied that such work could be carried out with the minimum of disruption to the valuable townscape of Pancester. The traffic department, however, points out that car use within the walls would increase by an estimated 35 per cent in the first year, which, as I'm sure we would all agree, is completely unacceptable.

'The second and cheapest option is simply to improve the current facilities. New signage and road markings would improve access to the current short-stay car park, whilst the long-stay facility at the station could be tarmacked, and extended to include a further new short-stay area. The city architect, however, points out that new signage and road markings within the walls would spoil the amenity value of the city, whilst the traffic department estimates that this solution would lead to a 9 per cent increase in city centre car use, where a decrease in real terms of 4 per cent is envisaged by the current city plan. The Tourism Office is concerned that the revitalised long-stay facility still represents a ten-minute walk around the ring road to gain access to the city proper, and that furthermore, the planned new short-stay area depends on the purchase of land from Railtrack, land which abuts on to the grounds of the Pancester Riverside Hotel, which might very well have grounds for objection.'

Juliana smiled, as though objections to her scheme were laughable.

'We have therefore decided to recommend to the City Council option three, an entirely new 1000-car facility on a greenfield site, just outside the city walls. The site we have chosen is Dole Acre, which is located, as committee members are well aware, adjacent both to the ring road and to the Pack Bridge, and so to the West Gate of the city. It is a two-minute walk from Dole Acre over the bridge and into the city proper. The plans that have been drawn up by the city architect, and which you can find on page seven of your report, show that a large part of the new car park would be built underground. Access to and from the ring road would be facilitated by the construction of a slip road and a new roundabout, which would be located in the south-west corner of the Dole Acre site. Although cars will be parked on the upper level, the plans allow for extensive landscaping and tree planting, which will, in my opinion, improve the look of the area, which at present is unkempt and badly cared for by the tenant.

'Traffic department figures show that car use inside the city proper will fall by a startling 43 per cent, whilst traffic on the ring road will be slowed by a useful average of eleven m.p.h. by the new roundabout, a figure which will reduce accidents on the Laikley turn-off by almost 17 per cent.'

As she talked, Juliana manipulated the overhead projector with an expert hand, so that the relevant facts and figures were projected on to its screen. The committee sat spellbound by the combination of jargon and heavyweight statistical ammunition with which they were being bombarded. Juliana sipped water from a glass, and continued.

'Whilst the actual ownership of the land is uncertain, it is beyond question that the use of Dole Acre has been under the control of the city since Sir Kenelm de Courtney's Charter of 1503. There being no living member of the Courtney family, the city solicitor is certain that almost 500 years of continuing use by the city constitutes a prima facie case for the city to be able to go ahead with this development. The land has been rented since 1973 to a Mrs Jocelyn Innes at a peppercorn rent of £100 per annum.

Mrs Innes currently uses the land as a donkey sanctuary, and at the time the report was commissioned, only six donkeys were on site. In point of fact, it has come to my attention that since we prepared the study, one of the donkeys has died. We recommend sympathetic handling of the donkeys, and Laikley Children's Zoo has expressed an interest in taking over care of the animals, and has already started planning a new attraction, Donkey World.

'As is well known, the income from Dole Acre is used to help the old folk, currently by financing the Pancester Dole. Profit from the new car park, once we have taken into account the costs of construction and running overheads, is estimated at £250,000 per annum. It does not take a mathematical genius, therefore, to see that by remaining true to the spirit rather than the letter of the Charter, the pensioners of Pancester would stand to benefit a great deal from the scheme. In addition to the Dole, a trust could be established which would administer the funds. Pensioners could be sent on holiday, for example, or helped to stay in their own homes by grant in aid, rather than move into the almshouses. Social Services, whilst reluctant to put a figure on how much such additional funds might assist their work, are enthusiastic. The relevant figures and projections can be found in the cost-benefit analyses in Table B in your report.

'In conclusion, I should like to say that in view of its current lack of amenity value, Dole Acre is the ideal site for the urgently needed new car park. All departments of the City Council are supporting the scheme. The Department of the Environment has given its informal approval. The pensioners win, the visitors win, the city wins. All that remains, ladies and gentlemen, is that you vote for the measure. I hope I have managed to persuade you of its benefits this morning. Are there any questions?'

She clicked off the overhead projector and smiled around the room.

Aolderwoman Armistead was the first to speak.

'Yes, Ms Blezzard. You say that Dole Acre has no current amenity value. What about the Eastering? The girls of Pancester have gone a-Eastering on Dole Acre for I don't know how long. What's going to happen to them?'

'Thank you, Aolderwoman Armistead. The plans have taken this into account. The new roundabout is to be sited in the south-western corner of Dole Acre, where the Eastering currently takes place. We envisage landscaping the centre of the roundabout, and establishing a small garden therein. I feel sure that it will prove a pleasant spot to spend a few hours lost in dreams of love.'

The committee laughed.

Gotcha, thought Juliana. 'Any more questions?' she said.

'I have one,' said Dexter Halton. 'Why did you not consider Park 'n' Ride?'

'In point of fact, in the preliminary stages we did examine the possibilities. The traffic department felt that the narrow streets of Pancester were unsuitable for buses, and that the construction of bus stops on the ring road by the Pack Bridge would be unsafe. The city architect failed to identify a suitable out-of-city site which took into account traffic flow both from the motorway and from Laikley, and the Tourism Office pointed out that in a 1993 survey, visitors to Oxford cited the Park 'n' Ride scheme as the main disincentive to a day trip to the city.'

Dexter grunted, and made a note. Several other Aoldermen asked questions of a technical nature, which were fielded by Nigel Morris and Polly Seagrave, and at ten past eleven, Trevor Mallinson said, 'Thanks very much to our friends from Tourism' (smiling at Juliana) 'and Traffic, as well as the city architect. This report has much in it for us to consider, and I must ask you now to leave us to our deliberations.'

Juliana, Nigel and Polly took shelter in the lounge bar of Ye Blacke Bull.

'That seemed to go very well,' said Nigel.

'Old Mother Armistead thought she had us, though,' said Juliana.

'I'm still a bit worried about the Eastering myself, as it happens,' said Polly Seagrave, who was trying for another baby.

'The thing about the Eastering is that it is the only one of our wonderful curious customs which attracts almost no visitors. A couple of deluded old bitches who can't afford IVF, and that's about it. Mostly it's just locals. Anyway, what's he called, squinty guy, pot-bellied, your landscaping expert ... '

'My husband. Colin.'

'Yes. Colin. Well, he reckons we can come up with something acceptable on the roundabout.'

'An eleven m.p.h. slowdown will be really something,' said Nigel.

'I know,' said Polly. 'But it'll never be the same.'

'Hey, what about Dexter Halton?' said Juliana. 'I thought he might throw us something a bit tougher than Park 'n' Ride.'

'So did I. He might yet,' said Nigel. 'If there's going to be any protests in the city, I reckon he'll be the ringleader.'

'He's an ugly bastard, isn't he?' said Juliana. 'Not like his brother.'

It was true. Dexter looked like the love child of Charles Laughton and Joyce Grenfell.

'Strange, isn't it?' said Nigel. 'Especially when you consider that they're identical twins.'

'I like Dex. He's a sweetie. He reckons they look so different because he's corrupted himself with politics, while Oliver lives in the pure atmosphere of literature,' said Polly.

Nigel laughed, but Juliana did not. She excused herself, and hurried to the Ladies to check herself in the mirror. She freshened her lipstick, but did not notice any deterioration in her complexion. Perhaps the corruption wasn't showing yet. Perhaps there were some who were involved in politics whose corruption failed to show on their faces at all, though she could not, off the top of her head, think of an example.

Maybe she'd get away with it. She drew back her lips and examined her teeth to check for smudges of lipstick.

Who was that fat prick last night who asked her if she was married? Well, she certainly didn't intend getting married, especially to blubbery losers like him. If ever the time came, she could do much better. She looked great. She looked like a mover and a shaker. London would suit her, she felt. Her mobile tittered.

'Hello?' she said.

'Hello? Juliana? It's Trevor. It's passed, darling. Congratulations. Six to one, Halton against, with Armistead and Plumb abstaining. So we're on to the next stage! Can I come round tonight?'

Juliana thought for a second. It would be useful to have Mallinson's account.

'OK,' she said.

'About nine?'

'Sure.'

And ... perhaps ... tonight will be the night? Now you can relax a bit?'

'Perhaps.'

She rang off and rejoined the others in the bar to tell them the good news, before heading back to her office.

Now, feminist readers will be feeling disappointed, if unsurprised, by Juliana's relationship with Mallinson.

'That is so typical,' they will say. 'Once again, a male novelist cannot imagine a successful woman who's achieved something without shagging the boss.'

They were not paying attention. No one said anything about shagging. Juliana was *sleeping* with Mallinson. She had never once permitted him to touch her in any way. All she would allow was for him to sleep beside her in her large double bed. It had been going on for a year. By now, he had got used to just getting into bed, making a feeble advance, hearing her say, 'Not now. Perhaps later,' and falling into sleep, where he dreamed of swiving Juliana all night. Trevor was beginning to despair, and his balls were turning petrol blue. Juliana never granted him access more than once a month, usually just before or after the planning meeting. But 'Not now. Perhaps later' drove Trevor insane with lust, and he continued to do her bidding.

She hated to be touched, by anyone, ever. Human flesh in contact with her own gave her a strong sense of formication, of creeping crawling creatures swarming over her skin. The thought of coming into contact with lips and tongues and mucous membrane made her feel nauseous. What was it? Fear of letting anyone close? An inability to let go, to find release? A desire, perhaps, for autonomy, for a total independence from others, rooted deep in her childhood? Juliana did not know, either, and had on occasion thought of going into therapy to find out. Somehow, it had never really worried her enough to do anything about it.

Besides, she was not without all erotic sensibility. Poor Trevor Mallinson couldn't know that sleeping next to people was Juliana's thing. Like Stephen Ward as portrayed by John Hurt in *Scandal*, she enjoyed the ache. She would lie awake, her body taut with pre-orgasmic pleasure as she sensed the rise and fall of her colleague's chest, the slight touch of his breath on her neck long into the night. She liked it with Trevor, if only he could have known. It would spoil it to tell him. Besides, she had a partner of choice, a favoured lover who shared her interest in erotic quietism, and it wasn't Trevor. It was someone else who both needed and hated Pancester, someone else who would be interested in Mallinson's report.

As Terry Whittaker left the cathedral, and started looking for somewhere to eat, Juliana walked from City Hall up to the Tourist Information Office, where they told her a fat man had asked for her in familiar terms that morning, and as Whittaker sat down in the Holly Bush to deal with Taffy Gabatini, she made her way home, to shower and eat and watch telly and to wait for Mallinson's report.

At nine, the doorbell rang. Trevor was never late. He had a bunch of pink roses and a bottle of champagne. She accepted them as he gushed at her, sidestepped his attempted kiss, and sat down in her armchair.

'I'll get some glasses, shall I, darling? And a vase?'

'Sure. So what happened?' she called through to the kitchen.

'Hang on . . . here I am. Give me the roses. That's it. Shall I put them here? And the bottle. Here we go! Ha! Hold out your glass . . . whoops! And for me . . . there. Here's to us!'

'So what happened, Trevor?'

'Piece of cake. It's such a superb scheme, it really is. Hardly any debate. Armistead said that she thought it was a very good scheme, but that she was worried about the Eastering, so she decided to abstain. Old Archie Plumb was asleep, so we counted him as an abstention too. Dexter Halton voted against, but that was more politics than anything. He is the opposition after all. Declared himself pro-donkey, and said that Mrs Innes had rescued the creatures from beach rides and zoos, and it wasn't right to condemn them to Donkey World. All they wanted in the twilight of their lives was rest. I noted his objection, and pointed out that there now followed a three-month period of consultation when he could raise these kinds of issues, before the thing goes to a full meeting of the council.'

'I suppose it has to?'

'Well, of course it does, darling. The council has to come up with the cash . . .'

'City treasurer says he can come up with it, no problem. Says we can sell the old short-stay car park for redevelopment. Traffic say they can put the recobbling of High Street on hold for a year.'

'Yes, I know, but the council still has to vote on it. It is a democracy.'

Juliana sighed. It was a shame.

'And then it goes through?'

'You know as well as I do. Of course. Unless any opposition groups try for a judicial review, or a public inquiry, or refer it to the Secretary of State . . . But that would only be as a delaying tactic. It'll go through. It's such a clever scheme. You clever thing!'

Do you think there will be any real opposition?'

'Not if we can make the donkey thing watertight, no. Of course not. Who'll have the nerve to take a quarter of a mill away from the pensioners? Poor old Dexter?' said Trevor.

Juliana snorted, and turned to the telly.

'What's on?' said Trevor, a note of resignation in his voice.

'*A Touch of Frost.*'

'Isn't it a repeat?'

'Yes.'

'Wouldn't you rather ... come to bed? With a bottle of bubbly? Licky licky?' he said, more in hope than expectation.

'Not now, Trevor. It's been a long day. Not now. Perhaps later.'

'Not now, thanks, Dawn,' said Whittaker.

'Perhaps later?' asked Dawn Gabatini.

'I don't know, I really don't. I'm stuffed.'

'Well, there's plenty more if you want it.' She put the bowl of trifle on the sideboard, sat down at the table, and lit herself a cigarette.

Taff had invited Terry back to his house on the estate to eat. The walls of the sitting room were covered with memorabilia – a Heinz gold record, one of Johnny Kidd's eyepatches in a display case, a signed photo of Gene Vincent, framed snaps of the five children in their graduation gowns, pictures of grandchildren on the windowsill, two paintings of dogs. Dawn had had no warning of Whittaker's arrival, and there had been a quarrel in the kitchen, until Taff produced the cheque, and Dawn screamed, after which Whittaker could do no wrong. Whittaker had liked Dawn at once. At least two feet shorter than her husband, and almost perfectly spherical, with short grey hair and a pair of specs large enough for Dennis Taylor, Dawn gave off an air of cheerful efficiency and can-do briskness which Whittaker found very attractive, and which had undoubtedly helped in keeping Taffy's various enthusiasms in check.

Oliver Halton was phoned, and he had come for dinner too, so that he could share in the good news. He didn't say anything, but Whittaker could see that he was excited from his shining eyes.

'... and the business reborn!' Taffy was saying for the hundredth time over. 'You and me, Ol.'

'And a new kitchen, and a holiday, and presents for the grandchildren ...' said Dawn.

'... and a new drumkit and new costumes for The Knight-watchmen.'

'... a car would be nice,' said Dawn.

'A bugger to park in town, that is,' said Taff.

'No, but we could keep it here, and just use it for runs out,' said Dawn.

'It's a thought, lovely girl. It's a thought.'

Whittaker was pleased that he could bring so much pleasure. He was smiling as he sipped his coffee.

'What about you, Tel?' said Taff. 'What now?'

'Well ... I guess we'll have to see a solicitor, work out the deeds and stuff. Then there'll be things for me to sort in London.'

'Sell your place, you mean?' asked Dawn.

'No, I'll keep it on. But I'll let it, maybe. No, all sorts of things. I'll probably need to ship in some trained staff for one thing, to judge from the service in Ye Blacke Bull. No offence.'

'None taken, Tel,' said Taff, leaning back in his chair and lighting a Castella.

'And then I'll have to get some design people in, and start tarting the place up. You haven't got a drinks licence, I guess?'

'God, no.'

'We'll need one. And a music licence, too, maybe. I thought I might put cabaret on in the basement eventually. And there'll be builders, and a menu to devise and tableware to buy and blah blah blah. It'll all take ages, Taff, Oliver. You needn't rush your plans. I know this has all been a bit sudden.'

Taff folded away the table, while Whittaker helped carry the dining chairs back into the kitchen.

'You not married then, Terry?' asked Dawn. 'Nothing like that to sort out? Girlfriends?'

'Not married yet, Dawn, but I've got my eye on someone.'

'A London girl?' asked Dawn.

'No. Someone I've met here in Pancester.'

'You're a bloody quick worker, boy,' said Taff, bringing through the last of the chairs.

'Oh, well,' said Whittaker coyly. 'You've either got it or you ain't.'

'Who is she then?' asked Taff.

'I met her in the Tourist Information Office. Her name's Juliana. Blezzard.'

Taffy looked surprised; concerned, even.

'No, old Ted Blezzard's girl? I know her. I used to play golf with Ted, years back. Laikley, they're from. He's got the bowls shop there. And she went off to Uni down south, and then she got a job working in tourism in Staines, by Heathrow, wasn't it, love?' Dawn nodded. 'And Ted told me she'd turned the place around, quadrupled the visitors. They called her "The Girl Who Put Staines On The Map". And she came here to head the Tourism Office a couple of years ago. Young, she was, for such a big job. Lot of visitors in Pancester. Very go ahead, she is. But I expect you knew all that.'

'No, I didn't.'

'Well, there you are then. Now you know. Juliana. Well, well. I thought . . . well, it just goes to show you how wrong you can be.' Taffy rubbed his gargantuan chin.

'Yes,' agreed Whittaker. 'Need a hand with the washing-up?'

'Hear that, Taffy? Isn't he lovely? No, Terry, bless you. I'll leave it till the morning.' They returned to the sitting room with a tin of beer each, and one for Oliver.

'I tell you what, Taff,' said Dawn. 'What about our Gwyneth?'

'What about her?' asked Taff.

'If Terry's looking for staff.'

'God, yes, that's a thought. That one's Gwyneth,' said Taff, pointing to a picture of one of his pretty daughters. 'Our youngest.'

'Works in London. She's a duty manager at the Savoy Grill,' said Dawn.

'No, really?' said Whittaker.

'Really,' said Taff with pride.

'And she was telling me the other night she'd like to find a job local,' said Dawn. 'Her best friend, Sally, who she shares a flat with, has been offered a job up here, so she wants to move back, if Sal takes this job. So I said, you'd be daft packing in a good job like that, and she said she'd rather pack the job than pack being friends with Sally, which I think is nice.'

'Give me her number,' said Whittaker. 'I'll give her a ring. I'll need a manager.'

'That would be reely kind of you Tel,' said Taff.

'No promises. But the Savoy Grill . . .' Whittaker was startled by a voice in his ear.

'I found some recipes,' said Oliver, in a surprisingly deep tone. 'Pop in tomorrow.'

'Er . . . yes. I will. Thanks, Oliver.' Oliver nodded, and smiled.

'Christ almighty,' said Taffy. 'Someone's in a good mood.'

'I think we all are,' said Dawn.

Terry phoned for a taxi, and headed back to the Pancester Riverside. Dennis was on again.

'Nice day, sir?' he said.

'Smashing, thanks. I love your city.'

'All mucked about since my day,' said Dennis. 'You should have seen it before they started mucking it about.'

Back in the Lady Abigail Suite, Whittaker made a list of everything he had to do. It was a long list, but he felt more relaxed than he had for months.

His holiday was over.

I Hope You Don't Mind My Asking . . .

No one could accuse Whittaker of being scared of commitment. He woke in his bed in the Lady Abigail Courtney Suite, bubbling with commitment to Pancester, where he had been for one day and two nights. His head was bursting with plans for the 4i's. He ate his continental breakfast, utterly committed to turning the 4i's into the most successful restaurant in the north of England. And he was chock-full of commitment to his new relationship with Juliana Blezzard. He had arranged to meet Taffy at his solicitor's at ten, and then planned to meet Juliana, if she was available, to outline his scheme. At nine, he took the precaution of making an appointment through her secretary, telling her something of his ideas, so that Juliana would agree to see him again.

'I've had a word with Ms Blezzard, Mr Whittaker,' said Gaynor. 'She'll be delighted to run through some of the help Pancester Tourism can offer to new leisure businesses wishing to establish themselves within the locality. Her eleven-thirty has cancelled. Will that suit?'

'I should say so!' said Whittaker cheerfully.

'This will be a surprise for her,' he thought. He'd play it straight, just turn up as though he were any other top chef wishing to make contact with the local tourism boss – and then he'd tell her about his ideas for the stencilling in the nursery. He imagined her pretty face alight with joy.

Terry Whittaker had had very few girlfriends. If you or I were counting, we'd say he'd had just the two. First, there was Susan Riley. Terry and Susan started going out when they were seven. They were in the same class at primary school in Ealing, and they held hands all through break and lunch. They became engaged at eight, and Whittaker started saving all his money, for a house.

'I hope you're going to wait for the wedding before you make me a grandpa. Your little winky-woo is much too tiny to be of any use, anyway,' joked Old Man Whittaker. Whittaker's mother would blush and mumble at him not to be so crude, but the old man would laugh and say that Terry was a chip off the old block, that girls would be putty in his hand, that the little tarts would be ripping off their knickers for him, that Susan was just the first in what would prove to be a long line of sexual conquests. This would make Whittaker's mother cry; he could still remember her standing in the kitchen, cutting crosses into the stems of Brussels sprouts, tears streaming down her cheeks, as his father boasted of how he'd fucked at least one woman for every station on the District Line. Terry resolved that he would never be like his father. He would be like a swan, mated for life. There would be just one woman for Terry, a pen to his cob, just one, and she would be everything to him.

By the time Terry and Susan first slept together, when they were fifteen, he had over £700 in his National Savings account. When he left school to train as a chef at sixteen, Susan stayed on to do her A levels. Despite the miserly wage he was paid while he learned his trade, by the time she left home for college, he had over £3000. He was clearly talented. Whittaker, like so many successful people, is a monomaniac. He can apply himself to the task in hand. He got his first real job at nineteen, as a commis in a smart French place in Oxford (where Susan was studying PPE), and the savings mounted until, at twenty-one, he announced to Susan that the time had finally come, and at last they could afford to get married. So Susan dumped him, and took up a traineeship at KPMG instead.

Terry was so numb with pain that he barely noticed when his mother died. Later, when he tried to reconstruct what had happened, he calculated that it was just over a month after Susan had left that his mother's diabetes took her away too. His old man hardly blinked; within a fortnight of Terry's mother's death he had moved a woman called Barbara into the family home, a fat and sluttish divorcée whom Whittaker *père* groped with malicious zest. Whittaker moved out for good, in pieces. If the One wasn't Susan, then who could it be? Aged twenty-two, Whittaker saw nothing but a life of monkish misery in front of him. He cut off all contact with his father, and concentrated on his career.

But then there was Francesca Salt. After Susan dumped him, Terry moved downriver to the Riverside at Bray, where he learned what great cooking really was, and how to do it for himself. He concentrated, he saved (he lived in), and he liked his job very much. He'd been there for six years when Francesca came in one day for lunch, and asked to meet the chef. It was Terry in charge that afternoon, and all he cared about from that moment on was how to make her his. She wrote a nice little piece for her paper (she had just started reviewing restaurants), and Terry bombarded her with flowers, chocolates, thoughtful little gifts, tears, suicide notes, until after four years she shagged him to shut him up, and found she quite liked it. She was married, yes, but she was crazy about Whittaker too, in her own way, and after three years of clandestine meetings, she finally left her husband and kids, and moved in with Terry. He was back in London now, head chef at Rococo, and the reviews and the celebrities and the Michelin stars were starting to roll in. They managed a year before Francesca could no longer stand being worshipped twenty-four hours a day. Her husband, that long-suffering man, took her back, and put up stoically with Terry's endless attempts to win her round. Then Terry got sacked, and decided to walk away like a real man. Two girlfriends, we would say.

But Whittaker made it four. Between Susan and Francesca there had been Mandy, who worked down the Spar in Bray. After a year or so of pleading with Susan, he had become fixated on poor Mandy, a friendly girl who always had a smile for her customers, and Whittaker needed no more encouragement than that. He would hover about in the shop when Mandy was working and he was off, and try to understand why she refused to go for a drink, or to the cinema. Her smile for Whittaker began to fade under his relentless attentions.

'At last she's starting to take me seriously,' thought Terry. 'She's gone beyond fancying me. Or else why has she stopped smiling?'

He would hang about to meet her after work, and her boyfriend, Ray, would hit him, often quite painfully. Each punch convinced him of his case. Why did Ray punch him? Because Ray was jealous. Why was Ray jealous? Because Mandy was in love with Whittaker. It was simple.

And what of sex? Surely you can't believe yourself to be 'going out' with someone in this day and age if you never have sex? Terry could. He had evolved an elaborate system of auto-erotic practices centred around Mandy which enabled him to cope with that side of things. If Ray had known what Whittaker was up to, he might have gone beyond merely punching him. Whittaker had a cardboard filing box which contained various totemic items to ignite his lust, including some intimate items which he had managed to steal from Mandy's clothes line. He had been lucky not to be caught. He kept this box on top of his wardrobe.

It lasted two years, and Mandy was in the process of applying for an injunction from the court, when Francesca asked to meet the chef.

Terry had also had two very serious crushes on famous women, but he had always managed to stay just this side of sanity, and didn't really count them as actual girlfriends. First he imagined that Chrissie Hynde from The Pretenders was singing 'I Go to Sleep' just for him, and for six months or so he couldn't stop imagining himself and Chrissie together. He understood that he would have to work in a vegetarian restaurant for that to come off, but he was prepared to make the sacrifice in return for Chrissie's cool slim hands stroking his forehead.

And then, shortly after Francesca went back to her husband, Terry realised one night that Kirsty Wark from *Newsnight* was sending him coded messages of desire. He started taping the show, and watching it ardently when he got home from work, for clues, little hints. For three months, he watched the tapes every night, rewinding them in slow motion, the better to interpret Kirsty's enigmatic smile.

'There's just time for a quick look at tomorrow's papers,' she would say, and Terry would read secret love letters for his eyes only from the headlines, without ever quite losing sight of the fact that it was only a game that he was playing.

So he didn't really count Chrissie or Kirsty. But now there was Juliana. Four girlfriends. And at last, Terry was convinced, this was the One, the Real Thing. It had to be. Her eyes had told him so.

Whittaker had to get through the meeting with Taff and his solicitor, Brian Carless, before going to see her.

Carless leant back in his chair, and whistled at the cheque held in his bony fingers.

'Well, I'll say this for you, Taff, you drive a hard bargain. Forty thousand pounds! Cash! Phew!'

Taff grinned, his eyes glowing with pleasure.

'How far is Pancester from London?' asked Terry.

'About 280 miles. Why?' asked Carless.

'Just wondered,' said Whittaker.

'Well, Mr Whittaker . . .'

'Terry, please.'

'Well, Terry. Once this baby has cleared, I'll transfer you the deeds. Easiest bit of conveyancing I've ever handled.'

'Thank you.'

Taff was hopping about with unrestrained glee outside the solicitor's office after the meeting, and insisted on taking Terry back to the 4i's for a coffee. He couldn't resist telling the staff the splendid news that they were about to become redundant whilst he, Taff, was in the money. Sandra the waitress shrugged, but Martha the cook was inconsolable, and wailed loudly, until Whittaker offered her a new job.

'But I can't do fancy restaurant things, Mr W,' she sobbed. 'I can only do homely things, like spaghetti on toast.'

'Well, to judge from your bacon sandwich yesterday, you do

the homely things very well. You cook with love. It's the most important ingredient. The rest I can teach you.'

Martha dried her eyes on her tabard.

'Oh, thank you so much. I don't know that I could face being at home all day with Dad and the cats, I really don't.' Terry wrote her a cheque for two months' wages in advance.

'I'm afraid you're going to have to put up with them for a bit. We're going to have to close for a big makeover. But this should keep you going till Easter.'

'Easter?' said Taff.

'Yeah. Reckon two months should be enough.'

Taff and Terry made some arrangements, sipping the 4i's' coffee-flavoured foam.

'I've got to go back to London this afternoon, really, Taff,' said Whittaker. 'Put my house in order, meet with some designers, get things moving. Maybe give your Gwyneth a call. I'll move into the flat next week, if that's OK?'

'Sure. You're the boss,' said Taff happily. 'I'll get talking with Oliver.'

Whittaker called in at Heavily Foxed on his way to the City Hall, where Oliver, just as promised, had dug out a book of local recipes – a pamphlet produced by the Townswomen's Guild in 1954 to celebrate the end of rationing called *Pancester Provender*.

'How much?' asked Terry, turning the pages.

'S'yours,' said Oliver.

'No, really, Oliver, how much?'

'Twenty pee.'

The deal done, Whittaker walked to City Hall. He thought of buying some flowers, but just managed to stop himself. 'Play it cool, Terry,' he said aloud.

In her office, Juliana Blezzard looked as fragile as a snowdrop, as pretty as frosted cobwebs festooned across suburban gardens on a winter's morning, Terry thought. She stood and shook his hand, smiling.

'Mr Whittaker. Nice to meet you. How can I help?'

'You don't remember me, do you?'

'Er ...' She looked puzzled for a moment, and then recognition struck, and she smiled again.

'Gosh, yes I do! You were one of the judges on last year's *Junior Masterchef*, weren't you? You wore a red bow-tie, am I right? Timmy Rubenstein was your fellow judge, wasn't he? The girl from Norwich won it. Well, well, well, it will be a feather in our cap if you come here to open a restaurant. I've thought for a long time we could do with a really first-class place.'

'Um, yes I was. How clever of you to recognise me.' I must have stayed in her mind, Terry thought. 'But we've met before? The night before last? Elver Day?'

Her smile faded. 'Oh. Oh, yes. I remember now. Did you enjoy the ceremony?'

'Very much. I loved it. I've fallen in love ...' he paused dramatically, and looked deep into her grey eyes, her all-knowing, all-seeing eyes, '... with your city.' But she knew what he really meant, he could see that. She was crazy about him. She had to be. Her eyes told him so, beyond all doubt.

So he told her all about his plans for the restaurant, how he was going to gut the kitchen, and redesign the interior, and modernise the flat, and how he was going to need a drinks licence, and maybe a music licence too, and she told him about Pancester Tourism's marketing ideas, and where she felt a revitalised 4i's might sit in Pancester's catering profile (very much at the top, it seemed). Terry watched her throat flex as she spoke, watched her skin move over her muscles. Sunlight caught tiny golden hairs on the nape of her neck. She had a series of small moles in the shape of a Y on her left forearm, he noticed. Whittaker couldn't remember when he had last been so happy. Twelve approached. Juliana stood, smiling once again.

'Well, Mr Whittaker. It's been a pleasure. If I can be of any assistance, please let me know. In view of your reputation, I really don't think there will be any problems with the drinks licence, or any internal alterations you might need to make, but please keep me informed, and I'll do what I can to oil the wheels.' She extended her hand, and Whittaker raised it to his lips, and kissed it. She shuddered, and pulled her hand away hurriedly.

'Come and have lunch with me,' said Whittaker. 'I'm off back to London this afternoon, and we won't be able to see one another again till next week.'

'I'm sorry?' said Juliana.

Whittaker repeated his invitation.

Juliana stared at him, goggle-eyed with incredulity, but she kept her temper, and said, 'I'm afraid I have an arrangement already. Perhaps another time?'

Which was enough to keep Whittaker buoyed up with ecstasy all the way back to the hotel, all through packing and checking out, and all the way back down the motorway to London. By Hilton Park services he got stuck in a jam behind a lorry carrying Lucozade, and he called the Truckers' Helpline again. The same West Country voice answered.

'Hello, Truckers' Helpline.'

'Hello again,' said Whittaker.

'Oh, hello sir. How can I help you this time?'

'Well, I'm behind another one of your lorries, V for Venus 723 L for love J for Juliana M for I'm getting married in the morning, and I'd just like to tell you that this lorry is being very well driven too. Even better than the other one in fact.'

'Are you taking the piss?'

'No. No, I'm just phoning to say how impressed I am.'

'Sorry. Sorry. It's just that . . . well, we don't get many calls. Especially nice ones. Thank you very much. Mr . . . Whittaker, wasn't it?'

'Terry. My God, you really don't get many calls if you can remember my name.'

'You have a nice voice. And you were the first person I can remember phoning in to say something positive. Even if you are only taking the mick.'

'Thank you. It's my pleasure.'

He arrived back in his flat at eleven that night, opened a tin of raspberries, and phoned directory enquiries.

'What town, please?'

'Pancester.'

'Name please?'

'Blezzard. J.'

'Thank you. Do you have an address please?'

'No . . .'

'That's OK. I have only one J Blezzard in Pancester.'

'Thank you.'

'Thank you.'

A robot gave him Juliana's number, which he immediately called. An Ansafone clicked into life. 'I'm not here at the moment. Please leave your name, number and a message after the tone.'

'Hi. It's only me. Just thought I'd phone and let you know I got back safely. I'll call tomorrow,' a message which puzzled Juliana a great deal when she picked it up upon arriving home. Who on earth was 'Only Me'? Arrived safely where? A wrong number, it had to be.

The next day was a busy one for Terry. He spent a couple of hours with a restaurant-designer friend, Penny Lester, telling her about Pancester and the 4i's. He lent her Clement Dadd's book so that she could read up on Pancester, and she agreed to come back up with him the following week to start drawing up plans. He popped into Rococo to pick up a few things, and made up with Ronnie Walton, whose head was still bandaged, but who had never been one to bear a grudge.

He called in to see his father, who was asleep. He watched the old man's chest rise and fall under the sheets, and thanked Christ that he wasn't like him. He left some money with the sisters so that they could continue to buy the sweets.

He phoned the Savoy, and asked when Gwyneth Gabatini was working next. He was told that she was working that evening, and Terry booked himself in for dinner. (Chefs of Whittaker's status have no trouble getting tables at short notice.)

He phoned Juliana, and she was outraged. 'It was YOU who phoned me last night!' she gasped. 'Where did you get my number?'

'From directory enquiries.'

'Well, please don't phone me on this number again. If you need any more information, you can contact me in office hours.'

'Sure thing, baby,' said Whittaker rakishly.

She hung up. Whittaker smiled. Playing hard to get, huh? Well, he knew all about that. He'd just have to get another box for the top of his wardrobe like he'd had with Mandy, that was all. She'd come round in the end.

Gwyneth Gabatini showed Whittaker to his table. Terry recognised her from the photos at her parents' house. She was tall, broad-shouldered, and handsome, despite a slight hint of her father's record-breaking chin. Her brown hair was cut short. She wore sensible shoes.

'I hope you don't mind my asking, sir,' she said as she seated him, 'but aren't you *the* Terry Whittaker? From Rococo?' She spoke with a slight Northern accent – Taff's Welsh affectation had clearly not influenced her at all.

'Yes, I am. No, I've left. You haven't spoken to your parents lately?'

'My parents?'

'You're Gwyneth Gabatini, aren't you?'

'Yes. How did you know? Do you know my parents?'

'Yes. I've bought the 4i's.'

'Shit!' said Gwyneth. Some nearby diners looked around. She smiled at them.

'What time do you get off?' said Terry.

'Midnight.'

'Come and have a drink with me, and I'll tell you all about it.'

'My friend usually comes and picks me up.'

'Is that Sally?' Gwyneth nodded. 'She can come too. We'll go to the Fork and Knife.'

'OK. Er ... this is François, your waiter this evening ...'

Whittaker had a very good dinner, and the service was everything he'd expect. What really impressed Terry, however, was that halfway through his pudding, Gwyneth ejected an aggressively drunk customer alone and with the minimum of fuss by pulling his arm up behind his back and guiding him to the doors. Whittaker doubted whether any of the other customers had even really noticed what was happening.

Arriving outside the staff entrance at midnight, Terry noticed a petite woman wearing a Barbour pacing up and down and looking at her watch whilst furiously sucking at a hand-rolled cigarette.

'Hello,' said Terry. 'I hope you don't mind my asking, but are you Sally?'

'Yes?' said the woman, with some suspicion in her voice. Her black hair was cut into a neat bob, and from behind her round glasses her dark eyes narrowed slightly as she stared at Whittaker.

'I'm a friend of Gwyneth's family. I'm waiting for her, too.'

'Oh,' said Sally, smiling. 'Are you the guy that's bought the 4i's? Gwyn phoned me.'

'Oh, good. Yes, I am. Terry Whittaker.' He extended his hand.

'Sally Gould.' They shook.

'Is that right you've been offered a job in Pancester?'

'Yes. Dawn and Taff tell you that, did they? Yes, it's a homeless project, working in Pancester and Laikley.' She spoke with a textbook Essex accent. Whittaker could imagine the owner of that voice in the passenger seat of a black Golf GTi while Kool and the Gang belted out from the in-car stereo.

'Run by the City Council?'

'No, by a charity. The St Oswald's Trust. I'd really like to do it. I love Pancester. At the moment I work as a social worker in Tower Hamlets, and it's doing my head in. I'd like to get out of London. Well, I expect you feel the same, don't you? Or why would you have bought the 4i's? It's crazy here now, it really is, isn't it? Where we live, in New Cross, well, I won't go on about it. But Gwyn's only been here a year, here at the Savoy, I mean, and she loves it, and where could she get anything like it up North. I mean, there's not many places even in London as good, are there, never mind in Pancester. So we don't really know what to do. St Oswald's have given me a week to decide.'

'Cou ...'

'I mean, I could commute, I suppose, come back here at

weekends, but then Gwyn works weekends. And it would be so expensive, wouldn't it? You wouldn't believe what we pay in New Cross, and the St Oswald's thing pays less than my current job and there'd be somewhere to get in Pancester, unless I stayed with Taff and Dawn, which might be a bit weird, and train fares, unless I got a car ...'

'Ah, here's Gwyneth,' said Whittaker.

Gwyneth kissed Sally, and said hello to 'Mr Whittaker', who insisted on Terry, and the three of them made their way to the Fork and Knife, London's premier late-night private drinking spot for those who work in the restaurant and hotel trade. Terry was quite well known there, and it excited some gossip amongst the members to see him in for the first time since his sacking. A saucier from the Savoy cornered him at the bar, got to hear Whittaker's version of events, and then said, 'Thinking of doing something with Gwyn? She's very good.'

'Really?'

'Really. Efficient, clever, friendly. Strong, too. Don't let her sucker you into an arm-wrestling contest, 'cos she's unbeaten. I thought she'd get on. Is that why you're here, with her, Tel? Thinking of giving her a job? You can't be after a shag, that I do know.'

'Maybe.' He joined Gwyneth and Sally at a side table, and started to tell them about the 4i's project. Gwyneth was wide-eyed.

'It's a great idea. Pancester is packed with tourists all year. Dad's been trying to sell since Gramps retired. It was his and Gramma's life, but Dad's always hated the caff. So he's going in with Olly at last? I bet Mum's pleased.'

'I'm surprised they haven't phoned.'

'They left a message to call them, now you come to mention it. Haven't got round to it yet.'

'Why are you so surprised, Terry?' said Sally. 'You've discussed Gwyn with them, haven't you? That's why you're here, isn't it? They told you what she did, didn't they? And about me and St Oswald's? You're going to offer her a job, aren't you? Aren't you?

61

You lovely man! Darling, he's come to offer you a job! Goodbye, Tower Hamlets! Hello, Pancester! Oh, this is wonderful. Isn't it? Didn't I say something would turn up? Didn't I? It's God's will!'

Gwyneth frowned at her and held her finger to her lips. Sally blushed, and lowered her eyes under dark lashes behind her glasses. 'You really are very pretty,' thought Whittaker. He laughed.

'Your name came up, yes. When your mum said the Savoy Grill. But there are other people I'd like to see. Danny Bateman, the Maître d' at Rococo for example. He's a mate of mine.'

'Danny Bateman?' said Sally. 'He's not fit to clean Gwyn's shoes.'

'Sally, do shut up. You don't even know him!'

Whittaker laughed again. 'No, but do you think you might be interested?'

'Of course she's interested, aren't you?' Gwyn nodded.

'Come to our party. On Saturday. Come on. Please,' said Sally.

'I'd love to.' They finished their drinks while Sally gave Whittaker detailed instructions on how to find their flat, before saying good night. Whittaker watched Gwyneth and Sally get into a taxi.

The next night Whittaker phoned Danny Bateman, but Dan wasn't keen to leave London. 'Sorry, Terry.'

'Sure thing, pal. That's cool. Do you know Gwyneth Gabatini? At the Savoy?'

'I do, yeah. I've heard good things. You know she just lost out as manager at Pharmacy?'

'No, I didn't.'

So over a couple of days, Terry formed a favourable impression of Gwyneth's abilities, and he looked forward to the party. He spent the time till Saturday on the phone, getting measurements from Taff, talking about dinnerware with Penny Lester, sketching out some preliminary ideas for a menu, and writing 'Juliana Whittaker' on pieces of scrap paper.

Brian Carless phoned him. 'The sale has gone through. The 4i's is yours. Congratulations. If you need representation in Pancester, I know that we here at Carless Peddler Spoke would be pleased to help.'

'Cheers, Brian. That would be great. You're hired. Could you get on your bikes and start the process of fixing up a drinks licence?'

'A pleasure, Mr Whittaker.'

Sally shouted with joy when he turned up the door of the small flat in New Cross. It was already crowded by the time Whittaker arrived. An Indigo Girls CD played quietly in the background.

'Everyone! This is Terry! He's going to give Gwyn a job, so we can go and live in Pancester!'

'Sally! Shut up!' said Gwyneth, ushering him across to the drinks table. Several beautifully painted Airfix models Second World War aircraft hung by nylon threads from the ceiling.

'Cor, those are smashing,' said Whittaker enthusiastically. 'I used to make those when I was a kid.'

'Er, I still do,' admitted Gwyneth. 'Helps me unwind.'

'Do you have a hobby, Sally? How do you unwind?' asked Whittaker.

'Smoking. You just can't top it for keeping your hands busy, can you?' She rolled herself a fag from her tin.

'I don't know. It ruins the tastebuds, you see.'

'Oh. Bad luck.'

There was only one other man present, who came across and introduced himself as Pete, an art historian from Goldsmith's. He and Whittaker chatted for a while.

'How do you know Sally and Gwyn?' asked Whittaker.

'Oh, from Meeting,' said Pete, enigmatically.

A large and hearty tennis coach called Mabel crossed the room with a bottle of whisky, and filled Whittaker's glass to the brim.

'You're a chef, aren't you? You like food?' she said. 'Did you hear the one about the guy who goes up to this ice-cream van?'

Whittaker shook his head, which was all the encouragement Mabel needed. For three hours Whittaker was weak with laughter as Mabel regaled him with whisky and her bottomless store of filthy stories, until by two, when the other guests had all left, Whittaker was blind drunk and snoring on the floor.

Gwyn took off his shoes, put a cushion under his head and a blanket over his body while Sally made some cocoa.

'He's OK, isn't he? Do you know what his staff called him?' said Gwyn.

'What?'

'Cuggles.'

'Ahh. Cuggles. Like a big fat squishy love ball. Think he'll be all right?'

'Yeah. Come on, let's go to bed. We've got an early start.'

In the morning, Whittaker awoke with a screaming headache and his stomach in revolt. He looked at his watch. It was five past eleven. The bedroom door was open.

'Hello?' he called, a pathetic catch in his voice.

There was no reply. Sally and Gwyneth had obviously gone out. He managed to get himself to his feet and into the small kitchen to make some tea. He was still sitting there shortly after noon, staring at the table top, when the girls got in, smiling and holding hands. Whittaker looked at them both, and at last the penny dropped.

'Um . . .' he said, 'I hope you don't mind my asking . . .' Sally and Gwyneth looked at each other, and let go of one another's hands.

'. . . but are you – you know, you two – are you . . . Christians?'

Sally whistled, and Gwyn sat down at the table. 'How could you tell?' she said.

'Well, little things. Your shoes. Sally's waxed jacket, and going to work for a charity, and then she said something the other night about God's will. Pete saying he knew you from Meeting. And who else gets up on a Sunday?'

'Oh, you won't tell Mum and Dad, will you?' said Gwyneth anxiously. 'They don't really know about Sally and me being . . . well, we're not exactly what you'd call "out".'

'Of course not. Hey . . . I hope you won't mind my asking, but I've always wondered. What is it you guys actually do?'

'Same as anyone. Stuff,' said Gwyn.

'We're Quakers. We don't really do what you would call a lot,' said Sally.

'Oh', said Whittaker. 'Er . . . could I watch some time?'

The girls laughed. 'It doesn't worry you then, Terry?' said Sally. 'It doesn't make you uncomfortable? It won't change your mind about giving Gwyn the job, will it?'

'Course not. It's the noughties. People are into all sorts of weird stuff. Live and let live, I say.'

'Oh, Cuggles!' shouted Sally. 'So you *are* offering Gwyn the job?'

Whittaker smiled weakly. 'Yes, Sal, I am. What do you think, Gwyn? Come and be my manager?'

'I'd love to, Terry. I really would. What are you paying?'

'Um . . . same as you get now, plus free accommodation.'

'Accommodation? Where?' said Sally.

'In the flat. With me. Both of you, obviously. There's loads of room, and it'll be no fun on my own.'

Gwyneth looked at Sally and smiled. Sally kissed Terry and then threw her arms round Gwyn, sobbing.

Gwyn looked over Sally's shoulder, and smiled again. 'That's a yes, then, Terry.'

'Good. Great. Er . . . where would be the best place for me to be sick?'

A Realignment of Various Energies

On Monday, Whittaker drove back to Pancester, Penny Lester in the passenger seat next to him, the boot and the back of the car piled with boxes and duvets and suitcases and everything that would enable him to set up camp in the flat above the 4i's, at least for a few weeks until the builders had finished and he could move in properly. Whittaker talked to Penny about Juliana; Penny pretended to listen, and then talked about Ulrich, a German producer with the BBC World Service who had been buggering her about for almost a year.

'He's a pig, Terry, quite frankly, but he's soooo dishy, and he has pecs to die for. I should stop seeing him, really, but when he phones me up and calls me Penelope in his sexy accent, I just melt.'

Terry pretended in his turn to listen to Penny's troubles, and so, between the two of them, they felt that they had had an intimate conversation. As Terry turned the corner on the Blackhampton road that brought the city into view, Penny sighed and said, 'How utterly precious.' Whittaker felt as though he were coming home, as though he had never been away.

Juliana felt that he had never been away, too. He had phoned twice more over the weekend, and on arriving in her office that morning, she had found a huge bouquet of flowers waiting on her desk. It was beyond a joke, quite frankly. She would have to do something.

Whittaker managed to find the short-term parking by the

National Museum of Crime and Punishment, and he took Penny into the Tourist Information Office. Juliana wasn't there, so they left a message, telling her he was back safely and not to worry, and then they headed down to Carless Peddler Spoke to pick up the keys for the 4i's.

Brian Carless handed over the keys, and got Whittaker's signature on the application for a drinks licence.

'I don't think we'll have any problem with that,' said Carless. 'If you need to change the outside of the building in any way though, Terry, you might have to apply for planning. Everything in the city proper is subject to approval.'

'Even signs?' said Penny.

'Officially, yes. I mean, I don't think they'd kick up too much of a fuss about new signs, especially since you don't intend changing the name, but it will be worth running past them, no doubt. Keep 'em sweet.'

At the 4i's Taff and Oliver were packing records into boxes in the basement. Taff grinned at Terry. Oliver looked at Penny and blushed.

'Gwyneth phoned last night. You're a bloody hero in our house, you are.'

'Well, I liked her. I heard good things. And Sally is great. She told you about sharing the flat?'

'Yes. Great. Nice to think there will still be a Gabatini in the old place.'

Penny was wandering around the café, taking photos with a digital camera and displaying them on her laptop. She didn't really need Whittaker, so he went to move the car, in order to unload his things into the flat.

He spoke to Taff and Oliver as he left. 'Will it be all right to leave the motor outside for a bit, Taff?'

'Yeah, for a bit. If you're living here, you'll be able to apply for a resident's permit. Hey, seen the new car park your girlfriend wants to build? Very swish.'

'Where?'

'Down on the Dole Acre. Some of the ladies are a bit fed up.

They go there at Easter. Been going there a long time, they 'ave. Still, you can't stop progress, can you?'

'Can't you? I thought Pancester stopped progress twenty-five years ago, at least. No new building inside the wall since the cathedral in 1894, all the city's medieval practices still intact. Your haircut. All unchanged.'

'Cheeky London poof! Still, you're right in a way. I've not made my mind up. Though I guess we do need a car park. You must have a look. See what you think. There's a computer mock-up of how it'll look on the front page of the *Mail*.'

'I'm sure if Juliana's involved it'll be great. Um, what's the best way from the car park by the castle back here?'

'I'll come,' said Oliver in his deep and little-used voice. 'Show you.'

'OK. Thanks.'

Whittaker and Oliver walked to where the Subaru was parked. 'Nice girl, Penny,' said Oliver, still blushing furiously.

'Yes. An old mate of mine. Top designer. She's going out with a ski instructor called Albert. Swiss, or something, she was telling me.'

Oliver nodded, and pulled his earlobe.

They reached the car. 'I'll drive,' said Oliver, holding out his hands for the keys.

'Oh . . . are you insured?'

'Um.' said Oliver. Whittaker gave him the keys, and climbed into the passenger seat. Oliver started the engine, put the car into reverse, looked over his shoulder, gunned the accelerator, and shot between two cars whose red-faced drivers waved their fists. He screamed backwards around the castle, out into the Guildhall Square, scattering pigeons and pedestrians, and through the narrow archway to Shy Street, where he jammed on the handbrake, swerved round in a 180-degree arc and skidded to a halt in front of the 4i's. He turned off the engine, nodded at Whittaker, who sat rigid with fear in the passenger seat, and said, 'Help you unload?'

'Er . . . no thanks, Oliver. I – actually, I think I'll just sit here for a minute and catch my breath.'

Oliver smiled, and nodded.

Penny stayed in Pancester for a week, drawing up plans for the building. Whittaker wandered around the shops, looking for suppliers. Gwyneth phoned him, and they made some plans. Sally was to arrive on the following Monday to start work with St Oswald's, Gwyn not for a month while she worked out her notice.

Whittaker did not neglect Juliana, whom he continued to bombard on a daily basis with flowers, chocolates and invitations for drinks. When this didn't seem to be getting him anywhere, he thought he might try something more unusual. He bought a huge poisonous cactus from the florist, with a sign on it saying 'Do Not Touch', in case she liked that sort of thing – in case she had been a Goth or something in her youth – just to show that he was a bit out of the ordinary line of suitor. Even the small interval between receiving the cactus and putting it into a bin liner to throw it out had been enough to raise a painful rash on her hands. The next day he sent her a pair of love birds, which he found in Pancester Pets; she donated them to Laikley Children's Zoo, who were grateful for anything that moved.

Penny, who knew something of Whittaker's past, urged caution one evening as they sat on chairs from the café in the large front room of the flat. 'Take it from me, Terry, it's not worth getting involved with anyone who doesn't have feelings for you. Look at me and Ulrich.'

'I hear you, Pen, but I rather think Juliana is starting to develop feelings for me.'

Which was true enough. Juliana already had very strong feelings for Whittaker.

On Friday night, Penny and Terry went out to see The Knightwatchmen. Taff had insisted. 'New kit, new uniforms, the lot. You'll have to come, or I'll sulk, see?'

They were playing in the Holly Bush, and had crammed their gear into the tiny bar, Taff's new drum kit in pride of place. The pub was packed; Terry and Penny bought two pints and found themselves a corner. Oliver came into the bar, bought himself a drink, and then came and joined them. He nodded at Whittaker, blushed at Penny, and sat down next to her.

'Hello, Oliver,' said Penny. 'How are you?'

Oliver turned a deeper shade of scarlet, and mumbled into his beer. Penny smiled politely, and turned to watch the stage.

The band came on stage to a huge cheer. They were all wearing new black leather suits and white shirts with thin leather ties. There was Taff, and Barry from the café, and two of Barry's mates, Kev and Chris, who were on guitars. Barry, Kev and Chris had just formed a thrash metal band called The Dead Wait and wanted out of The Knightwatchmen, and out of being Teds, but they had been playing with Taff for three years, since they were sixteen, and so they felt loyal to the poor old geezer, who had, after all, taught them a lot. They decided to go along with it for this one last gig. Taff wouldn't mind.

'I'm the John Mayall of Pancester rock 'n' roll, I am,' he boasted.

The Knightwatchmen, to Whittaker's horror, played Shadows covers. Barry, Kev and Chris twanged and stepped politely, and Taff tore into his new kit with all the enthusiasm of the natural-born amateur. One last time, they clattered through The Knightwatchmen's perennial repertoire. The crowd was enthusiastic, which worried Whittaker.

Taff looked a bit fed up when he came over to Terry, Penny and Oliver after the show, towering above them in his shiny new leather suit. 'Ah, well,' he said. 'Now I'll have to find a new lot to train up. I just 'ope they fit the new uniforms.'

'Never mind, love,' said Dawn, coming across and giving him a hug. 'You'll find some. You always do,' she added, looking at Terry.

'Yeah. There's always a demand for The Shads. Some things never go out of fashion, do they, Penny?'

'Hah!' said Penny. 'You're so funny, Taffy! Isn't he funny, Oliver?' Oliver smiled the smile that had broken a hundred hearts in Pancester, and nodded vigorously.

'How's the bid to capture the youth slash alternative market going?' asked Whittaker.

'Not bad. Not bad at all. I'm going downstairs with the records, and Olly's going up on to the first floor with the books and that. Stevie Medlicott is doing some alterations. The Fox Hole, we're calling it. Like a cross between Heavily Foxed and the Rock Cave. I liked the Heavy Cave, but Oliver wasn't having it, were you?'

Oliver shook his head.

'Is Steve Medlicott your builder?'

'The best in town. I can recommend him for whatever you need doing. I've got his card at 'ome.'

'Cheers, Taff.'

'What do you think of this new car park they want to build then, Terry?' asked Dawn.

'I've seen the pictures of how it's supposed to look in the *Mail*. It looks good. The figures made a lot of sense. But I'm surprised more people aren't objecting. I thought Pancester was the place where nothing changed. That's why I like it. And I've read about the Eastering, which sounds fun. Aren't the women a bit put out?'

'Yeah, I am a bit, to be honest with you, Tel,' said Dawn. 'Me and Taff did a lot of our courting down there. It's romantic, isn't it?'

'Olly's brother, Dexter, is trying to whip up a bit of aggro,' said Taff. 'Along with old Mrs Innes, who keeps her donkeys there, and a few others. We couldn't 'alf use it though.'

'I s'pose so,' said Dawn. 'But I used to like hiding in the bushes with my sisters, lighting candles and dreaming of boys.' She sighed.

'I 'ope you dreamed about me,' said Taff.

'Well, I had a nightmare once,' she replied. Taffy kissed her.

On Monday evening, after Penny had gone, promising some detailed plans by the end of the week, Sally arrived, with a suitcase and a sleeping bag. She was full of enthusiasm for the flat.

'Oh, it's so big! It's lovely, isn't it? It'll be lovely when you get some furniture, won't it? And paint it. It'll be lovely, won't it? Which one's mine and Gwyn's room? This one? That one?'

'Well, either. You choose. I've got this one, and the one at the back is for the nursery . . .'

'Ooh, are you having a baby? Is that what's in here, Cuggles?' she said, patting Whittaker's stomach.

'No. One day. Soon, I hope. Who told you they call me Cuggles?' He smiled complacently.

'Gwyneth. Who's the lucky girl?'

Whittaker made tea and told Sally all about Juliana. Sally looked solemn.

'So you're not so much her boyfriend as her stalker then, Terry?'

'You haven't seen her when she looks at me. We both know what's going on. She's just coming round to seeing it.'

Juliana had felt like coming round on several occasions. First, she had thought of coming round with a hammer, and trashing Whittaker's car. Then, she had thought of coming round with her solicitor, or perhaps a few . . . friends. Good sense, however, still prevailed. She had returned every box of chocolates to Terry, usually with an obscene note – all of which he kept – and had donated all the flowers to the almshouses, but still they came. At first, in her flat, she had taken to call screening, listening to all her messages before answering the phone, but after a week, she could stand Whittaker's increasingly rambling and incoherent declarations of love no more, and changed her number, taking care to ensure that she was ex-directory. She was still vulnerable at work. Gaynor was forbidden to let Whittaker's calls through, and even to take any messages, but Whittaker haunted the building, and Juliana had taken to forcing Gaynor to check that he wasn't hanging around outside before she went anywhere. Even so, he had caught her on a number of occasions, and had followed her down the street, chattering brightly of their future together, while she ignored him.

Once, as she was trying to duck into De'Ath's to get away from him, he caught at her arm to restrain her, and with a cheerful grin on his face, he patted her bum and said, 'Are you trying to get away from me?' Red-faced with fury, she pulled herself away, and punched him in the mouth with all her force.

'Fuck off!' she screamed. 'And if you ever touch me again, I'll see you behind bars, you sick bastard!'

Whittaker rubbed his jaw thoughtfully. 'Sorry, Ju,' he said. 'I was only mucking about.'

'And don't call me Ju!'

That afternoon, Whittaker bought himself a smart cardboard filing box from the stationer's to keep on top of his wardrobe. His father phoned as he was assembling the box.

'How are you, boy? Eh? Are you well? Are you buried up to your balls in a tight little pussy, are you? Did I catch you at a bad time?' Whittaker could hear the tumours rattling around in his father's chest as he spoke.

'I'm well, thanks, Dad. I'm opening a new restaurant, up here in Pancester.'

'You can't, boy. You can't leave me here alone to die.'

'Well, would you like it if I found you somewhere up here? I'm sure there are hospices in the North.'

'Leave London? What for? Leave London! Are you fucking mad? Are you wrong in the fucking head, boy? Eh?'

'Then I'll come and visit you as often as I can.'

'Every week?'

'Probably not. Not with this new restaurant I'm opening. And I've got a new girlfriend, so it won't always be . . .'

'Heh heh heh! New girlfriend? Give her one from me, son. Give her one from your old Dad! Eh?'

'But I'll get down to see you as often as I can.'

'I'll be dead.'

'Well . . .'

'You only started talking to me again 'cos you knew I was dying. 'Cos you wanted my money. Well, I haven't got any. Spent it all on tarts. So fuck you, lover boy. What's her name?'

'Juliana.'

'Fuck me, boy, she must be desperate, eh, to shag you. Eh, boy? Desperate.'

'Well, OK, Dad. Thanks for phoning. I'll come and see you when I can.'

'I'll be ...' Whittaker hung up, and thought about his campaign to win Juliana. Desperate, his father said. Whittaker smiled grimly. At least he knew what love really was, unlike the old man. At least he would never use women in that way. At least he knew how to keep his fly zipped. He finished putting his filing box together, and lifted it on to his wardrobe.

Juliana was beyond desperate. So when Whittaker's application to change the signs at the 4i's arrived in front of the planning committee, she saw a chance to stop him at last.

Penny had sent up the plans for the alterations and redecoration from London. She had chosen an optical theme for the 4i's. The diners would sit at glass tables in outdated optician's examination chairs, and eat from glass plates. Framed cases of antique spectacles would line the walls. Halogen lights would be directed to shine through prisms. The menu would look like a sight-test, with the starters in large print and the puddings in a tiny font at the bottom. The kitchen was to be completely gutted and rejuvenated, with new ovens, cookers and freezers. The frontage was to be altered only slightly. Penny suggested simply cleaning the plate-glass window which had been installed in the sixties, and replacing the old sign with a new one; four untreated steel bars, cut to the shape of lower-case i's, suspended on wires from a bracket over the door. 'This shouldn't present any difficulty with the planners,' she had written.

Some alteration was proposed to the flat as well, including a shower cubicle in Gwyn and Sally's room. Terry called Steve Medlicott, who came to see the plans. He was a small, thin man in his late forties or early fifties, with a hoary Hawkwind T-shirt bagging out from his pigeon chest. He had long straggly grey hair cut in a Peter Stringfellow style with a drooping mandarin moustache, which he chewed as he viewed the plans.

'What do you think, Steve?' Whittaker asked.

Steve pushed his tongue from between his lips and considered.

'The universe,' he said deliberately, 'is a matrix of energy.' His voice barely struggled out from under his moustache, so that Whittaker had to work hard to hear him. He had a marked tendency to pause thoughtfully and screw up his forehead in concentration in the middle of his somewhat enigmatic statements, as though he were searching for exactly the right words that would enable a bright five-year-old to understand his complex ideas.

'Oh, yes, I see, a matrix of energy, yes,' said Whittaker, who didn't see at all.

'In order to maintain equilibrium, it is necessary that we conduct ... the various energies that surround us in an appropriate manner.'

'I see.'

'This building ...'

'Yes?'

'... has certain energies. What you might call ... a vibe. Your project also creates energies within the vortices. The question is ...'

'Oh, yes?'

'... is do these two differing energies have harmonising potential?'

'And what do you think, Steve?'

Steve cocked his head, and flipped through the plans again. 'Yes, I believe they might,' he said.

'So you'll do it?'

'I will try to bring harmony to bear, yes.'

'Great. How much, do you think?'

'Mr Whittaker, money has a particular energy of its own. Sometimes it is strong ... other times, this money energy is not so strong ... How can I say, until I have completed the process of harmonisation, whether the energy will be strong ... or weak?'

'Guess.'

'Five grand. Give or take.'

'Done.'

So while Steve began work on the interior, having finished

work at the Fox Hole next door, Brian Carless prepared to present the plans for the exterior alterations to the planning committee.

'So that's all, is it, Terry? Old signs down, window cleaned and frames repainted, four steel bars, each of eighteen inches in length, to be suspended on a three-foot bracket? The planners won't even give it a moment's thought. Even easier than the magistrates' – who had granted Whittaker his drinks licence, unopposed, a few days earlier.

Juliana just managed to spot the item at the bottom of the planning committee agenda, and told Trevor Mallinson that she would be opposing it.

'But, darling . . . on what grounds?'

'I'll think of something.'

She arrived at the meeting on time, and sat anxiously through various routine applications until the last item was reached.

'Item . . . new signage at the 4i's café. Er . . . I don't really see any problems with this . . . really? Not really?' said Trevor, nervously looking at Juliana. The members of the committee shook their heads, and started to gather up their papers.

'Yes. The Tourist Office objects,' said Juliana, rising to her feet.

'Objects?' said Dexter Halton. 'On what possible grounds?'

'Because . . . because it will destroy the tourist trade here in Pancester. Not overnight. But it will kill it for ever.'

'I must say, I'm most sceptical, Miss Blezzard,' said Aolder-woman Armistead.

'But don't you see? Don't you understand? If you let Whittaker change the 4i's, then you admit the possibility of change. And why do all the tourists come? Because nothing here ever changes. Everywhere else has. But what would happen if Courtney's changed into yet another branch of Debenhams? Or if KFC bought De'Ath's? If Ye Blacke Bull got bought up by Ye Olde Worlde 100 Per Cent Authentic Taverns PLC? It would become like everywhere else. And the tourists wouldn't come. Tourism outstrips all other economic activity within the walls of Pancester by 82 per cent. How much does the council earn in business rates from all the antiques shops? From the already perfectly adequate restaurants, which are thronged with visitors day after day?'

'Yes, but they're not adequate, are they?' said Dexter. 'They're awful.'

'Aye, and the 4i's is the worst of the lot,' said Aolderman Dymock. 'It's full of rockers and bovver boys.'

'That's how people like it. They want waiters with long faces, not some halfwit wishing them a nice day when all they want is egg and chips. Pancester is like England before Mrs Thatcher ...'

'Lady Thatcher to you, young woman,' said Aolderman Dymock.

'Sorry, Aolderman, of course. But, you see, Pancester keeps not just the medieval stuff, but all the fifties, sixties and seventies things too. And people love that. If you let Mr Terry Whittaker come here and start serving ... I don't know, monkfish in crab juice and stuff, then no one will want boiled mutton and cabbage from Ye Blacke Bull, will they? The illusion will pop, and soon there'd be good food and friendly service all over town – just like everywhere else. And visitors won't come, not even to see people prancing about with elvers and apples. Oh, but young people will love it. They'll move here in great numbers. There'll be pavement cafés. They'll want community art projects and basketball courts. You'll see.'

'So we have to eat horrible food for ever?' said Trevor Mallinson, sadly.

'Oh, but the horror of the food is part of the fascination of the place. People like horrible things. If people want nice things, then how come Alton Towers is so popular? Why on earth would anyone go to Legoland UK? No, they want long queues, bad food. It's all part of the traditional British day out. This place is a theme park too, you know.'

'But what about the Americans?' asked Dexter. 'They're always complaining about the food. And they don't come here for seventies nostalgia, do they? They don't want authentic re-creations of the three-day week, do they? Surely we could afford one good restaurant? For the Americans?'

'Ah, but you're wrong, Aolderman Halton. When the Americans come to England, they want abbeys and castles and some easily digested history, sure, I admit that, but mostly they want to confirm the views of England which they've been spoon-fed by Hollywood. They want pea-souper fogs, and bobbies on bicycles, and red double-decker buses and City gents in bowlers. And they want bad food, poorly presented. It's what they've been led to expect, and they want it. It's becoming harder to find by the minute, outside our walls. Pancester stands alone. Gentlemen, Aolderwoman Armistead, Pancester stands for England!'

A hush fell on the room as the committee considered the solemnity of its duties.

'So you object to four steel bars hanging from a bracket, but you approve the destruction of our heritage so that you can have a new million-pound car park?' asked Dexter.

A rustle ran through the committee as it sensed trouble.

'The car park, Aolderman Halton, is outside the walls. Very different,' said Juliana, her eyes narrowing as she stared at Dexter.

'Yes, well, thank you, Ms Blezzard. If you'd leave the room, we'll move to a vote,' said Trevor.

Juliana stormed out. The new signs at the 4i's were approved six to two: Mallinson and Dymock against, and Plumb asleep.

Dexter phoned Whittaker and invited him out for a drink that evening. Sally and Taff joined them.

Whittaker felt hurt as Dexter told the story over a pint in the Holly Bush.

'Why is she being like this?' he asked no one in particular.

'Because she hates you,' said Sally. 'Please leave her alone. She doesn't sound very nice, but no one deserves to be bothered twenty-hours a day. Please try and forget her.'

'No, no one hates Terry,' said Taff. 'He's a beautiful man. Stevie Medlicott says his energetic aura is violet, and he doesn't say that about many people.'

'She said it was because you represented change,' said Dexter. 'You represent metropolitan values that run counter to the spirit of Pancester.'

'Oh, I hope I don't, at least not too much. I mean, I agree with her. You can't start changing this place, or you'll be in trouble. But one modern restaurant down a side street shouldn't be too threatening, should it? I think it's because she knows that we're meant to be together, and she wants to put up a bit of a struggle. Make it exciting.' Sally shifted uncomfortably in her chair.

'So if you oppose change, does that mean you oppose the new car park?' asked Dexter.

'Well . . . I don't know that it's entirely my place. I've only been here a couple of weeks.'

'Nonsense. You're a businessman, you'll be paying business rates. You're entitled to a say.'

'Well then, as a businessman, I think the car park makes a lot of sense. But if I were a Pancestrian, then I should say no. You can't just throw away six hundred years of history.'

'More,' said Sally. 'I was told the Eastering has been taking place since the time of the Romans, if not longer.'

'So come and join the anti-car park campaign,' said Dexter. 'I don't know.'

'It would show that Juliana what you're made of, bach,' said Taffy.

The world spun round inside Whittaker's head. His mouth went dry. He gulped at his beer. 'God, yes. Yes, it would. She'd see that I was responding to her opposition to the 4i's with an equal and, er . . . opposing force. Yes. It's probably what she wants. Probably, she only tried to stop the 4i's as a way of expressing her feelings for me. That's the kind of woman she is. Of course! How could I be so stupid? She wants me to prove my love by standing up to her.' He laughed, and stood up.

'Where are you going, Terry?' asked Sally.

'To find her, and tell her I've seen through her little ruse.'

Sally rolled her eyes to heaven. 'No, Terry, please don't,' she said. 'That . . . er, I don't think that would be . . . look, I tell you what. If you're going to be actively opposing her for a bit, I don't think you should contact her at all. I mean, you should play hard to get for once. If she sees that you are against the car park, she'll understand. She won't need to be told. She'll just know. Women are like that, they just know things, After a while, she might contact you herself. If you're right.'

Whittaker sat down again.

'I see what you're saying,' he said. 'But you don't think she'll be hurt if I don't contact her?'

'No, Terry, I don't,' said Sally emphatically. 'OK, yes, say she wants you to resist her. By opposing her, and not contacting her ... er ... she'll see you're a real man, and then maybe she'll fall into your arms. Or something.' Sally couldn't believe that she'd said it.

'Oh. Do you really think so?' Whittaker rubbed his chin, and Sally nodded vigorously. Whittaker sighed.

'OK, OK,' he said. 'If this is what it takes to get her to stop playing this silly hard-to-get game, then OK. What do you want me to do, Dexter?'

'Well, we're having a meeting tomorrow evening at Mrs Innes' house. Come to that, and we'll start making some plans.'

So it was agreed.

The next morning, Terry had arranged with Sally to run her into Laikley. He'd never been before, and wanted to make contact with the fishermen's co-operative there, feeling that they might supply him with fresher produce than Wiggins, the Pancester fishmonger, with whom he had been unimpressed. Sally already spent most of her time in Laikley, and had been going out on the bus.

'I'm looking for some premises to open a homeless shelter. There's no point in doing it in Pancester.'

'Why?'

'Well, there aren't really any homeless people, unless you count Edmund.'

'Who's Edmund?'

'Oh, you must have seen him. He's a real old-fashioned gentleman of the road, huge beard, smokes a pipe ...'

'Oh, yes, I have.' Whittaker remembered his first morning in Pancester, and the tramp scavenging for elvers.

'Well, he's beyond help. God knows where he sleeps, but he's happy enough. He's quite articulate, actually. But Laikley . . .'

They were coming into the outskirts of the town. They passed the shabby concrete entrance of the Laikley Children's Zoo, where two workmen were erecting a banner that read 'Coming Soon! Donkey World!' They passed three empty crazy golf courses. The promenade was cold and bleak. Parking was no trouble. The sea was nowhere to be seen; a great plain of wet grey mud extended from the prom to the horizon. A young woman in a Kappa tracksuit, her bottle-blonde hair bunched on top of her head, pushed a buggy against the wind. Several shabby arcades, still open even in the winter, offered prize bingo. Whittaker watched the Kappa girl push her buggy into one of the arcades and open her purse.

'Unbelievable, isn't it?' remarked Sally. 'All the resources go into Pancester, and nothing comes here. High unemployment, high crime, a rampant smack culture, and homeless figures that would shame a big city, never mind a run-down seaside resort. I tell you what, the money for that car park would go a long way here.'

She went off to work, and Terry found the fishermen's co-operative, where he made some satisfactory contacts. He also walked around the town centre. One in three of the shops was boarded up. Several people approached him for money. The shopping arcade was almost deserted, and smelt of poverty. He found Juliana's father's bowls shop, I'm All Right, Jack, but the 'Closed' sign was up, and when Whittaker looked in at the window, he could see no sign of life.

He walked into a newsagent's to buy a paper, and cast a surreptitious eye along the top shelf. There was certainly plenty to choose from. And didn't that foxy girl on the cover of *Razzle* have just Juliana's shade of red in her hair? He was reaching towards the mag when the shopkeeper called out to him.

'Hey, mate! I know you! I've seen you on telly!'

Whittaker's hand instinctively grabbed at a magazine about keeping tropical fish instead, and he whirled around, red-faced and smiling.

'Hey! Mother! Get 'ere! Look! It's 'im!'

An old lady in a green and white sari came through from the back room and stared at Whittaker.

'Hello,' said Whittaker.

'It's 'im, from *Changing Rooms*. Aren't yer?' said the clearly very made-up shopkeeper.

'Well ...' Whittaker began. The old lady snorted, and said something contemptuous in Urdu.

'Oh aye, that's right. *Junior Masterchef*. Where's yer bow-tie?'

'Um, I only wore it once, for the programme. I didn't really think it was me.'

'No, it were right smart. Is this what you want? *Cold Water Aquarium Monthly*?'

'Um ... yes. Yes please.'

'No, you don't want this, do you? I thought you were after one of the porn mags. You were, weren't you? And I put you off your stroke, so to speak. I'm sorry, it's just that we don't often get anyone off the telly in here. Go on, don't be embarrassed, I'll send Mother back into the stock room,' and he spoke sharply to his mother, who retreated with a disapproving frown. Whittaker replaced the fish magazine, and selected *Razzle*, which he hid inside his copy of the *Guardian* on the counter.

'That's better,' said the shopkeeper. 'I'll pop it in a bag for you, shall I? There you go. Well, this 'as bin a red-letter day for us, it really 'as. You'll 'ave made Mother's day, you really will. I'll phone me uncle in a minute, and tell 'im who I've 'ad in. He'll be that thrilled! What's yer name?'

'Terry. Whittaker.'

'Well, it were right nice to meet you, Terry. I'm Zahid. Any time you fancy knockin' one off, Terry, you come and see me. I'll sort you out.' And he took Whittaker's hand and shook it; as Terry left the shop, Zahid smiled and waved as he picked up the phone.

Terry tucked the bag with the mag under his coat, and hurried back to the car. When he got back to the flat, he put it into his new cardboard filing box, for later examination.

*

That evening, when Sally got in, and before he went off to his meeting, Whittaker gave her his car keys.

'No use to me, at least not at the moment. It'll make it easier for you to find your new premises, and I'll look less hypocritical opposing the car park. I've put you on the insurance.' She leapt into his arms, and covered his face with kisses.

'Oh, Cuggs. You lovely, lovely man. What a Christian thing to do.'

'Shhh,' said Whittaker. 'Someone might hear us.'

At seven, he walked down to Mrs Innes' house, a three-storey affair by the Great Gate. He rang the bell, and was greeted by a muffled, booming bark from inside. He could hear a highly cultured voice saying, 'Oh, do shut up, Rolly, you fat arse. Shut up. Come here. Down!'

The door opened. Mrs Innes, a tiny white-haired woman in her seventies with humorous blue eyes, was wearing a greasy pinafore and black wellington boots rolled down to her ankles. She was clinging to the collar of Rolly, a massively fat basset-hound with a suppurating tumour on his hind quarters, who panted and salivated at Whittaker in enthusiastic greeting. The whole rear end of his body waggled with ecstasy.

'Come in, dear, come in. Come through. I hope you don't mind dogs. He'll jump at you, I'm afraid, but I'm sure you won't mind. Come through.'

She led him down a dark book-lined corridor, which stank of meat, and into a dark and filthy book-lined sitting room, where Whittaker saw Dexter Halton and Steve Medlicott, sitting amongst piles of old newspapers. They nodded a greeting. Mrs Innes released Rolly, and he pushed his snout into Whittaker's groin, snuffling with joy.

'Sit down, dear,' said Mrs Innes. 'On the . . . whoa! Hang on! Look out! Don't sit there!'

Whittaker looked behind him, and saw a large dog turd on the sofa.

'Rolly! You naughty boy! How many times have I told you? Don't shit on the sofa! You know you're supposed to use the floor! Let me get that.' She pulled a tissue from her pocket, scooped up the turd, and threw it on to the fire.

'There. Here, put this under your bum, dear,' she said, handing Whittaker a yellowing copy of the *Daily Telegraph* from 1975. 'Now, tea?'

Tea was served in delicate bone china cups, nut-brown with the patina of tannin.

Mrs Innes talked. 'Now I'm sure you know our other members. Aolderman Halton of course, and Mr Medlicott, who assures me that he has been realigning the energetic structure of your fascinating new restaurant. Rolly and I will come in for a cup of tea one afternoon, show you some support. Now . . .'

'Er . . . sorry? Other members? Isn't there anyone else?'

'Not yet, dear, no. We're sure that as our media spokesperson and chief fund-raiser, you'll be drumming up support all over Pancester.'

'Media spokesperson?'

'Yes, dear, of course. You've been on the telly. I saw you. With Timmy Rubenstein. I like *Junior Masterchef.* I was surprised when the girl from Norwich won it, though. And the bow-tie didn't suit you. You'll have to tell me all about cogitating and digesting later. Now . . .'

'Chief fund-raiser?'

'Well, you're richer than any of us. Now, do stop asking questions, dear, and listen. We are going to hold a public meeting next Wednesday – chief speakers, Aolderman Dexter Halton, Mr Terry Whittaker, and myself – to whip up a bit of support. I shall be concentrating on the legal angle, and on how the Dole Acre plays a unique role in the life of the city. Aolderman Halton will be speaking on the subject of animal rights, with particular reference to donkeys. What will you give us, Mr Whittaker?'

'Um . . . how about something about new road schemes and car parks attracting more traffic? You know, a classic road-protester line. We could try and find out if the city has any eco-warriors, get them interested.'

'Marvellous! Mr Medlicott, are there any topics you would like to see covered?'

Steve licked his lips. 'I am in contact . . .' he paused, '. . . with certain – beings.'

'Oh, good,' said Mrs Innes.

'I have communicated with these beings, and they are not – you would say – happy with the possible consequences of energetic realignment on Dole Acre at this time.'

'Oh dear,' said Mrs Innes.

'They have assured me that they will send what you might call . . . a *representative* to our meeting.'

'Good. Good. Well, I look forward to that. In the meantime, if we could all tell our friends and families about the meeting, and perhaps each take a few posters around town? You can? Good.'

'What legal angle, Mrs Innes?' asked Whittaker.

Mrs Innes smiled grimly. 'It's all in the Charter, dear. Sir Kenelm de Courtney's Charter of 1503, which sets up the Dole. It's only the grazing rights which are granted to the city, not the freehold. Look.'

She dug around, and came up with a copy of Dadd's book.

'Look. There's a reproduction of the Charter, just here, look. It's all in Dadd. The freehold remains with the Courtney family, of that there is no doubt. Our opponents are counting on there being no living heir to the Courtney estate, which is true, poor Lady Lettice Courtney having disappeared in rather mysterious circumstances in 1972. But this does not mean the city takes over the freehold. Grazing rights, that's all the city is entitled to, and grazing rights, however you read it, can hardly have meant putting up a blooming great big new car park, can it? Hmmm?'

'No, Mrs Innes,' said Dexter and Terry together.

'The Charter, at the moment, is our main weapon.'

Medlicott opened his eyes wide, and looked around the room. 'There will be others, my friends. You can rest assured. There will be . . . others.'

And with that, the meeting adjourned to the Holly Bush.

End of Act One.

A Visit to the National Museum of Crime and Punishment

Bereft of Juliana's company, or what he perceived as her company, Whittaker found time hanging heavy. Gwyn was due to arrive, the energetic realignment of the 4i's was in full swing, and he had his speech to prepare for the public meeting. There was much to do, and he was very busy. But his days passed unleavened by the yeast of unrequited love, now that he was keeping his promise to Sally to stop contacting Juliana. As Captain Beefheart used to say, there was too much time.

Yes, and while we're on cultural references, y'know that bit in Proust where Swann can't go to Pierrefonds, because Odette is there, and it's not on because Pierrefonds is the only place he feels like going? Well, that's pretty much how it was for Whittaker. He really wanted to go up to the City Hall, and hang about in the entrance, because he needed to see Dexter Halton. But he didn't want to phone him in case . . . well, in case he was in, thereby blowing Whittaker's excuse for hanging about in the lobby. But he didn't go. He was strong.

But he did give in to his desire to visit the National Museum of Crime and Punishment, whose ticket office, as Whittaker knew full well, was in the Tourist Information Office, where finding Juliana was not unheard of.

She wasn't there. Just as well, he thought. Disappointing, but just as well. He bought his ticket, and entered through the gate of the castle into the courtyard, its cobbles rubbed smooth by generations of prisoners. The sun did not penetrate this dark place, and the temperature dropped several degrees. Ghosts seemed to be frozen within the massive walls of this temple to man's inhumanity to man, this granite paean in praise of horror and exploitation. Terry shivered in his jacket.

Then he hired a cassette guide from the gift shop, slipped it into his Walkman and began his exploration of the museum.

'Abandon hope, all ye who enter in, and welcome to the National Museum of Crime and Punishment. Come with me now as I take your hand on this short trip through some of the darker corners of the human psyche.' The voice was oily and sibilant in Whittaker's ears, like Bob Monkhouse with a lisp. There was a hint of an accent – Hungarian? Romanian? Whittaker walked up stairs and down corridors, under portraits of serial killers, through galleries packed with iron maidens and hanging stools and instruments of torture.

In each gallery there was a huge shaven-headed thug, each dressed identically in a black polo-necked sweater and a black leather jacket, all wearing Ray-Bans, and all carrying walkie-talkies. They stared malevolently at the visitors, and muttered into their handsets. Whittaker tried to ignore them as he went round the museum. It was a fascinating place, a cornucopia of crime. He gazed into cases of burglars' tools, examined the work of the great forgers, and tried a hands-on demonstration of how to open a combination safe by hearing the tumblers fall through a stethoscope. At the end of the tour he was gripped by a live demonstration in the computer room, where he was shown how to siphon off $4.9 billion from the Danish banking system and launder it through the Cayman Islands.

He had enjoyed his visit, but had conceived a heartfelt loathing for the oleaginous voice which hissed through his head. He abandoned the tape after the third gallery, which housed a large display of the instruments of capital punishment, sickened by a gloating note in the disembodied voice.

So he was surprised when, enjoying a bottle of Badoit and a caraway seed roll with butter in the rather excellent museum café after his tour, he heard the same voice close behind his ear.

'Mr Whittaker, isn't it?'

He jumped, and turned in his seat.

He saw a tall, reedy man with jet-black hair slicked away from his forehead. He looked a little like Robert De Niro, thought Whittaker: the same half-smile, the same hint of buttoned-down violence. He was around Whittaker's age – a little older, perhaps – and was wearing an Armani suit and blue-tinted spectacles.

'Mr Whittaker.' He smiled. 'Please, I did not mean to startle you. Allow me to introduce myself. I am Dr Q Sandahl, Director of the National Museum of Crime and Punishment.' He extended a limp hand, which Whittaker shook.

'I recognised your voice from the guide,' said Terry.

'Ah, I saw you wearing headphones.'

'You saw me?'

'Oh, yes. Security is our first concern. We have an excellent CCTV system here at the museum. We have harnessed what you might call the ideals of the panoptic prison in the service of learning. As you may know, Mr Whittaker, this place was a gaol until very recently. Imagine, if you will, the scenes of misery and degradation that these walls have witnessed over the centuries.' Sandahl licked his lips. 'I like occasionally to sit and watch our visitors in the afternoon. To see what catches their eye, which exhibits are the most popular, and so on. I knew you at once, of course.'

'Did you?'

'Mr Whittaker, you are famous. I am a great fan of *Junior Masterchef*. And I have spent many a pleasant evening in Rococo. You are an artist.' He bowed.

'Thank you very much. This place isn't half bad, as it goes. Far and away the best place I've found to eat. I think you might be my main rival.'

Sandahl smiled. 'Oh, no, Mr Whittaker, we are not rivals. In some areas you are far and away my superior . . . whilst in others . . .' He licked his lips again. 'Oh, no, Mr Whittaker, not rivals at all.'

'Oh, good.'

'In fact, Mr Whittaker, we have mutual . . . ah . . . acquaintances.'

'Do we?'

'You know Ms Blezzard, I have been informed.'

'You know Juliana?'

Sandahl smiled. 'She is a very dear friend of mine, Mr Whittaker. She tells me that she has heard nothing from you for a few days. In this, you are wise, Mr Whittaker. It is better if you stay away from her.'

'Yes, I guess you're right. Sally thinks so too, Sally my flatmate. She thinks I should show her how I feel by opposing the car park, instead of sending her flowers. But I'm not sure. You know how it is? When you just know that you are right for somebody, and they are right for you, but they don't see it? Maybe this car park thing will make her see sense.'

Sandahl raised his eyebrows. 'Oh! You *oppose* the Dole Acre Millennium Car Park, Mr Whittaker? On what possible rational grounds?'

'Well, we've got a few things going for us, I think. Mainly the point about grazing rights in the Charter. Mrs Innes thinks the City Council will have to fight all the way to the High Court to prevent animals from grazing the land.'

'I see. That's very interesting, Mr Whittaker. There is a meeting tomorrow, I think? I shall attend, and hear what Mrs Innes has to say for myself. And now . . .' he waved his hands around at the museum, 'I have much to attend to. Research, and so on. Good day, Mr Whittaker. If there is anything you wish to see in the castle, please let me know. A pleasure to meet you.'

They shook hands again. Terry stood and made his way through the archway, out from the castle courtyard and back into the street.

Sandahl watched him go, turned smartly on his toes and made for his office high in the tower, its walls lined with monitor screens. He flipped on his intercom and spoke to his secretary. 'Mrs Wiseman, do you think you could ask Messrs Draper, Johnson and Sturges to step into my office, when they have a moment?'

He sat back in his swivel chair, his long fingers pressed together, and turned to watch the screens through narrowed eyes.

*

Unlike most evil geniuses of his ilk, he hated cats. They made him wheeze. Juliana liked them, and had brought two up with her when she moved back to the area from Staines, but she got rid of them a week after meeting Q.

Another week later, she got rid of her old catty furniture, and replaced it with brand-new hair-free stuff. She replaced the cats with Beanie Babies, once she had checked that they did not set Q off. She now had over 120, which she displayed in wine racks around the flat, the labels in their ears still firmly in place.

Q quickly learned of Juliana's horror of physical contact, and he was quite happy for her to lie beside him at night in a state of mild excitement. She knew that he knew that she hated to be touched; on the rare occasions he did touch her, she took it as a sign of his displeasure, and was filled with a fear which bordered on panic. Although she knew she could never care for another man, she was terrified when she first started seeing him that she would lose him, as she felt unable to satisfy his vile, though perfectly legitimate carnal needs. But it quickly became obvious to her that power was Q's thing, and that he felt, in his turn, that sex involved the loss of his power, the sapping of his strength. Q could not surrender himself to another, could not put his desires into another's hands. And he had a point, for what is good sex if not a mutual surrender, an exchange of power? Q did not want to exchange his power for anybody else's. His own power was what he wanted, what he sought to advance. So the arrangement suited them both very well.

She knew now, after three years, what he liked in other ways, too. Above all, he liked the telly. Her flat was silent when he arrived. She heard his key in the lock and the sound of his feet in the hall. She smiled at him as he sat down beside her on the sofa.

'Is there anything worth watching?' he asked, and she passed him the guide.

'Would you like some water, Q?'

'Yes, thank you.'

By the time she came back from the kitchen, he was watching *Vets in Practice*. They sipped their water together. When the show ended, Q sighed with pleasure, and turned to Juliana.

'My dear, I met a friend of yours today.'

'Oh?'

'Mr Whittaker. A very interesting man.'

Juliana smiled.

'He told me rather an interesting fact.'

'What did he tell you, Q?'

'He told me that he intends to oppose the car park.'

Juliana reddened. 'Oh, my God, will I never get a moment's peace from that dreadful man?'

'Dreadful, yes, but useful. He made the mistake of telling me something of their thinking. It seems they intend to give you a hard time over the terms of the letting of the ground. As I understand it, they seem to be arguing that grazing rights mean the right to graze animals, just that and nothing more. Whittaker mentioned the High Court.'

'They have a point. The city solicitor thinks we can establish the freehold, but he's not sure. Strictly speaking, the land belongs to Lady Lettice Courtney. Damn! I knew this would be a problem!'

'But no one has seen or heard from the Courtney woman since 1972. Pre-empt them. Go to court and apply to have Lady Lettice declared dead.'

'Even so, it's going to take time. Bugger the Charter.'

'Well, my dear, all things are possible. What if it were not a few medieval practices that the Charter permitted, but full use of the land?'

'But it doesn't. I've read a transcription.'

'Transcriptions, or indeed reproductions, are not permissible in law. Only the real thing will do. And what if the real thing was to be ... altered?'

'You mean – you mean, steal the Charter and destroy it?'

'My dear, your mind is so quick, and yet, on occasion, so vulgar. We would not wish to destroy so fascinating a document. No, we will take the Charter, insert a new clause, and replace it. Draper and Johnson have had a look at the Lady Courtney Gallery's security system, and they assure me that they can be in and out in ten minutes, without disturbing the authorities in any way. Jack Sturges is already sharpening his quills and preparing some appropriate inks. Any other members of my research staff who can assist your cause in any way are, of course, entirely at your disposal.'

'When, Q? When's the job?'

'I thought ... with your permission ... tomorrow evening. During the public meeting.'

'Q. Of course.'

'My dear, whatever you say.'

'I say anything that can stop that man is OK with me. Anything.'

Whittaker had stopped at a newsagent's, after his visit to the Museum of Crime and Punishment, to buy the *Pancester Mail*. Once again, he had allowed his eyes to stray towards the top shelf – and there, to his delight, on the front cover of *Barely Legal*, was a woman with breasts exactly as he had imagined Juliana's. I'll get it from Zahid tomorrow, thought Whittaker. He hurried home and pulled his box down from the top of the wardrobe. He had a small collection of magazines now, all bought from Zahid's. There was the girl in *Razzle* with Juliana's hair, a copy of *Club* with a model whose forearms and hands reminded Whittaker of the blissful morning in her office discussing his plans for the restaurant, and even a copy of *Ugly Birds* with some photographs of a girl who had just Juliana's particular hint of over-bite. When he ejaculated, he always closed his eyes, and called out for Juliana.

In the morning he hitched a ride over to Laikley with Sally.

'I just wanted to check the fishermen's co-operative's shrimps. I don't see how I can leave Laikley Bay shrimps off the menu. They're world-famous.'

'Sure. You OK to catch the bus back? Or if you can hang around till lunchtime, I can run you back.'

'No, no, I'll catch the bus.'

She dropped him outside the co-op's small shop, and he ducked inside, tasted again the shrimps boiled in sea water which he had already decided he liked weeks before, and then nipped round to Zahid's.

"'Allo, Mr Whittaker. Back again? What can I do you for today? *Barely Legal?* You'll start going blind, you will! Eh? Start going blind?'

Whittaker smiled in his humiliation, but felt too embarrassed to start a new porn-buying relationship with another, possibly less coarse newsagent. Besides, he was too well known in Pancester to feel quite comfortable buying this kind of stuff. Zahid had proved discreet, in his own way. And he had such a superb selection.

Zahid put *Barely Legal* in a paper bag and said, as he always did on these occasions, 'How's business?' and Whittaker replied, as he always replied, 'Good, thanks, Zahid. Fine.' But he never really knew which business Zahid was referring to. The TV business? The restaurant business? The wanking business? It was a puzzle.

He put the bag under his mac, and caught the bus into Pancester.

Back in the flat, he pulled out his box, and added his latest acquisition to the pile. He stared at his favourite pictures for a few minutes, before getting undressed and fetching a pair of nail scissors from his washbag. He sat naked on his bed, and began to cut out various features of the girls which he thought most resembled Juliana: the hair, the arms, the teeth and now the breasts.

He started to pull at his erection, staring hard at the scraps of paper. His mobile phone rang.

'Hello, boy! Hope I didn't catch you at a delicate moment. Hope I didn't catch you about to lose your mess!'

Whittaker's knob started to shrink away rapidly. 'You did, actually.'

'All right for some. No chance of that for me with my prostrate.'

'So were you wanting anything in particular?'

'Was I . . . ? You ungrateful little sod! After all I've done for you!'

'Like what, exactly?'

Whittaker's father fell silent.

'Dad? Like what, exactly?'

'Well, if you don't know that . . .'

'You told me a joke once, about a plumber, that I still tell at dinner parties.'

'About a plumber?'

'You know. With the parrot.'

Whittaker could hear his father's wheezing laugh. 'Oh, that's a good 'un, that is. Well, there you are then. After I told you that joke, you should remember I'm your father and be grateful.'

'Yes, Dad. But I must get going now.'

'Oh, yes, that's right. Some people still have balls that work.'

'That's the one, Dad. Bye!' Whittaker cut off his father, and returned his attention to the scraps of paper on his bed.

Once he had finished cutting meticulously around his selections, he started to rearrange them on the bed cover, as though he were making one of those cardboard dress-up dollies. And once he had arranged them to his satisfaction . . .

'Juliana!'

He put away his box, showered away his shame, pulled on his dressing gown and began to prepare his speech for that evening's meeting.

The meeting was held in an airless hall belonging to the cathedral. Doleful plaster Madonnas watched a small crowd fill up the first four rows of the hall. Taff and Dawn sat with Sally and Oliver in the second row. Women outnumbered men by two to one. Juliana and Q crept in at the back as Mrs Innes called the meeting to order.

She began by outlining her points about the grazing rights, and then fulminated loud and long on the subject of the traditional prerogative of Pancester women to spend one night a year on the Dole Acre, dreaming peacefully of love. She sat down to an enthusiastic reception.

Dexter Halton followed with an impassioned plea on behalf of the donkeys. He showed some slides of donkeys: donkeys in mineshafts, on treadmills, on desolate summertime beaches.

Juliana rolled her eyes and muttered. 'Bloody donkeys. I wish you could do something about them.'

Q smiled, and raised a finger to his lips.

Dexter concluded with a scathing attack on the Laikley Children's Zoo, and made much of the fact that its owner, Mrs Miranda Dandyworth, had been convicted in 1989 of cruelty to a lemur.

'Any woman who can be cruel even to this most innocent of God's creatures is hardly someone to whom I would wish to entrust these pathetic and helpless donkeys.'

Dexter sat down to louder applause still.

Mrs Innes introduced Terry. He was wearing a handmade chalk-stripe Savile Row suit, and a Jermyn Street shirt and tie. In his left hand he held his notes, which he referred to from time to time, over the top of an entirely theatrical pair of half-moon spectacles, bought that afternoon.

'Ladies and gentleman, I stand before you, a newcomer to your beautiful city, to object this evening to the proposed car park on the Dole Acre. The traffic department figures from . . .' (and here Whittaker rolled off some dates and figures) 'which show a reduction in city centre car use of . . .' (and so on) 'and the projected percentile reduction in accidents at the Laikley turn-off, do not allow for a projected overall increase in ring road traffic of . . .' (etc., etc., etc.) '. . . between . . .' (la-di-da) '. . . and . . .' (blah blah blah) '. . . nor do they allow for an increase of . . .' (more numbers from Terry) '. . . thereby increasing chances of collision on the Blackhampton Road . . .'

'Blampton,' whispered Mrs Innes.

'What?'

'It's pronounced "Blampton", dear. Not "Black-hampton".'

'I do beg your pardon. That's ignorant incomers from London for you,' said Terry.

The audience laughed.

'Thereby increasing the chances of collision on the *Blampton* Road,' he smiled at Mrs Innes, 'by a worrying 17 per cent.'

The audience liked this stuff. Juliana was fuming, and made to stand up. Q reached out his hand and touched her knee with the lightest of pressure. She quivered, and sank back into her chair.

'By spending the projected car-park budget on new rolling

stock for the trains from the main line at Preston, and by a mid-term commitment to reopening the branch line to Laikley, our figures show that overall traffic use in Pancester *and* Laikley would fall by as much as 36 per cent over a three-year period, thus removing the need for a new car park altogether. Ladies and gentlemen, I ask you now. Will you please help us stop this unnecessary, inhumane and sexist car park?'

The audience stood and shouted their approval, clapping and whooping and stamping their feet. Whittaker held out his hands, pulled Dexter and Mrs Innes up from their chairs, and held their arms aloft with his own.

The crowd cheered again. It took some time for Mrs Innes to restore order, so that other voices could be heard from the floor, a committee formed, some decisions taken, another meeting arranged.

'I think we should leave, my dear,' said Q. 'It was only necessary that we were seen.'

As the crowd filed out, Mrs Innes shook Terry's hand. 'Wonderful stuff, Mr W.'

'Was that the sort of thing you had in mind?' asked Terry.

'Beyond my wildest dreams. Where did you get all those figures?'

'Made 'em up, Mrs I.'

'Good lad. All that guff about improving the railway convinced me, anyway. I think we'll call it the "Whittaker Plan". What do you think?'

'I'd be honoured. Though perhaps we should get an expert in, to see if there's any truth in it at all?'

'Nonsense, dear. You *are* new to politics, aren't you?'

Sally hugged him and told him she loved him and could she have his babies? Taff thumped him on the back, Dawn pinched his bum, and Oliver nodded. Terry was fascinated to see Oliver next to his brother for the first time. It really was extraordinary. They were identical in name only. Dexter's rumpled face beamed up at him.

'Did you see Blezzard and Sandahl lurking in the back? Hoo hoo, you gave 'em a scare tonight, my boy!'

'Do you think I impressed her?'

'You put the wind up her, Terry, I know that. I was watching her.'

'Is that good, Sally?' asked Terry.

Sally smiled brightly. 'Oh, God, yes,' she said. 'Women love having the wind put up them.'

Whittaker nodded sagely. 'Good.'

Steve Medlicott approached him, accompanied by a long-faced and goofy man in his late fifties. He was wearing a pair of charity-shop trousers, a prison shirt and a Marks and Spencer sweater, his curly grey hair cut amateurishly into a horrifying footballer's mullet.

'Mr Whittaker, the other evening I spoke of certain – beings with whom I have established contact,' said Medlicott. 'This – is one of these. His name's Syd.'

'Hello, Syd.'

'Hello, Terry,' said Syd in the bright tones of the minor landed gentry, holding out his hand for Whittaker to shake. 'Pleased to meet you. Sydney Montague-Forrester. Absolutely smashing job you did up there tonight. Really first-rate. Couldn't agree more. The thing must be stopped, so much is clear. Steve's told me all about you. Says your aura is violet. Splendid! Look, the thing is, Terry . . .' Syd's voice dropped to a whisper. 'Steve thinks you should be told some of the secrets of Dole Acre.'

'Secrets?'

'Mr Whittaker . . .' said Steve, licking his lips. 'How can I explain to you? There are – pathways in the vortices. Where these pathways – converge – certain energies accumulate. Powerful energies.'

'I see. And this is the secret of Dole Acre?'

'Shhh, Terry. We can't really talk here.' Syd looked over his shoulder at Mrs Innes. 'Look, can we meet?' he continued. 'The three of us? In private? Something fearfully important to tell you.'

'My flat, tomorrow evening?'

'Marvellous. Until tomorrow then.' Steve and Syd wandered off, while Whittaker went with Sally and Taff and the others to the pub for a celebration drink.

In the morning this mild triumphalism seemed horribly premature. The faint whiff of victory which had been generated by the meeting evaporated with the arrival of the *Pancester Mail*. The news was bad.

During the public meeting objecting to the construction of a new car park on Dole Acre, somebody had audaciously stolen a number of valuable artefacts, including the Charter of 1503, from the Lady Courtney Art Gallery and Museum.

The police were said to be baffled.

The Easter Rising

'It's certainly baffling, Mrs I,' said Whittaker to Mrs Innes, who had dropped in at the 4i's with Rolly around eleven.

'I'm not so sure it is. How very convenient this is for Ms Blezzard. She must feel that the destruction of the Charter will help her case in some way. I can't see how, though. The Charter could be proved, I should have thought, even if it were destroyed. And yet I feel convinced that Ms Blezzard and that creep Sandahl are up to something.'

'I don't see Juliana breaking and entering, somehow. Besides, they were at the meeting. And the paper says other things have been taken too. The Clangers, for example.' Whittaker poured evaporated milk over a bowl of tinned fruit salad, and started to slurp.

'That's just for cover. And it will be one of Sandahl's aides, dear, who carried out the job. That castle is full of the most unsavoury types. Guides, curators, Sandahl's "research assistants" . . . where did they get their expertise, do you think? No, this could go all the way to the top. Don't lick your sores, Rolly. Nasty.'

'Mrs I, you've been watching too many *X- Files*.'

Steve Medlicott had finished putting in Whittaker's state-of-the-art kitchen, and the restaurant now only awaited the arrival of the furniture and optical displays from London, so he had turned his attentions to the flat, where he was putting the final touches to Sally and Gwyn's room. He stopped for tea, and joined his allies.

'Mr Whittaker, much of what Mrs Innes has told you is true. Why do you think Pancester is free from so called "crime"? I'll tell you . . . it's because all the great criminal minds of our day work at the castle, and they don't want the authorities' attention turned this way. Their function...? They are teachers, Mr Whittaker, professors of crime. Young criminals flock here to get educated. Pancester is becoming the Oxbridge of crime. Dark energies ... emanate.'

'Good grief! Really? Are you kidding me? Why doesn't anyone put a stop to it?'

'Because Pancester is crime-free, my dear,' said Mrs Innes, a little shamefacedly.

Whittaker opened his mouth to protest, but stopped. He had to admit there was something to that. It was nice to learn that self-regulation worked in at least one sector of the British economy. He dipped his spoon into his bowl.

'And this is where my energetic path – diverges from your own, Mrs Innes,' said Medlicott. 'I do not think the powers-that-be at the castle would show their hand in this way. I think it's an outside job.'

'Well, we'll see. I notice you were with Syd last night, Mr Medlicott. I didn't get a chance to speak with him. How is he? How long has he been back?'

Medlicott smiled. 'He just is. And he has never been away.'

'Yes, well, do try and persuade him to give me a call.'

'He has. His energies have called out to you often.'

'Yes, I meant a telephone call, dear. Well, goodbye, gentlemen. I shall see you at the committee meeting on Wednesday. Come along, Rolly.'

'Who is Syd then, Steve?' asked Whittaker, when Mrs Innes and Rolly had cleared the building.

'Amongst many other – incarnations – he is Mrs Innes' nephew.'

'And what's the big secret?'

'When Syd's here,' said Medlicott, returning to his work.

Whittaker spent the day in his new kitchen, working on the menu. Sally came home early and was pleased to find that Medlicott had just finished their room.

'Ooh, it's fabarooni! It's splendiferous! It's . . . can we get some furniture now, Cuggles?'

'The energy patterns on the walls are still unstable,' said Medlicott.

'Sorry?'

'The paint's still wet,' said Terry. 'But it'll be ready to move your things in when Gwyn gets here.'

Gwyneth was due to arrive that weekend in a Transit full of stuff, driven by Mabel. A pantechnicon-load of furniture and fittings for the restaurant was due on Monday, and on Tuesday, Gwyn and Whittaker were interviewing staff. Terry felt that an evening with Steve and Syd was the last thing he needed, but nevertheless, he had agreed, and was stuck. Besides, he was intrigued to hear the Secret of Dole Acre.

The conspirators arrived together, punctually at nine.

'You don't mind Sally being here, I trust?' Whittaker asked Syd.

'Not at all, Terry. Be pleased to have a lady's view of things. Mind if I skin up?'

'Go ahead. Tea, coffee, wine, beer, tinned fruit?'

'Cheers. A beer would just hit the spot.'

'Could I have – a glass of wine, Cuggles?'

'Course you can, Steve. But please don't call me Cuggles.' Medlicott smirked, and Sally tittered.

'This is your fault, Sally,' said Whittaker, 'and I'm going to get you for it. And I suppose you want a drink?'

'Yeah, wine please, Terry.'

Whittaker clattered around, brought drinks through, put on a CD.

'Well,' he said.

'This is nice,' said Syd, gesturing around at the flat.

'Be nicer when Steve's finished and we can get some furniture in.'

'Goodness, yes. Much more to do, Steve?'

Steve shook his head. 'Harmony is close,' he said.

'What colour are you having it in here?' asked Syd.

'Oh, just a neutral cream. We thought that would suit everyone, and I've got quite a few pictures to put up. Pictures look better against a neutral background, I always think.'

'Ooh, that'll be nice. Are you getting new curtains?'

'Look, will you stop going on about soft furnishings and tell us about the Secret of Dole Acre?' sighed Sally.

'Oh, gosh, yes, right, OK, sorry. Well ... where to start?'

'The Festival,' said Steve. 'Start with the Festival.'

'OK, right. The Festival. Well. It's 1972, and I've just been chucked out of the Army for smoking this stuff.' He waved his joint around. 'Couldn't very well go home, as Father had been a brigadier in the old regiment, and was not a happy bunny about me getting cashiered. So I came to stay with my Aunt Jocelyn, Mrs Innes, that is, and I was at a bit of a loose end. Decent of Auntie to put me up, and all that, but I didn't have anything to do all day. Used to sit in the 4i's, as it goes, gossiping about pop with Taff. Must go and see the new premises. Love Taff. Anyway, here I was, bored as hell after Ulster ...'

'You were in Northern Ireland?' asked Sally. Syd sucked his joint, and passed it to Medlicott.

'That's where I ended up, yes. I was other places too, Cyprus, Aden. Career officer, you know, Sandhurst and all that. I was in for the best part of ten years. It was ... well, it was awful in the end, but I was missing my men like absolute heck, the *esprit de corps* and all that, when I met old Lettice Courtney. A superb woman, you know. A wonder. A few years older than I was, of course, past her middle thirties, but that didn't worry me. A superb body. Tits like puppies in a basket. And full of go. Knew everybody, Beatles, Jagger, you name 'em. Had just come home herself after a rather unfortunate affair in London. There was talk of Mars Bars, if you know what I mean. With a Cabinet minister. At a Buck House garden party, as it happens, which I always thought was a bit impulsive, but Letty said that they were jolly unlucky to get caught. And lucky to keep it out of the press. Anyway, the thing is, me and Letty were an item. And we were bored. So we got it into our heads to organise a Free Festival. Everyone was at it at the time, y'know. And with my organisational skills, and Letty's contacts, we thought the whole thing would be a bit of a spree.'

Medlicott offered the joint to Whittaker and Sally, who shook their heads, so he passed it back to Syd.

'Cheers, m'dear. Course, it wasn't. It was awful, really. It was daft of us to try to do it in late September, I suppose, but all the other dates were taken – festivals here, happenings there. We didn't want to clash. And then old Letty's stock was running a bit low, what with one thing and another, and we couldn't get the bands we wanted. And my ability to run a Company didn't immediately translate into the skills necessary to run an event of this kind, to be frank. But still, we managed to wangle it with the council that we could do the thing on Dole Acre. It was Letty's land, after all, in a way. So there we were. The big weekend came. We'd managed to knock together a stage, and get a generator down there. And there were some good bands, after all, even if they weren't quite out of the top drawer. We had The Pink Fairies, Brinsley Schwarz . . . who else, Steve?'

'Fat Mattress. The Knightwatchmen.'

'Yes, we had to have them. Taff lent us the public address system. So there we were. Not too many of us, actually. Letty and I had relied on word of mouth to publicise the thing, thinking we'd get thousands of Beautiful People from all over the shop. But it wasn't to be. Pissed down with rain all weekend. How many did we count on the Sunday night, Steve?'

'Eight. Including Fat Mattress. And they . . . went.'

'Yes. Not exactly Woodstock, was it? And then the bloody generator packed in, and that would have been that, if Letty hadn't discovered the mushrooms.'

'The mushrooms?' said Whittaker.

'God, yes, the mushrooms. Ever tried psilocybin? No? Extraordinary stuff, really. Nature's acid. Marvellous, if you think about it. Well, there we all were, eleven o'clock on the Sunday night, it's pouring with rain, we've no power, no music, and everyone was getting ready to pack up and toddle off, when suddenly old Letty pipes up that she's found a load of 'shrooms. That livened us up, I can tell you, and we all wandered about with torches peering at the ground, and blow me if she wasn't spot on. Thousands of the beggars, fresh as a daisy. They were sprouting up faster than we could pick 'em. So I don't know how many we got, but it was a fair old few, and Letty had the idea that we should brew 'em up into tea, and pass it round like a loving cup. So we lit a fire, and got a bloody great big field pan, and we all put our mushrooms into the pot, hundreds and hundreds of 'em, and we boiled 'em up with tea-leaves and sugar and milk, proper sergeant-major's tea. And then we all drank it.' He sighed. Medlicott smiled.

'Well, you know, that many ordinary magic mushrooms would have sent us all on quite a trip. But this is the secret we found out that night. The mushrooms on Dole Acre are not ordinary magic mushrooms at all. They are about a hundred times more powerful than your common or garden mushie. I'm afraid we all went a bit doolally.'

Steve coughed.

'Yes, sorry, Steve, not you, I know. Steve began to acquire his new way of looking at the world that night. Not all bad, was it, eh, Steve? Maybe other people had a nice time too, but I don't really know. I didn't. I walked into a nightmare. I was back in Aden. Screaming. Gunshots. My best friend, you know. Face blown off, next to me. We were running up the side of a sand-dune. Tried to put it from my mind, till then.'

His lip quivered, and a tear ran down his cheek. Sally moved across the room and hugged him.

'Thank you. It's . . . never mind. Thank you, Sally.' She stayed next to him, holding his hand.

'Well, I ran away. Didn't stop running till I got to Manchester. Then I booked myself into the bin for a few months. When I got out, I tried to contact Letty, find out what had happened. But by then, it was too late. She'd gone.'

'Where?' asked Whittaker.

'That's the thing. No one knew. She'd just gone.'

'Yes, I knew she'd disappeared.'

'That very night. Last anyone ever saw of her she'd torn off all her clothes and was running towards Laikley. No one's seen hide nor hair of her since.'

'They never found a body?'

'No, not a thing. Some people thought she'd done herself in, but I don't believe it, not even in that state. She was too full of life. No, I still think she's about somewhere. Steve thinks so too.'

'I still feel her energetic patterns. On occasion.'

'But she was the last of the Courtneys, you see. They shut up Courtney House after she'd gone. You know it? The big old house in the close by the castle? The locals call it the New House because it replaced the old half-timbered hall that was burnt down in the Great Fire of Pancester. Still empty now. I don't suppose anyone's set foot in there for twenty years or more.'

'So this is the Secret of Dole Acre? The mushrooms?'

'Of course. One of them. There's dozens, I expect. You should get the county archaeologist to come and have a poke around. The place is probably stiff with secrets. But this is ours. Steve here kept his head, whilst all about him were losing theirs. The cover-up began straight away. Steve let it be known that we'd all had a batch of bad acid, and got round all the people who'd been there over the next day or so, and persuaded 'em to keep quiet. And then he began researching, learning about the mushrooms. Finding out about dosage. Developed his skills. Became what he is today.'

'A builder,' said Sally. Steve smiled.

'A bloody good builder, though,' said Terry.

'And you've kept it quiet, all this time?'

Steve nodded. 'As I told you last night, Mr Whittaker, many pathways through the vortices – what *you* might call "ley lines" – converge on the Dole Acre. It crackles with energy. The mushrooms focus this power. Until others learn how to use these energies, we must be cautious.' Medlicott shrugged.

'It's amazing that heads from all over the place aren't camped out there,' said Terry.

'Well, this is our idea, you see. Steve thinks that if we let it be known what grows on the Dole Acre, we'd have every hippy in the country parked up down there to defend those mushrooms. Hundreds of 'em. Vans, buses, the whole convoy set-up. They'd dig tunnels, build tree-houses, all that Swampy stuff. I don't think they would need much encouraging, do you?'

'God, no. This is a great idea!' said Whittaker.

'Yes, but won't they all go bonkers once they've scoffed the mushrooms?' asked Sally.

'Steve here thinks he can warn them off. Help them with dosage.'

'One mushroom, Mr Whittaker, is more than enough. Hippies aren't stupid.'

'Well, it's a hell of a plan. Shall we run it past Mrs Innes and Dexter at the committee meeting?'

'Ah ... I'd rather Auntie didn't know. Still a bit down on me about the drugs thing. Whole family is, to be honest.'

'Oh, we won't tell the committee about the 'shrooms. We'll tell them that Steve's hippy contacts are willing to help. They won't need to know more than that. It's whether they want them, that's the question, if they think they'll do more harm than good, in case they alienate the locals or something.'

And so it was agreed. Steve and Syd would make contact with their allies in the traveller world, so long as the committee approved.

'And what about you, Syd? What are you up to now? Are you going to stay and help?' asked Terry.

'Thought I might. I've got a place in Portugal. Market gardening. Grow a bit of this, for family and friends,' and he held up his bag of grass, 'but mostly I do succulents. Cactuses and so on. Good business. But it can run without me for a bit. I've not been back to Pancester for a year or so. Nice to be here again. I'd like to see the Dole Acre saved. For Letty, as much as anything.'

Even as the pace of life picked up, Whittaker still felt the loss, as he saw it, of daily congress with Juliana. Love is ... well, you know. Not always easy. And although we may feel superior to Terry, and want to say to him, this isn't love, this is a silly infatuation, and although we may feel that our own pain, our own losses, our own sufferings are much more legitimate than his, that ours have some basis in reality, whilst his are all self-inflicted, self-invented even, we must at least grant him the right to his own feelings, however alien they may seem to us. He called it love. And who has not longed for an unattainable stranger, or cried themselves to sleep over a hopeless crush? Work saved Whittaker, work and his friends. But Whittaker wanted more. He wanted Juliana to be there at the end of the day, loving and gentle. He wanted children to hold, to grow up with. Both the car park campaign and his secret box of desire seemed like poor substitutes.

But Sally was keeping him on the straight and narrow, and keeping him to his promise not to bother Juliana. He liked having her about. Whittaker and Sally had happily shared the flat for a month, and they had both privately felt a little uneasy that Gwyn's arrival might upset the dynamic. But Gwyn was so pleased to be with Sally, and so excited about the 4i's, and so thrilled to be back in Pancester and close to her family, that any worries Whittaker and Sally might have had evaporated almost as soon as she and Mabel arrived with the van.

Taff and Dawn were at the 4i's, ostensibly helping to unload.

'I met Syd Montague-Forrester the other night. Steve brought him round. He was telling me about the Free Festival,' said Terry.

Taff scratched his chin. 'Was he now?' he said.

'Yes, he was. You played, didn't you?'

'Yes, we did. Can't say I enjoyed it much. We were on on the Saturday night, just before The Pink Fairies. I think there was only Dawn watching who wasn't one of the organisers.'

'How many times you seen The Knightwatchmen, Mum?' asked Gwyneth, arriving in the flat with a box of her Airfix models.

Dawn came panting in behind her with a box of CDs. 'Too bloody many,' she gasped, setting down her load and collapsing beside Taff on the newly delivered sofa.

'That's it, love. You have a sit down. Our Gwyneth'll make us all some tea.'

'I bloody well will not.'

'I'll make some tea,' said Whittaker, standing up. 'Come and tell me about Lettice Courtney, Taff.' Taff stood, rubbing his knees, and followed Whittaker through into the kitchen.

'Ah, Letty. She was a wonderful lass. Big lass. Knockers like wasps' nests. Full of vim, she was. We didn't see her much when she was growing up, she was always off at school, and university.

Her Mam died when she was only sixteen, and she was always a bit wild. Dawn used to read about her in magazines, always going out with some pop star or jet-setter. A very fast lot she used to hang about with. One of those sixties rich girls who turned into a hippy. In fact, I think she went to Morocco with Brian Jones and Anita Pallenberg. But then something happened down London, and she came back here for good, and woke the place up.' Taff smiled with the memory.

'Full of plans, she was, and every night at Courtney House there was a bloody great big party. She used to light it all up with candles and laughter. She was great, Terry. Everyone loved her, you know. Syd was mad about her. Pancester is always better with a Courtney living in the New House. But there you go. Since Letty's gone, so has the Courtney family, and the New House is boarded up. Very sad.'

'What do you think happened to her?'

'You know about the last night at the Festival?' Whittaker nodded.

'Silly beggars, taking all that bad LSD. They all went mad, those of 'em that were left down there. Monday morning, the site was empty, except for Steve Medlicott, who wouldn't shut up about energy patterns. Syd had gone, no one knew where, and Letty had been spotted running down the Laikley Road, naked as a baby and howling like a dog. Old Mr Franklin, who used to live behind us, was out walking his whippets last thing. He saw her and tried to catch hold of her, but she jumped over the hedge into the field where the maggot factory is now, and he lost sight of her. No one ever saw her again.'

'Yes, but what do you think happened to her then?'

'Oh, she went into the river, no doubt about it. There was a tide running that night. Once she got in, that would have been that.'

'But they never found a body?'

'No, but that's no surprise. The Athon is a nasty river when it wants to be. She'd have been down at Laikley Point and out to sea in no time.'

'Where's that tea?' called Dawn from the front room.

'Come on, Taff. We'd better go and get moving stuff about.'

On Monday morning the pantechnicon from London arrived, full of opticians' chairs and glass tables and cases of antique spectacles and optical charts. Medlicott supervised the unloading, and began the final fitting of the furniture in the restaurant. On Tuesday, Whittaker and Gwyn interviewed staff. Brian Styles, an old and unambitious, though talented, friend of Whittaker's from his days at the Riverside was coming up to be Terry's sous chef, and Brian's wife, Mindy, was coming up with him to be the chef de pâtisserie. Both solid professionals, Whittaker was pleased to get them, and he looked forward to having them around. Martha, the cook from the old 4i's Coffee Bar, was already hanging about, ready to start as one of the commis. As the second commis, Whittaker hired Kevin, the ex-guitarist from The Knightwatchmen, who'd just finished his course at the Pancester and Laikley Technical College, and who showed a good deal of promise. Waiting staff were more problematic, but Gwyneth and Whittaker chose half a dozen enthusiastic and inexperienced youngsters, whom they felt it would be easier to train in modern restaurant etiquette, in preference to some old stagers from De'Ath's and Ye Blacke Bull, who were permeated with the Pancestrian tradition of bad temper and suspicion towards outsiders.

But Whittaker argued that his restaurant would have lacked something of the authentic Pancester feel without a dash of fatalism, so he chose old Dennis, previously the night porter at the Pancester Riverside, as his new kitchen porter.

'Why do you want this job, Dennis? What's wrong with the Riverside?'

'Ah get fed up dealing wit' public. Ah can't stand t'public.'

'You might find us a bit new-fangled, Dennis.'

'Aye, but at least I won't 'ave to smile at t'bloody public at three int' bloody morning.'

Whittaker found that he couldn't quite resist taking him on, against Gwyn's better judgement. Martha was pleased when she heard, however.

'Dennis Alvey? Ooh, I remember when I was at school, we all used to fancy Dennis. He were centre forward for Pancester FC. Dishy Dennis, we called him. Do you know, he asked me to the pictures once, but Dad said I wasn't to go. Said he were too old for me to walk out with, and, besides, there were the cats to see to. Ooh, I've a right soft spot for Dennis, I have.'

On Wednesday, the newly constituted Committee Against the Car Park agreed that it might be a good idea to move in the hippies and eco-warriors if the Dole Acre scheme got the go-ahead from the full council.

'At least they'd hold things up a bit, if we had to get it referred to the Secretary of State,' said Dexter. 'But let's wait and see what happens at the full council meeting before we give them the nod.'

'Yes, I agree,' said Mrs Innes. 'And I'm going to stir up the women at Eastering. We'll make bloody sure this car park doesn't go ahead, even if we have to lie down in front of the bulldozers.'

'Mrs I! I never had you down for a radical.'

'Well, there you are, you see, dear. I'm full of surprises.'

The committee also liked Syd's idea of getting the county archaeologist along. With only two months to go before the meeting of the full council which would decide on the fate of Dole Acre, it was felt that every potential ally was worth contacting.

'Such an obvious idea, too. I feel a bit ashamed that I didn't think of it before my naughty nephew,' said Mrs Innes.

On Thursday, Penny Lester came up on the train to see the results of her plans for the 4i's.

'What do you think, Terry?' she asked, smiling around at the cases of glasses.

'It's amazing. Hasn't Steve done a great job?' The dingy old café had been transformed into a light and airy state-of-the-art restaurant, sparkling with colour from the prismatic lights.

'Yes, he has. Really good. There's nothing for me to criticise. So when are you opening? Menu all ready?'

'Yep, just about. Brian and Mindy Styles get here next week, and then we're going to spend a couple of weeks training. So I reckon Easter Monday.'

'Funny day to choose.'

'This is a funny place. But apparently, the women of Pancester don't cook for a week after the Eastering. Traditionally, all the men were supposed to cook, but these days they tend to get takeaways, or take their wives out for dinner. Dawn assures me we'll be packed. Can you come back for the big night?'

'Of course.'

Terry's mobile rang. It was the Mother Superior in charge of the hospice where his father lay dying.

'He's much worse, I'm afraid, Mr Whittaker. I think it advisable that you come and see him.'

'Oh. This is a bad time, to be honest.'

'Well, that's up to you, of course. But I'm very much afraid that if you don't come now, you'll miss him.'

'Miss him? Oh, I see what you mean. Erm . . . OK, OK. I'll try and make it down tomorrow. Thank you, Mother Superior.'

Terry sighed and pulled a face.

'What is it?' said Penny.

'My dad. He's got cancer of the everything. That was the hospice. They don't think he's got much longer.'

'Oh, Terry, I am sorry. I didn't know. How awful for you, just when you're trying to get this place going. It must be very difficult.'

'Well, yes, it is a bit of a bore. It means I've got to go down to London tomorrow. I'll come on the train with you.'

'A bit of a bore? That's hard.'

'Is it? You don't know my father.'

'You don't get on?'

Terry reddened. 'I hate him, Pen. I really hate him. I didn't speak to him for about fifteen years after my mother died. Then he phoned me up about a year ago to say that he had cancer, and could we make it up. So we have, in a way. But he disgusts me. He tells me he loves me, but he doesn't know what love is. What I feel for Juliana . . . that's something he could never understand. Sex, that's all he ever cared about, sex and his gut.'

'Like Ulrich. What did he do, your father?'

'What, for a job?'

Penny nodded.

'He was a driver on the Tube.'

Penny giggled.

'Don't be such a snob,' said Terry.

'I'm sorry, Terry. I am a bit, I know.' She bit her thumbnail, then continued, 'How are your neighbours?'

'What, Taffy and Oliver? They're getting on well. Why?'

'Oh, I don't know. I might pop in and see them, actually. Not that Oliver will talk to me, or anything, even though I gained the impression last time I was up that he was quite keen.'

'He's our computer whiz, you know. Taff says that he does all his communicating by e-mail. Finds it much easier, apparently.'

'Does he? I use it a lot myself. It is rather fun. I'll make sure I get his address.'

On the London train the following morning, Whittaker watched England unroll past his window while Penny read a book. It didn't stop raining until Milton Keynes Central. Over Tring, Whittaker saw a cloud which reminded him of Juliana's mouth. At Euston he said goodbye to Penny and caught a cab to the hospice. The sisters smiled at him as he walked down the corridor to his father's room. His father was out of bed, sitting in his armchair watching TV, a blanket over his lap.

'Hello, boy. How are ya? Getting yours all right, are ya?'

'Hello, Dad. You're looking ... well.'

'Ha ha! I'm feeling well! Old bitch Mother Superior, I gave her a right fucking scare the last few nights. Woke up this morning feeling better than I have for months. Cancer. Strange, or what?'

Terry smiled weakly, and went to find one of the sisters.

'Oh, your father seems to be much better this morning, Mr Whittaker, much, much better. I think it must have been the news that you were coming down to see him that perked him up.'

'Good. Good. I'm glad,' said Terry.

He lunched with his father in the room. Terry had salmon and new potatoes, his father drew mush painfully through a straw. Terry almost felt sorry for him.

'How's it going with your new bird, boy?'

'I'm playing hard to get, Dad.'

'Hard to get? Silly bugger. Take her. Fuck her. That's what they want. Mastery. Take the little tart. That's what I used to do.'

Terry felt his chest tightening with anger. 'I'm not like that. I think you're wrong.' But he blushed, and thought of the time he had patted her bum.

'No, of course you're not like that, boy. That's 'cos you're a cupboard queer.'

Terry stood up, breathing heavily. 'Goodbye, Dad,' he said. 'Glad you're feeling better.'

'Don't go, boy. Don't be a pansy. I was only mucking about. Don't you know when I'm mucking about? Can't you take a joke? What about the plumber and the parrot? I thought you liked a joke? Please don't go.'

'Goodbye, Dad. I'll ... call you.'

On the train northward, Terry thought of his mother's hands. At Crewe, the rain started again.

A week before Terry's opening, Olly and Taff started trading in their revitalised premises, the Fox Hole. Medlicott had done a good job here, too. He'd opened out the ground floor, where there was now a large selection of new CDs and some DJ vinyl, as well as the pick of Taff's second-hand stock. The first floor, where Whittaker had never been before, was now a well-lit bookstore, where garish graphic novels and a carefully selected choice of new books were arranged alongside what was any good of Olly's old stuff. There were photocopying and fax facilities, and even an online computer terminal, where Pancestrians could log on to the Internet. A coffee machine and two tables surrounded by chairs were placed by the counter at the back.

'This is civilised!' said Terry, holding a glass of wine at the launch.

'Hey hey! I should say it is, bach! And look at the crowd!' said Taff, sweeping his arm around at a room full of young people wearing anoraks and flares, middle-aged people wearing mountaineering gear, and very old people wearing Afghan coats and purple velvet cloaks.

'Looks like there really is a youth slash alternative market in Pancester, after all,' said Terry.

'I knew there would be. Pancester is much more alternative than you think, boy.'

Dexter came up, smiling his most rumpled smile.

'Olly says we can have free photocopying, and he's going to help us put together a website!'

'Oh, that's great! If that's OK with you, Taff?'

'Course! We talked about it. It's our way of saying thank you, Tel. For making this possible.'

Whittaker blushed. 'Leave it out, Taff,' he said.

The pace of life began to pick up further still. Days were spent in the restaurant, running the staff through the new menu. Martha, when she wasn't flirting with Dennis, showed Mindy Styles the secret of how to bake apple plummettys. Nights were spent in meetings and discussions. The county archaeologist called to say that he would visit the week after Easter.

All three flatmates were exhausted in the evening. Sally was still struggling to find suitable premises in Laikley for a shelter. She worried about Edmund, the only homeless person in Pancester proper, whom she felt sure wouldn't go into the shelter when it arrived. 'He's too proud, the daft old sod, that's his trouble.'

In Good Friday's edition of the *Pancester Mail* there was an open letter from Mrs Innes, calling the women of Pancester to arms. She pointed out that this could be the last ever Eastering on the traditional site, and would a broken-down municipal garden in the middle of a roundabout really be the same? She urged the women of Pancester to come in numbers to the Eastering, so that it could be decided what should be done.

Juliana was worried, and spoke to Q about it in the evening when he came round to watch *Dangerfield*.

'My dear, all you need to worry about is the council meeting.

These hags shouldn't concern you at all. You have the council in your pocket.'

'But, Q, if they stir up enough trouble, the councillors will worry that the car park will cost them votes.'

'It's a storm in a teacup. Everyone knows that the car park makes perfect sense. You should write a reply to the paper, emphasising the benefits for Pancester's poor downtrodden pensioners. Taking a quarter of a million pounds a year away from the old folk – now *that's* a vote loser.'

'Dear Q. I'm sure you're right, as always.'

'And after all, there's nothing to stop you going to the Eastering yourself. To see what they're up to.'

'Ugh, no thank you. I've never been that fond of women, never mind the cold. Still, I could make Gaynor go . . .'

The evening of Easter Sunday came around, and many of the men of Pancester watched their womenfolk set off for the south-western corner of Dole Acre, armed with sleeping bags and candles. Judging from the number of men in the pubs that night, it looked as though Mrs Innes had got the record attendance she had hoped for. It would be nice to go with them, and report what Mrs Innes said, and how the women of Pancester responded. But I really think we too must watch them from a distance. We can stand on the Pack Bridge, and listen to the sluggish pulse of the Athon whilst we watch the light from hundreds of torches pick a route through thistles and donkey dung. We can stand on the city walls, and watch the women's candles flickering on the Acre, looking like a cross between a ghostly convention and a Barry Manilow gig. But as readers of Clement Dadd's *Account* will be well aware, the Eastering is a women-only space, and I think I have to respect that.

It is perhaps worth quoting Dadd's views in full.

The Eastering

For evidence that pagan rites have been transformed into Christian festivals, one need look no further than the Dole Acre on the night of Easter Sunday (see 'The Pancester Dole').

On this most holy of nights, any unmarried young women who

wish for a sweetheart, or any married women who wish to find themselves in the blessed state of expectancy, take candles to the south-western corner of the Dole Acre, which they guard until extinguished, at which point they lay down to sleep the night in the open.

It is my belief that the location chosen has some significance accruing to it from pagan times. Perhaps it was the site of a fertility cult of some kind. I am hopeful that an excavation will shortly be undertaken to test this thesis.

It is said that married women often find themselves with child shortly after the Eastering (as the practice is known), and furthermore, that maidens will dream of their husband-to-be as they sleep in the old meadow. It is fair to assume that some of these young creatures go on to bake plummettys for the object of their affection later in the year (see 'Apple Plummeting')!

I am sorry to report that this is the only one of Pancester's ancient ceremonies which I have been unable to witness for myself, as the women refuse male company. From what I have been able to discern, it seems clear that an amount of bawdy talk is indulged in!

This is surely an opportunity for a lady folklorist, who would be able to venture where the present author, alas, is forbidden to go!

So even Clement Dadd himself, expert on all things Pancestrian, never dared to venture on to Dole Acre on the night of the Eastering. The Pack Bridge is the closest we can legitimately get to whatever it is that goes on.

Gwyn didn't go, as she needed an early night, given that the 4i's was due to open the next day, but Sally slept out, and came back shivering to the restaurant in the morning with a piece of news: a consequence of the Eastering which was about to become public knowledge, and so important for all to know, male or female.

Whatever else had gone on, one thing was for sure. Mrs Innes, Steve Medlicott's wife, Sandra, and Dawn Gabatini had founded a Women's Anti-Car Park Camp, and were all going to stay on the old meadow indefinitely.

The Battle for Dole Acre was hotting up.

The 4i's Opens

The 4i's had been fully booked three weeks in advance of opening night, as the people of Pancester and fans of good cooking from all over the north-west queued up to see what Whittaker would produce. The big night itself, on Easter Monday, was reserved for friends, local dignitaries, F-list celebrities, hangers-on, liggers and food writers from the national papers – including Francesca, who, feeling that she must be safe from Terry's imprecations after not hearing from him for so long, and being genuinely keen to see what his first solo venture was like, had taken her life in her hands and caught the train up from London.

She was impressed by the decor, and said so to Penny Lester, who was sitting at the same glass table.

'Nice job, Pen.'

'Thank you, Francesca. Gosh, it's brave of you to turn up, though. Aren't you worried he'll come out and start weeping all over you?'

'Not really. He phoned me for the first time in months to invite me up for this do, and it was nice, except when he called Tony a fat Mick Hucknall lookalike who couldn't cope if he lived more than a mile away from his mum, but he told me all about this place, and he told me he'd met some new woman ...'

'Ah ...'

'Ah?'

'Ah. Her name's Juliana. And as far as I can tell she's his latest target, more than his latest woman.'

'Dear God. Poor cow. He won't ever leave her alone. I should know ... and here he is.'

Whittaker's whites were whiter than white, his tall hat sparkling with starch as he passed amongst the tables, smiling and shaking hands.

'Hello, Penny. Hello, darling!' Terry bent over Francesca and kissed her on both cheeks. 'How lovely to see you! Hasn't Pen done a wonderful job?'

'Lovely to see you too, Terry. Yes, she has. How are you?'

'Lost to London for ever, I think. I really love it here.'

'Do you? It always comes as a surprise to me that there is any life outside London, apart from a few old yokels in smocks and mill workers in clogs.'

'London is like a knot, a vastly complicated knot. My fingernails weren't long enough to unpick it, in the end. It's much more simple here. Less tangled. And you get to see the weather,' said Whittaker.

'Don't you in London, then?'

'No. There's no horizon. The sky is too low.'

Penny nodded, to her own surprise.

'And here you get time to do things other than work. I've even started playing politics.'

'No!'

'Yes indeedee. You are looking at the media spokesperson of the Stop the Car Park Campaign.'

'Good grief. And ... er ... is *she* here?'

'Penny's told you about Juliana, has she? Yes, she is. Sitting over there. The guy with her is her soon to be ex-boyfriend.' Whittaker spoke through clenched teeth.

It was true. The opening of the 4i's was too prestigious an event for Juliana to avoid. Both she and Q were invited, and both had accepted – Q with enthusiasm, Juliana because it would have looked strange at City Hall if she had declined. They were seated at a table with the Halton twins, and no one looked especially comfortable.

'That doesn't bother you, then, the fact that she has a boyfriend?' asked Penny.

'Heavens, no. Never has before.'

'Oh, don't pester the life out of her, Terry,' said Francesca. 'Find a nice single girl.'

'I'm not pestering. I'm proving my devotion by opposing her scheme to build the car park. I make no contact with her at all. Except on the odd occasion like this.' He nodded towards Q and Juliana. Q nodded in return; Juliana turned her face away.

'Cunning plan, Mr Whittaker. You should have tried it with me.'

'Tried what?'

'Ignoring me. Just sometimes.'

'I've ignored you for months.'

'Not now. It's too late to ignore someone after you've split up. That's easy. When we were together, then you should have ignored me more. Let me get on with it, you know?'

Whittaker couldn't help but look sad, which made Francesca sorry. She changed the subject. 'So what are you giving us tonight?'

'Aha! My manager, Gwyneth, will be around with the menus in a bit. I'll just pop over and say hello to the woman from the *Telegraph*, make a little speech, and then we'll be off. Enjoy! Alice! So nice to see you ...' Terry passed on to the next table, and Francesca strained her neck to get a look at Juliana.

'Hmm. She's pretty, I'll give him that. Bit of an over-bite though.'

'Do you think he stands a chance?' asked Penny.

'You should never write him off. Persistence really does pay, sometimes. And the boyfriend looks a nasty piece of work. Terry's bonkers but he's a sweetie. But tell me, who is that gorgeous man sitting at the table with them who keeps looking over at you?'

Penny smiled. 'Oliver Halton. Bookshop owner, and terribly shy. Never speaks. He's rather sweet, actually. He keeps e-mailing me.'

'God, you lucky cow. Beautiful and silent. What more could a girl want? I'd be in there like a rat up a drainpipe,' said Francesca.

Penny laughed. 'I thought you were a respectable married woman these days,' she said.

'I am. I am. But I can dream. And he's a spunk, as they say so innocently in Australian soaps.'

Penny looked thoughtful. 'Yes,' she said. 'Yes, he is rather.'

Whittaker clapped his hands. The room fell silent.

'Mr Mayor, Aoldermen, ladies and gentleman. Welcome to the 4i's, which we are hoping to turn into the north-west's most exciting restaurant. In a moment, my staff will distribute the menu, but first I'd like to call for a big hand for my designer, Penny Lester, without whom this place wouldn't have existed, and for Steve Medlicott, the craftsman who put it all together. Penny and Steve!'

The diners applauded enthusiastically.

'Steve is here on his own tonight because his wife, Sandra, is camped out at the Dole Acre, in opposition to the Dole Acre car park. And to support her, and the other women who have decided to make a stand against the dominance of the motor car, I shall be donating the first week's takings from the 4i's to their campaign!'

There was some more applause, still enthusiastic from the table where Sally sat with Steve, Taff and Syd, but muted from elsewhere in the room. The Mayor did not clap, and Juliana stood to leave. Q touched her hand, and she sat down again, blushing with anger.

'So, ladies and gentlemen, I hope you enjoy your meal. I'd better stop talking and get off to the kitchen. Gwyn? If you're ready?' Gwyn nodded at her waiting staff, who started to hand around the menus. The room began to hum as the diners saw what was on offer.

Terry has given me his permission to reproduce the menu here, but has asked that I do not give the prices, which, he points out, are subject to fluctuation. That's understandable, I think.

4i's

Goujons of smoked eel with a fennel and lemongrass purée
Pancester black pudding in apple and quince sauce

Marsh puffballs in batter, with a rowanberry jus
Laikley Bay shrimps potted in chef's tapenade
4i's Easter salad

Roast seasonal vegetables in a chilli oil coulis with saffron rice
Salt marsh lamb's tail pie with barberry jelly and laver sauce
Tartare of Athon salmon with an aniseed and dill marinade
Blackhampton stewed steak with horseradish dumplings
Roast wild duck with a gooseberry and walnut stuffing

Chocolate cream and strawberry Nick cakes
Brown bread ice cream with poached pears
Green tea and lime sorbet
Apple plummetty
4i's fig tart

Even Juliana had to admit that Whittaker could cook.

'I still hate him ... but ... mmm.' She licked chocolate cream from her spoon.

'He is an artist, my dear. You should be thankful that he is interested in you.'

'Well, I'm not. And he'll never stop my car park, however many stupid old slags camp out there.'

'Did Gaynor go last night? To the Eastering?'

'Mmm, mmm, yes, she did. It was Mrs Innes who put them up to camping, and there's only a few actually staying down there for now, but Gaynor says that lots of the women were on their side. And Aolderwoman Armistead has changed from an abstainer into a no-sayer, apparently.'

'It is of little consequence. That is still only two votes against. And by the way, Jack Sturges tells me the Charter is ready to be returned into circulation.'

'Shh, Q, for goodness' sake. Not here.'

Q laughed. 'You are over-cautious, my dear. Over-caution is the handmaiden of recklessness.'

Francesca was in ecstasies, and stayed on for a drink with staff and friends.

'Oh, Terry, it was superb. God, you're a genius. And Gwyneth, the service – it was wonderful. Friendly, helpful, just right. He's paying you all too much. Or why else would you all be so lovely?'

Whittaker grinned, and Sally hugged and kissed Gwyneth.

'I've got good staff. What did you have?' asked Whittaker.

'Well, I started with the puffballs, 'cos I'd never had them before, and they were lovely, earthy, nutty, crisp batter, tart sauce, super. Oh, but then I had the lamb's tail pie. Ah! What? Wow! Exquisite. The pastry!'

'Made by this young lady,' said Terry, indicating Martha, who blushed into her champagne. Old Dennis, who was standing by Martha's side, gave her a squeeze, which made her blush harder still.

'Shouldn't you be getting on with the washing-up, Dennis Alvey?' she said, clearly pleased.

'And then I had the apple plummetty,' said Francesca. 'Nice, I thought, but not out of this world, only Christ, don't they look amazing? The case is like folk art or something.'

'Martha again. Or at least, she showed Mindy Styles how to do them. And it is folk art. The Pancester women throw apples into the river, and then bake these for the men who catch them.'

'Gosh. Well, it was a shame to eat it, it looked so lovely. Cuggles – my deepest congratulations. My editor might want to do a feature.'

'Thanks, honey. Thanks to you all! Really well done. Cheers.' He raised his glass to his staff, and they raised theirs in return with a ragged cheer.

'Well,' said Whittaker, 'we'd better get our coats on, Taff.'

'Coats on? Where are we going?' asked Penny Lester.

'To the Women's Anti-Car Park Camp, of course. It may be late, but I don't see why the lasses should miss out. Come on . . . here, you carry these, Taff . . . Gwyn . . . good, you've got them . . . Sally, you carry this and the torch . . . that's it. Olly, if you take this . . . Steve . . . hang on, that's hot, use a cloth . . . Coming, Fran, Penny?'

It was touching to see the two women from London carrying

plates and hot boxes, dressed as though they were still in Knightsbridge, picking their way through clumps of thistles and heaps of donkey turds by the uncertain light of Sally's torch. She had been there the night before, of course, so had a good idea of the best way, and the expedition from the 4i's soon made out the glow from the protesters' campfire.

'Halloo!' called Sally.

'Halloo, yourselves,' called back Mrs Innes from a makeshift bench by the fire. Dawn Gabatini and Sandra Medlicott came across to help with the food. Gwyneth kissed her mother.

'You all right, Mam? Not too cold?'

'Course I'm all right. We've got it right cosy in there.'

From somewhere, Mrs Innes had conjured up an old bell tent, and as the women fetched out glasses, it was obvious that they had indeed made it very comfortable. Mrs Innes claimed that this was due to her pioneering spirit, that she had been up and down Kilimanjaro in a day with nothing more than a stout stick, a pair of good walking shoes and half a dozen bearers, and that she knew all about making life pleasant in the bush. But Sally suspected that it was Sandra Medlicott, a veteran of countless festivals, who was the expert at creating luxurious spaces in adverse circumstances.

The hot boxes were opened, and food served to the campers.

'What were it like?' Dawn asked her husband, who was squatting next to her as she balanced a plate of lamb's tail pie on her lap.

'Horrible,' whispered Taff to Dawn. 'I 'ad the fish, and it was raw.'

'Poor love. You can knock yourself up some egg and chips when you get home. You'll manage OK? While I'm down here?'

'Of course I will. You make a stand, sweetheart. I'll come and visit you every day.'

'Ah, bless you, Taff.'

It was strange to be sitting in the Dole Acre by night. The city squatted on its hill, the castle lit up by spotlights, while the sluggish old river gurgled under the walls close by the camp. On the ring road, occasional cars hissed by, one or two of them hooting as they passed the signs the protesters had put up, which read 'Honk Your Horn, Say No To The Car Park.'

Whittaker sat next to Mrs Innes, firelight flickering over her pretty face.

'This is rather lovely, Mr Whittaker,' she said, her mouth full of pie.

'So is this,' said Whittaker, indicating the camp.

'Yes, it is. I think we'll be fine. But I don't think your girlfriend will be very pleased, do you?'

'Let's hope not, Mrs I. Let's hope not.'

'Now, a little bit of business, Mr Whittaker. The county archaeologist is coming tomorrow at eleven. Think you can be here?'

'Of course.'

'And we've been using my phone as the main contact number, which is no good while I'm camping. I've had a word with Dawn, and she thinks it will be fine to use the Fox Hole. What do you think? Taff, will that be OK with you and Olly, if we use the Fox Hole as our headquarters? Yes? Olly can cope with answering the phone?' Olly nodded. 'Good fellow!'

'Will you really be OK down here?' said Whittaker.

'Oh, yes, we'll be fine. Rolly is in his element. And Steve Medicott is bringing us down his and Sandra's yurt.'

'What's a yurt?'

'A sort of Mongolian bell tent, I think. Very comfortable, I'm told.'

'Do you know, I've never actually been down to the Dole Acre before.'

Penny and Francesca sat in their best frocks, perched on the little makeshift log benches that Sandra had knocked up, shivering as they tried to get as close as possible to the fire. Oliver sat next to Penny, and offered her his jacket, which she accepted with a grateful smile. Gwyn and Sally were walking hand in hand away from the camp towards the river. Taff and Steve were kissing their wives good night. Terry took pity on Penny and Francesca, and made ready to take them back to the Pancester Riverside. Sally and Gwyn had the torch; he could see it flickering down by the river. He asked Penny and Francesca to wait while he went to fetch his flatmates.

It was difficult walking on the Acre in the dark. Whittaker walked towards the torch, the only other light a faint glow from the castle floodlights. He almost tripped over some thistles. A large shape on the ground in front of him, which he took to be a small mound of some kind, stirred and rose braying to its feet as Whittaker came close.

Whittaker jumped as the shadowy donkey trotted away. His pulses racing, he walked a little closer to where he could make out Sally and Gwyn's figures on the river bank . . . and slipped down a muddy slope feet first, his hands flailing for support. His feet, his legs were in the river, and he felt himself being sucked away from the bank, when his hand hit a tree root, which he grabbed at; it felt as though it was pulling out from the mud, but it held for the moment.

'Help! Help, I'm in the river. Help!'

The current was strong, and Whittaker was tired. Already his hands were slipping on the slimy root. Its shape was vaguely familiar under his palms. He was reminded somehow of Juliana, even *in extremis*.

Sally and Gwyneth came running, shouting towards the camp. Sally shone the torch at Terry. The mud bank down which Terry had slipped was perhaps six feet high. He watched the terrified faces of Sally and Gwyn above him.

'Hold on, Terry!' screamed Sally.

'There's a branch here,' shouted Gwyn. 'Come and help me drag it over, Sal. Dad! Steve! Help!'

More shouting voices, and the sound of running.

'It's OK. Hold on, boy bach. Well done, our Gwyneth!'

'Grab this, Dad, Steve. Sally, shine me down the torch.'

Whittaker could see Taff and Medlicott holding the branch as Gwyneth climbed down towards him. She held out her right hand, the other holding on to the branch as she leant out from the bank.

'Come on, Terry, grab hold. Grab my hand. That's it . . . now let go of the root and grab the branch . . . OK? . . . Pull! Dad, pull! Come on, Terry! That's it . . . gotcha!'

As Whittaker grabbed the branch he felt the root finally pull away from the mud bank, but he was gripping it too hard, too desperately, to release it, and he clung to it as Steve and Taff helped him and Gwyn to the top. Whittaker collapsed on the wet grass, soaked and shivering.

'Here you are, Mr Whittaker,' said Sandra Medlicott, hurrying up. 'Come on, stand up, we'll get you back to the fire. Wrap this around you. That's it. Put that old root down. Come on, you're safe now.' Sandra prised Whittaker's hand away from his life-saving root.

'Put that down, Mr Whittaker, you're safe now . . . Ooh, look, you could send that to Esther Rantzen, look.'

Whittaker looked at the root. Sandra Medlicott was right. No wonder the shape had been so familiar; it was a shape he felt under his hands night after tortured night as he lay haunted by dreams of Juliana. He dropped the root in disgust as Sandra wrapped a space blanket around his shoulders. A campfire was never so inviting.

'Been for a swim, Mr W? Here, I've made some tea.'

'Th . . . th . . . thanks, Mrs I. And what about Gwyn? Are you all right?'

Gwyneth grinned, her face covered with mud.

'I'm fine, boss. Couldn't afford to lose you, not with all the bookings we've got.'

'You saved my life.'

'My heroine,' said Sally, hugging Gwyn again, and covering herself in mud in the process.

'I t . . . tell you what though, Taff,' said Whittaker.

'What's that, lovely boy?'

'I believe you about Lady Lettice. If you were on your own a . . . and you fell into . . . th . . . that river, and y . . . y . . . you were on your own . . . no way could you survive. N . . . No way.'

No one would have blamed Whittaker for oversleeping, but he awoke on time to meet the county archaeologist. He even managed to arrive at the camp a few minutes earlier than expected. He and Mrs Innes walked over to the river.

'Do you think Letty went into the Athon, Mrs I?' said Whittaker, looking cautiously into the swirling flood.

'Yes, dear, I do. Oh, look, this is probably our man.'

'Hello! Mrs Innes? Mr Whittaker? Hello. Hi, I'm Neil Winterburn. The county archaeologist.' Winterburn had butter-yellow hair and a teasing smile, and the trousers of his disgraceful egg-stained old suit were tucked into a battered pair of black wellington boots. He was carrying a long red and white surveyor's pole with a sharpened end, which he rested in the hollow of his shoulder as he shook hands.

'Shall we have a wander about, do you think? Where shall we start?'

'Over by the camp, I think, Mr Winterburn, by where we have the Eastering.'

'Sure. Lead on, MacInnes.'

Mrs Innes pursed her lips.

'You know something of the archaeological history of the Dole Acre, Mr Winterburn. Have there been excavations here before?' asked Whittaker.

'Yes, just before the first war. They didn't really find anything of value, to be frank. Surprising, really, when you think of everything that's happened here.'

'Oh? Like what?'

'Well, the battle, for one thing.'

'The battle? What battle?'

'In 996. Between the upstart Viking and the fearless Anglo-Saxons. You know, when they got the Ramstheng,' said Winterburn.

'What happened?'

'It's a story known to all the schoolchildren of Pancester, Mr Whittaker,' said Mrs Innes, 'how the Lady Wildaburga rallied the women of Pancester around her, and led them into open battle with the raiders, here on the Dole Acre. And how they repulsed the Norsemen, captured the Ramstheng, drove them into their ships, and generally gave them a thick ear.'

'Where were the men?' asked Whittaker.

'Legend has it that they were off playing something very akin to Wally Oop in Blackhampton,' said Winterburn.

Whittaker laughed. 'So you're following in a fine tradition, Mrs I.'

'Mr Whittaker, you'll make me blush.'

'Is this your camp? Round here, you think? Let's have a quick prod around. Morning, ladies. Fancy coming for a quick prod around in the bushes with me?' said Winterburn.

'You watch your tongue, you saucy bugger,' said Dawn Gabatini, who was balancing a kettle over the fire.

Winterburn wandered off. Whittaker followed him.

'Hmm, I don't know,' said Winterburn, poking his surveyor's pole into the soft marshy ground of the Acre.

'What don't you know?'

'I'm in a difficult position. Pancester City Council won't be overjoyed with the county if I slap some sort of an order on the place, and the county doesn't have the budget to do a full-scale speculative dig on a bit of old agricultural land, however potentially interesting. It's hard enough to get the funds even to do the bits and bats of rescue work that we're obliged to do by law. Hmm, I just don't know.' He plunged his pole into the ground again, and rubbed his chin. 'I can't feel anything, but . . .'

'What?'

'It is interesting, though, isn't it? There must be *something*, I'd have thought. Records show the place in continuous use for the best part of a thousand years. And why do all the women come and sit just *here* when they're trying to get pregnant? Just on this corner of the field, nowhere else. And there was a battle, well a skirmish, anyway. Shame they didn't come up with anything in 1913. Even a few clues from back then, and I could have spared my geofizz guy for a couple of days. That's what it needs, really, but . . .'

'Come and have a look down by the river. Perhaps you'll see something there.'

'I doubt it, old love, but I'll come and have a gander if it makes you happy.'

They walked down to the site of Whittaker's brush with death, but the tide was high, and there was nothing to be seen. Winterburn poked at the ground with his pole.

'Nothing, I'm afraid ... Hello! What's this?' He pointed at Whittaker's discarded root on the riverbank.

Whittaker laughed. 'That's my lucky root. I grabbed it to save myself from going into the water. We thought of sending it off to a TV show, about humorously shaped vegetables, but I don't know what we'd do now *That's Life's* off the air.'

'Root? Root? You mean you found it in the riverbank, just by here?'

'Yes.'

'That's not a root. Look.' Winterburn picked it up, and scraped away at the mud.

'Root, my arse,' he said. 'It's earthenware! Bugger me! Or, rather, don't. It's a clay dildo.'

'Really?'

'Yes! Look. Fascinating, isn't it?' Winterburn's face was illuminated by his beaming smile.

'So last night a dildo saved my life. It's a bit big, isn't it?'

'Oh, they like 'em big. When have you ever seen a realistically sized dildo? What would be the point?'

'What does it tell you?'

'Well, it tells me that Ann Summers parties have been going on a lot longer than we previously thought. And it tells me that we have *got* to come and do something here, definitely. I've seen these in museums, usually from the Greek settlements in Sicily. But I've never heard of one being found in England before. So we *must* do something. But what? When can we fit you in? Hmmm?'

He pulled a face, and looked through his diary, then he looked up at Whittaker with a smile.

'Tell you what, though. You know we've just found a big Roman town up in the north of the county, towards the Cumbria border? See that? It was on *Time Gang*?'

Whittaker nodded. 'I remember Timmy Rubenstein telling me about it when we were on *Junior Masterchef* together.'

'Well, next week we've booked a plane for a couple of days to do us a complete aerial survey of the place. This is pretty well en route, as it happens. Why don't I get the pilot to do a quick flyover, snap a few snaps, have a look. It would be something, wouldn't it?'

Whittaker agreed that it would. Back at the camp, Winterburn accepted a cup of tea, and told the protesters of his decision.

'Better than nothing, sweet captors of my heart. Sorry I can't do more. But perhaps we'll come up with something, other than this ugly great thing.' He showed the ancient dildo around the campers, who giggled.

'Shall I take it with me, girls, or shall I leave it with you?'

'Cheeky monkey. What would we want with that filthy thing?' said Dawn.

'Maybe you're right. We'll get it cleaned up, and dated, and I'll let you know. And perhaps the aerial survey will come up with something. Fingers crossed.'

And with that they had to be satisfied.

Whittaker walked Winterburn back to his car, and hurried to the station in time to see Penny and Francesca off.

'Are you sure you're all right, Cuggsy?' asked Francesca. 'We wouldn't want you catching cold after your swim.'

'I'm fine. Let me know about the feature, if your editor's interested. Look after yourself.'

He kissed her, and hugged Penny, who said, 'How's your father?'

Francesca looked surprised. 'What's this?' she said. '*The News Huddlines*?'

Whittaker smiled. 'Best offer I've had all day. No, he's a little better, thanks, Penny. Still hanging on in there.'

Penny nodded. 'Good. And good luck, Terry. Let me know if you have any problems with the fittings. I'm sure you won't,' she said.

He watched the train pull out of the station, and crossed back into the city over the Pack Bridge. He was surprised to find the entrance to Shy Street blocked by police cars.

'What's going on, officer?' asked Whittaker of the young policeman who stood by the entrance.

'There's been an incident, sir. Mr Whittaker, isn't it? Perhaps you'll wait a moment?'

He spoke into his walkie-talkie.

'Yes, if you'd like to go through, sir, Inspector McCracken will meet you.'

Feeling guilty, as you do whenever the police stop you for anything, because God knows you've got plenty to feel guilty about, Whittaker hurried through the arch to see a uniformed inspector emerge from the door of the 4i's. Whittaker saw Taff and Oliver watching anxiously from the doorway of the Fox Hole.

'Mr Whittaker? If you'd like to follow me, sir.' McCracken led the way through to the kitchen, where, entirely implausibly to Whittaker's mind, Sally and Gwyn sat with Edmund, the Pancester tramp, who was wide-eyed with fear. He had pulled the end of his filthy matted beard into his mouth and was sucking hard. A rich smell of goats' armpits filled the room.

'What's going on?' asked Whittaker.

'That's what we're trying to find out, sir,' said McCracken.

'Edmund's found the Charter, Terry. Look!' said Sally. She pointed to several clear plastic bags on the chopping table.

'What!' shouted Whittaker. Edmund pulled his beard from his mouth and covered his eyes with its damp ends.

'It's true, Terry. They were in the dustbins. Our dustbins,' said Gwyneth.

'Well, how did they get there?' asked Whittaker.

'That's what we're trying to find out, sir,' said McCracken.

'Tell him, Edmund,' said Sally. 'Don't be afraid.'

Edmund took his beard away from his face, and looked at Whittaker.

'Good dustbins, Mister, you got good dustbins.' His voice was deep and rough, but he changed it from time to time, so that his next statement, 'I dine there orften,' was delivered in cod posh, whilst for, 'I likes eels, I do,' Edmund felt that a West Country accent most clearly conveyed his meaning.

'I'm glad. So what happened?'

'That's what we're trying ...'

'Oh, for goodness' sake, Inspector. I know what you are trying to do. Can we please hear what this gentleman has to say?' said Whittaker. Edmund nodded at the inspector.

'Well, this morning, I thought I might have a rummage through them bins, see if you had any eels. I like the pie, too. Been coming here for a few weeks, while you've been learning all them to cook. And I finds some eels, all right, but I finds these too.' He pointed to the bags.

'And they were just as we see them, sir, is that right? Conveniently wrapped in police evidence bags?' said the inspector.

'That's right, inspector,' said Edmund in a strange high-pitched nasal voice.

'So what did you do, Edmund?' asked Terry.

'Well, Terry,' said Edmund, 'I knew what it was as soon as I looked at 'em. My mum used to take me to the Courtney Museum when I were a kid. I knowed the Clangers straight away, bless 'em. I'm a Clanghandler, I am. I know what the Clangers look like ...'

'Stuffed woollen socks that sound like swanee whistles,' said Whittaker. Sally laughed, but the Pancestrians looked stern. It does not do for incomers to mock the traditional life of the city.

'So what did you do, sir?'

'I whistled up Miss Sally. Still in bed, she was.'

Sally shrugged. 'It was a late night. I was taking the morning off.'

'Still in her nightie. Still in her nightie, she was.' Edmund rubbed his thighs.

'Yes, thank you, Edmund. So I called the police, and they came screaming up ten minutes or so before you arrived. More than that we don't know.'

'Well, Inspector,' said Whittaker. 'What do you think?'

The inspector looked at the bags, at Edmund, and then at Whittaker.

'Well, sir, as far as I can tell, everything that was stolen from the museum seems to be here. I can't tell if there's any damage, we'll have to see what Mr Turner, the curator, thinks. But if everything's OK, it looks to me as though whoever nicked this lot found that they couldn't sell it. I mean, who would want a set of medieval handbells, or a piece of old parchment? Who's going to buy them? So I reckon they just panicked, and dumped them.'

'Yes,' said Whittaker. 'But in evidence bags? What kind of thief has access to those?'

'Very highly trained and skilled criminals, sir. The break-in was a lovely job. Strange they chose such difficult stuff to sell.'

'Well, surely the staff at the castle must be obvious suspects.'

'The castle, sir? You mean the National Museum of Crime and Punishment?'

'Well, I thought it was the university of crime.'

'The university of crime, sir? What a funny idea. I think if anything like that was going on, the Pancester police would know, don't you, sir? We don't go about with our eyes closed, you know. No, I think whoever they were, they just dumped the gear when they found they couldn't sell it. You shouldn't have moved them really, miss. Still, we'll dust 'em over for prints. I'll get my constables in, get them to take some statements from you all, but I don't think after that we'll need to keep you any longer, ladies and gentlemen.'

After the police had taken statements, and the forensic boys had been to dust down the bags and put them into yet more bags, Terry, Sally, Gwyneth and Edmund sat in the kitchen, drinking coffee and running over all that had happened. Whittaker said, 'Do you think that policeman was covering up for the castle? Or was he just being stupid?'

'Stupid,' said Sally and Gwyneth together.

'Mister,' said Edmund, 'hey, Terry. Got any of them eels?'

Do You Not Have Gentlemen's Lavatories in Pancester?

The first week's takings from the 4i's proved more than satisfactory, and at Wednesday's committee meeting, held in Sandra Medlicott's yurt, newly erected on the Dole Acre, it was decided that the campaign could now afford proper legal advice.

The next morning, Brian Carless came nervously down to the camp to meet the committee. He sat on one of the benches around the fire, listening to Mrs Innes' case, and looking anxiously over his shoulder.

'I see . . . an interesting point. Could "grazing rights" be taken to mean car-parking fees, though, I wonder?'

'Of course not, Brian,' said Dexter, 'and anyway, the Charter clearly states that the freehold remains with the Courtney family. If a Courtney heir, or even Lady Lettice herself, were to turn up, then the council would be in a mighty sticky situation. We might have to give them the car park, after spending one and a half million quid of council taxpayers' money. Without the freehold, I can't recommend going ahead to my constituents.'

'Haven't you heard?' said Carless. 'The council has applied to have Lady Lettice Courtney formally declared dead. And there certainly isn't an heir of any kind. Lady Letty was the last of the Courtneys.'

'The evil, manipulative . . .'

'Evil is a strong word, Mrs Gabatini. I urge caution. And I think the first thing we should do is go through the Charter with a fine . . . Whoa! Get that thing away from me!' Brian Carless had shot up from the bench, and ran round to the other side of the fire, away from the donkey who was walking towards the camp.

'All right, my dear, don't worry.' Mrs Innes stood and shooed the donkey off. 'Goo on, Edith! Goo on! You're not scared of donkeys, are you?' The donkey moved a little way away from the group.

'Yes, I am, Mrs Innes. Can't stand the creatures. Whaaa!' He dived inside the yurt as the donkey walked back towards the meeting. Whittaker stood next to Mrs Innes, and the donkey stopped, staring at him.

'It's almost as if the donkeys want to come to the meeting, isn't it? After all, it is them who'll be evicted from their home,' he said, fondling the donk between her ears.

'Have they gone yet?' called Carless from inside the yurt.

'No, stay put for a minute, Brian,' said Whittaker. 'Now look here, Mrs Donkey. Mr Carless is trying to help us keep you here, and it's no good if you keep scaring him. You run along, and Mrs Innes will come and tell you later what was decided.' He smiled, and the donkey trotted off.

'Mr Whittaker,' said Mrs Innes, 'it looks as though we shall have to add donkey whispering to your list of talents.'

Brian Carless was helped out from the yurt, white-faced and sweating.

'It's OK, Brian. They won't be back,' said Whittaker.

Carless reluctantly took his place again. He gulped at his tea, his hands shaking. He continued, keeping an eye on the donkeys.

'Well, anyway, as I was saying, the thing to do is to go through the Charter with a fine-tooth comb. And then think about what to do next. But if you're right, this grazing rights business might take us all the way to the High Court.' He licked his thin lips. 'I've never had a case go all the way to the High Court before.'

'And what about the case to declare Lady Letty dead? What happens if they succeed?'

'Well, then, I'm afraid, Mrs Innes, the whole thing about grazing rights might become an academic issue. Without a Courtney heir, and given that the city has had the use of the land for the best part of five hundred years, the council will have a very strong case for establishing its right to the freehold.'

Whittaker and Dexter helped Carless through the field, fending off any donkeys who threatened to come too close.

'Thanks, Mr Whittaker, Aolderman Halton.' He mopped his brow with trembling hands, and laughed with relief at reaching the safety of the ring road. 'I'll get on to Mr Turner at the museum to get me a transcription of the Charter. We'll take it from there. And have a think about why Lady Letty shouldn't be declared dead.'

Dexter and Terry walked back together into the city.

'What about the donkeys, Dex? Any movement on this one?'

'Yes, I've been in contact with some animal rights campaigners. They're very upset. A very emotional issue, donkey welfare. They're hoping to run a big demo here in a couple of weeks' time. I'll let the committee know when it's confirmed. I doubt that poor old Brian will be joining their ranks, though, don't you?'

All the evidence suggested that the 4i's was a brilliant success. Night after night it was packed with locals and tourists. One elderly American couple who asked to see the chef were actually in tears as Whittaker approached the table.

'We'd been here a week, trying to trace my husband's family, before we found this place, and dear God in heaven, the things we've eaten . . .' She sobbed. Her husband patted her arm.

'It's OK, honey,' he said, his wrinkled cheeks stained with tears of gratitude. 'It's OK now.'

So Whittaker was very busy. A rave review appeared in the *Telegraph*, and Francesca called to say that her editor had agreed to a feature, and she was sending up a photographer.

'But I'll do the interview by phone if that's OK, Terry. Tony's still a bit sensitive about me seeing you too much.'

'Tell him I'm a one-woman man.'

'How's it going?'

'Well, she keeps coming into the restaurant, anyway. That must mean something.'

It was true. Juliana had been twice more since the opening, once with Q, and once with Trevor Mallinson.

'Isn't this romantic, darling?' asked Mallinson of Juliana as they sat across from one another at the glass table.

'Do shut up, Trevor. Shall I have the black pudding again, or try the puffballs, I wonder?'

She found that Whittaker's cooking was haunting her dreams. She would wake up at night with the memory of his chocolate cream and strawberry Nick cakes on her tongue, and the smell of his tartare of salmon in her nose. At work, she found it harder to concentrate, despite the fact that the full hearing in front of the whole council was getting closer and closer. Sensual experience was new to her, new and frightening. I hate you, Terry Whittaker, she thought.

Q was becoming mildly concerned. 'My dear, you must keep your mind on the job in hand. The city solicitor is preparing the case to prove Lettice Courtney dead, and any day now someone is going to discover our little . . . ah, amendment to the Charter. Do not succumb to the pleasures of the flesh.'

'I know, Q, I know. But it's taking me over. I've never felt like this about anything.'

'Then you must fight it, my dear. We live by the will, and it is only in the public sphere that the will can operate. You and I, Juliana, we understand that the quest for personal, private happiness – the modern idea that real life only happens behind a mortgaged front door, and that the public world is bogus and frightening and cannot be controlled – we know this is false. We know that private happiness is unattainable, and that icy calm, sensual indifference and an erotic quietism are the most we can wish for. We project our lusts and desires onto the world, not on to ourselves, or one another. We know that the public realm is the only possible realm for action. I am me. You are you. Nothing can be changed. But traffic flow at the Laikley turn-off, that we can reduce by 11 per cent. Ancient charters we can steal and alter. We can change history. We can destroy thousands of years of custom and belief simply by building a roundabout. We must not allow the passionate senses into our lives. Passion is weakness, passion is destruction. In order to master the world, we must master ourselves. I shall not be taking you to the 4i's again, until you understand this.'

Juliana hung her head. 'Yes, Q.' But still she dreamed of food.

One morning, when Whittaker had gone as usual to chat with Taff in the Fox Hole, a phone call came through from Neil Winterburn.

'Mr Whittaker? Good news. Looks like we might have found something.'

'What?'

'Can't say for sure. But I've just got those snaps in from the aerial photographers, and it could be big. It looks like there might be a structure of some kind under the camp, and a further two smaller structures down towards the river. And we think they might, taking into account our little find the other day, just might be Roman or Romano-British.'

'So what does this mean?'

'Well, in the first instance, it means we can come and do a bit of geofizz, and make a proper report. Take it from there. We'll be up next ... hang on a mo ... next Tuesday and Wednesday. Mind you, it'll have to be something pretty out of this world before I can do anything other than recommend. But it's a start, *n'est-ce pas?*'

Whittaker liked to walk down to the camp most mornings, to make plans with Mrs Innes and to tickle the donkeys, of whom he was becoming increasingly fond, and this piece of news put a spring in his step as he hurried over the bridge and on to the Dole Acre. In the night two new tents had appeared, as Emma and Gemma, twin sisters from Laikley, had arrived, saying that they wanted to defend their traditional right to fall pregnant. They reminded Whittaker of the girl he had seen on the prom at Laikley; same hair, same tracksuits. Mrs Innes had thought them a little young, and indeed had whispered to Terry, 'I rather think they should be at school', but in the end she was pleased to get some new campers.

'They'll learn more here, Mr W, than at Laikley High. And actually, while they're with us, they're much *less* likely to get pregnant.' They grinned at Whittaker from the doors of their tents as he arrived at the camp.

All the protesters were pleased about the news from the county archaeologist. 'There had to be something, didn't there? Well, now we shall see,' said Mrs Innes.

But for every oohjah there is a wotsit, as Bertie Wooster might say. The next morning Whittaker received a call from Brian Carless. 'I've got to talk to you. Something rather tricky has come up. But please, not in the middle of those ruddy donkeys.'

Mrs Innes was summoned up from the camp, and she and Dexter sat with Whittaker and Carless at the tables upstairs at the Fox Hole. Carless spread out some papers.

'It's the Charter, I'm afraid. It looks like we've been getting it wrong all the time.'

'In what way?'

'Well, I got in touch with Mr Turner at the museum to see about getting a transcription. And he said that the council had already been on to him to say that nothing but a new transcription would do, since the last one was Dadd's in the 1890s, and who was to say that his reading was accurate? So he got a pal of his up from Cambridge to prepare a new version. That's good, I said, could I have a copy when he's done? Got it yesterday afternoon. This is it. And I've been over and over it, and there's absolutely nothing about grazing rights at all. It quite clearly grants the "use" of the land. And there's another thing. In the event of there being no Courtney heir, the Charter states unequivocally that the freehold should pass to the city.'

'Show me that!' said Mrs Innes. 'Oliver!' Olly looked up from the computer, where he was still trying to set up an Anti-Car Park website. 'Have you got a copy of Dadd's *Account*? Well, fetch it over, there's a good lad. Now, where's my glasses? Here we are. Now ... ah, here it is. A transcription of Sir Kenelm de Courtney's Charter of 1503 establishing the Pancester Dole.'

She read the new transcription over, and compared it to the old one. There were only two differences, but they were just as Carless described. She looked up, pushed her glasses to the top of her head, and said, 'Well.'

'Looks like old Clement Dadd made a bit of a pig's ear of it. A shame. Strange that the only mistakes he made are the two that matter so much in this case,' said Carless.

'Strange, Mr Carless? Dadd was the foremost Pancester scholar of his day. He wouldn't make a childish mistake like this! Don't you see? The thing is a forgery.'

'Now, Mrs Innes, you can't go making allegations like that about people. Mr Turner's friend is the top man in his field, I'm assured.'

'Not Mr Turner's friend. The castle! The castle is behind the whole thing! This is why they stole it, so that they could alter it. The cunning weasels. And they knew about it up at City Hall, too. That's why they ordered a new transcription. What do you think of Ms Blezzard now, Mr Whittaker? Hmm?'

Whittaker was troubled, and spoke to Sally about it when she came through the kitchen on her way home from work that evening.

'Sally, she couldn't do this. I know her. She's a moral woman, I know. Please won't you let me talk to her?' Whittaker tipped back his head, and guzzled down the syrup from a tin of peaches.

Sally shook her head. 'The committee are getting their own expert in to examine the Charter, presumably?' she said.

Whittaker nodded sadly.

'Well, at least wait and see if your expert can tell whether it's a forgery or not. If it is, you can tell Juliana the gaff is blown, and you're going to the police, unless she puts her hands up. If not, then you're going to have to let her have this one. You've still got plenty to fight her on. And that's what she wants, remember? She wants you to stand up to her all the way, and then . . . well, you'll have to see. But don't call her, please, Cuggs. Please?'

Syd Montague-Forrester and Steve Medlicott attended the next meeting on Dole Acre, as did Aolderwoman Armistead, to see if any case could be made for stopping the council from declaring Lettice Courtney dead.

'Well, I was her last lover. And although the old festival was a bit of a flop, I can tell you that there is no way at all she was in

140

the least bit suicidal. She absolutely fizzed with life, did Letty,' said Syd.

'But, Syd, I fell into the river stone-cold sober. If Gwyneth hadn't acted quickly, I'd have been well past Laikley Point and halfway to Ireland by now. On your own, and tripped off your face, there's no way you could get out. She didn't top herself, Syd, she just fell in,' said Whittaker.

'Ah, but Steve's seen her,' said Syd.

'Have you, Steve? Really seen her?' said Dexter. The committee took a collective deep breath, and leant forward.

Medlicott sighed. 'Not with my eyes. But there are other – organs of sight. I sense her pattern. She's what you think of as alive.'

'Can you prove it though, Steve? asked Terry.

Medlicott smiled. 'In your sense . . . no.'

The committee sighed, and leant back on their benches.

'I don't really think we've got anything to take to court, do you?' said Mrs Innes.

Aolderwoman Armistead coughed.

'The Chair recognises Aolderwoman Armistead.'

Aolderwoman Ursula Armistead, ten years or so younger than Mrs Innes, was at least twice as large. She dwarfed the home-made wooden bench on which she sat. The thick tweed suit and brogues which were her habitual uniform for council business had been forsaken, on the occasion of her visit to the Dole Acre Donkey Sanctuary, for a hacking jacket and jodhpurs. Whittaker felt rather overawed by her.

'Thank you, Mrs Innes. I . . . I hope I'm amongst friends?'

The committee murmured assent.

'I'm afraid I agree with Mr Whittaker. If Letty was alive, I'm sure she would have been in touch with me. She was washed away by the river a long time ago. But – well, I want you to know that I wouldn't be telling anyone this for all the world, if it wasn't for this damned silly car park. And because I loved Letty. She was my best friend, you know, though we drifted apart in later years.' She cleared her throat.

'We were the only Pancester lasses at our school, which was

right away in the Midlands, in Malvern, and we were the same age. And she was so kind to me. I was the swotty one, and I helped her with her books, you know, but she was the popular one, the one all the girls adored, and she made sure that I was included in everything. I'll always love her for that. But she was wild, you know, and all the boys of the town loved her too, and one night she came up to me in the dormitory in tears, and told me she was going to have a baby. She was fifteen. I hugged her, and told her everything was going to be all right – but of course, it wasn't, not in 1952. She was sent away from the school, and old Lady Abigail, her mother, you know, pretty much locked her up in Courtney House. No one saw her, and as far as I'm aware, the whole thing was hushed up. And when I came home at the end of the school year, I called for her, and Lady Abigail, who was on her last legs, though we didn't know it at the time, wouldn't let me in to see her. But she sent me a note. Look.'

The Aolderwoman unfolded a piece of expensive notepaper, embossed with the Courtney crest. The committee read.

Dearest Ursula,

Everyone has been a pig, especially Mummy. I had the baby a month ago, a darling darling baby boy. Mummy got some awful nurse up from London to deliver him, and I hardly got a proper cuddle before they took him away. I cried and cried, but Mummy said it was for the best. I don't know what they did with him, but that nurse took him away, and they won't tell me where. Mummy's going to have to let me out soon, and then I'll come and see you. Hope you enjoyed the last term at St Theresa's.
    Love,
    Letty

The committee looked up from the letter.

'And then about a month later, of course, old Lady Abigail died, and after the funeral Letty headed out of the house and away to London and university and her wild ways. And by the next time I saw her, a couple of years later, I didn't like to mention it. And she never said a dickie bird. But you know, she was never the same.'

Aolderwoman Armistead wiped away a tear with the sleeve of her jacket.

'Gosh,' said Whittaker.

'So you see, as far as I know, somewhere there *is* a Courtney heir, unless he's dead too. But he might have had children of his own. That must be our strategy – to find the heir of the Courtney's.'

The committee looked at one another.

'Thank you, Ursula,' said Mrs Innes. 'Thank you very much for coming and telling us this. It can't have been easy, and we very much appreciate it.'

Aolderwoman Armistead smiled in thanks.

'Perhaps it's the Courtney energy patterns you've detected, Steve, rather than Lady Letty herself,' said Syd.

'Perhaps,' said Steve, thoughtfully.

The weekend saw the arrival of Dexter's animal rights protesters. Two minibus loads of middle-aged ladies and suspiciously well-dressed hippies disgorged in the Guildhall Square. They wandered about a little aimlessly, but Dexter, armed with a megaphone, marshalled them towards the Guildhall steps. He spoke to Whittaker while the protesters milled about, trying to press leaflets into shoppers' hands.

'They can be really useful to us, Terry, if things get bad. We can use them as shock troops. You just have to know how to press their buttons. Watch.'

He spoke into his megaphone, and the animal rights activists came to wide-eyed attention.

'Excuse me! Excuse me … thank you.' Dexter turned and winked at Whittaker before addressing the crowd.

'Africa is being devastated by AIDS! And the multinational drug companies do nothing to help, but direct all their resources towards an affluent minority in the West!' The activists shuffled, and flapped their leaflets.

Dexter continued. 'All across Asia, millions of women work in conditions of near-slavery, making consumer goods for sale at vastly inflated prices in the so-called developed world!' Some of the activists looked at one another and shrugged. 'Whilst here in Pancester, five donkeys are being inconvenienced!'

This set them off. They bayed and screamed at anyone who looked faintly anti-donkey.

'Murderers!'

'Haven't you got a conscience?'

'Donkey killers!'

'I'm going to kill you!'

'We know where you live!'

'We're going to bomb your children!'

'See how you like it.'

'Good, aren't they?' said Dexter. 'Shall we get them back for the full council meeting?'

'Yes. Oh, God, yes. They'll intimidate a few waverers. They intimidate me.'

'Oh, don't be daft. Here, you have a go ... excuse me! Excuse me! Thank you. We are now going to have a few words from Mr Terry Whittaker, spokesman for the anti-car park campaign! Here we go, Tel.' He passed Terry the megaphone.

'Thank you. Thank you for coming here today to show your opposition to the new car park. Er ... as you know, the council is planning to build this car park on the Dole Acre, a piece of land which resonates in the hearts of all Pancestrians. And in something more than the hearts of many of the women of Pancester.' He smiled hopefully, but there was not so much as a polite titter. 'An environmentally friendly transport policy would remove the need for this new car-parking facility. As environmentalists yourselves ...' The activists looked puzzled. What was an 'environmentalist'? '... I'm sure we can count on your support as we try to preserve the beauty of Dole Acre from the ravages of the motor car.' The activists scratched their heads. Dexter snatched the megaphone away from the faltering Whittaker.

'Oppose the live transport of donkeys!' he screamed at the crowd.

'Murderers!'

'Haven't you got a conscience?'

'Donkey killers!'

'I'm going to kill you!'

'We know where you live!'

'We're going to bomb your children!'

'See how you like it.'

'And so on. You've got to get them just right, or they won't react. And never mistake them for environmentalists. And lay off the jokes. They don't like 'em. But keep it simple, and we should be able to use them fairly effectively,' said Dexter.

'I'll never be a proper politician, Dex. You've got the magic touch.'

'Oh, it's just practice. That, and the abandonment of all principle. Look, I think I'll get them down the Acre now. Mrs I can tell them all about donkey rescue. They'll like that. See you later . . . excuse me! Excuse me! Follow me to the donkeys, please. This way to the donkeys!' And off they all went.

Over the weekend more and more tents appeared on the Dole Acre. Some of them were gone again by Monday, only to reappear the following weekend, but Mrs Innes reckoned that if you counted the weekenders as halves, there were now twenty-two women living permanently in the Women's Anti-Car Park Camp. Or sixteen, if you didn't count them at all.

'It breaks my heart to say it, but I'm going to have to ask you all to budge over for a day or so,' announced Neil Winterburn when he turned up with his geophysicist. 'We need to cover the area of your campsite with all our wires and boxes. It's a bore, I know, but you can come back when we've done. Only a few metres over that way would be enough.' He pointed towards the ring road.

'What about the yurt?' asked Sandra Medlicott. 'It's a right cow to move.'

Winterburn looked at his geophysicist, who nodded.

'Oh, that'll be fine. We can work round that. I'm sorry to put you to this inconvenience. Only for a couple of days. We'll give you a hand shifting your stuff.'

The campers liked Neil and 'the geofizz guy', and for two days they made endless brews, worked as unpaid assistants and cooked for the two archaeologists. Mrs Innes even forgave Neil his overfamiliar manner. 'He's rather charming, actually,' she said.

Emma and Gemma were particular fans, and willingly held tapes and poles and reels of wire for the two men until well after the sun had sunk over Laikley Bay. By Wednesday evening they had finished covering the areas where they suspected they might find some structures, and were treated to a farewell meal after they had helped move the camp back to its original site.

'Well, *mes braves*, that was luscious, but we're going to have to love you and leave you, I'm afraid,' said Winterburn, standing up. 'Do you think you can live without me till Friday afternoon? We'll run the stuff through the computer tomorrow and knock together a preliminary report. And I'll come and show you on Friday. OK?'

Whittaker, Dexter, Steve Medlicott, Sally, Gwyneth and Taff were all waiting with the protesters to hear the report when Winterburn came back on Friday afternoon. He smiled around at the assembled company, and opened his document case.

'Well, you are a bunch of saucepots, ye ladies of brave Pancester, aren't you? You've been coming out here for, excuse the pun, donkey's years, without really knowing why, except that your mothers and grandmothers did it before you. And presumably, because it works. Lots of you fall pregnant after sleeping out here, you little naughties. Well, for the first time in almost fifteen hundred years, I can show you why.' He unrolled a computer-generated map.

'Now, this is what we've come up with. The computer has extrapolated one or two places where the evidence has mostly vanished, but I think this is a fairly accurate picture. As you can see, we are not dealing with three separate structures, as we originally thought, but with one very large one. These two adjacent circular structures down by the river quite clearly share a continuous curving wall, and are linked to the larger bell-shaped structure under the site of the Eastering by a long shaft-like corridor. The entrance . . .' (he looked at his diagram and moved a few paces to his left) 'a slit-like opening at the tip of the larger part of the structure, would have been about here. Come and have a look.'

The protesters gathered round the map. Some of them giggled, and Mrs Innes blushed.

'Let's 'ave a look,' said Taff, craning his neck to see. 'Well, it's a funny-looking building, isn't it? Where 'ave I seen a shape like that before?'

'You surprise me, Signor Gabatini,' said Winterburn. 'Do you not have gentlemen's lavatories in Pancester? I've rarely if ever visited a public loo without a shape very like this carved into the door.'

'Oh, Christ, yes. It's a bloody great big . . .'

'You are with us. It is, yes. An absolute whopper, isn't it, girls? We are standing on the site of the most important fertility temple in Europe, unquestionably. Dedicated to the cult of Priapus, or some similar deity. In fact, that would be a good working name. The Temple of Priapus. Yes, I like that. We think it late Roman, maybe. That's just a guess at the moment, though a pretty good one, taking into account the dildo, which I am prepared to bet my last pfennig is associated with activity in the temple. We've sent it for carbon dating. And now, if you don't mind, I think I'm going to jump up and down and whoop with joy, because if this isn't the most fabulous find of my whole career, then I'm a Dutchman.' But he contented himself with smiling broadly at everyone who looked at his map.

'But what does this mean for the campaign?' asked Terry.

'Oh, didn't I say? The campaign is over. You've won. This thing is utterly, totally unique. There is no way in the world that anyone can build over this. Monday morning, I'm back in the office slapping a preservation order on the whole site. We'll be excavating for at least two years, and then when we've uncovered this wonderful thing, you'll be able to apply to put up a little visitor centre or something, if you want one. Even more tourists, I'm afraid. Where *are* they all going to park their cars?'

And pedestrians on the ring road, walking from the station towards the Pack Bridge, were startled by a loud burst of cheering from behind the hedge.

Burning the Midsummer Ring

By Saturday morning the news of the find had swept through Pancester like a fire in a stick factory. The weekend campers, returning to the Dole Acre, found that a large party was being organised to celebrate victory over the forces of progress. Juliana was beside herself with misery until Q came down from the Castle to visit her in her flat.

'The thing is, I should be pleased. I am the Chief Tourism Officer, and this is a find of international importance. Oh, but I did so want my lovely new car park. And we do need it, Q, we really do. And if we'd got it, it would have made my career! The whole heritage industry would have known my name. And then I could have applied for a job in London, or Edinburgh, and got out of this shithole!' She leant on his shoulder. Tears streamed down her cheeks on to his expensive jacket. He pulled back impatiently, and wiped away the tears with a silk handkerchief.

'My dear child, how easily you give in at the first sign of adversity. I thought more of you. The whole City Council, with the exception of a handful of ostriches whose heads are buried in the sands of time, support this scheme. The County supports it. The Secretary of State has rubber-stamped it, at least in principle. We have powerful political allies. One might even say pawns. Go and have a shower, and then come back in here and start telephoning round. Beginning with your dear friend Trevor Mallinson.'

'Yes, Q. Of course. Of course. We've come too far. You're right again.' She managed a smile.

*

Whittaker and Gwyneth couldn't go to the party on Dole Acre, as they were working, but all the rest of the campaigners lit a giant bonfire, made a huge cauldron of fearsome punch, sang songs and danced to the sound of Pancester's ceilidh band, The Marsh Men, who had brought their instruments down to the camp and were whipping up a storm. Sally even persuaded Oliver to get to his feet and dance a jig or two with her by the light of the fire. The only dance Taff could do was his own strange version of the jive, and he yanked Dawn about, and dragged her through his legs until she thought she was going to be sick.

On Sunday, everyone slept late, and on Monday morning they started to pack up the camp.

Until Neil Winterburn phoned Whittaker at the Fox Hole.

'Better sit down, Terry. You're not going to believe this. My masters have been on to me. There is no way at all that they are going to allow a preservation order, no way that they are going to allocate any extra funds to the project, no way they are going to allow me to stand in the way of Pancester's, I quote, "sorely needed new car park". It's out of my hands, I'm afraid.'

'My God. They can't do that, can they?'

'I didn't think so, but they have. You can apply to the Secretary of State, but it's unlikely that he will want to intervene. Someone has been playing politics on a grand scale.'

'What can we do?'

'Well, keep plugging away, as you have been. Use every means at your disposal. This must be stopped.'

'And what can you do now?'

'Oh, me? Well, I thought I might come and bunk down in Pancester for a month or two, start a volunteer dig. They'll try and stop me, but I don't see how they can. Not now I've resigned.'

'You've resigned?'

'Of course! Obviously. There's no point in having a County Archaeologist's department if they dump on us like this, is there? I'll come and see you all tomorrow. Think you can put me up for a night or two?'

'Yes, that's fine. I'd better shoot off and stop the campers leaving the site.'

'You do that. See you tomorrow.'

As Whittaker arrived at the gate to Dole Acre, he found Emma and Gemma gloomily carrying their tents towards the Laikley bus stop.

'Follow me,' he ordered. 'Something's come up.' Emma and Gemma started smiling again as they crossed the field in Whittaker's wake.

'Stop!' he shouted to the protesters, Steve Medlicott in particular, who was pulling the tarpaulin away from his yurt. 'Stop! The fight goes on!'

'What's happened?' shouted Mrs Innes.

'They've stopped Neil Winterburn from putting up the preservation order.'

'What?'

'They can't do that!'

'But they have.'

'Who have, exactly?' asked Dawn.

'Neil's bosses. County. Whoever, I don't really know. He's coming down tomorrow to tell us all about it. He's packed his job in.'

The protesters who were left murmured appreciatively.

'Good for him,' said Dawn.

Emma and Gemma were cheerfully re-erecting their tents. Steve Medlicott shrugged, and started pulling the tarp back over his yurt. Mrs Innes sat down heavily on one of the benches with a sigh.

'What are we going to do now?' she said.

Whittaker found that he was shaking with anger.

'We're going to stop these bastards,' he said. 'We're going to prove that the Charter has been forged, we're going to go all the way to the Secretary of State to save the Temple of Priapus, and get Neil his job back, we're going to surround City Hall with rabid animal rights activists, we're going to fill the Dole Acre with eco-warriors and hippies and travellers, we're going to find the Courtney heir. And you, Steve, are going to use your "organs of sight" and help us find Lady Letty, if need be. We're going to fight. And keep on fighting. There may be months of struggle. Mmm, some of us may fall by the wayside. It will not be easy. Mmm, but we will not give in. We will never surrendah. And if we are strong, the day will come, mmm, howevah far away it may seem now, the day will come when we have stopped this evil car park, and donkeys and archaeologists and women and hippies are free, once again, to call the Dole Acre their own!' He sat down, shaking, to cheers.

'Mr Whittaker! You don't just look a bit Churchillian, do you? You walk the walk, as they say!' exclaimed Mrs Innes.

'And I will try to – detect – Lady Lettice. I know she's here somewhere,' said Steve.

'And I'll put my head together with Ursula Armistead, and try and work out what could have happened to Letty's baby,' said Dawn.

'And we'll help Neil,' said Emma and Gemma together.

'And our expert is coming to examine the Charter next week,' said Mrs Innes.

'And Dexter will unleash his harpies,' said Whittaker. 'And maybe the time has come for Syd to unleash his hippies. And now, and I don't care what anyone says, I am going up to City Hall to see Juliana.'

It was a brief meeting. Gaynor tried desperately and failed to stop Whittaker bursting into Juliana's office. He stood in front of her desk, breathing heavily.

'I don't think you have an appointment, Mr Whittaker.'

'I don't need one. I've only got one thing to say to you. No, hang on, two.'

'Well, I'm afraid you still need an appointment . . .'

'Oh no I don't, Ms Blezzard. Not to tell you that I don't care how low you sink, or how dirty you fight, or whatever you do, I still love you, and I'm going to stop you building this bloody car park.'

'I see. Well, you haven't done very well so far, have you? And what is the second thing? You might as well get it out while you're here.'

Whittaker leaned across her desk.

'You are barred from the 4i's.' And Whittaker whirled around, and out of City Hall.

She sat in her office after he had gone, staring at the wall. Not that, she thought. Don't make me give up that. And she tried to hear Q's voice, 'We must master ourselves.' But it was going to be hard. She still hadn't tried the potted shrimps.

Neil Winterburn arrived the following morning with a car full of equipment and a small bag of clothes.

'You can kip in the nursery, and eat with us in the kitchen. Here's a key,' said Whittaker.

'I very much appreciate this, Terry.'

'You're welcome. Oh, and you're co-opted onto the Committee Against the Car Park.'

'Well, I call that an honour. And now, if it's okay with you, I'm off to start digging.'

'Don't you need permission?'

'Yep.'

'And have you got it?'

'Nope.'

'Will they try and stop you?'

'I expect so. But who would you back in a fight – a bunch of council officials with a handful of writs, or Mrs Innes and her fearless crew?'

Whittaker smiled.

'Good luck, Neil,' he said.

'See you later, Terry,' said Neil.

And now days, weeks passed in a flurry of activity. Aolderwoman Armistead and Dexter Halton spent countless hours patiently canvassing their fellow councillors, trying to persuade them to vote against the car park in full council. Dawn Gabatini spent a long time trying to get Social Services to give her a clue as to how she might track down the Courtney heir, but records were sketchy that far back, and she was unable to locate a birth certificate. The committee's expert came up from London, and they trooped with her to the Lady Abigail Courtney Museum and Art Gallery, where she pored over the Charter, and in particular the suspect clauses, while the committee breathed over her shoulder.

She looked up after an hour, a jeweller's glass still screwed into her left eye socket.

'No go, I'm afraid,' she said. 'If this has been forged, it has been done by an absolute master. But I don't think it has. You might try getting permission to have it X-rayed, but the Museum will kick up a fuss, and even that might be inconclusive. If you ask me, old Clement Dadd just made a blunder. Sorry.'

Whittaker had made several more trips into Laikley to visit Zahid, and his virtual Juliana now had legs, eyes and, frankly, pudenda, which he had spent quite a while choosing. And, although he had been fighting his tendency to stalk, he had weakened, and had spent a couple of mornings lurking by some garages behind Juliana's flat. He had only seen her twice: once when she came out from her back gate into the alley with some rubbish bags, and once when she had pegged out some clothes to dry on the line in the little yard behind the flats. And, it has to be faced, Whittaker disgraced himself.

As he watched her peg out her washing, he could see several lacy black items, which he felt that he had to make his own in order to hang on to his sanity. He waited, and then, after making certain that the coast was clear and that Juliana had set off for work, he tried the gate to the yard. It was bolted from the inside. So, taking his life in his hands, he scaled the wall and grabbed a pair of knickers from the line. Holding them to his delicate and highly trained nose, he detected a definite whiff of smoked fish in a rich mushroom ketchup. His heart beating fast, he stuffed them into his pocket, before unbolting the gate and slipping nonchalantly back into the alleyway, and bore them proudly home, to add to the contents of his box.

In his defence, although the knickers came to play an

important part in his auto-erotic existence (and as he stretched them badly out of shape as he forced them over his hips), he did feel a sense of guilt each time he mopped up, and he promised himself never to violate Juliana's privacy in this way again, a promise which he broke most nights after work.

Neil Winterburn, with only Emma and Gemma to help him, was making slow but steady progress on the ground. After more careful surveying work, he had decided to cut a trench down towards the river, over that part of the Temple of Priapus everyone quite understandably called 'the Balls', but it was heavy work in the boggy ground, and he expected results to be slow in coming. He also spent time on the telephone, calling ex-colleagues, English Heritage, the Department of the Environment, anyone he thought might be able to help. And one morning he came down to the camp with a piece of very exciting news.

'I've been schmoozing with a researcher at Channel Four I met last year. And I've sent her loads of stuff, and her producer got back to me this morning, and guess what?'

'What?'

'We're going to be on *Time Gang*! They're going to come and help us excavate the place!'

'No!'

'That's fabulous!'

'When?'

'Ah. That's the thing. Next February.'

'Oh, but Mr Winterburn, the council meeting is next week. The day after the Midsummer Ring,' said Mrs Innes.

'I know. I know. You know what the telly are like, though. They have schedules and plans. February is the absolute earliest. But we can hold on till then, I know we can. We're going to have to.'

Whittaker felt himself attracted to Neil Winterburn, and the two men had taken to lunching together, or sharing a beer after the restaurant had closed. Terry told Neil about Juliana, and Neil made a face.

'Doesn't sound too great to me, I'm afraid. My wife used to treat me with indifference and mounting hostility, but it didn't mean that she loved me.'

'No?' said Whittaker.

'No,' said Winterburn, his voice hardening, 'It meant that she was shagging our next-door neighbour.'

'Oh.'

'Of course, she got the house and custody of our daughter. I mean, it's only fair, isn't it?'

'Um . . .'

'I get access, obviously. Except that they moved to Torquay after the divorce. So access isn't especially useful. I only get to see my daughter in school holidays now. When Diane lets me. It isn't always convenient, apparently.'

'It must be hard.'

Winterburn pulled a face and gulped at his beer.

'Yes,' he said, 'yes, it is.'

'How old is your daughter?'

'Twelve. She's twelve.'

'What's her name?'

'Megan. Anyway, Terry, the thing is, I'd forget about women altogether if I were you, especially ones who don't love you.'

'But Juliana does love me, that's the whole point. It's just that . . .'

'What?'

'She doesn't realise it. Yet.'

The week passed busily by. Public meetings were held, leaflets were distributed, councillors were pressurised, and more and more women felt that they wanted to join the Camp, now that the council meeting was drawing close, and the weather was so much nicer, until on the morning of the Burning of the Midsummer Ring, when the city was packed with tourists, the Committee Against the Car Park held its final meeting down on Dole Acre, to collate the various objections to the car park.

Dexter ended the meeting by announcing that his animal rights protesters would be staging a demonstration on the City Hall steps in the morning to greet the councillors as they arrived.

'You don't think they'll do more harm than good, Aolderman Halton?' asked Mrs Innes.

'Well, we'll see, I guess. They're scary, if nothing else. Hello? Who's that old geezer?'

Dexter pointed to the riverbank, where a tiny old gentleman wearing an award-winningly huge pair of shorts and the sort of bobble hat that small boys jeer at in the street was gazing into the brown water of the Athon. Mrs Innes declared the meeting closed, and Whitaker and Dexter strolled across the talk to the newcomer.

'Excuse me!' called Whittaker. 'I wouldn't stand so close to the riverbank if I were you. It can be dangerous.'

The old gentleman looked up from the river, peered at Terry and Dexter, and produced a magnifying glass from one of the pockets of his voluminous shorts.

'Look,' he croaked in an ancient voice, 'come and see.' On the ground in front of him was a glass jar containing a small amount of river water.

'Look! Look!' he said, pressing the magnifying glass into Whittaker's hand. 'Look! Do you see? Do you see it? In the jar. There. Climbing up the jar. Look, look.'

Whittaker squinted through the old man's glass and made out a very tiny snail with an intricate pink shell inside the jar, climbing up the side.

'Oh. Very nice,' said Whittaker. 'Do you want a look, Dexter?'

'Yes!' said the old man. 'Yes! Look!' Dexter took the glass and looked into the jar.

'It's lovely,' said Dexter. 'Well done.'

'Yes,' said the old man, and he started to cackle. 'Yes, hee, hee, hee, it's lovely, hee, hee, hee, very nice, yes, well done.'

'Well,' said Whittaker, 'we'll leave you to it. Careful of the river.'

'No!' said the old man. 'No! Look. Do you know what it is? Do you know what you've seen?'

'A snail?' suggested Dexter.

'Yes, a snail. Hee, hee, hee, a snail, yes. Yes. But what snail?'

'Um ... couldn't possibly say. It's not an eater, I know that,' said Whittaker.

'No, no, not an eater, no. No. That, kind sirs, that snail, is Planorbis Pancestrum!' Planorbis Pancestrum!' And he started to hop around, cackling, holding his jar up to the sun.

'Is it rare?' asked Whittaker. The old man stopped dancing and stared open–mouthed at Terry.

'Rare? Is it rare? Is Planorbis Pancestrum rare? The Athon Ramshorn, is it rare? It's the rarest of the rare. This,' and he indicated the riverbank, 'is its only known habitat. I've been coming here every year for fifty years, and I've never seen one before. And here it is, hee, hee, hee. Here it is!' And he smiled at Whittaker and Dexter through the glass of the jar, so that his toothless smile was ghoulishly magnified.

'Perhaps you would be kind enough ... Mr ... er ...'

'Daggers. Enoch Daggers. Professor Enoch Daggers,' said the old man.

'Perhaps you'd be kind enough to come across to our camp and tell our friends about the snail? I'm sure they would be very interested.'

'Ooh, yes. Yes, I'm sure they would be, yes. They could hardly fail to be interested. It's the rarest snail in Europe. Who wouldn't be interested in Planorbis Pancestrum, hee, hee, hee?'

'Who indeed, Professor Daggers?' said Terry, looking at Dexter. 'Who indeed?'

Professor Daggers was seated by the fire and given a mug of tea. His jar was handed around the campers. Planorbis Pancestrum may only be three millimetres long, but it has never had a more appreciative audience.

'Please, Professor, tell our friends what you've just told us,' said Whittaker.

The professor smiled around him, lifted his mug of tea in salute and began to speak.

'My name is Professor Enoch Daggers. You may have heard of me? *Water Snails of Europe*? It's the standard work. I have spent my life criss-crossing the continent looking for water snails and examining their habits. The war was a bit of a nuisance, as I found it hard to get around. And so I was forced to spend six years or so here in Blighty, compiling *Water Snails of Great Britain*, hee, hee, hee. It's an ill wind that blows nobody any good, though it's out of print now, subsumed into my later volume. Still, I did some useful work. There are seventy or so species of water snail in Britain, did you know? And in those six years, I saw them all, catalogued them, classified them. Even discovered a new one, Lymnaea Daggerius, hee, hee, hee, my snail. I saw 'em all. Except him. Except Planorbis Pancestrum. The Athon Ramshorn. Oh, I've seen him in the museums, I've even found a few shells, but until today, hee, hee, hee, until today I've never seen him alive! Alive! And here he is. My life's work is complete.' Professor Daggers sipped his tea, and smiled beatifically round at the campers.

'I believe you said, Professor Daggers, that this is the snail's only known habitat?' said Terry, looking at Mrs Innes.

'Yes, yes, this stretch of riverbank, nowhere else. Though I once found a shell a little lower down. Washed up there, though, I hypothesise.'

'I see,' said Mrs Innes. 'So if someone decided to build something here, a car park, for example, then this unique species would be threatened with extinction?'

Oh, no. No, no, no. You can't build here. A car park? Are you mad? You can't build a car park here, young woman. Imagine the disturbance. And the run-off – oil, petrol, anti-freeze. No, it would be the end for our little friend, I'm afraid. Impossible. No.'

'Wow! Maybe this could be our ace in the hole,' said Dexter. 'We can apply for triple-SI status – Site of Special Scientific Interest,' he added for the benefit of Emma and Gemma, who were looking puzzled. 'No Secretary of State in their right mind is going to be able to say no, not when you add in the Temple, are they? Look, Professor, would you mind coming and telling the council about this tomorrow?'

'My pleasure, hee, hee, hee. Always happy to talk snails.'

'Where are you staying, Prof?' asked Whittaker.

'In Ye Blacke Bull, where I always stay. Full of tourists, again.'

'It's the Burning of the Midsummer Ring tonight. The city is packed,' said Whittaker.

'Well, it takes all sorts, I suppose,' said the Professor tolerantly.

'Hey, and another thing,' said Whittaker. 'This is going to wind the animal rights types up even more, if they know a whole species is under threat.'

Dexter shook his head. 'Afraid not, no.'

'Whyever not?'

'Not furry.'

Whittaker made a silent 'Oh' shape with his mouth. He was beginning to understand.

Whittaker had given Gwyneth the night off, her first since the 4i's opened almost three months ago, so that she could go with Sally to the Midsummer ceremony in the Castle Courtyard. They joined the crowds, thousands of people, locals and tourists alike, crossing the Pack Bridge, winding up through the honey-coloured streets, up through the Guildhall Square and on to the castle. In Pancester, which is much further north than you might imagine, it does not really get completely dark at Midsummer. The sun does not disappear over the horizon until past eleven, and even then the afterglow lasts all night, moving north and eastward around the distant hills until the sun rises again before four. The ceremony does not begin until ten, so that the burning hoops can be seen to some advantage. Sally and Gwyneth held hands in the twilight as they took their place in the cold of the courtyard.

Sally was excited, Gwyneth much less so. She'd grown up with the thing, had listened to the boasts of the boys in her class at Our Lady's High, about how they were going to dive through the flames and be crowned 'King of Midsummer'. She'd never been that impressed. But Sally had wanted to come. Large areas were roped off to contain the thousands of spectators who had come to see the young men of Pancester leap through the shrinking hoops.

In front of the roped-off areas, the five hoops of iron covered with woven straw, each slightly smaller than the next, were arranged in front of a series of sisal landing mats. At ten, the Alarumist stepped into the arena, and sounded the Ramstheng. Almost everything in Pancester starts with a blast on the Ramstheng. As its discordant note died away, a small procession emerged into the Courtyard, led by the three Burners, all previous Kings of Midsummer, and all carrying flaming torches. Behind them were the seven Divers, each of them bare-chested and bare-footed. The crowd yelled and cheered, their shouts echoing around the walls of the dark Castle.

Burning the Midsummer Ring is taken very seriously in Pancester. According to Dadd, it has been taking place in the Castle since at least 1398. Even Gwyn, despite her scepticism, was shocked by Sally's joke about the morning after eating curry. Contestants are trained throughout the spring by the Burners, and are whittled down to the traditional seven over the months proceeding the contest. You have to be eighteen to take part, and it is very rare these days to see any Divers over more than about twenty-two or three. The contest is surprisingly free from ceremony, probably because it is so potentially dangerous. Here's how it goes. All the participants bow to the crowd, the Burners light the first of the hoops and the Divers stand in line. The flames from the Ring flicker eerily on the Castle walls. The ghosts hide from the purifying flame, but high in the Castle tower, a light still burns. Someone is still working, watching it all on CCTV.

The crowd falls silent as the first Diver runs forwards, and springs through the fire, somersaulting on to the landing mat. The crowd cheers, the Diver bows, and the crowd falls silent again as the next contestant makes his run up, his dive, his somersault. It is very rare that all seven do not complete the first jump, but as the Burners light the second, slightly smaller hoop, the crowd can see that several of the contestants like it less than the first. And, sure enough, two of the Divers make their run-up and turn away at the last moment. The crowd sigh with disappointment, but there are never any boos, it is never seen as shameful to refuse the leap. I mean, would you fancy it? So then there are five, and the next hoop is lit, and more Divers fail the test, so there are only three left, and then, after the next, only two young men, their torsos shining with sweat, breathing heavily, their hair stuck to their heads, stand in front of the final blazing hoop of straw. It is difficult to see how anyone can get through it at all, even when it is not alight. The first Diver eyes the Burning Ring, rocks back on his heels, eyes the hoop again, and makes his run. At the last moment, he turns away, his face turned skywards, a look of self-loathing on his face. And now there is only one Diver left. He stands, he takes a deep breath, he runs, he dives . . . and somersaults through the burning gap. The crowd scream and cheer and throw their hats in the air. The victorious Diver bows, a huge smile on his face, and leads the contestants and the Burners back into the Castle.

That's how it generally tends to go, anyway, and this year was no exception. Gwyneth felt as bored as ever, and in the years since leaving school had become even less impressed by sweaty boys. But Sally was jumping up and down with excitement, and held her hands to her mouth to contain her screams as each Diver leapt through the Rings. And to add to her joy, she knew the winner.

'Oh, Gwyn, it's Barry, who used to play bass in your dad's band. Oh, well done, Barry!'

Gwyneth sighed, and smiled at Sally.

'It is rather wonderful, isn't it?' she admitted. 'I guess . . . we used to be taken as kids. You know how teenagers get. You end up sneering at everything, even the things you love. But I'm glad I came. I'm glad you enjoyed it.'

'Yeah, it was amazing. Really. Thank you. And you needed a night off. Hello. Look who's heading towards us.'

'Oh, my God. And she's smiling.'

'Not at us, surely?'

'Hello,' said Juliana. 'It's Gwyneth, isn't it? My dad used to play crazy golf with your dad.'

'Er . . . yes.'

'And aren't you Sally Gould? They like you over at the Laikley office. They say we'll get more visitors there now you've got the scum off the street.'

'What do you want, Ms Blezzard?' said Gwyneth.

'You got the night off, did you? To come and see this? Instead of...' she licked her lips '... being in the restaurant?'

'Yes. What do you want?'

'What's the Special tonight?'

'I believe it's steamed turbot in an oyster sauce.'

'Mmm. I've never had turbot. And the salad? I see it's a Midsummer salad now, rather than the Easter salad.'

'Uh-huh.'

'And is that very different from the Easter salad? What's in that?'

'Look, Ms Blezzard...'

'Juliana, please.'

'Look, what is it you want?'

'I ... I don't see why we should be enemies, just because we disagree about the silly old car park.'

'I'm sorry, Ms Blezzard, I don't see how that's possible. We try and keep Terry off your back, but we'd do that for any woman. And if you're trying to get around being barred from the 4i's, you can forget it. Until you admit that you and Sandahl forged the Charter, and tell us how you nobbled the preservation order on the Temple of Priapus, there's no way you're getting so much as a bread roll.'

Juliana narrowed her eyes.

'In your dreams, you sick pair of tuppence-licking perverts,' she said.

Gwyneth rolled her eyes to heaven, bunched her fist and lamped Juliana on the chin.

'And now you'll also have to apologise to Sally before you get back in,' Gwyn said.

'You stupid bitch,' spat Juliana through swollen lips. 'I've got powerful friends. You'll be sorry.'

Gwyneth held her face up to Juliana's.

'And I've got chocolate cream and strawberry Nick cakes, you sexless cow. You already are sorry. And if you ever say anything like that about Sally or me again, you'll be sorrier still. Goodnight, Ms Blezzard.'

She took Sally's arm and led her through the crowds and out of the Castle.

'Gwyneth!' breathed Sally.

'Homophobic bitch. At least she'll look awful at the council meeting tomorrow.'

There were more demonstrators on the City Hall steps than Mrs Innes had hoped. There were the committee, with Taff, Oliver, Syd Montague-Forrester and Sally; most of the staff of the 4i's and the women from the Anti-Car Park Camp and their supporters, of course; but the news of the archaeological find under Dole Acre had firmed up a lot of opinion in the city, and Mrs Innes reckoned that there were perhaps a hundred or so people holding placards, waiting for the councillors to arrive. And then forty or so animal rights activists turned up in three minibuses. Terry was in charge of them this time, as Dexter was going to be in the meeting. He arranged them on the steps opposite the main demonstration and told them about the snail. As Dexter had predicted, it did not set them off in the slightest. So he waited for the right moment to light the blue touchpaper.

Aolderwoman Armistead and Dexter Halton were the first to arrive, accompanied by Professor Daggers holding aloft the jar containing Planorbis Pancestrum, and they were greeted by applause from the demonstrators. Dexter shook hands with those in the front row and hugged his brother, Oliver. They weren't even the same height, Sally noticed. They could go into *The Guinness Book of Records* as 'Least Identical Identical Twins'. Armistead and Halton entered the building with the Professor.

Next it was the turn of Trevor Mallinson and the Pancester Independents. Whittaker shouted, 'Donkey abusers!' and the animal rights group were off, screaming, spitting, throwing eggs, issuing bomb threats. The pro-Car Park councillors ran up the steps but were covered in eggs and spittle by the time they entered the building. Next came a few waverers, like old Archie Plumb, who had been asleep at the vote of the committee meeting, but, as an abstainer, was still felt to be a potential ally by the Anti-Car Park Committee, and Cordelia De'Ath, Dexter's fellow Independent Pancester Independent, who had been keeping her counsel, but whose vote Dexter was fairly sure of. Whittaker held his troops in check. Finally, there were the City's expert witnesses, Polly Seagrave, the City Architect, Nigel Morris, Head of Traffic, Ken Perry, the City Solicitor, and Juliana Blezzard, Head of Tourism, looking rather lovely, Whittaker felt, with her thickened lips. I'll get her to think about having a collagen injection when we're married, he thought. She looks foxy, and I don't think she'd like it if Gwyn keeps hitting her.

'Donkey molesters!' he shouted. The air was filled with the shrill cries of the animal rights activists.

'Murderers!'

'Haven't you got a conscience?'

'Donkey killers!'

'We know where you live!'

'We're going to bomb your children!'

'See how you like it.'

Eggs and globs of phlegm rained down upon them. Several strands of opaque spit streaked Juliana's face, and I can't really tell you what Whittaker thought about that, as this a family show, except to say that he hoped, with Juliana's consent, to deposit something which looked not dissimilar there or thereabouts in the future. Whittaker saw a photographer from the *Pancester Mail* capturing the scene, and he made a mental note to see if he couldn't get a print of Juliana in this state for the cardboard box.

Juliana turned at the door of City Hall and flashed a V sign at the demonstrators before disappearing into the building. The Committee followed her, as they were to sit in on the vote.

The Council Chamber was packed. Some routine business had to be got through, all of which passed on the nod. Everyone was keen to get down to the main business of the day.

Eventually, the mayor said, 'Item Five. The proposed Millennium Car Park on Dole Acre. Aolderman Mallinson to propose.'

Trevor rose to his feet, and Juliana was almost proud of him as she heard her words, her facts and figures in his mouth. Nigel

Morris was called, to give an account of the benefits for traffic flow in the City, and Juliana herself spoke, with a little difficulty through her swollen lips, of how tourist access would be improved.

The Mayor called Dexter to speak against. He spoke of how the Charter only granted grazing rights, and how, even if the new transcription was true, a car park was surely against the spirit of the bequest, if not the letter. He called the council's attention to The Eastering, a centuries-old tradition which was threatened by the development. He spoke movingly of the plight of elderly donkeys, forced to move from the happy retirement home that they had thought they were going to be able to enjoy for the rest of their lives. He spoke with outrage at the fact that the council were prepared to grub up and destroy the newly discovered Temple of Priapus. And he obtained the council's permission to allow Professor Enoch Daggers to address the meeting. The old gentleman held aloft his specimen jar.

'Ladies and gentleman. In this jar which I am holding is a representative of a species which has inhabited this stretch of river for millions of years. This is Planorbis Pancestrum, hee, hee, hee, the Athon Ramshorn. If the Dole Acre belongs to anyone, it belongs to him. It is his home. He is to be found nowhere else on earth. But if you build your car park, he will die. He will be extinct, yes he will. And we will all be the poorer.'

'Well done, Prof,' whispered Dexter as he sat down. 'Good stuff.'

Dexter stood again to make his final appeal.

'And finally, Aoldermen, Aolderwomen, in view of Professor Daggers' revelation, we will be applying to the Secretary of State for triple-SI status, no matter the outcome of the vote today. The Dole Acre, once a site of local importance, has been elevated to an area of national and even international concern by our recent discoveries. I urge you, in the name of science, if nothing else, to vote against this car park!'

His supporters in the gallery applauded and cheered, and were hushed by the Mayor.

Trevor Mallinson stood, and picked off Dexter's objections one by one. The Charter said nothing about grazing rights, but clearly granted the use of the land, and anyway, once it was proved at the High Court in a few months' time that Lady Lettice Courtney was dead, the freehold would pass to the City in any case. The Eastering was to be accommodated in a newly commissioned municipal garden, built in the middle of the proposed round-about. The donkeys were to be sensitively rehoused by the Laikley Children's Zoo. Part of the car park budget would be allocated for two weeks' rescue archaeology before the bulldozers moved in.

'And finally, I thank Professor Daggers for his contribution. It is fitting that a snail should be the symbol of those who oppose this car park: slow moving, old fashioned, and of no earthly use to anyone!'

The council laughed, and moved to a vote.

Pancester City Council, meeting in full session, approved the building of the Millennium Car Park, twenty-four votes to seven.

The Committee's faces told the story to their supporters, who were waiting outside.

'What now, Terry?' asked Sally.

'Well, we start an appeal to the Secretary of State. We apply for special status. And Syd. . . ?'

'Yes, old thing?'

'Activate the hippies.'

'With pleasure, Terry. Absolutely. Now the fun will really begin.'

New Mycological Friends

'Where's Syd gone?' Whittaker asked of Steve Medlicott in the Fox Hole over coffee one morning, a few days after the council meeting. 'I told him the time had come to get the hippies and now he's buggered off.'

'Mr Whittaker, a look at your calendar would tell you where Syd had gone. Or you could watch your television after you close the restaurant. You might see him.'

Whittaker rustled through his paper for the TV schedule.

'Oh. Glastonbury.'

'Of course. Every significant traveller, eco-warrior and shroom head in the land is camped out in the Green Fields of the travellers' camp at Glasto this week. Syd has gone to spread the word. In a week or so, we'll see some action.'

'You didn't fancy going yourself, then?'

Medlicott smiled. 'I am there in what *you* would call "spirit". And besides, I couldn't hack it without my old lady.'

Sandra was still living down on the Dole Acre. The weekenders still came too, and all the women were just as committed to carrying on the struggle as ever, but some of the more naïve ideas about people power had taken a blow since the vote in council. Some of the brio, a little of the pep, had been knocked out of the Camp. Mrs Innes was struggling to see a way forward and was having to work very hard to keep her spirits up. Professor Daggers spent his days by the riverbank looking for another specimen of Planorbis Pancestrum, and his evenings in his room at Ye Blacke Bull writing up a report on a typewriter which had probably been quite the thing in 1915, when he was a boy. He came to hand over his report, a week after the defeat in the Council Chamber, and to say goodbye.

'This is for submission to the Secretary of State on the reasons why Dole Acre should be accorded SSSI status. The E on my typewriter is jammed, so I've used X instead, hee, hee, hee. Call me if you need me, or if there's anything you don't understand.'

'Goodbye, Professor. And thank you,' said Mrs Innes.

Neil Winterburn was keeping Emma and Gemma smiling and busy, marking off a huge area of the field with pegs.

'Thing is, Mrs Innes,' said Neil, drinking tea by the fire one morning, 'what with these hippies coming to camp here too, it's vital we outline the area of the Temple, so that we can work there. How many are coming, do you know?'

'Not really,' said Mrs Innes, thoughtfully washing pus from Rolly's tumour. 'Not too many, I shouldn't think. Last time my nephew tried to fill this place with hippies, only about half a dozen turned up.'

'That sounds like defeatist talk, Mrs I. Not to fear, I'm sure we'll get a few.'

A meeting was called at the Fox Hole with Brian Carless to prepare the appeal to the Secretary of State. It was decided to have Professor Daggers report retyped, opening as it did with the words,

```
Unfortunatxly, during thx prxparation of this rxport
on thx habitat of Planorbis Pancxstrum, it bxcamx
xvidxnt that the lxttxr bxtwxxn 'D' and 'F' on my
typxwritxr is no longxr fully functioning as it
should. Rxalising this, I havx substitutxd thx
lxttxr 'X' whxrxvxr thx lxttxr bxtwxxn 'D' and 'F'
would ordinarily bx xxpxctxd to appxar.
```

Carless tapped his fingers on a large file appertaining to planning appeals.

'I've been boning up on this stuff, and we should have a cast-iron case, what with the snail and the Temple. But then, Neil Winterburn thought he had a cast-iron case already, and he was overruled. Someone's been pulling strings, and heaven only knows whose strings they might try and pull next.'

'They'll be putting together their evidence for the appeal to the Secretary of State,' said Juliana to Q one afternoon in his office.

'And this worries you?'

'Of course. They've finally managed to come up with a case. The Temple, the snail. The Secretary of State is going to have to give it very serious consideration.'

Q leant forward and flipped a button on his desk intercom.

'Mrs Wiseman? Could you bring me the file on the Secretary of State for the Environment, please?'

'You have a file on him?' asked Juliana.

'My dear, I've got a file on every MP at Westminster, except Martin Bell, obviously. When will these people learn? Once again, I give thanks that I have managed to unshackle myself from the demon of sexual desire. Ah, thank you, Mrs Wiseman. I'm looking forward to this evening. Yes. Here we are ...'

He shook some photographs out on to the desk. Juliana leant over his shoulder.

'Oh dear,' said Juliana. 'Pink's not really his colour, is it? And what on earth is he doing with that stirrup pump?'

'So, you see, my dearest Juliana, if the Secretary of State gives us any trouble ...'

'Goodness me, yes. Tut tut. Mucky old devil.'

'One day I'll show you the Lord Chancellor in action. That will make your eyes water.'

'What did you mean when you said to Mrs Wiseman that you were looking forward to this evening?'

'It's her birthday. A small party of her colleagues from the Museum are taking her to the 4i's for dinner.'

'You too?' asked Juliana, wide-eyed.

Q nodded.

'You're going to the 4i's tonight? But you can't! It's not fair.'

Q took her wrist and held it lightly between his thumb and forefinger.

'I am not banned from Mr Whittaker's excellent restaurant. And I advise you – do not ever tell me what I can and can't do.'

'No, Q. I'm sorry. It's just that . . .'

Q tightened his grasp, almost imperceptibly.

'Yes, Q. I'm sorry.'

Q smiled and released her wrist.

'All forgiven, my dear. I'll make sure to tell you what we had.'

'Thank you, Q. You are kind.'

Q looked surprised.

'No one has ever called me that before,' he said.

In her dreams, Juliana tasted the delicate yet piquant goujons of smoked eel, the earthy robust aroma of the Blackhampton stewed steak, and again and again the chocolate cream and strawberry Nick cakes. Each morning, her pillow was wet with saliva.

Her hair in a scarf and her eyes hidden behind a pair of Ray-Bans, she followed the party from the Museum of Crime and Punishment as far as the 4i's. It was packed as usual. She watched through the window, which was damp with condensation, as Gwyneth showed Q and his party to their table. Q looked up and Juliana turned hurriedly away, pretendeding to study a display of old punk albums in the window of the Fox Hole. She thought she might as well give in, just go round to the kitchen door, admit the Charter was a forgery to Whittaker and get stuck in to the menu. But the thought of owning up to that disgusting man, of telling him that she was in the wrong, filled her with loathing. Her flesh crawled with horror when she thought about the fat, cheerful, friendly, well-meaning son of a bitch groping at her, slobbering and puking his sentimental goo over her. Love? He didn't have a clue what it was, who she was.

No, when the Millennium Car Park had picked up a few architectural awards, then she would apply for a job in a real city, and she would be able to dine in world-class restaurants night after ecstatic night. So she hurried away from Shy Street, and walked a little way round the city walls to where she could overlook the Dole Acre. She closed her eyes and saw her new roundabout, the landscaped upper parking level, the ramp leading down into the superb underground areas. She didn't see the vermilion splendour of the sunset over Laikley Bay, or the way the light caught the tops of the distant mountains to the north. She didn't see the ponderous progress of the Athon as it made its stately way to the sea, or the smoke rising from the fires at the Women's Anti-Car Park Camp, or hear the laughter carried on the wind from the direction of the tents. She turned for home.

The following morning, Oliver, who was still trying to get his Anti-Car Park Website functioning, received a call in the Fox Hole from the secretary of Dame Margot Prosser, MP for Pancester and Laikley, to say that Dame Margot would be in the area and would like to visit the camp at two that very afternoon. Oliver told Taff, who called Whittaker, who walked down to the camp in glorious sunshine to make everything ready.

'Is there an election coming up?' asked Dawn Gabatini. 'She never comes here otherwise.'

'We are honoured,' said Mrs Innes. 'Is she still Labour?'

'I think so. I vaguely remember a red rose on her election manifesto last time,' said Dawn.

Dame Margot had once been regarded as an ally and confidante of Edward Heath, with whom she had entered Parliament, and she had even served as a junior minister in his government. She had been astute enough in the mid-seventies to ally herself with Margaret Thatcher, with whom she was thought to be very close. This closeness did not translate into a job, but she had been the most loyal of back-benchers throughout the Thatcher years, and had even cleverly voted for her in the first ballot in 1990, before switching her allegiance to John Major. Once again left out in the cold, despite her fervent support for 'Back to Basics', she crossed the floor in 1996 to become a New Labour MP. She was sure of two things: that Pancester's fear of change would ensure that she was re-elected regardless of party, and that she liked to be on the winning side.

Whittaker stayed for lunch in the camp and, at two, watched as three huge minders in nurses' uniforms helped navigate Dame Margot's electric wheelchair through the thistles and donkey todds.

Mrs Innes and Whittaker walked down the Acre to meet her. The minders held on to the bags of plasma and urine which swung from a pole on the side of the chair.

'Dame Margot! This is a surprise! We hadn't expected you for a few more years.'

Dame Margot's beady eyes peered over the top of her oxygen mask, and her one good finger flickered over her keypad. A voice, sounding rather like Steven Hawking with a head cold, issued from a speaker built into the back of the chair.

'As I was saying to Tony only last week, we must never forget that we are in Parliament to serve our constituents, Mrs Innes. I always enjoy coming back to dear old Pancester. And how are you? I hear that you are going to have to re-house your donkeys. I'm sure it's for the best. We can't stand in the way of progress, can we? The young people must have their chance, I always think.'

'But, Dame Margot, it's not as simple as that. They can't be allowed to build it here.'

And Mrs Innes told Dame Margot of the appeal to the Secretary of State, of the unique character of the Dole Acre, of the Temple of Priapus, of Planorbis Pancestrum.

'Good,' said Dame Margot, 'all of which I would wish to support. But what we have to remember is that the income from the car park will be going to the old folk. The old folk are behind this development 100 per cent. Think of the old folk, Mrs Innes, lying in their hovels, shivering under moth-eaten blankets with only a crust of mouldy bread for their lunch and a mangy cat for company. Is that really what we want for our old folk?'

'We could try giving them proper pensions,' suggested Sandra.

Dame Margot's eyes flashed.

'Mrs Medlicott, isn't it? If only it were so easy, my dear. And of course, pensions have risen under New Labour by 34 per cent in real terms. But this extra source of additional funding could make all the difference between the old folk being able to stay in the modest houses for which they have worked so hard and being forced into rat-infested residential homes. And we don't want that, do we?'

'No, of course we don't,' said Mrs Innes.

'So I can tell the City Council you'll be giving up your protest?'

'No, Dame Margot, you cannot. It is unfair to bring this issue of the pensioners into it. The ends do not justify the means,' said Mrs Innes. 'And I'm afraid Rolly has peed on the battery of your wheelchair.'

It was true. Sparks crackled from under the chair. Dame Margot jabbed at her keypad to no avail. The system was down. Her yellow skin took on a faint glow of pink. Her cruel, ancient eyes blinked furiously. She gestured angrily with her good finger, and her nurses pushed her hurriedly away across the field.

'Still,' said Whittaker, 'at least we know there's no point in asking her for help.'

'We knew that all along, Terry,' said Sandra.

'And besides, the pensioners are not 100 per cent behind the car park, anyway,' said Dawn. 'You should hear Taffy's dad go on.'

'Really?' said Whittaker.

'Aye, really. Have you never met him?'

'No.'

'I'm going up to St Homobonus' this afternoon. Come and have a word, if you've got time.'

Whittaker looked at his watch.

'Sure. I'd like to.'

Dawn and Whittaker walked into town, pausing on the Pack Bridge to stare down into the river.

'Did you ever drop an apple for Taff to go plummeting after?'

'No. Taff couldn't dive off here. It would ruin his hair.'

The Hospital of St Homobonus is still housed in its original premises, built in 1483. It is built around a cobbled courtyard, made bright with plantings of roses, to the quadrangular design so popular at the time. Little has changed. If there is good weather, the pensioners sit out in the sun in their black and red robes; when it rains, and in the evening, they sit in the refectory and talk and play cards. All of them have a television in their rooms, which, although these days are rather luxuriously appointed, are still known as cells. Life is pleasant for the pensioners; their one duty being to process to prayers in the Parish Church each morning, and afterwards to watch the pensioners of St Gilbert's Hospice collect and eat the Pancester Dole.

As Whittaker and Dawn walked into the quadrangle, their ears were assaulted by a barrage of noise from around the medieval courtyard.

'They're all watching television after lunch,' yelled Dawn by way of explanation.

'What?' shouted Terry.

Dawn knocked loudly on the door of one of the cells, to make herself heard above the din.

A lively-looking old gentleman leaning on two sticks opened the door and smiled at his visitors.

Nicolo Gabatini was always pleased to see Dawn, who often popped in to see him after lunch. He was a large man, almost as tall as his son, so his trousered legs stuck out a good way from the bottom of his robe. But at eighty-three, he was not as limber as he once was, and now had to be pushed to church each morning in his chair, often by his friend Dolly Halton, mother of Oliver and Dexter, and, at seventy-two, the youngest of the current crop of pensioners, a year younger than Mrs Innes. Again, like his son, Nicolo had the Gabatini chin, and perhaps as a consequence of this he had always had difficulty in finding dentures which fitted properly. When he spoke, it sounded as though he had a kazoo hidden in his mouth. His Italian accent was still pronounced after seventy years in Pancester.

'Dawn, my darling,' he buzzed. 'Please, come in, come in.'

'This is Mr Whittaker, Papa Nico. The man who bought the café from Taff.'

'Ah, Mr Whittaker! I have often heard Dawn and Paolo speak

of you with great respect. Please, Mr Whittaker, come in. Sit down here, on the bed. Perhaps Dawn will make us a cup of tea?'

Nicolo clicked off his cacophonous TV and sat down in his armchair.

'I'm sorry that we haven't met before, Mr Gabatini. It would give me great pleasure if you would come to dinner one night, as my guest, of course, and see what we've done with the place.'

'I should be delighted, Mr Whittaker. It was a good business, but Paolo was never interested, only in BANG BANG BANG, BOOM BOOM BOOM. I am glad that it has passed on to such a great chef and now restaurateur as yourself. And Gwyneth is a good girl.'

Whittaker bowed his head slightly.

'I'm lucky to have her, sir,' he said.

Papa Nico smiled and nodded.

'Here we are, Papa Nico,' said Dawn. 'Sit in your chair, and I'll sit next to Mr Whittaker. That's it. And how are you?'

'I'm OK. The sunshine is good for my knees. Yesterday, today, I have walked home from church. I think Dolly wishes I could walk to church, eh? Then she wouldn't have to push me up the hill, eh?' He laughed wheezily. 'I'll call her,' he said with sudden resolution. 'HEY, DOLLY!' He banged his stick on the wall of his cell. 'DOLLY!' An answering knock came from the other side of the wall, followed shortly by a very glamorous lady coming through the door, who made her black and red robe look as though it were by Versace. Whittaker stood up.

'Ah, Dolly. This is Mr Whittaker who has the café now. Come, join us. Dawn will make you some tea.'

'Hello, Dolly,' said Dawn. 'Milk, no sugar?'

'Thank you, dear, no, I won't. Otherwise I'll keep having to go to the . . .' and here her gentle voice disappeared, and she mouthed the next three words silently, '. . . you know what.'

'I'm friends with both your sons, Mrs Halton, but neither of them warned me that they had such a charming mother,' smarmed Whittaker.

'Oh, I say, Mr Whittaker. Flattery will get you everywhere.'

'Your boys, Dolly, they are helping Mr Whittaker and Dawn stop the car park coming,' said Papa Nico.

'They're good boys, both of them. Dreadful idea, a car park on the Dole Acre. Who'd have thought they had the nerve?'

'The City Council like to give the impression that the pensioners are all for the idea, since they stand to benefit,' said Whittaker.

'No, we don't want their filthy charity!' said Papa Nico. 'All we want is what we've got coming to us, our bread rolls, the Pancester Dole, Sir Kenelm's bequest. That's all we want.'

'But, Papa Nico, St Homobonus' hasn't been in receipt of the Pancester Dole since 1952. You only get the Dole when the Clanghandlers win the Wally,' said Dawn.

'Since the boys were born,' said Dolly dreamily.

'Who cares? That's not the point. The point is, old Sir Kenelm, he wanted us to pray for his soul, so he give us a *chance* of the bread rolls. We don't want them unless we win them.'

'Yes, but the Clanghandlers hardly ever win the Wally, Papa Nico, because they've got to go uphill to score, but the Ringlers attack downhill. If we had the car park, you could all have bread rolls,' said Dawn.

'We don't want charity. We just want the chance to win the rolls in the Wally. We like winning, not rolls.'

'So would you say that most of the pensioners agree with you?' asked Whittaker.

'Of course, dear,' said Dolly. 'This is Pancester. We like things just how they've always been.'

'Even St Gilbert's. I was talking about it to old Charlie Styler this morning while he was eating his roll, and they're against it too,' said Papa Nico.

'We should have made more of this before the meeting,' said Whittaker.

'It's not too late, my boy. You must keep fighting,' said Papa Nico.

'One thing I've been trying to do is follow up this story of Aolderwoman Armistead's about an heir to the Courtneys,' said Dawn. 'You never heard anything about that, did you, Dolly?

Ursula told us that Letty had a baby that was taken away from her. The date we were given is 1952, the same year you had the twins. There was no gossip in the clinics, or anything like that? You never heard anything?'

'No, dear. I never heard anything like that.'

The next morning Taff came hammering on the door of the 4i's before Sally, who was always first up, had left for work.

'Sal, wake 'em up!' said Taff. 'Syd's back!'

Whittaker and Gwyneth pulled on their clothes and hurried down to the kitchen door.

'Come on!' said Taff, and the four of them climbed into Whittaker's car, and drove out on to the ring road. It was gridlocked; Whittaker, Taff and Gwyn hopped out of the car, leaving Sally to sit in the queue so she could get over to Laikley, and they jogged through the traffic to find the source of the trouble.

At the gate to Dole Acre, Syd was directing vehicle after vehicle through on to the field, where Neil Winterburn was marshalling them on to the areas away from the Temple of Priapus. It was a slow process, and this was delaying the traffic on the ring road. Mrs Innes was remonstrating with a bemused policeman whose only interest was in keeping the traffic moving.

'Please be patient, officer. Another ten minutes and we'll have the road clear.'

'Aye, well, Mrs Innes, but they're holding up the traffic.'

'Another ten minutes, officer. Come on, Syd! Hello, all!'

'Morning, Mrs I. Looks like Syd hit the jackpot,' said Whittaker.

The Dole Acre was filling fast, with old buses and trucks, and converted vans pulling trailers, and ambulances reinvented as homes. A battered Transit van with the makings of a tepee strapped to its roof was stuck in the ditch beside the gateway, and four large hippies were trying to push it out. Whittaker hurried across to help.

'Thanks, man ... Ready, Carl? One two three, now!'

The driver gunned the accelerator, and the four hippies, with

Whittaker's help, heaved the van out of the ditch and back on to the track through the gate.

'Cheers!'

Whittaker walked across to Syd, who was waving the vehicles through from the ring road.

'This is amazing, Sydney. Truly amazing.'

'Yes, I've managed to raise a few,' shouted Syd over the roar of engines. 'I took a couple of dried mushrooms with me to Glastonbury. After that, I couldn't beat them off with a shitty stick. And I got some experienced road protesters too. I'm looking forward to helping them dig in. Grandfather was in the trenches, you know.'

The last of the travellers' vehicles swung through the gate into Dole Acre and traffic started to move on the ring road once again. Sally pulled Whittaker's car into the gateway and rolled down the window.

'How many?' she asked.

'As many as there were in the Convoy. It's the Convoy back from the dead,' said Terry.

'No, more,' said Gwyneth, looking at the field. 'Loads more. They've brought all the dance crews, too.'

Sally raised her thumb, rolled up the window and pulled back on to the ringroad towards Laikley.

The field was alive with hippies, parking up their buses, unpacking tepees and yurts from vans, looking for wood to light their burners, exercising dogs, drumming. Rolly ran around the site barking and waggling with joy.

'I've called a meeting for ten with some of the big wheels,' said Syd. 'Hope that's OK for everyone?' It was.

The Women's Anti-Car Park camp was dwarfed by the population explosion on the Acre, which now thronged with life. While most of the new inhabitants continued to settle in, four of their elders came for a powwow around the women's campfire.

There was Phil the Painter, walking with his stick, his mutton-chop whiskers framing his lined face, veteran of the Battle of the Beanfield and Convoy old-timer; Ronnie of the Pink Bus, younger, representative of the ravers, dressed in clothes that would have shamed Edmund the Pancester tramp, his hair matted into dreadlocks, but with a smile that made the ladies in the camp ignore his manly aroma; Ash the Scrap Metal Man, oldest of the old, on the road since 1956 and wise beyond all reckoning, his portable forge and blacksmith's shop housed in the back of the huge Mercedes van that was also his home; and Tony the Tunneller, youngest of the four, his face streaked with ingrained mud from his exertions at Newbury and the Manchester Airport extension, his huge hands ready at a moment's notice to start digging. Mrs Innes smiled at them all.

'Thank you so much, all of you, for coming to help preserve the Dole Acre. I'll just tell you something of the reasons why we're all here ...' which she did, 'before introducing Mr Neil Winterburn, our archaeological expert, who will explain why we're asking you not to camp on the pegged-out areas ...' which he did in his turn. The hippies nodded, and asked intelligent questions, some of them rather technical. Neil was delighted.

'I've worked with travellers before. Strange how many of you have worked on digs. I'm looking for volunteers, if you want to put the word about the site.'

'And now I'd like to introduce Mr Steve Medlicott, who apparently is going to tell us something about ... mycology, was it, Steve?'

'Yes, indeed. Thank you, Mrs Innes. My colleague Syd will have told you something of the *sacred* nature of the mushrooms on this site. Three ley lines cross here. It is a place of immense power. It is vital that you treat the mushrooms, when they start appearing in a few months, with the utmost ... respect. I have a supply of dried shrooms, which I will distribute about the camp. Once you have tried them, even in tiny doses, you will see that caution is essential. When the crop appears, I will be on hand to give advice on collecting and preserving. You will not go unrewarded for your efforts here.'

The hippies nodded again.

Phil the Painter coughed and said, 'It's ironic when you think about it.'

'What is?' said Mrs Innes.

'Well, you trying to stop them building a car park. And us coming here for a park-up.'

Ronnie of the Pink Bus said, 'Can we have some tonight? Can we, man? Can we have some holy righteous shrooms tonight? Now? Can we have some now? To celebrate our arrival? I can't wait, man, I can't fuckin' wait.'

Medlicott smiled. 'Impatience is the fear of time,' he said. 'Do not be distressed by the passing of time. Time and space – are the same thing. If you can't handle time, you can't handle space. That's Einstein. But I think tonight we might have a little celebration.'

The hippies seemed content, and after some questions about wood and water supply they returned to tell their comrades about what was going on. Syd went off with Tony the Tunneller, to talk about where they might start digging.

Mrs Innes smiled. 'Well, Mr Whittaker. It looks to me as though we have found some powerful allies.'

'And it looks to me as though we might be in for some serious parties, Mrs I.'

'Isn't it sweet of them to come all this way, just to get some mushrooms? You'd think you could get them anywhere, wouldn't you?'

'These are rather unusual mushrooms, Mrs Innes,' said Medlicott.

'Well, it's still sweet, all the same. Do you think there will be music at the party? I'd quite like a dance myself. I'm feeling rather jollied up since our new mycological friends arrived.'

Apple Plummeting

Whittaker felt too tired after work to hack down to the party, but he heard all about it in the morning from Sally as he was eating his morning tin of tangerine segments.

'It was cool, Cuggs. Ronnie of the Pink Bus fixed up a sound system, and The Marsh Men came down, and Ron and a couple of his mates DJed while the Marsh Men fiddled, and loads of people were drumming, and Steve Medlicott brewed up this tea while I watched, and I swear to you, Terry, he put no more than five dried mushrooms into a huge pot, and made sure that everyone who wanted some had a sip, and they all went ape, and got their kit off and leapt about like loonies around this huge fire while the sounds just banged away. It was something else. We left at three, and there was no sign at all of them shutting down.'

She sucked her roll-up and grinned.

'Did you and Gwyn try the 'shrooms?'

'No. But we might, in the autumn. I'll take a few days off work, though.'

'And do try not to call me Cuggs. Mr Whittaker is fine.'

'Sorry, Mr Whittaker.'

'And so you should be, young lady.'

Mrs Innes phoned. 'Oh, good morning, Mr Whittaker. Just to tell you that Dawn and I have decided to come off the site for a while. Dawn's been so busy trying to find out about Letty's baby, and I'll be spending a lot of time with Brian Carless arranging the appeal, and he doesn't like the donkeys, poor man, so we thought that since we've got such an influx of numbers, we could probably do more good in town.'

'Couldn't get any sleep, then, Mrs I?'

'Dear God, I thought I would die. The drumming! On and on and on. And they all took their clothes off, and at my time of life I don't want to have things like that waggling about in my face. I think Rolly's a bit disappointed, though.'

And so a new regime was established on Dole Acre. The travellers knew how to live in the open with style. At least thirty living vehicles, five tepees and three more yurts had been added to the camp. The elders sat outside Phil the Painter's caravan, which was painted in lurid fairground colours, talking of this and that and drinking chai, while the practically minded gathered at Ash the Scrap Metal Man's blacksmith's shop, making props for the tunnels. Tribes of naked children rorted around the site, laughing and playing with dogs. Where once an observer from the city wall would have seen one or two campfires by night, now there were dozens. A pall of smoke hung permanently in the air, which throbbed day and night with music from The Pink Bus. The donkeys were free to wander where they liked, and were welcomed in the camp, especially by the children, but in practice they largely retreated to the far side of Neil Winterburn's dig, which was beginning to make progress now that he had so many skilled volunteers. And over by the gate, Syd and Tony the Tunneller had started a dig of their own. Mounds of earth from the expanding network of trenches and tunnels began to heap up by the entrance.

Juliana was incandescent with rage. Since the arrival of the hippies, visitor numbers to the city had dropped by 3 per cent. People didn't want to see a mess like that, right by the Pack Bridge, right on Pancester's front doorstep. The police were urging caution.

'There's a lot of 'em, miss,' said Inspector McCracken, 'and we can't just go charging in, more's the pity. When the Secretary of State gives the all-clear for the car park, that'll be the time. We've already started making plans in conjunction with the sheriff's office, have no fear.'

Her nights were torture, as she tried to live without dinner at the 4i's. Time and again, she hid herself behind the restaurant, trying to calm her shattered nerves by sniffing the rich aroma from the kitchen. One night she got a shock when Edmund emerged from one of the bins, his beard glistening with fish scales, and offered her a slice of pie. Her heart pumping, she hurried home, swearing that she would never stoop so low.

The next evening, Gwyneth caught her, bottom up, head down in the bin.

'Go home, Ms Blezzard. Or I'll give you another thick lip.'

In desperation one Saturday, she caught the train into Preston, and bought herself a padded bra to put on under a new dress which she chose because it was exactly the sort of thing she would never wear. A wig, a pair of Ray-Bans and a thick middle European accent completed the disguise.

Her heart beat faster as she stepped through the door of the 4i's. 'Ey hef booket a tabel. My name is Frau Moellereiss.'

Gwyneth sighed and looked up from her booking schedule. 'Ms Blezzard, you look ridiculous. Go away.'

Whittaker was in agonies. How could a love as great as his be unreturned? It would make a mockery of the whole thing. He knew how much he wanted Juliana, and he knew how much she wanted him, or at least his chocolate cream and strawberry Nick cakes, and yet still Sally remained resolute.

'No contact, Terry, until after the Dole Acre has been saved. And then she'll be yours, I promise,' she said unblushingly.

And so Terry felt he had no option but to continue to patronise Zahid's shop in Laikley. He had been frustrated for some time in his search for a suitable bum for his patchwork Juliana, but at last, in an issue of *Peaches*, he found just the thing he was looking for. He cut it out, and laid it beside all his other scraps. She was complete. She didn't look anything like Juliana, of course. She didn't look like anything other than a grotesque parody. None of her components was to scale, but the curling pieces of glossy paper seemed to bring Whittaker some comfort, as he sat on his bed, staring at his simulacrum, the purloined knickers stretched tightly over his hips.

This was not enough to assuage his longing. He started to patronise telephone sex lines, and found himself phoning girl after girl from his mobile, alone in his room in the afternoons, looking for one with a northern accent. All the girls sounded bored and indifferent, which made Whittaker's heart pump with excitement; but none of them sounded remotely northern and he would ring off without speaking.

But at last, one afternoon, he struck pay dirt. The voice was a little broad, but it would do.

'Hello, dahling,' said the voice, 'would yer laike t' play wi' me? And if so, please can I 'ave yer credit card details?'

Whittaker, his breath coming in short gasps, gave her his number.

'Now, what game would yer laike ter play?'

'Um, I'd like you to be called Juliana.'

'Yer looky, sweet 'eart, that is m'name. Juliana, that's me. What else would yer laike?'

'Um, I know it's a bit unusual, but can you roll your Rs?'

'That's not unusual, dahling. Of course ah can. Ah'm rolling me arse for yer now. Ah've got a lovely arse, all soft and creamy for yer.'

'Ah, no. No, I mean can you rrrroll your Rrrrs. You know, like in the old Hovis advert?'

'Ee, yourrr the cheeky won, arrren't yer? Laike that?'

'Yes, that's great, thank you.'

'And I'm still rrrolling me arrrse, an' all.'

'Juliana!'

'Yes, love?'

'No, sorry. I've finished. Goodbye.'

'Bloody 'ell. That werrre a quick 'un. No wonder you can't get a f—'

Whittaker replaced the receiver, removed the now sticky panties, and carefully packed away his scraps. He did not feel proud of himself.

Juliana was not proud of herself, either.

'My dear,' said Q, listening once again as she begged him on bended knees to bring her back a doggy bag from the 4i's, 'I can take no more. There is only one thing to be done. Mr Whittaker must be disposed of, and then we can have our lives of ordered calm back again.'

Juliana smiled with relief. 'Oh, thank you, Q. I'll be fine once you've had him killed.'

'My dear, dear Juliana. You know that I cannot authorise an operation of that kind on our doorstep. The raid on the Courtney Museum was risky enough. My clients would not be at all happy if we drew attention to ourselves in this way. No, you'll have to do it yourself.'

'Kill him? But how?'

'In the same way that so many women in Pancester have disposed of unwanted lovers.'

'You mean . . . ?'

'Yes. You must tell him that you will be his, if he plummets from the Pack Bridge after an apple. Certain death awaits a man of his age and build who is foolish enough to make the attempt. No other method can I authorise.'

'It will be a pleasure, you brilliant man. Sheer pleasure.'

The summer passed, as summers do. And where do they go? Into our memories, filtered through our longings, our imaginings. The weather was wonderful that year, it never rained. We were happier then, for a time, happy and in love. Or so we imagined.

The 4i's was running like clockwork, and Whittaker felt confident enough in Brian Styles and the rest of his staff to take a few days off. He borrowed the car from Sally, and completed his planned trip to Scotland. Travelling up the M6, he phoned the Truckers' Helpline again. The voice of the same woman as before answered him.

'Hello, Truckers' Helpline.'

'Hello again. I don't suppose you remember me?'

'Mr Whittaker? How can I forget you? How many people do

you think phone me here? I mean, I don't know why some half-witted dolt with a degree in marketing thought it would be a good idea to put this number on the back of trucks, 'cos do you know how many calls I get? Do you?'

'Er . . . no.'

'About one a week. One call a week, and I sit here like a lemon waiting for it to happen.'

'You could write a book, or something.'

'What, about my experiences on the Truckers' Helpline? That would be a riveting read, wouldn't it? Chapter Seven, nothing happens. Chapter Eight, an old lady from Kidderminster calls to say that a wagon has flashed his lights at her heading northwards on the M5 for no better reason than because she was going at thirty-five m.p.h. in the middle lane. I can see them queuing up to buy it now.'

'No, I meant, given that you've got all this time on your hands, you could use it to write a detective story, or something. Or do the Open University, or something like that.'

There was a stunned silence on the other end of the line.

'God, you've got a point. That might be fun. God, yes. A detective story! God knows I read enough, sitting here week after week. Yes! My detective could be a trucker, couldn't he?'

'Or she.'

'Oh, my God. That's brilliant. I could call her . . . er . . . Madge Hardwick.'

'Hmm. Not very mysterious, is it? Detectives should have an air of mystery about them. How about . . . Dorcas Moon.'

'Yes. God, yes. *Dorcas Moon Investigates . . . Murder at the Midway Truckstop.* Thank you. It'll make a change from crosswords, anyway.'

'Well, I'm happy to have been of service.'

'And were you phoning just to inspire me, or was there something you wanted to tell me about trucks?'

'Well, it's just that I'm stuck south of Carlisle behind one of your trucks, registration number L for London bus, 451 C for Cliff U for Una W for We're all going on a summer holiday, and I just wanted to tell you I couldn't be more impressed, I really couldn't.'

The woman laughed. 'You're funny,' she said. 'What's your first name?'

'Terry. What's yours?'

'Rowena. Phone me in a week or two, and I'll tell you how I'm getting on with the book.'

'OK. Good luck.'

The traffic cleared, and Whittaker drove on, through Gretna, through Dumfries, and headed north-west for Ardrossan, where he caught a ferry for the Isle of Arran. He spent a couple of nights there before taking another, smaller ferry from Lochranza in the north of Arran across to the Mull of Kintyre, trying not to whistle the song. He drove across the breadth of Kintyre, and as he breasted the highest point of the road, he saw the west open up before him, the far west; the Paps of Jura, Islay, Tir Na Nog. He stayed for a night in Tarbert, and then from Kennacraig caught a ferry out to the lonely island of Colonsay. He stayed in the hotel there, sitting in the sand-dunes by day, beating off midges, composing love poems for Juliana in a little notepad and eating tinned fruit, which is big in Scotland. The evenings he spent in the bar, drinking 30 Shilling beer and talking with the locals. Remember? The perfect summer?

Feeling relaxed and confident after three days on the island, he travelled home to Pancester. His first stop was the Dole Acre.

Even more hippies had arrived on the site, and when they were not partying, they were digging, either on the temple site with Neil Winterburn, or in the tunnels with Syd and Tony, both of whom had taken to sleeping underground. Whittaker crawled through the labyrinth to visit them. They were smoking a large bong in a room-sized opening they had carved out, held up by metal props from Ash's workshop, and lit by candle lanterns.

'What ho, Terence. Have a nice trip? Don't think the Hun'll get us out of here too easily, do you?' said Syd, smoke curling from his nose.

'Is it safe?' said Whittaker.

'As houses, old boy. As houses.'

Sally and Gwyneth looked careworn on Whittaker's return to the 4i's.

'What's up? No problems, Gwyn?'

'Not with the restaurant, no . . .'

'It's Juliana, Terry,' said Sally. 'She's been ringing every day, asking to speak to you. Please be careful.'

'Really?'

'Yes. She said she'd ring again tonight.'

'At last, she's ready to tell us how they faked the Charter, and stymied the preservation order. And fall gratefully into my arms.'

'Terry, remember who you're dealing with. Q Sandahl is behind all this, I know. Please be careful,' said Sally.

'Careful shmareful. She's crazy about me, like I've told you all along.'

Whittaker took the call from Juliana on the kitchen phone that evening. She had to shout to make herself heard over the sizzling and bubbling pans.

'Mr Whittaker? Terry? It's Juliana here, Juliana Blezzard. Look, I was wondering if we could meet some time soon. I've got something very important to discuss with you.'

A hundred images popped into Whittaker's mind. Juliana's capitulation over the car park, Juliana's willingness to sleep with him, Juliana's ideas for the seating plan at the wedding reception. It could be any or all of them. He realised with a start that the box would no longer be necessary, and resolved to destroy it as soon as possible. Before she came into his room, naked but for her perfume and an ankle chain, and asked him what was in it.

'Sure thing, babe. Would coffee in De'Ath's suit you? Tomorrow at eleven?'

'I'll look forward to it, Terry.'

Whittaker spent the rest of the evening singing, which disconcerted his staff, and worried Gwyn.

'Be careful, Terry.'

'Ha! *La la la lali lali morning, ding dong dee deedle deedle doo . . .*'

*

The carillon sounded the hour as Whittaker arrived at De'Ath's Café. Juliana was already there, chewing her lip.

'Good morning – Terry,' she said, forcing a smile.

'Good morning good morning good morning. How lovely you are looking this morning. Here,' he rummaged in his pocket 'I've written you these poems.'

'Thank you. That's – very kind. I – I've been thinking about you, too.'

'I know, I know. It was inevitable.'

'Yes. Yes, I suppose it was.'

'So are you ready to help us get a preservation order for the Dole Acre?'

'Oh, Terry. It is so sad that this one thing keeps coming between us. It looks to me as though you don't care about me. I mean, if you cared about me, you'd see how important it is to me to have my car park.'

'Oh, lovely Juliana, I care about you desperately. Can't you see how you've been sucked into this car park thing by the wiles of Dr Sandahl? That's what I've been trying to help you see. Give it up, Juliana, give him up, be mine. Eat at the 4i's every night.'

'Terry, if only it were that simple. The car park is so important. If only I had some proof that you really, really loved me, then maybe I could give it up.'

'I've written you these poems.'

'Yes, Terry, and I'm sure they're wonderful. But I need something more.'

'Like what? Just name it.'

'I want you to try and catch my apple. At the Plummeting.'

'Really? That's all?'

'Yes, Terry. That's all. Catch my apple, and I shall give up the car park, safe in the knowledge that we are destined to be together.'

Whittaker leant across the table and grabbed her hand. 'Oh, my darling Juliana. Of course we are destined to be together. Of course I will catch your apple. When is the Plummeting?'

'In two weeks. Two weeks this Sunday.'

'And after that, we'll be together?'

'Yes, Terry. If you catch my apple, of course.'

'I will, my darling, I will.'

Juliana smiled, and pulled her hand away from Whittaker's. 'Until then, we must not see one another.'

'No?' said Whittaker sadly.

'No. It's part of the tradition.' She stood up. 'Until the Plummeting, then, Terry.'

'Yes, my love. Until then.'

Whittaker bounced into the kitchen of the 4i's.

'Gwyn! Gwyn! It's on! Between me and Juliana! She's going to give up the car park, because we're destined to be together.'

Gwyn did not seem to share Whittaker's delight.

'Is that what she told you?'

'Yes! Yes! Oh, hip hooray! Oh, happy day!'

'Just like that? She told you she's giving up the car park? As easy as that?'

'Yes! Yes! If I can pass a simple test.'

'Which is?'

'Oh, she just wants me to catch her apple at the Plummeting, to prove I really love her. Then she'll help us secure the preservation order, and we shall be together for ever!'

Gwyneth went white, and held her hand to her mouth. 'Terry . . .' she whispered.

'What?'

'Terry, you're coming with me.'

'Where?'

'To see Mrs Innes.'

'Why?'

'Terry! Come on!'

Mrs Innes' house was not appreciably cleaner after her stay on the Dole Acre. Rolly was clearly demonstrating how he felt about leaving the wonderful campsite by leaving little markers of protest on all the furniture. They sat in the kitchen, a huge saucepan full of overpoweringly strong-smelling offal simmering on the stove. A sheep's head, whose dead eyes seemed to follow

Whittaker around the room, sat revolving slowly in the bubbling mess.

Gwyneth wouldn't let Terry speak, as she told Mrs Innes about Juliana's demand.

Mrs Innes pursed her lips.

'Mr Whittaker, you are a newcomer to Pancester, and no doubt apple plummeting strikes you as a rather quaint, indeed romantic tradition. And certainly these days, most of the girls who throw apples for their beaux are full of good intent. But it was not always thus. Apple plummeting has its dark side. You've never heard the old nursery rhyme?'

'No.'

'It's one of the lesser known ones, I suppose. It goes:

'Sally Plumb
Dropped an apple,
In the Athon foaming brown.
Billy Heath
Tried to catch it,
Broke his head and he did drown.

'Like so many of the old nursery rhymes, it is based on a true story. Billy Heath loved Sally Plumb; indeed, they were betrothed. But Billy went away, to fight for the king in the Civil War, and while he was away, pert little Miss Plumb found someone that she liked better, and planned to marry him instead. But Billy came back from the war, and demanded his right to Sally's hand. He was most insistent, and made himself something of a nuisance. So Sally told him that if he should catch her apple, then she would be his, and Billy agreed. But Sally was very clever, and instead of dropping her apple vertically from the bridge, she threw it some way to the right, where she knew perfectly well there was a treacherous gravel bank, barely covered even at high tide. Whether Billy knew this, and jumped in despair, or whether he had forgotten the topography of the river bed during his enforced absence, we shall never know. But he jumped, and broke his neck, and was drowned. And although Sally's case is the

most well known, there have been other instances of unscrupu-
lous young women demanding that their lovers jump, when they
knew certain injury, at least, was bound to ensue.'

'So?'

'So, Terry, you idiot, Juliana is trying to kill you,' shouted
Gwyn. Whittaker laughed.

'No, Mr Whittaker, I'm very much afraid Gwyneth is right,'
said Mrs Innes. 'I know you see open hostility as a come-on, but
in nine hundred and ninety-nine cases out of a thousand, open
hostility means that someone dislikes you very much. I don't
know why you can't see that, I really don't. Has Ms Blezzard ever
shown you any sign of affection before this?'

'No, but . . .'

'Then under no circumstances must you dive from the bridge.
It is very dangerous even for fit young men whose lovers only
wish them well. You are no longer in the first flush of youth, and
you're carrying at least a stone overweight. And Ms Blezzard has
only evil intent towards you and yours. You must see that,
surely?'

'I'm a good swimmer, and I've done a bit of diving. I'll be fine.
And I do get a bit fed up with everybody bad-mouthing Juliana.
She's just been led astray by Q Sandahl, that's all. You'll see. I'll
catch the apple, and she'll come round to our side.'

'Mr Whittaker, I hope you won't take offence, but you are a
fruitcake.'

'No offence taken, Mrs I. You'll thank me when we get the
preservation order.'

'Brian Carless thinks the Secretary of State is obliged to grant
our appeal. We'll get the preservation order anyway. Please, Mr
Whittaker. Don't kill yourself for nothing.'

'I won't, I promise.'

Now each morning Whittaker cycled out to the swimming pool
in the leisure centre on the Laikley Road to practise his diving,
and to lose a little weight. Sally and Gwyneth refused to speak to
him.

Neil Winterburn, who was still staying in the Nursery when he wasn't excavating the temple, tried to talk some sense into Terry over a tin of beer one night, after the restaurant was closed.

'If there's anything I've learned in life, Terry, it's that women are out to de-bollock men. Christ, look at me. There I was, drifting along quite happily, number two in the archaeology unit at the university, when my wife fucks off with a fucking Itie waiter.' Winterburn mimed the action of cranking an unnaturally huge pepper grinder.

'Black pepper for the laydee? I have a great big one. Hmm? Isn't that right, laydee, much bigger than your husband's.' Accents were clearly not Winterburn's strong suit.

'I thought he was your next-door neighbour?'

'He was, the greasy little shit.'

'And he was a waiter?'

Winterburn sighed. 'Well, strictly speaking, no. He was the head of the sociology department at the university. That's why I applied for the job with the county. I couldn't stand seeing him every day with his smarmy hair and his shiny suits, the double-dealing little wanker.'

'But he was Italian?'

'Er . . . no. Well, I think his mother was, Sicilian or something. His name is Bernardo, anyway.' Winterburn stared angrily into his beer.

'But Juliana told me she loved me. She's not going to leave me for a waiter, or a sociologist, for that matter, not if I catch her apple.'

'Oh, isn't she? That's what Diane said. That she loved me, that she would love and cherish me, all that bullshit. Said it in church, in front of all our families. Wasn't worth a worm's turd. Take my advice, stay alive, mate, get on with your work, and forget her.'

'I can't, Neil.'

'Then, my son, you are a pig-headed twat. You'll see.'

Taff and Olly took him to the Holly Bush one lunch-time to show him the list of apple plummeting fatalities painted on a plaque on the wall. But he continued to train. At first, his diving was rusty, and time and again he landed in the water with an agonising belly flop. But as the days went by, his skills returned, and his dives became increasingly elegant and successful. There were several other men in the diving pool, clearly training for the plummet – the oldest of them could have been no more than twenty.

'Excuse me, grandad, but you're not training to jump off the bridge, are you?' he asked Whittaker one morning.

'Yes, I am actually.'

'You know you'll be killed, don't you?'

'Nonsense. I'll be fine.'

'Er, no. You'll be killed.'

But Whittaker's confidence was unshaken. When you really want someone, and want them really bad ... what wouldn't you do to show them? Are there any lengths to which you wouldn't go, any depths to which you wouldn't sink? If you're not prepared to go all the way, then you don't really want them, do you? And Whittaker really wanted Juliana. And everyone had misjudged her, surely. She was wonderful. She had been so romantic. You couldn't fake all that, not the things she had said in De'Ath's. Kill him? Ha! He dived again.

The evening before apple plummeting, Gwyn and Sally went round to Juliana's flat. They rang the doorbell, and she answered in a white kimono, her wet hair tied back from her forehead. When she saw who it was, she tried to slam the door shut, but Gwyneth stuck her foot in the door, and grabbed Juliana's arm.

'What do you want?'

Sally put her face into Juliana's. 'Just to tell you not to be on the bridge tomorrow, 'cos if you are, Gwyneth here is going to break your pretty nose. So you won't get a chance to drop your apple, anyway.'

Juliana smiled, and twisted away from Gwyn's grasp.

'Oh, surely you're not going to deny Terry and me the chance of happiness? Do you think I'm like naughty little Sally Plumb?' she said.

'And if he's hurt, we'll be after hurting you. Badly,' said Gwyn. 'So be warned.'

'Oh, I am. I am warned. And now I'll be after phoning the police, unless you get out of my flat.'

'We're going. Just don't show your evil face on that bridge tomorrow.'

Juliana slammed the door, and hurried to call Q. It seemed she might be needing a little back-up.

While Gwyneth and Sally were out visiting Juliana, Whittaker nipped upstairs from the kitchen, grabbed the box from the top of the wardrobe, and burned the contents in the newly restored front-room fireplace. Whittaker worried momentarily that burning the panties might have some voodoo significance, that Juliana's pubic regions might be visited by a terrible burning sensation, but he dismissed the thought as superstitious nonsense.

Besides, he thought, if they are, I can kiss them better tomorrow night.

On the morning of the plummet, Gwyn, Sally and Taff tried to barricade Terry in his room, by the old-fashioned means of propping a chair under his door-handle. This always works in films, but they had forgotten that Whittaker's door opened inwards, and he yelped as the falling chair caught him on the toe.

'Look, guys. You can't stop me doing this. So please don't try. High tide's at ten. I'd love it if you came down to the Pack Bridge with me.'

'Oh, we're coming, have no fear. We're coming to stop that bitch.'

'Oh, don't be daft. You're going to be the best of friends, I know. We'll all look back on this and laugh, in years to come.'

'We won't, Terry, BECAUSE YOU WILL BE DEAD!'

'Come on, Sal, don't be like that.'

'Like what? Like a friend who is trying to save you from making a terrible mistake?'

'Have a bit of faith. You'll see.'

'Leave me the 4i's in your will, Tel, will you?' said Taff. 'Then I can sell it again to some other stupid London ponce who doesn't know his arse from his elbow.'

'Taff, I know what I'm doing.'

By a quarter to ten the bridge and riverbanks were packed with spectators. A dozen or so young men paced up and down in their bathing costumes, while a similar number of girls sat in the roadway, tying lengths of ribbon around their apples. This makes it easier to distinguish one apple from another. Terry and his three friends walked out on to the bridge. His mobile rang from the pocket of his bathrobe.

'Hello?'

'Hello, son.' His father's voice sounded weak and far away.

'Oh, hello, Dad.'

'I haven't caught you at a bad time, have I? You're not just about to unload, are you?'

'Yes,' said Terry.

'I'm dying, boy. Doesn't that mean more to you than shagging?'

'No. Goodbye, Dad.'

'But—'

Terry turned off his phone, and removed his bathrobe. He stood in the roadway of the bridge in his bathers, and started to warm up with some stretching exercises.

'*Fat* stupid London ponce who doesn't know his arse from his elbow. I left out fat,' said Taff.

There was no sign of Juliana.

'We've scared her off, Gwyn.'

'Don't you believe it. Look.'

Juliana came through the West Gate of the city and on to the bridge, accompanied by two of the guards from the National Museum of Crime and Punishment. Gwyn and Sally tried to get to her, but the heavies pushed them away.

'You touch those girls, mate . . .' said Taff. The heavies looked at him over the top of their shades.

'The old rocker is scaring me, Wayne,' said the first.

'Oh, me too, Jason. I'm all a-tremble,' said his friend.

'Thanks for the warning, sickos,' said Juliana. 'I thought it best to bring a few friends. Now then : . . . what colour ribbon shall I tie round my apple? Blood-red, I think, don't you, boys?' The heavies laughed.

'Hey now, Juliana. Soon we'll be together, and you're all going to be friends. So let's not be horrible, hmmm?' said Whittaker, walking across.

'Oh, Terry, I'm so sorry. I didn't think. I do you hope you catch it. The apple, that is.'

'Of course I will, my darling. Look, I think everyone else is ready.'

The girls of Pancester stood leaning over the parapet of the bridge, holding their apples at arm's length above the swirling brown water. Juliana took her place at their extreme right.

'Terry. You must not do this. Remember Billy Heath,' said Gwyneth.

'Terry! I'm ready! Come and catch me.' Juliana smiled and waved her apple in the air. The boys started clambering on to the parapet. Whittaker climbed up beside them, with a little help from one of Juliana's minders.

'Thanks, mate,' said Whittaker cheerfully. He stood and looked around him. The high walls of the city, built from massive stones, loomed above him to his right; the smoke from Dole Acre rose to his left. No traffic moved on the ring road. Below, the water eddied and rippled as it reached the top of the tide.

Actually, Whittaker thought, it did look, now you came to see it from this angle, really rather a long way down. There was a moment when the crowds on the bridge and on the banks fell silent. The girls took a breath, leaned over the parapet . . . and dropped their apples.

They seemed to hang in the air, like balloons. Terry watched Juliana's drop away to the right, the far right. He watched it, he watched it . . . and the first of the boys was diving, and the crowd started to cheer and shout, and the boys were gliding down after the love tokens, and Whittaker rocked back on his heels, and dived.

Now he watches his apple hit the water, rushing up towards

him, *don't watch the water, watch the apple, catch the apple,* and he hits the water, arms first, brown estuary water in his nose, in his mouth, and down he goes and down … and he sees the apple, the red of its ribbon rising up, bobbing back towards the surface, and still going down he reaches for it, feels it slip away, grabs it, holds it, and the river is shallow here, too shallow, and with an agonising crunch his left shoulder cracks into the bed of the river, into Billy Heath's shoal, and he gasps, and swallows water, water in his nose, in his lungs, *but I must hold the apple, I must hold on to this stupid bleeding apple and kick upwards, Jesus this hurts, Jesus save me, Jesus I caught it, kick up, close mouth, up up hold it sweet fucking Jesus hold it up up up* and with a gasping rush he breaks the surface of the river, choking and breathing again in sucking gulps, his left arm useless, his right hand holding the apple. And there close behind him is the bridge, and he kicks towards it, leans against it, leans against the bridge while the tide, starting to turn, tries to carry him downstream, and *use the bridge as support though it flays off the skin from your arm, and kick for the shore,* and there are hands, and voices, his friends, 'Terry, Terry, here, hold my hand,' and Gwyn is in the water, pulling him out of the river again, crawling choking gasping on to the gravelly bank by the bridge.

'Look, Gwyn. I got it. I got the apple. I'm born again.' And the pain in his shoulder, and the shock, and the water in his lungs …

After that, he didn't remember anything more.

The Second Pancester Free Festival

'Terry?'

'Mother?'

'Terry, can you hear me?'

'Can you hear me, Mother?'

'My God, he's turned into Sandy Powell.'

'Mother, have you come to take me across?'

'Cuggles, can you hear me? Try opening your eyes.'

By an act of will, Terry forced his eyes open, and was almost blinded by brightness. He shut them again.

'Mother, it's much brighter than I imagined. Doris Stokes always used to say that it was blue. Is Dad here yet?'

'Terry, stop going on about your mum. It's us.'

'Oh, hello, Sally. Are you dead too?'

'No, and neither are you. Open your eyes.'

Terry tried again, and watched his friends' faces swim into focus above him.

'Who is Sandy Powell?' he said.

'An old-time comedian,' said Mrs Innes. '"Can you hear me, Mother" was his catchphrase.'

'Oh. Where's Juliana?'

'I can't believe you, Terry Whittaker,' said Gwyneth. 'She's just tried to kill you, and still you're after her.'

'Where am I?'

'In the Infirmary. And bloody lucky, too,' said Sally.

'Hey, but I got the apple, didn't I? Where is it? Aoow!' Terry had tried to sit up, and found that it hurt a great deal. He lay back again.

'Ow ow ow!' he said. 'What have I done?'

'You have dislocated your left shoulder, boy bach ...' said Taffy.

'And broken your collar-bone ...' said Sally.

'And you have nine stitches on your upper arm. And concussion. You've been out for a couple of hours,' said Gwyneth.

'Which means, Mr Know-It-All clever boy, that although you are very lucky not to be dead, you are out of commission for a while, and will do just what I tell you,' said Sally.

'Yes, Sally, I promise. But where is the apple?'

Sally sighed. 'It's here, if you must know. Look.'

She passed him the apple, still tied around with a bedraggled red ribbon. He smiled triumphantly.

'And I hope you're satisfied,' said Gwyn.

'Oh, I am. It's all been worth it. But where is she? I thought she'd be here.'

'Oh, I'm going home,' said Mrs Innes. 'I really can't stay and hear him witter on any longer.'

'I'll come with you, Mrs I,' said Taff. 'Perhaps the girls can beat some sense into him.'

'What?' said Terry. 'What's up?'

Sally and Gwyn told him what was up. 'She hates you. She tried to kill you. When she told you that she would shag you if you caught the apple, she was lying through her sticky-out teeth.'

'Really? Do you really think so?'

'YES!'

'Well, then, I guess my only hope lies in the car park thing.'

Gwyn held her head in her hands. Sally said, 'You have no hope. There is no hope. She tried to kill you. Give it up.'

'But ... I can't give up ... if I haven't got somebody to love, then ... I don't know. What's the point?'

'Don't you love me and Gwyn? Mrs Innes? Taff?'

'Well, yes, of course, but I'm not *in* love with you.'

'What are you, a star-struck teenager? You're thirty-eight! You can't just be in love with the first person who comes along any more.'

'Can't I?'

'No. Or at least not unless they like you too. As a rule of thumb, don't fall in love with people who want you dead. And I'm the boss, remember?'

'Yes, Sal. Whatever you say.'

'Good.'

Whittaker spent two nights in the Pancester Infirmary. He fretted about the 4i's, and was in a great deal of pain, so sleep was hard to come by. When they let him out, he was very tired, but he found he could sit on a chair in the kitchen for an hour or so in the evening, nagging at his staff, which calmed him down. He began to feel rested, and had time to catch up on the kitchen gossip.

Most excitingly, Martha was having the walk-out with old Dennis the kitchen porter that her father had forbidden so many years before. And everyone feels cheerful when love is in the air, even Dennis.

'I plummeted in my time, Mr Whittaker. O'course, it were much more dangerous in them days, before that global warming.'

'Oh, how's that then, Dennis?'

'Well, the river were much shallower in them days. Stands to reason, dun't it, with your global warming. The water level's rising.'

'Shut up going on, Dennis. You're as bad as the cats, with all the noise you make. Come and get these pans out of my road,' said Martha, smiling.

Whittaker's arm, which was strapped around his chest so that he couldn't move it, started to throb a little less, and a few days after coming home, he went for a walk with Taff around the Guildhall Square.

It was Thursday, market day, and the square was packed with stalls. Whittaker loves markets (what cook doesn't?) and Pancester's market is still traditional enough to have fish and meat and dairy and greengrocery, as well as discounted cheapjack clothing and shoe seconds and drapers selling offcuts and pirate video stalls and all the rest of it. Many of the stallholders had heard about Terry's plunge from the bridge. Frank Welford, from whom Whittaker bought milk, eggs and butter for the restaurant, came out from behind his stall and shook his good hand.

'Aye, very well done, Mr Whittaker. It's opened a lot of people's eyes. I used to be for the car park, but when I heard that Ted Blezzard's lass had tried to do a Billy Heath on yer ... well, we need you more than we do a load more visitors. Glad to see you on the mend.'

'Thanks, Frank. Thanks a lot.'

'Aye aye, Terry. Here comes trouble,' said Taff.

Juliana was walking with Q through the market. They stopped when they saw Whittaker. Sandahl smiled, and Juliana looked at her feet.

'Juliana, Dr Sandahl,' said Whittaker.

'Piss off,' said Juliana, looking up.

'Shh, my dear. We are lucky that Mr Whittaker is still with us. Your ... temporary feelings for him ... could have had tragic consequences. Mr Whittaker, Juliana wishes to apologise for letting a short-lived schoolgirl crush endanger your life. She is sure that you will understand that while she no longer wishes you to prove your devotion to her, she in no way intended harm in any shape or form. Isn't that right, Juliana?'

Juliana bit her bottom lip, and nodded.

'Say sorry to Mr Whittaker, Juliana.'

Her eyes flashed at Q. He touched her upper arm with his forefinger.

'Say sorry, Juliana.'

'Sorry,' she mumbled. Sandahl took his finger away.

'There. So now we can all be friends again,' said Q. Taff had bunched his fists.

'Well, thank you,' said Whittaker. 'Apology accepted. Oh, and Dr Sandahl?'

'Yes, Mr Whittaker?'

'You are banned from the 4i's.'

'But, Mr Whittaker ...'

'But, Dr Sandahl. What I say goes. Neither you nor any of your staff are welcome in my restaurant any longer. And now, if you'll excuse me, I was talking to Frank.' He turned his back, and started to ask Frank Welford about cream supplies. Q and Juliana stood staring at his back for a moment before turning and walking off among the stalls.

'Hey hey, Terry! That's telling 'em,' exulted Taff. But he could see a large tear running down Terry's cheek.

In the evenings Neil Winterburn would bring news from the camp. 'We've been concentrating on the Balls, and making great progress. If you want willing diggers, you really can't beat those travellers, and Emma and Gemma are turning into first-rate little archaeologists. Syd and Tony's tunnel network is still growing too. But Monsieur Medlicott tells me the first mushrooms are due any day now, which might well slow us down.'

A week after coming home, Terry felt fit enough to get along to a committee meeting. There was little to report. Brian Carless had compiled all the information necessary for the appeal to the Secretary of State objecting to the council's decision, and had sent it away to London.

'So now there's nothing to do but wait,' he said.

Mrs Innes had helped Nicolo Gabatini compose a letter to the *Pancester Mail*, outlining the pensioners' objections to the scheme.

'We popped a copy in with the stuff we sent off to the Department of the Environment. It really is quite an impressive case,' she said.

And so the late summer started to turn into autumn. After a fortnight, Sally agreed that Whittaker could get back to work properly, although his arm was heavily bound, and he still experienced some discomfort. The restaurant was as successful as ever and, much as Juliana had predicted to the planning committee when trying to stop the new signs, its influence had started to spread throughout the city. Ye Blacke Bull had hired a new chef, and was working hard to improve its menu, while De'Ath's had sent their waiting staff on a course to teach them how to smile at customers. Juliana herself had enrolled on a cordon bleu cookery course at the Pancester and Laikley Technical College, but was the first to admit that she didn't really have the knack, and her new-found sensual appetite was hardly slaked by burnt *œufs bénédictine* or runny *crème brulée*.

While he lay in the hospital, and while he was convalescing, Whittaker found himself thinking about his father. Although he had been receiving weekly reports from the hospice, he had not spoken to the old man, apart from the truncated call on the bridge, since his visit to London some months before. Thinking about his father was like pressing a bruise. Terry tried to recall happy moments from his childhood with his father, and could only come up with two: once when the old man had knelt down while Terry was in the bath, and had talked him through the new drivers' manual issued by the Underground; and once on a walk through the park when his father had told him the joke about the plumber. Terry could still remember the feelings of importance caused by his father choosing him to talk to about his work, could still remember the joke word for word.

And he remembered his mother's face, her eyes red with tears, his father's mocking voice taunting her with his latest conquests at Ruislip Gardens or High Barnet.

But mostly, all that Terry could remember was an absence, and his own longing, never fulfilled, for his father's attention. He talked to Sally one evening about how he felt about his father's impending death.

'You should write to him and tell him how you feel,' said Sally.

'Really? No, I don't think I could.'

'Why not? It's never too late. Write to him, and tell him how you feel about him never being there for you, about how you felt when your mother died, about everything.'

'What good would it do? You don't know my old man, really you don't.'

'But isn't it worth a try? You only have one more chance. He could die tomorrow, next week. Tell him how you feel, and ask him for an apology.'

'Whaaaat?'

'No, really. It's a standard practice in therapy.'

'I don't need therapy. Do I? Do you think I need therapy?'

Sally pursed her lips and lit a fag. 'Hmmm. Well, it's not for me to say. But this really is your last opportunity to resolve this stuff with him while he's alive.'

So Terry sat down at his desk, and composed a long and emotional letter to his father. He told him how his merciless sexual teasing had undermined his confidence; how the cruel treatment of his mother had felt, and what it had done to her; about how he had never paid Terry any attention or given him any thought; about what it was like to see his father's latest mistress move into the house only a week after his mother's funeral; about how, while the joke was funny, it was hardly enough; and about how everything could be made all right if only his father would acknowledge Terry's feelings; and apologise. It felt good to write the letter, but Terry felt hopeless as he posted the envelope. It was all too late.

At weekends, Whittaker had taken to going with Gwyneth and Sally on long walks into the countryside. They had helped him choose a fleece and some walking boots from Pancester's climbing shop. Some days, with his arm bound up beneath the fleece, and the empty sleeve pinned to his chest, looking like Nelson on a management-training weekend, Sally would drive them up into the hills. They could look back over the Athon estuary and see Pancester rising on its hill from the flat country and Laikley sprawling along the bay. But Whittaker's favourite walk was along the river itself, to the Falls of Athon, where the fresh water from the hills tumbled over rocks to meet the salt-water tideway. He loved the view of the city from the Falls, as did Turner, whose famous painting, *Pancester from the Falls of Athon*, can now be seen in the revamped Tate Britain. The view has changed hardly at all.

There is an old pub by the falls, the Tickled Trout, where

Whittaker and his friends would enjoy a couple of pints after the walk up from the city. Never particularly crowded, as access by road was difficult, the landlord would often come over and chat, and boast of the unique privilege which came with the pub.

'Do you know,' he would tell them time and again, 'I'm the only private citizen in England entitled to keep sturgeon?'

'Yes. You've told us.'

'No, but I am. Anywhere else you get sturgeon, they have to be presented to the Queen. But not here. Any sturgeon caught between Laikley Point and the Falls belongs by right to the landlord of the Tickled Trout. What do you think of that?'

When the landlord first told them, Whittaker had asked, 'When was the last time anyone caught a sturgeon in the Athon?'

'Seventeen eighty-three. But you never know, do you? There could be another any day. And I tell you what, Mr Whittaker, if there is, I'll get you to come and cook it for us.'

'I'll look forward to it.'

By late September, the fresh mushrooms had started to appear on the Dole Acre, and more and more hippies and travellers were crowding into the site. Syd and Tony the Tunneller were careful to guide new vehicles along the only route through the site which they could guarantee as subsidence-free. Things were heating up. The Pink Bus, having previously pumped out music twelve hours a day, now moved into a twenty-four-hour shift system. The fires got larger and larger as dancers filled the Acre. The drums grew wilder and wilder, the smoke drifted higher and higher. Medlicott sat night after night outside Phil the Painter's van dispensing his tea, and persuading the travellers of the necessity of treating the fresh 'shrooms with kid gloves. Both he and Sandra were now living in the yurt full-time, still in its original position on the site of the Eastering, to make sure that no one over-indulged. Bands turned up, acoustic at first. Cajun bands from Manchester, ceilidh bands from Kendal, The Tango Band from Radnorshire, all came and played on the small stage that Ash had built and Phil had decorated. And once Ash the Scrap Metal Man had got his generator up and running, electric bands turned up too, bands like Ted Milton and Blurt, and The North Lancashire Feedback Co-operative. One night the legendary Nik Turner played for five hours to a swaying crowd of wildly hallucinating travellers.

An informal committee had been formed, comprising Syd Montague-Forrester, Steve and Sandra Medlicott, Phil the Painter and Ronnie of the Pink Bus. Water bowsers were organised, camping areas for short-term visitors designated, a welfare tent erected. Music came from all over the site – from the Pink Bus, from the stage, from the drummers, from small sound-systems and ghetto-blasters – and blended into a Babel of sound which hung in the smoke-filled night air. Flags and banners flew from the roofs of the living vans. Fairy lights were festooned about the site; blanket traders turned up, and sat alongside the main track through the site offering hair-wraps, henna tattoos and head gear, pipes and bongs. Small cafés and bars sprang into existence outside the buses and in tepees, selling chai, brandy coffee and veggie burgers. The Dole Acre never slept.

Whittaker, who often came down late at night after work, was amazed at the discipline on the site. The dig was left untouched, and the donkeys remained undisturbed on the part of Dole Acre which was furthest away from the camp.

'We respect the ancient Earth mysteries,' Phil the Painter would say, somewhat to the annoyance of Neil Winterburn, who tried to argue that it wasn't really that mysterious, but should rather be seen as highly unusual but entirely explicable evidence of a Romano-British fertility cult.

'It's ironic, if you think about it,' said Phil.

'What is?' asked Neil.

'Well, you being a dead clever archaeologist who knows lots of stuff and all that, and yet you're, you know . . .'

'What?'

'Out of touch. Not connected with what's really going down.'

Whittaker had taken to smoking a little spliff of an evening, which eased the pain in his arm and helped him slide into sleep. He always sat with Ash, whom he liked and admired. No one knew Ash's age for sure, but Whittaker reckoned from his stories that he must have been in his early sixties. He had left home in Liverpool in the mid-fifties, and had been on the road ever since, becoming one of the pioneers of the hippy trail, picking up his skills in metalwork as he went. His proudest boast was that in all that time, he had never once signed on. He was almost as good-looking as Oliver Halton, with blue eyes, tanned skin and perfect teeth, but unlike Oliver he had an easy, charming and entirely consensual facility with women, which Terry envied. Ash, Syd, Winterburn and Terry often sat together for an hour or so, passing a pipe and watching the party.

'Do you know what occurred to me today, Terence?' said Syd one night by the glow of Ash's small fire.

'No, Sydney, I don't. What occurred to you today?'

'It occurred to me today that what we are witnessing here is the Second Pancester Free Festival. Letty would be chuffed to bits.'

Terry stayed away from Medlicott's mushroom tea, which was proving so efficacious, but one Saturday night Sally and Gwyneth had a go. As they danced wild-eyed around the huge fire by the Pink Bus, they started to undress one another, and Whittaker had to work very hard not to look as they kissed and caressed. Very hard. Very, very hard. Regretfully, he thought it best to go back to the flat, rather than invade their space with his fascinated gaze. He almost regretted that he'd burnt the box.

The girls came home at half past nine the following morning, and hauled Whittaker out of bed.

'Mr Whittaker,' said Sally, 'you know you asked if you could come and watch us some time ...'

'Well, it was hardly my fault, was it? You were shameless. I didn't know where to look. Well, I did, but ...'

'What are you on about, Terry? When we met you, in London, you asked if you could come to Meeting? Remember?'

'Oh, yes. Yes, that's right. I was joking, kind of.'

'Well, we're going, and so are you.'

'Yeah,' said Gwyn. 'The mushrooms have turned us into evangelical Quakers. Get your coat on.'

'Oh, all right.'

Pancester's Friends' Meeting House had been built in 1709, and Whittaker had always admired the elegant simplicity of the brick building, the earliest so constructed inside the city walls. It had somehow survived the Great Fire of Pancester of 1712, unlike the original Courtney House, which had been largely destroyed, along with much of the medieval city. Inside, the Meeting House was bright and white, and full of scrubbed oak benches arranged in semicircles, which held a good-sized and silent congregation.

Whittaker sat down with the girls. Nothing seemed to be happening. After a bit, he said, 'Have they started?'

Gwyn poked him, and held her finger to her lips.

Whittaker thought about Juliana. Where was he ever going to meet anyone else like her? I bet she will like me more when we stop the car park, he thought. I just bet she will. But I'll give up if she doesn't, I promise. I gave up the box, after all, which shows I can't be all bad. In fact, now I have given up the box, perhaps Sally and Gwyn's God will be on my side, and give me a break. Yes. I've made a sacrifice, a burnt offering. I'm not giving up, not after that. Only I won't tell anyone I haven't given up trying to go out with her yet. It'll be our little secret, mine and God's. She's just so . . . He dozed off.

Coming to, Whittaker realised with a start that the congregation was standing, and he stood as quickly as his arm would allow.

'Is it a hymn?' he whispered.

'No, loony, it's finished,' said Sally. 'Come on.'

'Oh, is that it?'

'Yeah, it was amazing, wasn't it?' said Gwyn.

'It just blows me away that we are part of all this,' said Sally, gesturing around her. 'And that all this is part of us. Don't you think, Cuggly-wuggly?'

'I guess I'm just not as spiritual as you. And not off my gourd on mushroom tea, either.'

'Heathen. Come on, let's go and cook breakfast. I'm starving,' said Gwyn.

Taff was waiting for them outside the 4i's, grinning from ear to ear, and looking, like Jacob Marley, as though the bottom part of his face was ready to fall off.

'Hiya!' he said. 'You coming down the festival tonight? About eight?'

'Well, no. We're open tonight.'

Taff looked crestfallen. 'Ah, no, Terry man. Please come down tonight. It'll be worth your while.' Terry looked at Gwyn and Sally, both of whom were dancing again, this time to silent music, and shrugged.

'Actually, come to think of it, perhaps it would be wise. I'll put a sign up saying we're closed due to staff incapacity. Look at the state of your daughter.'

'Well, you're only young once, aren't you, and Stevie M knows what he's doing. I'll see you all later.' He went off whistling 'Telstar'.

'Oh, no,' said Gwyneth, who stopped dancing, and stared in horror at her father's retreating back. 'You don't think . . .?'

'Oh, yes, I'm afraid I do,' said Whittaker.

It was The Knightwatchmen's first gig with the new line-up. They stood on the stage that Ash had built from pallets, and which Phil the Painter had decorated. The three new lads whom Taff had unearthed from somewhere were looking awkward in the new leather uniforms, which had so far only had one outing, the one which Whittaker had been unfortunate enough to catch with Penny Lester.

The band twanged through the perennial set, which the festival-goers seemed to love, fuelled as they were with mushroom tea and four decades of ironic pop sensibility.

'Worst yet,' said Gwyn to her mother afterwards.

'Yep. Appalling. Here he comes.'

'Hey hey hey! Wotcha think, pop-pickers?' said Taff.

'Best ever line-up, Dad,' said Gwyn.

'Yes, I agree. Wonderful as ever,' said Dawn.

'Yeah, we're getting there. The guitarist is only fifteen, and he's not much good, reely, but he fits the uniform a treat. Hey, we're the only band from the first Free Festival to play here this time. We're historic!'

'Prehistoric,' muttered Gwyneth under her breath.

Walking back across the site after the gig, Whittaker was surprised to bump into Penny Lester. She looked embarrassed.

'Hello, Pen. What on earth are you doing here?'

'Oh, hello, Terry. I . . . I've been meaning to pop in and say hi.'

'I should think so too. What, are you here for the festival? I should have thought that you'd had enough of The Knightwatchmen after the last time.'

'Yes. Yes, you would. I'm . . . yes, I'm here for the festival, yes.'

'And are you camping down here? I wouldn't have thought that that was your style at all.'

'Wouldn't you? No. But . . . I am.'

'You know you can come and stay with us in the flat if it gets too cold.'

'Can I? Thanks. But I seem to be keeping warm enough.'

'Oh, look, here's Oliver! Oliver! Over here.'

Oliver Halton walked across to join Penny and Terry.

'Hello, Oliver. You remember Penny?'

Oliver smiled and nodded. Penny smiled too, and blushed. 'Hello, Oliver,' said Penny.

Oliver raised his eyebrows.

'Well, look, you two,' said Terry, 'I've really got to get back to the restaurant. We closed for the night, so it means I can get ready for tomorrow, get some stuff done. Will you be all right in Oliver's hands, Pen?'

'Oh, yes. Yes, I'll be fine in Oliver's hands. You get on, Terry. Don't worry about me.'

'OK. Well, it's great to see you. Fancy old Penny turning into a camper, Olly.'

Oliver looked puzzled. Penny said, 'I've told Terry all about me camping here at the festival, Oliver.'

Oliver smiled again, and said, 'Ahh.'

'Right. Best get on. Pop in and see your handiwork, Penny, won't you?'

'Yes. You get on. Bye, Terry.'

'Bye, Penny, Oliver.' Terry walked back to the 4i's, and found himself, to his horror, whistling 'Apache'.

Sally had been having an exciting time at work, and had, at last, found premises in Laikley to serve as a centre for the homeless. On Monday morning, she took Whittaker with her, to see what he thought of the building.

'Yeah, it's OK. Easy to heat. Good and central. Oh, look,' he said, leaning from the window, 'you can see Juliana's dad's shop. I wonder if he's open. I've always meant to introduce myself.'

'Why?'

'Well, just to be polite.'

'You're not still imagining him as your future father-in-law, are you?'

Whittaker laughed. 'No! Of course not. Don't be silly. Of course I'm not, no, no way.'

Sally looked at him through narrowed eyes. 'Hmmm. Well, you can go and have a look. I'm going to be another half-hour or so, and then I'll run you back.'

'Thanks, Sal. Meet you back here!'

'And don't get carried away.' But he'd gone.

The 'Open' sign was up in the door of I'm All Right, Jack. Whittaker looked at the window display of bowls and bowling accessories. There were two mannequins, one male and one female, each sporting the appropriate bowling wear. A bell rang as Whittaker pushed open the door. A man looked up from the counter. He was wearing a green Pringle sweater and a pair of golfing slacks, and, like his daughter, had grey eyes and a slight over-bite.

'Good morning, sir. How can I help you?'

'Oh, I'm just looking, really.' Whittaker looked at the shelves, which were stocked with more bowls, more bowling accessories and more bowling wear. It was, after all, a bowling supplies shop.

'Looking for anything in particular?' What was Whittaker to say? Some bowls? He didn't know the first thing about the game, and they looked expensive. He scanned the shelves in desperation. 'Er ... a hat.'

'A hat, sir? A bowling hat? Let me come and have a look . . . here we are, sir. Finest selection of bowling hats in the north. Try this one . . . very nice, sir. You'll cut a rug on the greens in that.'

Whittaker saw no way out but to buy the thing. As Ted Blezzard took his card details, Whittaker said, 'I think I know your daughter. Juliana?'

'Oh, is that right? Oh, you must be Mr Whittaker, the chef fella. I've seen you in the *Mail*. And weren't you on that *Junior Masterchef* last year?'

'That's right.'

'Friend of our Juliana's, are you? She's a rum 'un, though. She were a right nice lass before she went away down south. She picked up a few airs and graces when she were at university, but she always had time for you. Not like now.'

'You don't see her much?'

'She's not been round to see me and her mother this last six month.'

'Oh dear.'

'It were Staines that ruined her. We were right proud of her when she got that job. But she were that full of herself, there were no talking to her. "The Girl Who Put Staines On The Map", they called her. She left here a nice Laikley lass, and she came back a bloody Surrey ponce. No offence.'

'None taken. I'm a Middlesex man myself.'

'Here's your hat, Mr Whittaker. No, I'm afraid more and more of the young people are like it these days. It's just me me me . . .'

The telephone rang. 'Hello, I'm All Right, Jack', said Mr Blezzard. Whittaker raised a hand in silent farewell. Ted nodded.

Back at the soon-to-be shelter, Sally was waiting for Whittaker.

'What have you got there?' she asked.

'A bowling hat.'

'Why?'

'Well . . . in case I ever play bowls.'

'What, with your father-in-law, for example?'

'Yes.'

'Terry, I take it back. You do need therapy.'

Hanging Nick

By late October, although the mushrooms were still appearing, the non-stop party on Dole Acre was starting to wind down. Too many nights had been wet and windy, and the cold was just beginning to bite. Syd declared the Second Pancester Free Festival officially closed. Several of the vehicles left the site, whilst others started to prepare for the coming winter, sending expeditions up-river to collect wood and checking over the canvases for leaks. Medlicott was still serving tea to those who wanted it, but he was also running a meditation group for those who were interested in exploring the mushroom's capacities beyond the admittedly entertaining 'Hey, let's all get naked and dance' level. The site had become quieter, more serious, more 'spiritual' according to Sally, more 'real' according to Medlicott.

Steve was true to his promise to attempt to track down Lady Lettice, and ran several chanting circles and a sweat lodge to see if they would help him find her, but, to no one's surprise but his own, he had very little luck.

'I still feel sure that she is about. But I am no longer certain that she is what *you* would call alive. I've tried channelling, I've tried sending, we've chanted in the sweat lodge – but I've come up with nothing. She was very – energetic. Her chakras were unblocked. Perhaps such a force has left an imprint on this side. I'm sorry.'

'That's OK, Steve. It was a long shot,' said Terry.

By the night of Hallowe'en, lots of children had appeared in the streets with their effigies for Hanging Nick. Pancester, in common with other predominantly Catholic towns, does not celebrate Guy Fawkes night with any great enthusiasm. Hanging Nick, which takes place on Old Bonfire Night, ten days later, is the city's great autumnal fire festival. Traditionally, the children make dummies of the devil, rather than Guy Fawkes, which they dangle from long poles, from which practice the festival gets its name. But as well as the devil, it is usual for other villains to make their appearance. Sir Alexander Honeyball, Pancester's most famous mayor, he who had installed the carillon, could still be found occasionally hanging by his neck. Clement Dadd, in his *Account of the Antiquarian Customs and Curious Survivals of Pancester*, notes that he had seen Napoleon, General Smuts and the Mahdi 'burn merrily in Guildhall Square', but he was writing in 1903, and Terry failed to make out any of these late Victorian shibboleths.

This year, the devil still predominated, and lots of little Satans were to be found on street-corners, their creators collecting money for fireworks. But Whittaker also saw a few Alexander Honeyballs, a couple of Hitlers, a Tony Blair, a Saddam Hussein and one female model, with orange wool for hair and a pair of goofy teeth that he didn't recognise at all.

'Who's this? Janet Street-Porter?' he asked the little girl sitting by the effigy.

'No, silly. It's that woman who wants to build a car park.'

'Juliana Blezzard?'

'That's her. Me mam helped me do her. She's down on the camp.'

'Well, good luck to you. Have a fiver.'

That night, after work, Whittaker was feeling blue. He shouldn't have encouraged the girl with the Juliana dummy. And Juliana's hair was strawberry blonde, and a slight over-bite hardly amounted to great big sticky-out teeth. Everyone always thought the worst of her, when it was that monster Q Sandahl who had led her astray. They should burn *him* in effigy, that would be fairer.

He walked around the castle, hoping to catch a glimpse of his rival, so that he could give him a piece of his mind. The city was dark and quiet. The walls of the castle towered above him. As he turned the corner of the path around the walls furthest away from the castle gate, he could see a phosphorescent light burning in the window of the attendant parish church, St Gilbert's. There was something about it that Whittaker found fascinating. It shouldn't have been there. He should phone the police on his mobile. But he didn't. Instead he felt compelled to go closer; he felt drawn to it. He walked up to the great door of the church, and turned the handle quietly. It was open, and he entered the building.

The source of the light was sitting on Sir Kenelm de Courtney's tomb. It was an old man, shining with a ghostly grey luminescence. He had grey hair and a silver pointed beard, and he shimmered slightly. Whittaker, the hairs standing up on the back of his neck, realised that he was almost transparent. He was wearing a Manchester City away shirt, Adidas tracksuit bottoms and a pair of Reebok trainers.

'Ohhh, by St George, somebody's come at last. I thought that none should be drawn by my light this year, and it is only ten minutes until my dematerialisation. There is much for you to tell me, mortal.' His thin voice quavered in the still air of the church.

'Bubba, fubb, ababa . . .' stuttered Whittaker.

'There's no time to be frightened, I'm afraid. I'm not going to hurt you, I'm too, ahem, "loved up". Just answer me this. Who won the Premiership this year?'

'M . . . M . . . M . . . United.'

'God's teeth! And the Cup?'

'M . . . M . . . M . . . United again.'

'Is there no justice? How I detest the Red Scum! And City, how are City doing this year?'

Whittaker made a face and shook his head. The ghost groaned, a terrible moaning groan which shook the windows of the church. Whittaker covered his ears.

'Do not cover your ears, mortal! There is much to get through. Who's Number One?'

'I've no idea, I'm afraid.'

'You should be ashamed of yourself! You must try and keep up with the young people. I do, and I've been dead five hundred years. Is it The Spice Girls?'

'I don't think so. Geri's left, though.'

'I know that, mortal. That's old news. Now, what's happening on *Corrie*?'

'Er ... Ken Barlow is having a big row with Mike Baldwin about something, and Hayley's having a baby. Look, who are you?'

'I? Who do you think I am? I am Sir Kenelm de Courtney, buffoon. This is my tomb. My name and picture appear on the side. Look, that's me, in my armour. See? Who else would be sitting here? Hmmm? My posse call me Kenny. Do the young people still say "posse"? Or would "massive" be more appropriate in this context?'

'Oh, I don't really know. Do you ... if you don't mind my asking ... regularly haunt the church?'

'Regularly, yes. Frequently, alas, no, or else I'd get them to put a telly in. One feels so out of touch! Once a year, on All-Hallows' Eve, I materialise for an hour, and I like to catch up on things, if I can lure a mortal in here. Only two minutes left,' he ended sadly.

'Sir Kenelm, Kenny, please, we need your help. Did you leave the freehold of Dole Acre to the city?'

'Certainly not! I left the grazing rights, that the pensioners might pray for my soul. A good job they're doing too. But the Acre still remains within the Courtney family. Why are you asking me? It's all in the Charter. Now, give me the, ah, "4–1–1" on the family. Is Lettice still missing?'

'Yes. The city wants her declared dead.'

'Hmmm. I don't think she is. I've never come across her on the other side, anyway. Mind you, it's big. But with her being family, you'd have thought she'd have looked me up.'

'What's it like there? Is it blue?'

'The afterlife is something of a curate's egg, to be frank with you. It's blue in parts. But what's been happening in Pancester?'

'The City Council wants to build a car park on the Dole Acre.'

'Whaaat? The addle-pated drones! How dare they?'

'My friends and I are trying to stop them.'

'Good for you, mortal. You must stand up to them what I believe is known as "24/7". You must make it your "365".' Sir Kenelm scratched his ethereal beard, and looked puzzled. 'Or is it the other way round? "7/24"?' he said.   'Kenny, you're starting to fade.'

'Oh, no! Argh! No! Tell me quick . . . who won Wally Oop this year?' But with a pop, and a faint smell of almonds, Sir Kenelm disappeared, and his light was extinguished before Whittaker could tell him that the Ringlers had taken it again.

When he got home he woke Sally and Gwyn in a fever of excitement to tell them what he'd seen, and they put him to bed with a hot toddy.

'Delayed shock,' said Sally, tucking him in. 'Not unusual after concussion.'

'But I met with him. He told me he appeared every year. Loads of people must have seen him at one time or another. Old guy, see-through, City supporter.'

It took Mrs Innes coming round in the morning to convince Terry that no one had ever reported seeing the ghost before.

'Sorry, Mr Whittaker. There's just no tradition of Sir Kenelm haunting the church. Hundreds of other ghosts in there of course. I don't suppose it could have been Headless Keith Hutchinson, the Blackhampton Highwayman, mucking about? He's been spotted plenty of times, and is said to have something of a sense of humour.'

'No, this guy definitely had a head. And he looked just like the pictures of Sir Kenelm.'

'Well, you're the first to report him, dear.'

'So I'm going mad then?'

'Going?' said Gwyneth.

'No, of course not, dear. You took a nasty knock when you dived off the bridge. The mind can play funny tricks after a thing like that.'

'Well, he told me that the Charter only grants grazing rights. And that he doesn't think Lady Lettice is dead.'

'Did he?' said Mrs Innes. 'Now that is interesting. Maybe you did see something after all.'

'Oh, Mrs Innes. Please don't lead him on,' said Gwyneth.

'Well, you never know,' said Mrs Innes. 'Dawn must keep looking for Lady Letty and her son. And I'll try and persuade the museum to let us send the amended Charter for X-ray. Nice to know old Sir Kenelm himself is on our side. Quite a feather in our caps.'

After a lie-in the following morning, Terry got up to find a letter from his father on the doormat. He made himself a cup of tea, and sat down to read.

His father's hand was shaky, barely legible, but the letter was short, and Terry already knew what it would say.

You can fuck off. I knew how to live, that's all. You had your Mother running around after you the whole time. She never had no time for me after you were born. I was entitled to a life of my own, wasn't I? You can think that it was my fault you could never get fucked all you like. I don't give a toss. I'll probably be dead by the time you get this, and don't think I'm leaving you my money, cos I'm not. I'm leaving it to the nuns. At least they have more of a sex life than you, you sad little mummy's boy.
Your Dad, though that doesn't mean anything to you,
    Alex Whittaker

Terry put his head in his hands and wept. When Gwyneth came into the kitchen for her morning tea, she found him still snuffling, his cheeks stained with tears, his eyes puffy and red.

'Cuggles, darling, whatever's the matter?' She hurried across to him, and took his hand. Terry showed her the letter.

'The hateful old man. What a horrible thing to write. No wonder you're upset. Poor Terry.'

Terry looked up at Gwyn. 'I love him, though, Gwyn, you see. He is my dad, after all. He's never done anything except make me unhappy, but he is dying, and I do love him, and he is my dad.

And I can never make it better now, not now. And I tried, I really tried.'

Gwyn squeezed his hand. 'I know you did.'

'And now I'll never see him again.'

'Well, you still can, if you want. You could go down to London, and see him. You could keep trying, couldn't you? You don't have to leave this as the final word.'

Terry pulled out a sodden tissue, and blew his nose.

'No. What would be the point?'

But later that afternoon, Terry phoned Brian Styles, asked if he would run the 4i's that night, and caught the six o'clock train to London. It was dark, and he stared miserably out of the window, watching the lights stutter past. Outside Rugby, the train sat for half an hour, and he fell uneasily asleep.

He was looking down on the Dole Acre from above. He seemed to be flying. The camp, the archaeologists, all had disappeared, and their place had been taken by what looked like a crop circle, trampled into the thistles by the donkeys, in the shape of a tombstone. There was an inscription and Terry tried and failed to read it. He hovered closer, and watched the donkeys treading out a text. It read, 'Love, RIP'. Terry choked, lost the ability to fly, and fell spiralling towards the ground.

He awoke with a jolt, sweat beading on his forehead, as the train started to move again. He stood shakily, and made his way to the buffet car for a brandy miniature.

This is stupid, he thought, incredibly stupid.

The train got into Euston just after eleven, and Terry took a cab out to the hospice in St John's Wood. The sister on duty was surprised to see him. His father was asleep, grey and breathing painfully. Terry sat in the armchair beside the bed, and dozed fitfully.

As the dawn paled the sky, Terry woke to find his father sitting up, and looking at him with a smile.

'I loves ya, boy,' said Alex.

'I love you too, Dad. I just wanted to tell you.'

'I'm not sorry I wrote you that letter. I'm not sorry for

anything. At least it got you down here. At least you still remember the plumber joke.'

'I arrived last night. The sister said you haven't been too good.'

'Of course I'm no good, you useless wanker. I'm dying. I've got cancer. How could I be good? Have you brought my sweets?'

'No. The shop was closed. It's probably still a bit early. I'll pop out and get them in a bit.'

Alex winced. 'No, it's all right, the sisters'll get 'em. They always do. Stay with me for a bit.'

'OK.'

One of the nuns popped her head into the room, and brought Terry some tea. Terry stepped outside to talk to her.

'How is he, sister?'

'Not long now, the doctor says, Mr Whittaker. But he'll be glad to see you, that he will.'

Back in the room, Terry sat and held his father's hand, while the old man slept.

'I'm sorry I ran away, Dad,' whispered Terry.

Alex opened his eyes.

'You didn't run away. You've got your own life, that's all. Things to get on with. That's what I used to say to your mother. Leave him be, he's got his own fucking life. Leave him be. He'll be all right. Won't you? You'll be all right?'

'Course I will. I wish you could see my restaurant.'

Alex smiled painfully. 'Spect you'll have to get back to it, won't you?'

'Later. It'll be all right too.'

'You get back, boy. You get back. We all got our own lives. I love ya. I'm glad ...'

'What?'

'I'm glad you came.'

'So am I.'

On the train back to Pancester that evening, Terry thought that he'd very much like to kiss Sally and Gwyn. Men need women so much more than women need men.

The fifteenth of November in Pancester, and the time had come again for the ancient tradition of Hanging Nick, which marks the transition from autumn into winter. In the late afternoon, Whittaker watched the children march through the darkening streets with their effigies hanging from the ends of poles, singing their traditional song:

'Wake up, thou sluggards,
And give Nick a penny,
And may ye sleep not,
If you give us not any.'

The children knock with the guys at the upper windows of the houses, supposedly to wake the inhabitants, all of whom are actually downstairs cooking tea and watching *Neighbours* and *Pet Rescue*. No one goes to bed at sundown any more, even in Pancester, even when there's not much on telly. But still the children knock, and the good people of Pancester tear themselves away from the goggler to give them pennies and sweets. Whittaker paid up cheerfully, even to the little girl with Juliana on a stick.

It is later in the evening, after the children have been round all the houses, that Pancester hots up. A huge bonfire is lit in the Guildhall Square. All the adults come out to watch the children dip their effigies into the fire, and then hold them aloft, so that the crowd can watch them burn. And then, one by one, slowly at first, everyone steps forward and throws a bone into the fire, and wishes for good fortune, or mutters the name of an enemy under their breath.

Whittaker refused to go. The restaurant was open, anyway, and he was feeling back to full strength. His arm had been unbound the day before, so he gave Brian and Mindy Styles their first night off since the dive from the Pack Bridge, and enjoyed himself in the kitchen, two-handed again at last.

Gwyneth came into the kitchen smiling all over her face.

'You'll never guess who's in,' she said.

'Arthur Miller and Marilyn Monroe.'

'No.'

'Arthur Mullard and Marilyn Manson.'

'No. Last guess.'

'No, I give up.'

'Oliver Halton and Penny Lester.'

'You're kidding me.'

'I'm not. Look.'

Whittaker peered around the kitchen door. Penny and Oliver were sitting at a table for two, holding hands. Penny was talking, Oliver listening, a broad smile over his beautiful face.

'Bloody hell,' said Terry. 'I wonder how long that's been going on? Should I go and say hello?'

'Most certainly, *mon capitaine*. Go get the juicy.'

Whittaker walked into the restaurant.

'Penny! How lovely to see you again! You're becoming quite a fixture in Pancester.'

Penny let go of Oliver's hand.

'Oh, ha, hello, Terry, yes. Yes . . . I'm . . . I've . . . Oliver invited me to come and see Hanging Nick. We're going on to the Square after dinner. Weren't the children sweet?'

'Oliver invited you? How?'

'Don't be rude. By e-mail, of course. He can get quite eloquent when his fingers do the talking. Can't you, Olly?' She seemed to shudder with pleasure as she smiled at Oliver, who nodded at Terry.

'Are you telling me that you two . . . well, you know?'

'You nosy thing,' said Penny. Oliver winked at Terry without Penny noticing.

'Oh, come on. How long has this been going on?'

'None of your business, you nasty man. Haven't you got a kitchen to run?'

'Oh, you old sly boots. You weren't camping for the festival at all, were you? You were staying in Olly's flat!'

'Well, what do you think? I'd rather set my eyebrows on fire than go camping. You've known me long enough for that, I'd have thought.' She smiled at Whittaker, who gave her a hug in return. He shook Oliver's hand.

'Well, good luck to you both. Best news I've had in months. Dinner on the house, of course.'

'So I should hope. And do get a move on, Cuggles. We want to go and see the bone fire in the Square.'

Sally brought back a report of the Square packed with tourists, all cheering as each successive burning effigy was pulled from the fire, and of everyone coming forward with their bones and throwing them into the flames. She brought home some Nick cakes too, from the vendors around the town.

'Mmm, these are good. I'll try and go next year.'

'And I saw Blezzard and Sandahl, too, not too proud to take their turn at throwing bones on to the fire. Were they looking for good fortune, or cursing us, do you think?' said Sally.

'It amounts to the same thing, doesn't it? Their good fortune would be a curse for us anyway, wouldn't it?' said Gwyneth.

Whittaker smiled ruefully, and told Sally about Oliver and Penny.

'Do you know, I thought I saw them. Good for her. Do you think they'll get married?'

'Blimey, it's a bit soon for that, I'd have thought. Besides, Penny is much too much of a snob to marry a second-hand bookseller. But they seemed happy. I'm jealous.'

'You never fancied Penny, silly,' said Sally.

'Jealous of happiness. Jealous of love.'

And so the autumn has quietly passed by, and the clocks have gone back, and everyone is starting to think about Christmas. The Mummers' Play Committee, chaired by Taffy Gabatini, begin preparations for their performance in January. The first frosts start to bite. Winter is here. Time for Act Three.

Put the kettle on. Skin up.

The Pancester Plough Monday
Mummers' Play

'Good morning, Edmund.'

'Top o' the morning to ye, Terry.'

'Come into the kitchen and have a bite. It's much too cold to be rooting around in the dustbins.'

'That's very kind of you, sur. Though food always tastes much nicer when it's stolen. But thank you, I will ... oh. Good morning Miss Sally.' Edmund bobbed a curtsy, holding up the tails of his coat as though it were a skirt.

'Good morning, Edmund.' Sally was waiting in the kitchen for the old tramp.

'I'm doing bacon and eggs,' said Whittaker. 'That suit you?'

'Er ... aye. Thank you kindly, young master.'

'Now then, Edmund. I've been looking for you,' said Sally.

'Oh?'

'Don't give me oh. I've been leaving notes for you on dustbins all over town.'

'Oh, they were from you, were they, Miss Sally? You shouldn't leave me notes in the pantry, miss, or cook might scold me.'

'You know they were. And you know what they're about. And I'm scolding you.'

'Look, Miss Sally, I don't want charity.'

'It's not charity, Edmund, it's your right. There's a bed for you in Laikley if you want it, that's all. It's far too cold to be sleeping rough. Why not come in, just for the winter? You'll catch your death sleeping on the streets.'

'I don't sleep on the streets. I've got a place I can lay up.'

'And can't you tell me where it is? Please, Edmund. If I knew where you slept, if I knew you were all right, I could get a bit of sleep myself.'

Whittaker set down the bacon and eggs.

'Thanks, Terry. Miss Sally, I knows you mean well, but I don't want people poking their noses into my affairs. I'm a free man. I don't want no letters from the council. I stay warm and dry, and thank you for asking. And I like me bacon a bit crispier'n this, as a rule, if you don't mind my mentioning it.'

And no more would the old man say.

All through December, Whittaker travelled up and down between Pancester and London. His father's lucid moments were fewer now, and he was seldom aware when his son sat watching pain and morphine-induced rest take their turns to cross his face.

In London in the armchair in his father's room, dozing in First Class on the train, in bed at home at night, Terry was troubled by unpleasant dreams. His least favourite was the one where Juliana, naked except for a pair of nipple clamps, parked thousands of cars on his grave, in which he lay alive, gasping for breath. The nipple clamps hardly began to make up for the sensation of feeling crushed under tons of metal. And after his meeting with Sir Kenelm in the church, Whittaker had become increasingly jumpy. Sleep was harder and harder to come by as he tried to control a growing sense of panic.

A couple of times a week, Whittaker still liked to go down to the site to share a pipe with Ash. It was too cold to stay outside, so the two would sit in Ash's van. One of the things about the travelling life that most concerns people who live in houses is the cold. 'Aren't you cold in that old van?' they ask, but the real problem is with the heat. Ash's home-made wood-burner kicked out more BTUs than Krakatoa in July. The two men would sit sweating in T-shirts, no matter how cold it was outside.

One night towards Christmas, Terry told the old traveller about both his dreams and his encounter with Sir Kenelm.

'So I think I'm going mad. I can't sleep. My heart won't slow down at night.'

Ash sucked at the pipe full of his own grass, cropped from small plantations hidden in the Mendips, where he usually overwintered, and passed it to Whittaker.

'What you call mad, Steve Medlicott calls being in touch with reality. What keeps you awake at night – with your pulses banging like steam engines, your dreams, your visions – is the thing that makes Steve calm. Who is right, do you think?'

'Well, Steve, I suppose. He's the calm one.'

'But perhaps he's deluded. Perhaps you are right to feel frightened. There is loads out there, and in here, for that matter' (he touched his heart) 'to be frightened of, after all.'

'What do you think?'

'I think your subconscious is calling out. The ghost, the dreams, it's all about your father dying. And this fucking stupid state you've got yourself into over this girl. And the car park. It's no wonder you can't sleep. You are trying to tell yourself something, that's what I think.'

'I wonder what I'm trying to tell me.'

Ash started to refill his pipe.

'How's business?' he asked Whittaker.

'Yeah, great. We hit our yearly profit target after seven months. I'm going to look at doing up the basement. We might start doing lunches and coffees down there, maybe music and a bar in the evenings if we can get the soundproofing right.'

'Why?'

'Well, so we could have music downstairs without disturbing the diners in the restaurant. I mean, only like a bit of cocktail piano, or something. Not The Knightwatchmen, or anything loud like that.'

'No, I mean, given that you've made the money you hoped to make in a year in seven months, why do you want to do more work, rather than less?'

'Oh ... well, to keep the business growing.'

'Why?'

'Because that's how business works. You grow or die.'

'Yeah, and that's how it all starts. You have a good idea, you do it well, you make a good living, you get recognition, but something nags away at you that it's not enough. It nags at you to work harder, expand, open more restaurants, franchise the idea, go global, make a couple of million, turn into a monster. Now, I have my own demons. Look at me. I should be living in Speke with a wife and grandchildren and a Cortina up on bricks in the drive. But I've always hated all that. I've striven for more freedom, less responsibility. My demon nags me into living like this, and you could say that's me taking things to extremes. Well, that's our super-ego bossing us about, our conscience as opposed to our conscious, and that's what fuels your need for hard work and money, and mine for moral superiority. Super-ego. Guilt, yeah?'

'Tell me about it. Guilt's my middle name.'

'Listen. The super-ego, the father's voice, Terry, the little nagging voice that says, "You must do this, you must do that", that we need to try and ignore, if we want to hear our subconscious voice, our mother voice. And your ego, your conscious self, the You voice, well, that's trapped, like mine, in an Orwellian society, a society where the proles drink alcopops and watch soap opera and only really care about the lottery, just like Orwell said they would, while the middle classes are bound up in bureaucratic nightmare and are straitjacketed by convention, by disapproval from the neighbours, all for the benefit of the vast faceless multinational corporations who run the whole shebang. And the ruling elite just want us all to have fun, because it makes us more biddable and increasingly less worried about what they get up to. The only thing on the political agenda is the management of capitalism. Real change, visionary change, is now unthinkable. Who has vision, after all? Only the CCTV operators who watch us day and night, and play back the tapes as entertainment, and if that isn't pure Orwell then I don't know what is. And when we have dreams – which are postcards from our subconscious, our id, our mother, yeah? – what place do they have in a world run only for profit? Where can they go? What are they trying to tell any of us, and why are we so unprepared to listen?'

'I don't know.'

Ash sucked his pipe. 'Neither do I. But at least I'm *trying* to hear mine. You just think you're going mad. In short, you are being much too rational. If you want to stop this car park, maybe you should think less, and dream more, for a while, at least. There's been some mighty weird shit going down in all this business. Now you're coming up with some weird shit of your own. Why? I'd say let it come. Tune into your strangeness. Embrace the unknown. It'll be hard, it always is. But I bet it will have something useful to bring to the party. Your father is dying, so your own super-ego is trying to overcompensate for his absence. Has been for years, probably. Quiet that voice. And at least you'll find out what you're trying to tell yourself.'

'Sally said I needed therapy. Thanks for that.'

'That wasn't therapy. That was a stoned rant.'

'You smoke too much broccoli, old man,' said Whittaker, accepting the pipe.

'There's no such thing, my boy. No such thing.'

The morning after Ash and Whittaker had talked about dreams, Neil Winterburn invited the committee down to the Dole Acre to see part of his realised.

'Ladies and gentleman, may I proudly present the Balls.'

Together with increasingly confident help from Emma and Gemma, as well as from a willing army of hippy diggers, Winterburn had uncovered the remains of the two large interlinked circular structures on which he had been concentrating his efforts since the summer. The committee stood and looked at the low walls, uncovered for the first time in fifteen hundred years. Each of the structures was fifteen metres or so across its diameter.

'And just there, look, is the doorway into the base of the shaft. Whaddya think? Super, aren't they? Biggest pair of plums I've ever seen, and I played rugby at school.'

'It's amazing, Neil, it really is. Can we climb down?' asked Whittaker.

'Yes, if you're careful. There's a ladder over there. But look out, it can be a bit hairy down there. Bit hairy? Oh, suit yourselves.'

Whittaker, Winterburn, Dexter Halton and the Medlicotts all climbed down the short ladder to the dig. Mrs Innes and Rolly peered over at them, while Winterburn conducted a guided tour.

'It's the usual local stone, easy to get here by river. I don't think the building can have been much less than ten metres high. Look at the thickness of the walls. Superb. This is a really massive find.'

'Well done, all of you!' called Mrs Innes. 'No Secretary of State is going to want this buried under a car park, are they?'

'Of course not, dear Mrs I. It's too beautiful. As beauteous as thine eyes,' said Neil.

'They look like a series of low walls to me,' said Dexter. 'I mean, very important and interesting low walls, obviously,' he added hastily, when Winterburn glared at him.

'What next, Neil?' asked Whittaker.

'Well, it's all getting a bit much for us. It's not my period, you know, not at all. I specialised in industrial archaeology before I became county archaeologist. Medieval watermills in particular. I'd be able to tell you more about the old sluices they used to turn this into a water-meadow. Much more my kind of thing. But there, the county have washed their hands of us, and English Heritage won't move until the Big White Chief in London has spoken, so I'm the best we've got, I'm afraid. So we're waiting for *Time Gang*.'

'Oh, yes, of course. How exciting!' said Mrs Innes. 'When are they due? February, isn't it?'

'I've got one of their researchers coming next week. We're still on schedule for February, I hope.'

'And then?' asked Dexter.

'Well, then they uncover the shaft and bell-end, or at least establish beyond doubt that they are there. And help me with interpretation. And with the eyes of the nation turned upon us, the City Council finds funds for a proper excavation and a visitor centre. Victory for us, humiliating defeat for our enemies.' He pulled a face. 'And it will be the making of my career, I suppose. Which will make certain smarmy Sicilian sociologists sick.'

'What is he on about? Why is he making up tongue-twisters?' whispered Mrs Innes.

'Don't go there, Mrs I. Don't go there,' said Whittaker.

While Whittaker and the committee were congratulating Winter-burn, Taff was preparing for the first rehearsal of the Plough Monday Mummers' Play, due to be held that evening in the Guildhall.

In his day, the Reverend Clement Dadd had been England's leading authority on the ancient folk plays which still survive, here and there, to the present day; with the best will in the world, a lay audience can hardly be expected to understand his comments on the Pancester play, which are scholarly and abstruse. But essentially, a cast of twelve men, drawn from the losing side at Wally Oop, take highly stylised parts in the play, the text of which has been handed down from at least the sixteenth century. The play has been copied and recopied many times, and today there are parts of it which make little or no sense, either because the copyists have made errors, or because the original meaning has been lost or altered over time. But the Pancester Mummers, Clanghandlers to a man, would no more dream of consciously altering or updating the play than they would of giving the Ringlers an easy time in the Wally. There is one section of the play which the text does not cover, however, where the Doctor, aided by Jack Finney, attempts to revive St George, and it is traditional that this part is reinvented every year. The Doctor and Jack indulge in a bit of old-fashioned business on St George with garden shears and rubber hose behind a sheet, and swap wisecracks about the year just past while they operate. It will be seen, therefore, that the Doctor is one of the stars of the piece, and Taff, as well as producing the whole thing, had played the part for twenty-three years to great critical acclaim.

The costumes for the play are stored in the Guildhall in two large wicker hampers, and Taff always enjoyed digging them out each year, and seeing how they had stood up to the ravages of time. St George's armour was fine, and the Recruiting Sergeant had had a new jacket only a few years before, but Father Christmas was beginning to look a little moth-eaten. It might do one more year with a bit of patching, although Old-Hind-

Before's broom clearly needed renewing. Taff's own costume, a bloodstained tailcoat and top hat, needed nothing more than a little mildew brushing away. He took his silk topper from the antediluvian hatbox where it lived most of the year, and balanced it on his head. It was still too small. So Taff's head had not shrunk in the year just gone, which was always a relief.

He put the hat back in its box, and went to fetch some beers from the Holly Bush, ready for the rehearsal, which was due to begin at seven. It was just a read-through, really. The cast had been unchanged for seven years, since the time when Taff's next-door neighbour, old Brian Fowler, had died, and his son, Brian Junior, had taken over the part of Beelzebub. Brian Junior (known simply as Brian after his father's death) had brought some much-needed new blood to the thing, and had lowered the average age of the cast from fifty-eight to forty-nine at a stroke. Nicolo Gabatini was currently the oldest member of the cast, and had played the undemanding role of Johnny Jack for several years without incident. He couldn't make the rehearsal due to ill-health, much to Taff's relief; Nicolo saw himself as Dadd's successor, and liked to criticise everything that Taff did.

The full text of the play appears in Appendix Four of Dadd's book. It is not, quite frankly, a great piece of theatrical writing, and nor does it pretend to be other than what it is: a folk piece, a curiosity.

The read-through was held largely to check that everyone had memorised their handful of lines from the year before, and that the costumes still fitted. Frank Welford, the dairyman, who played Jack Finney, had put on a few pounds since last year, and made an appointment with Taff to go and see Dawn, who took care of any repairs and alterations which needed doing.

'You should lay off the cream, Frankie,' said Taff. 'You're becoming a fat bastard.'

'Yeah, and you should lay off the Brylcreem. You're becoming a bald bastard.' Taff and Frank grinned at one another. Friends since school, their broker's men schtick was the high point of the show, and they planned to stay behind after the rehearsal to start preparing their gags for the performance.

Taff adjudged the read-through a success. No one had forgotten their lines at all, and it was unnecessary to refer to the script. Dadd felt that this was probably the case in most years, except when a new cast member was introduced, and argued that the play was therefore in a process of slow evolution. Conscious alteration might be unthinkable, but as the memories of the actors reprocessed the text from performance to performance, slow change was inevitable. It would be interesting to test this theory by making a new transcription and matching it against Dadd's own.

Taff and Frank worked on their jokes for a while after the other cast members had gone to the pub. The car park, the Temple of Priapus and the hippies all promised to provide some rich material. At first Taff and Frank thought that jokes about the cooking at the 4i's, always a favourite source of hilarity in years gone by, would have to be rewritten, but they had been doing those jokes for almost a quarter of a century, and in the end they decided they couldn't bear to part with them. Frank helped Taff to pack away the costumes, except for his own and Father Christmas's, which were both going to need some attention from Dawn. As Taff opened the hatbox to replace his topper, he noticed that the red silk which lined the box was becoming unstitched and was coming away at the edges.

'I think I'll take this for our lass to have a look at, an' all,' he said.

'Righto, Taff. You done? Come on then, let's go and get a pint.'

'All right, boyo. You carry this bag with the costumes in, I'll carry the hatbox.'

Dawn had joined the rest of the cast at the Holly Bush. 'Hello, love,' she said. 'What you got for me this year?'

'Father Christmas and Fat Jack Finney. And this hatbox is falling to bits. It ent half heavy.'

'Let's have a look.'

She opened the box, and removed the hat. 'Well, this'll all want replacing,' she said, pulling at the silk. 'I'll have a look tomorrow.'

Dawn was too busy to have a proper go at the box. She had measured it up, and bought some silk from the market, but it had been forgotten in the Christmas rush, and she had her hands full letting Frank Welford's costume out and patching up Father Christmas. Taff had to carry the topper to rehearsals in a cardboard box.

Whittaker closed the 4i's for a few days over Christmas, and headed back to London. He had been getting down to sit with Alex as often as possible, and now he stayed at his father's bedside full-time, dozing in the armchair and reading the papers. The lucid moments had now gone for ever, and Alex was being fed by tube. On Christmas Day Terry presented his father with an illustrated copy of the *Kama Sutra*, which he lay on the old man's counterpane. His father did not regain consciousness, so the book sat on the end of the bed all day, while Terry watched his father's laboured breathing.

'And all you ever gave me was a joke about a plumber, Dad,' said Terry. 'But I must love you, whatever that means. 'Cos I'm still here.'

The nuns were all wearing party hats, and would pop into the room with smiles and glasses of whisky and meals for Terry; they would look at Alex, and shake their heads.

Sally and Gwyneth stayed in the flat, but spent the day itself with Taff and Dawn. Bethan, Gwyn's older sister, who lived in Glasgow with her husband, Andy, and their three children, had brought her family down to stay. Rhodri, the next youngest after Gwyneth, popped by in the afternoon with his wife, Ellen, and their yappy little dogs, but the visit was not a success. Ellen's father owned the maggot factory, and Dawn always said she gave herself airs. Papa Nico had come down from St Homobonus' and sat smiling at his daughter-in-law, grandchildren and great-grandchildren, and moaning at his son. Dai, Bethan's twin, worked at a university in Japan, and was much missed. Everyone took turns to speak to him on the phone. He was well, he was missing everyone, he was dating a Japanese girl. The third brother, Seiriol, came round in the evening with his girlfriend, Frankie, but only when they were sure that Rhodri and Ellen were gone, as Frankie and Ellen didn't get on. And Seiriol and Frankie brought their four kids, who bickered noisily over a PlayStation while the grown-ups played canasta. Ten for lunch, even with the girls helping, had taken a great deal of planning. And then tea with Her Majesty and poor old Rhodri, and supper with Seiriol and his noisy lot. Dawn had to borrow four chairs from Mrs Fowler next door, who was only having Brian and his wife.

Dawn loved having everyone together, and especially seeing the grandchildren, but it was hard work. She had been enjoying post-menopausal zest for a year or two, so much so that Sally called her PMZ Dawn, but Christmas always left her feeling like a limp dishcloth. Small wonder that the hatbox had been forgotten.

It was not until the day after Boxing Day, when the family had all taken off again, that Dawn gave it a thought. She fetched her sewing things from the sideboard, and took down the hatbox from the top of the wardrobe. The first job was to take out the old lining, and she set to with her scissors. The old red silk came away easily; underneath it, the box had a further lining of what looked like ancient yellow paper. Dawn pulled at it gingerly, frightened that it would crumble to pieces in her hand, but to her surprise, it felt soft and buttery to the touch, and came away easily. She looked at it. There was handwriting. She pulled a magnifying glass from her basket, and looked closer. And though she was by no means an expert on autographs of the late medieval and early modern period, what she saw made her call Taff.

'Hey, love, look at this. It's all covered in handwriting, old-time writing, and loads of numbers.'

Taff put on his specs and peered over her shoulder. 'Oh aye. That's been there a long while.'

'It has. Look, Taff, look here. A date. 1503.'

'The year of the Charter. By Christ, that is old!'

'And look. Don't you think that word there looks like Courtney? And these here, couldn't that say Dole Acre?'

'Aye, it could at that. What do you think it is?'

'I don't know, do I? But I'm phoning Mrs Innes. It could be important.'

Mrs Innes insisted on coming down to see it for herself. 'We probably shouldn't take it out into the air, in case it falls to bits. Do you mind if I bring Rolly? He's got the runs again, and I don't want to leave him on his own.'

She pulled up outside the Gabatinis' house in her old Austin Maxi, and stumped up the path with a sad-looking Rolly in tow.

'There you are, darling. I've brought his blanket. Can I put it by the fire, Dawn? Thank you. He's not feeling too bright. Too many mince pies always give him the gyp. There we are. Now, let's see what you've found.'

Dawn fetched her find, and spread it out on the table. She explained the parts she had managed to decipher, and handed Mrs Innes her magnifying glass.

'Oh, this is vellum. How lovely! No chance of it falling to bits, anyway.' Mrs Innes ran the glass over the document, her mouth moving silently as she tried to make out the words.

'Well,' she said at last. 'Well, well, well. Of course, I'm no expert, but . . .'

'What?' said Taff and Dawn together.

'I think it's a bill, made out for the attention of Sir Kenelm de Courtney. And it seems to mention the Dole Acre, just as you thought, right here, look, and then again here. And I don't know what you think, but couldn't this word here be "Charter"?'

Taff and Dawn leant over her shoulder, and agreed that it could.

'What do you think we should do?' asked Dawn. 'We can't really sew it back into the box, can we?'

'Good lord, my dear, of course we can't. It could be important. It could give us a clue. I think we should take it to Mr Turner at the Lady Courtney Museum. He might be able to make sense of it. I think they're open tomorrow, aren't they?'

Taff nodded, and Rolly farted, filling the Gabatinis' front room with a noxious fug.

'Oh dear, I am sorry. Perhaps I'd better get him home. Shall I take this with me? What shall I put it in?'

One of the grandchildren had been given a *South Park* poster for Christmas, and the tube it came in was sitting outside the back door, waiting for the bin men. Taff rolled up the vellum document, and slid it into the tube. They all agreed that it should be safe enough in there.

In the morning, Mrs Innes went to see Mr Turner at the museum, and she showed him Dawn's find.

'Absolutely fascinating!' said Mr Turner. 'I imagine that it was used to line the hatbox early in the eighteenth century, some time after the Great Fire of Pancester, when the Guildhall was damaged, and many of the city's papers were lost or destroyed. I agree with you, Mrs Innes. It certainly looks like a bill of some kind. But it's not really my period, you know. I'm afraid I can't read it any more than you can. But I could photocopy it, and fax it through to my friend in Cambridge, the one who did the new transcription of the Charter. He could tell us what it is straight away.' Mrs Innes agreed, and a copy was sent.

'It shouldn't take him long. He always stays in college for Christmas. I'll call you in a day or so.'

Four days after Christmas, the nuns, in consultation with the doctors, called a priest to Alex Whittaker's bedside.

'We're not Catholics, Father. At least, I don't think so,' said Terry.

'Well, no matter. It's nice for the sisters to have the comfort of it.' He set out his oil and water and lit some incense.

'Now then, Mr Whittaker. I'm just going to say a few prayers, and then I'm going to put a little of this oil on your forehead. We're asking God for forgiveness for all your sins, Mr Whittaker. If you could make a sign of some kind, that would be wonderful.'

The priest intoned his prayers, and touched a drop of the oil on to Alex's forehead. The old man turned in his sleep, and groaned. The bedclothes fell away, showing Alex in his shabby winceyette pyjamas, tubes and wires from his nose, his mouth, his arm, his prick. The priest smiled at Terry.

And then, as Terry and the priest watched, Alex moved his hand down his body, agonisingly slowly, and scratched long and hard at his testicles. And equally slowly, with the last of his fading strength, he raised his fingers to his nose, and sniffed. He smiled in satisfaction, and his hand fell back to his side.

'Well, now, that was a beautiful thing to see,' said the priest, packing away his kit.

'Was it?'

'Oh, yes. I've seen it time and again.'

'Oh. So does that mean he's going to be saved?'

'That's for God to say, not me. But I'm feeling upbeat.'

'Good.'

Later that evening, with Terry holding his hand, Alex died. Terry kissed his head, and tried to squeeze out a tear.

Whittaker came back to Pancester for New Year's Eve. He couldn't face sorting out the old man's flat just yet. He sat on the train, stunned and silent. The sensation that he was trying to suppress – of relief, of liberation – was surely not appropriate. He was not sure what he was supposed to feel, but this felt wrong, somehow. Gwyn and Sally told him how sorry they were when he arrived back at the flat, but Terry was not sure that he shared their regrets, not entirely.

He was interested to hear of Dawn's find. The travellers were throwing a huge party down on the Dole Acre site, and the committee and the stalwarts of the women's anti-car park camp were all invited. Whittaker, Sally and Gwyn, Taff and Dawn, Oliver and Penny, Dexter, Mrs Innes and Neil Winterburn, Steve and Sandra Medlicott, and Emma and Gemma all joined arms at midnight with the hippies and sang 'Auld Lang Syne'. After the singing, and its concomitant snogging, Ronnie fired up the Pink Bus's sound system. Ash and Whittaker stood by the fire, watching the dancers.

'What's your New Year's Resolution, Ash?' asked Whittaker.

'To eat more fruit. I'm bunged up like a bastard. What's yours?'

'To silence my father voice. My father's voice. To get in contact with my subconscious. Or something.'

Ash touched him on the arm, and passed the pipe. 'Good man.

You should try the mushrooms. They'll get you in touch with everybody's subconscious.'

'Maybe. I'll think about it.'

On New Year's Day, Whittaker walked with Sally and Gwyn to the Falls of Athon for a reviving pint in the Tickled Trout. It drizzled, which just suited their mood. Strange how New Year's Eve is always a riot, and New Year's Day an anticlimax. It's the drink, very likely.

The restaurant reopened the next day. In the afternoon, as Whittaker and Gwyneth were running over the stock figures, Mrs Innes came by with a piece of momentous news.

'I've just come back from seeing Dawn. I thought she should hear it first, since she found the thing.'

'Hear what?'

'About the parchment. The one she found in the hatbox. It is a bill. But you'll never guess what for.'

'Go on.'

'The Charter! It's a lawyer's bill, made out, just as I thought, to old Sir Kenelm.'

'Dear Lord. I bet it's astronomical, too,' said Whittaker. 'You should see what Brian Carless charges me. It's the one thing that's just as expensive here as in London. Poor old ghost.'

'Do you want to hear?'

'Oh, yes, sorry, Mrs I.'

'It's the bill for the drawing up of the Charter. Or should I say ... Charters?'

'Charters? Plural?' said Gwyn.

'Exactly. It shows quite clearly that two copies were made, one for the city, and one for the Courtney family! So all we have to do is find the Courtneys' copy, and then we can establish once and for all that the city's copy is a fake, and that they have no right at all to build their blessed car park!'

'Great! Oh, that's great. And where are the Courtney family papers?' asked Whittaker.

Mrs Innes pulled a face.

'We don't know. They could have been destroyed in the Great

Fire, when the old Courtney House burnt down. But we don't know that for sure. Somewhere out there, maybe lining another hatbox or something, there might be another Charter which would save the day.'

Whittaker sighed. 'Yes, and somewhere out there could be Letty's son, and even Letty herself. And we've not found them yet, either.'

'Never say die, dear. The Courtneys have always come through for Pancester. You'll see. We'll find one of 'em, that much I'm sure of!'

But Whittaker found it hard to share the old lady's optimism.

He went back to London for his father's funeral. He was the only mourner. He watched as the conveyor belt took the coffin through the curtains into the incinerator, and afterwards waited to collect the ashes, which were in a small oak box. He tried, and failed, to feel something. Terry put the box in his bag. When he got home to Pancester, he put it on top of his wardrobe.

Plough Monday, the first Monday after Twelfth Night, dawned clear and sunny. The pubs are always open all day, and Taff assembled his players at the Holly Bush for a last-minute briefing. His father, resplendent in Johnny Jack's hunting pink, was clearly agitated.

'You OK, Papa?' asked Taff.

'Yeah. Maybe. I don't know. Where's Dawn?'

'She's in the Guildhall, helping with the Feast.' Readers of Dadd will recall that the losers of Wally Oop prepare a Feast to be shared by all comers after the play. In practise, of course, this means that the wives of the losers prepare the Feast.

'I need to talk with her.'

'Well, you can after the Feast, Papa. OK, boys? Everything set? Here we go!'

The Pancester Plough Monday Mummers' Play is held on the Guildhall steps at ten in the morning. Inevitably, the Square is always thronged with visitors. Inevitably, the play starts with a blast from the Alarumist on the Ramstheng. The actors queue up to say their lines, all swept on to centre-stage by Old-Hind-Before. St George and the Bold Slasher fight. St George is killed, Molly Tinker calls for a Doctor, and the Doctor and Jack Finney go into their routine. They put St George under a sheet, and pretend to cut him open with a pair of shears. Then they pull a series of incongruous objects from under the sheet; a length of rubber hose, a cheese grater, all the time keeping up their patter. Let's enjoy a sample.

'You should get one of those hippies to cure him with a crystal, Doctor.'

'Them crystals couldn't cure a ham!'

'I see they've a new man at the 4i's, Doctor.'

'Aye. But they've still got the same old pies!'

'You should take St George down to that Temple on't Dole Acre, Doctor.'

'No, I don't want to look like a prick!'

Bit risqué, this one, and it drew a few disapproving looks, especially from Papa Nico, but it shows the standard of the material, I think. Let's not dwell on it. You can have too much of a good thing.

Well, eventually, the Doctor and Jack Finney pull back the sheet, St George rises from the dead, and kills Bold Slasher. The Doctor declines to bring Slasher back to life, and various minor characters, including Johnny Jack, come on and make gnomic statements. Old Papa Nico was still distracted, and forgot one of his lines, which was unfortunate since he only had four. The Mummers sing the Pancester Carol to the accompaniment of a concertina, they dance into the crowd, holding out hats to collect money, and with the ringing of the Feasting Bell at ten-thirty, the performance is over for another year. The helpers at the Feast bring out great steaming platters of roasted meat from the kitchen at the Guildhall, while the audience climb the steps to help themselves to a slice or two. Dawn was lending a hand with the serving, and she waved at Whittaker, Sally and Gwyn, who walked up the steps to say hello.

'What did you think, Terry? Weren't Taff and Frank funny this year?' said Dawn.

'Oh ... er ... yes. Very.'

'Mum! Perhaps Terry isn't feeling like laughing right now.'

'No, I did. They were very funny.'

'Couldn't cure a ham! I thought I'd wet me knickers. There he is, look! Taffy!'

Taff was helping his father up the steps. 'Papa wants a word, love.'

'And I want one with him. Fancy forgetting your lines. Here, I'll get you a chair, Papa Nico.' A chair was brought from inside the Guildhall, and his granddaughter helped him to sit.

'OK, Papa Nico?' asked Gwyneth. The old man nodded.

'There you are, love. Have a bit of pork. Now, what is it that ails thee?' said Dawn.

Papa Nico was flushed – whether from climbing the steps, or with embarrassment at his poor performance in the play, Whittaker couldn't tell. It turned out to be neither.

'Can I speak freely? I am among friends, yes?'

'Papa Nico, you are among a huge crowd of tourists eating slices of pork. But they can't hear you, so fire away,' said Dawn.

'I have found out what you wanted to know. Dolly Halton told me, last night in bed. I think she wanted to tell someone before she dies.' His breath was short; he was excited.

'She'll outlive the lot of us, will old Dolly,' said Taff.

'Did he say "in bed"?' whispered Gwyneth to Sally.

'What did she tell you, Papa Nico?' asked Dawn.

'Dolly tells me many things. But this thing, I never knew, and Dolly never told no one before! No one! Do you know what she told me?'

Everyone shook their heads and said, 'No, Papa Nico.'

'I tell you what Dolly told me. She told me she knows where we can find Letty's son. She told me who he is!' And he broke into a huge grin.

'What!'

'How does Dolly know?'

'Who is it?'

'Who is it?' repeated Nico. 'Who is it? Why, it's so obvious I could kick myself. Stupid we are for not seeing it before. Who is it? Think. Someone who has lived here all his life. It's obvious, that's who it is.'

'Yes, Papa Nico, but who is it?' said Sally.

'All his life, people joke about why the twins not look like one another. Now we know why they not look like one another. They not even brothers.'

'You mean . . .?'

'Yes, I mean. I mean it's Oliver Halton, of course. Poor silent Oliver. He is Letty's son.'

And Papa Nico stuffed a slice of pork into his mouth, and smiled at the open-mouthed company.

Inside Courtney House

It fell to Dawn to push Papa Nico back to St Homobonus' to hear Dolly's story.

'I think she will find it hard to talk, Dawn. She never told her husband, and she's never told the boys.'

'But she didn't swear you to secrecy or anything?'

'No, no. She wants me to tell you. She wants to talk to you. She wanted you all to know, you see, because of the car park. But she is very sad. It hurts to admit that Oliver is not really her son.'

'Oh, but he is. He always will be. Nothing can change that. But if she's really not his birth mother and Lady Lettice is, well, then yes, Papa Nico, it's important that we know that. A Courtney heir would mean that we could stop the car park. Well, if he wanted it stopped, and Oliver does.' They arrived at the hospital, and Dawn pushed Papa Nico to the door of Dolly's cell. He knocked on it with one of his sticks.

'Dolly?' he called softly. 'Cara? It is Nico. I have Dawn with me.'

Slowly the door opened, and Dolly Halton answered. Dawn had never seen her without make-up before. She had been crying.

'Come in,' she said. 'Will you be wanting a brew?'

Dawn manoeuvred Papa Nico into the little room, and parked him next to the bed. Then she said, 'I'll make it, Dolly. You've had an upset.'

'Oh, you are kind, Dawn. Thank you, dear.' Dolly sat down heavily in her armchair, and started to cry again. Dawn made the tea. Papa Nico held Dolly's hand as she sobbed.

'Now then, Dolly, what's this you've been telling Nico about Oliver?' said Dawn, sitting down on the edge of the bed.

Papa Nico handed Dolly his handkerchief, and she blew her nose.

'Thank you, Nico.' She sipped her tea.

'You want to tell Dawn what you told me?' asked Papa Nico.

Dolly nodded, wiped her eyes, took a big gulp of air and began.

'Oh, Dawn, I'd always meant to tell the boys, but I never felt brave enough. I never told their father, because I knew he'd be funny about it, but he's been dead five years, and I should have told the lads. And then when you told me Ursula Armistead's story, I knew I should tell you, but I just couldn't. Because, you see, if I told anyone, it should be the boys. But I just couldn't tell the boys. I don't know what . . . I mean, they'd be so . . . so . . .'

Tears started to roll down her cheeks again. Nico dabbed at her eyes with his handkerchief. Dolly gulped again.

'So I told Nico,' she said.

'Well, you've been very brave, I think. And now you've told Papa Nico, it should be easier to tell the boys.'

'Oh, Dawn, I can't tell the boys. I just can't. Nico said . . . he said you might tell them.'

'Oh, Dolly, I can't, really I can't. You'll have to be brave, Dolly, you will.'

'No, I can't. Please, Dawn. Please.' Tears were still coursing down Dolly's cheeks, and Papa Nico was giving Dawn his most beseeching look, which she could never resist. She sighed.

'Oh, all right, Dolly. I'll tell them. Stop crying now. Come on. Stop crying and tell me about the boys.'

Dolly smiled, and dried her eyes. 'I don't know if you know, Dawn, but the year before I had the lads, I had a little lass. Stillborn, she was. I had her at home, people did in them days. I was heartbroken, Dawn, I really was. And old Mrs Partridge, the midwife as attended me, she was very upset for me, you could tell. We became friends. Right old she were. She retired a bit after I had . . . Dexter, and went to live in Southport. But she were a good pal to me, old Mrs Partridge. Aye. So she used to come round for a cup of tea and a chat, and she were right pleased for me when I told her I'd fallen pregnant again. She'd come round more often after that, just to keep an eye on me, see that things were all right this time, you know. And she booked me into the Infirmary, just to make sure.

'Then a few weeks before I was due, she came and told me about this lass who were putting her baby up for adoption. Said she couldn't tell me who it was, but that if people ever found out she was pregnant, there'd be a right to-do. Said she didn't even want the adoption done through the normal channels, but wanted to give the baby away, secret like, to someone she knew would love it as her own. Said that me and her had the same due date. Then she asked me how I might like to have it, to have the poor baby whose mother couldn't keep him. Because I should have had two babies, Dawn, I should, and Mrs Partridge knew that. She said it'd have to be a secret, just between me and her. She made me promise, but I don't suppose it matters now. I didn't have to think, really, Dawn, I just knew that I should have two babies. So I said yes.

'Well, Mrs Partridge said we'd have to time it right, if it were going to work. It were Mrs Partridge who came up with the twins idea, and I just thought how lovely it would be to have two babies, and how they could help one another, and play together, and grow up together, you know. So that were that. I went into the hospital a few days early, I don't know how Mrs Partridge wangled it, but she did. And then we waited, best part of a week. Mrs Partridge kept telling me to hold on, but you can't, can you, Dawn, not when your time has come. So me waters broke, and I were right upset, but Mrs Partridge told me it was all right, they'd just started "up at the New House", they'd phoned through. So I could guess whose baby it was. Who else would have a baby in the New House, and folk had been saying that it was funny they hadn't seen Lady Letty back from school. I knew right off.

'Well, I had Dexter, and you know what that's like, Dawn. I had a time with him, you know, a bad time. And Mrs Partridge said we couldn't have a doctor in, or he'd know right off that I weren't having twins. But it were all right in the end, and there he was, all wrinkly in his cot, and I just loved him straight away, and

I forgot about the pain. And then in the night, Mrs Partridge came into the room with a little bundle, and she pulled the blanket away, and I saw little Oliver, the prettiest baby you ever saw. And I loved him straight away too. I fed him, and we put him into the cot with Dexter. And I had my two babies, Dawn. I had two babies.'

'How did Mrs Partridge know about it all?' asked Dawn.

'I don't know. They had a nurse in at the New House. Perhaps she were friends with Mrs Partridge. I don't know why I think that, but I just have an idea about it. And then again, her brother-in-law was old Lady Abigail's gardener. Perhaps it were Lady Abigail who told her what was happening.'

'What did your husband say?'

'Alan? He were amazed. We hadn't prepared for twins. I couldn't really tell him, could I, Dawn? I mean, they are twins astrologically, if you think about it, because they were born at the same moment. Nearly, anyway. So it wasn't like I were lying. But he was right pleased. And I loved my boys. I knew Oliver had to be Letty's, from not seeing her about for so long, you know, and them talking about the New House. And of course, he looks like her, doesn't he? A right bobby-dazzler was Lady Letty. I put two and two together, didn't I? I knew right off, I did, right off. I asked her, Mrs Partridge, and she put her fingers to her lips. But old Mrs Partridge, she'd said to me, she'd said that the mother wouldn't know where the baby had gone, that the nurse from the New House was handing her over to Mrs Partridge, and no questions asked. So it was only me and Mrs Partridge knew the truth, and Mrs Partridge went to live in Southport not long after, Dawn, like I told you. I think they must have dropped her a few bob, because it's not cheap, is Southport.'

'So on the birth certificates ...'

'Well, I registered them both as mine and Alan's, didn't I? And I brought them up the same, and I loved them both the same, just like Mrs Partridge knew I would. That's why I told everyone they were identical twins. They were identical, leastways to me. And no one ever guessed, did they?' She smiled weakly at Papa Nico and Dawn.

'Well, what now, Dolly? You really want me to tell your lads? This changes their whole lives. You can't want me to tell them, not really.'

Dolly sighed. 'Yes, Dawn love, I do. It hasn't been a lie, you know. They really are twins, to my eye. And I can't quite believe it isn't true, you know, that they really are both mine and Alan's. When I see them, I wouldn't know how to start.'

'You're sure?'

Dolly nodded.

Dawn rolled her eyes to heaven. 'I suppose I'd better give them a ring, then.'

'There's a telephone you can use in the refectory,' said Nico.

Dawn pushed Papa Nico into his cell next door, and helped him into his armchair.

'So that's that, eh, Dawn? You have your Courtney heir. Now everything is all right.'

'No, Papa Nico, it isn't, I'm afraid. You heard what Dolly said. She registered Oliver as her own. The only person who really knew about it was Mrs Partridge, and she's long dead. Even Dolly doesn't know for definite who the baby's natural mother was. No, it's a lead, a very good one, I admit that. Then, you see, so's the news about a copy of the Charter. But we can't prove either of them. We're just as stuck as ever.'

Dawn settled Nico in his chair, and walked across the quadrangle to the refectory, to arrange a meeting with the Halton twins later that evening.

'And you buggers are coming with me,' said Dawn to Terry and Taff when she got back to the kitchen of the 4i's, where they were waiting with Sally and Gwyn.

'Oh, God, no love, please no. He's my best friend. He wouldn't want me there,' said Taff.

'Why not? If he's your best friend?'

'Well, that's just it. You don't want your best friend around while you talk about your mam. We just don't do things like that.'

'Who's we?' asked Dawn.

'Men,' said Whittaker. 'Please don't make us go. We'll just try to change the subject, and start talking about steam engines, or stamp collecting, or Laikley's chances in the FA Trophy, so that we don't have to talk about the sort of stuff you all talk about. You'll be far happier on your own, Dawn.'

'Cuggles?' said Sally.

'Mmm?'

'You're going. '

'Oh, no, please . . .' whined Whittaker.

'And so are you, Paolo Gabatini. End of discussion.'

'B –'

'End.'

That evening Dawn rang the doorbell of Dexter's small house on Church Street, with Taff and Whittaker ploughing along woefully in her wake like captured galleons, their flags lowered in defeat. He ushered his guests into his small sitting room, where Oliver sat drinking beer. He smiled a welcome.

'Now, then, Dawn? What's all this about Mam?'

So Dawn told them. They smiled and nodded throughout, except when Dawn told them about Oliver actually being Letty's. Then they laughed. Taff and Whittaker sat with their hands under their thighs, staring at the floor.

'Well, you've taken it very well, I must say,' said Dawn.

Dexter laughed again. 'But we've always known that we aren't really brothers, well, we are, but not in the sense of having the same parents. I mean, I look like our dad, and Oliver looks like Rudolph Valentino in *The Sheikh of Araby*. Everything about us is different. We even have different blood types, which makes us very funny identical twins. I think we've always known, haven't we, Oliver?' Oliver nodded.

'But . . . you never said. I mean, you always went along with the twins thing,' said Dawn.

'Well, we didn't want to upset Mam. We always thought it was funny, didn't we?' Oliver smiled and nodded. 'I mean, fancy no one questioning us being identical twins. It just shows you, doesn't it, that folk'll believe anything.'

'But you didn't know about Letty?' asked Dawn.

'No. That's why we laughed. We seem to have been a bit dim ourselves, not connecting Ursula Armistead's story about Letty's baby with ours, and we should have seen it right away. But there you go, we know now, and we're off to see Mum now, and then Brian Carless first thing in the morning. Aren't we, Olly?'

Oliver nodded.

'Why Brian?' said Dawn.

'To put a claim in on the estate, of course. That'll make them think twice about declaring Letty dead. And while they faff about deciding what to do, we're going to apply to have Lady Abigail's body exhumed for DNA testing. And we think it best if Oliver takes a new name. Make the claim look more convincing. And, of course, we shall be claiming the baronetcy, too. Stand up, Sir Oliver Courtney!'

And Oliver stood up, smiling graciously, and raised a hand.

And Dawn and Taff and Whittaker stood up too.

'Erm . . .' said Taff. 'How do you fancy Laikley's chances Saturday, then? Sir Oliver?'

Oliver made a face, and the meeting was over. Taff and Dawn went home, Whittaker went back to his kitchen, and the Halton twins went to see their mother.

The following morning, Dawn caught Nico on his way back from church, and he told her that Dolly had been smiling all morning, and that he was very proud. 'They are good boys, and you are a good girl, Dawn. Too good for Mr Boom Boom Bang Bang. The boys, they came to see Dolly last night, and all is well. I thank you.'

In the afternoon, after the appointment at Carless Peddler Spoke, Dexter phoned Bill Brewer on the *Pancester Mail* to tell him the story, and it was the lead in the next morning's edition of the paper. Hundreds of Pancestrians filed through the shop to look at Oliver, who smiled and shook hands with everyone. He didn't feel compelled to speak.

Juliana had seldom seen Q so rattled.

'I am beginning to lose patience with these clowns,' he said, putting down the paper angrily.

'I've never known you to lose your patience before,' said Juliana.

'It's the principle of the thing. If we could have persuaded these peasants to accept the car park because it is a rational and forward-looking plan, no one would have been more pleased than me. But no, they talk of tradition, and history and snails and donkeys, and they import an army of unwashed hedonists, and throw every obstacle in your way. So we have been forced to employ sub-legal methods in defence of rationalism, against our will, of course.'

'Of course, Q.'

'And now this. Sir Oliver Courtney. Pancester is to be saved by an aristocrat. Do these people not realise that their time has gone, that this is the time when rational men, men who know what must be done, will take centre-stage? Even when the Secretary of State turns down their appeal, they will try to delay us with this childish hoax, when I have given you my word that you will have your car park. Well, enough. The time has come for me to act again.' He banged his fist on the breakfast table, and rattled the marmalade jar. Juliana was worried.

'Q, we'll be hearing from the Minister in a week or so. We know what he's going to say, and they don't. And the minute I get the authority, the police and the sheriff's men will be moving in straight away, same day, to evict the protesters from the Dole Acre. The plans are all drawn up. So don't worry. Even if that halfwit is Letty's bastard, they won't be able to stop us. So please, Q, don't take any risks. We've won.'

'So you say. But I have more weapons to deploy yet, if need be. I have not been idle. I will not be beaten by those ... those ... *Untermenschen*.'

'I love it when you speak German. Kiss me, Q.'

'Ach, there is no hope. Now even you are reduced to the level of the beasts.'

'No, Q, I'm sorry. I didn't mean it. It was a joke.'

'Hmm. Well, you are forgiven, for now. I will give you

something greater than my tongue slobbering in your mouth. I will give you . . . a car park!'

'Yes, Q, yes. A car park. I want a car park, I really do.'

'Well, then, a car park is what you shall have, my dear.'

The Committee Against the Car Park agreed unanimously that Sir Oliver Courtney should be invited to join their number. As Taff always said, Pancester was happier when there was a Courtney about the place. Oliver had very little to say, of course, so he was elected President of the group. Presidents, it was felt, should confine themselves to smiling and nodding and shaking hands.

Dolly was puzzled but pleased by her son's new-found status. 'Everyone's always ignored Oliver because he never talks, but now they all kowtow to him, and about time too. He always was a special little boy.'

Whittaker got a phone call from Penny Lester.

'Hello, darling. What can I do you for?'

'Terry, it's the strangest thing, but Oliver has asked me to marry him.'

'Good God.'

'I know. We've been seeing one another for a few months now, but I never imagined . . . well, I did, but . . . you know.'

'Why are you telling me?'

'Well, I just wanted to ask about this Courtney business.'

'Oh, yes?'

'Is it true? Or has the poor chap gone bonkers?'

'What's he told you?'

'Well, that he is the long-lost heir of the Courtney family, that he's a baronet, and that as soon as everything can be sorted out, he'll be as rich as Croesus.'

'That's about it.'

'So it's true then?'

'Oh, yes. As far as we know.'

'Well, I'm buggered.'

'So what are you going to do? Do you fancy being Lady Courtney?'

'It does have a ring, doesn't it? Lady Penelope.'

'Yus, m'lady,' said Whittaker through his nose.

'Oh, ha ha. Still . . . opening garden fêtes. Speech day at the Girls' High School. Hermès scarves. I could do much worse.'

'You certainly could. What are you going to tell him?'

'That, Mr Whittaker, is between Sir Oliver and me. How's your dad?'

The question came like a blow.

'He . . . he's dead, Pen. He died just after Christmas.' He found an unexpected catch in his voice.

'Oh, darling, I am so sorry.'

'That's OK. He was in a great deal of pain, you know. It wasn't what he would have regarded as life, not in the end.' Now tears were streaming down his face.

'Oh, Terry, I am so dreadfully sorry. You must be terribly upset.'

'Yes . . . I . . . I'd better go . . .'

'Oh, Terry.'

'It's not your fault. You didn't know.'

Terry put the phone down, and sank on to the sofa. Great racking sobs shook his body.

'Daddy,' he said. 'Oh, my daddy.' And all the years he'd never cried for his father, for his absence, for his indifference and cruelty, came crashing through Terry's defences. Tears poured from his eyes, rivers of snot ran down from his nose on to his lips.

And then, quite suddenly and without warning, he was so horny that he thought his balls would explode. He washed his face, walked into his bedroom, and saw the illustrated copy of the *Kama Sutra* that had been meant for his father. He flipped the pages, kneeling by the side of his bed. Position No. 23, 'Honey Bees Swarming', looked something else. He pulled out his old man, and tried to concentrate on the picture. But . . .

'Juliana!'

He mopped at the mess on the carpet with a tissue, and climbed into bed, where he fell gratefully into a heavy sleep.

*

Carless applied for authority to exhume Lady Abigail's body, and sent details of Oliver's claim to the Family Court, which was preparing to decide whether Lady Lettice should be declared dead. But Gwyneth, never one to stand on ceremony, was unimpressed by the fuss about Oliver.

'I mean, he still hasn't even got the website up and running. He's useless,' she ranted at Terry, one night after work, her fingers sticky with glue from the model Lancaster Bomber she was working on.

'He's a symbol,' said Whittaker, sucking blackcurrant pie-filling from a spoon.

'Of what?' asked Gwyneth.

'Um ... well, like the Queen. She's a symbol.'

'Yes, but of what?'

'The nation.'

'Well, even if she is, which she isn't, but even if she is, what is Oliver a symbol of?'

'The city? Pancester? Anti-car park opinion will focus on him.'

'Rubbish! You've all been treating this as if it were some kind of breakthrough, when it was Mum who found the real clue, in the hatbox. We should be looking for the other Charter, not trying to prove Oliver is a Courtney.'

'How do we do that? No one knows where the Courtney papers are kept.'

'Well, no one's checked the house, have they?'

'What, Courtney House?'

'No.'

'Well, no one seems to have a key. But if Oliver's claim goes through, then he'll be able to get into the house somehow and find out if the papers are there.'

'It'll be too late, Terry. Why has Juliana been so quiet? You don't think she's waiting patiently for the Secretary of State, do you? They're up to something, her and that worm Sandahl, and we should find out what and take them on.'

'So what should we do?'

'Look for the Charter. Inside Courtney House.'

'Break in, you mean?'

Gwyneth smiled. 'Well, kind of. When we were kids, me and my friend Andrew, we found a way in. It was our big secret. We only did it a couple of times, and we never went any further than the kitchen. We were too scared. But I reckon I could still find the way. What about it, Terry? Shall we go and poke about in the New House?'

'Yes,' said Sally, her eyes shining with excitement as she looked at Gwyn.

Whittaker listened for a moment, to see if he could hear his father's voice telling him not to be naughty, but it was absent, or at least faint to the point of imperceptibility. He smiled.

'Oh, why not, if you think you can do it without being spotted. It's an outside chance, though. Mr Turner thinks it most likely that most of the Courtney papers were destroyed in the fire.'

'Yeah, but long shots are fun. And we won't know if we don't look. We go in tomorrow night.'

'We?' said Whittaker.

'Me and Sally. Neither of us is on the committee. Then you can deny us if we get caught. Which we won't.'

The next evening was Gwyneth's night off, and she and Sally had laid their plans carefully. Sally's almost Blytonesque enthusiasm for the project had been growing all day.

'Torches, rope, screwdriver . . . what have you got in your bag?' said Gwyn.

'Ah. Well, you see, it's a wire coathanger and a sheet of newspaper. Then if we get nabbed, and locked in a room, say, we just slide this sheet of newspaper under the door, push the key out of the lock with the coathanger, and *voilà*, we are free! Assuming they leave the key in the lock, obviously.'

'Yes, *and* that there's no carpet to stop you getting the newspaper under the door. Villains have read Famous Five books, too, Sally. Anyway, what else have you got?'

'Flask of coffee, sandwiches,' replied Sally.

'It's not a picnic, Sal. Here we are, daring cat burglars, preparing to undertake the crime of the century, and you're thinking about light refreshments.'

'Do you really think it's a crime? I thought of it more as a prank.'

'Well . . . it is illegal really. It's breaking and entering. But we're not going to get caught, either by the police or by some hypothetical villain.'

'You really don't think we'll be caught?'

'We never were as kids. And the windows are all boarded up, so no one will be able to see our torches from the outside. We'll be fine. Ready?'

'Ready.'

'Then let's go.'

The streets of Pancester were dark and silent. Nothing moved except the flickering screens of ATMs outside the banks. The clock on top of City Hall struck one as the two women made their way through the city towards Courtney House.

The house was rebuilt by John Lucton in 1720, on the site of the medieval structure which was destroyed in the Great Fire of Pancester. For those who are interested in such matters, perhaps I should say that it is built of red brick in English bond, and that it is five bays long and three storeys high with a hipped roof. The main doorway has an apsed hood supported on two Tuscan Doric columns. Although the Friends' Meeting House is older, Courtney House, whilst sorely in need of attention, is still the finest brick-built building in a city constructed largely from stone.

Lady Abigail had spent a large sum of money having the roof repaired just before the war, and the house might have remained in a reasonable state of preservation had Lady Lettice stayed in residence. But in her absence hooligans had broken all the windows, which were now boarded and barred. The front door had been replaced by a steel security door, which was heavily chained and padlocked, as were the doors into the garden from the back of the house and the side tradesmen's entrance. No one was sure who had the keys, or who was responsible for the upkeep of the house. The city's case to have Lettice declared dead would take such anomalies into consideration.

Gwyneth didn't need doors. She led Sally into the churchyard of St Gilbert's, and they picked their way by torchlight through the darkened graves. A bat spun past, and Sally's heart started to thump. Courtney House backs on to the churchyard, and Gwyneth shone her torch on to the tombs which leant crookedly against the high brick wall of the garden.

'Sir Alun Overton, governor of the castle, and his wife, Cecille Overton, deceased 1712 in the Great Fire of Pancester, *The Lord maketh his ministers as a flame*; Bartram Tyler, late Alarumist of this parish, died 1620, *Blow the trumpets in Zion*, ah, here we are. Sir Alexander Honeyball, thrice Mayor of Pancester, died 1731, *A golden bell and a pomegranate*. Enigmatic, I always thought. The bell I understand, since he put the carillon in, but what's the pomegranate doing?'

'Perhaps whoever chose the epitaph couldn't find many references to bells in the Bible, so they just stuck this one down and hoped no one would ask about the pomegranate,' whispered Sally.

'Yes, perhaps. Still, here's where we get over the wall. A great man, Sir Alexander, I'm sure, but vainglorious. His tomb is at least half a metre higher than the others. Here we go; I'll give you a leg-up. That's it. Take the rope and my torch. Good . . . hup. There. Now this is where it gets a bit scary. You give me a leg-up, and I can grab the top of the wall, and sit up there. Then you hand me the stuff, then I pull you up. OK?'

'It's exciting!'

'Shush. Are you ready?'

'Yes!'

'Come on then . . . hup . . . that's it . . . got it.' Gwyneth pulled herself on to the wall, and sat astride the top.

'Pass us the stuff . . . well done.' Gwyneth kept her torch, and dropped the rest into the garden behind her. There was a faint tinkling as the bag hit the ground.

'I hope that's not my flask,' said Sally.

'Oh, you didn't really bring a flask, did you?'

'Course I did. I told you. Now I'll have coffee all over my sheet of newspaper.'

'Well, I'm sorry. I thought you were joking. Give me your

hand . . . come on, baby. Sally, come on . . . pull!' Sally scrabbled up the wall, and sat next to Gwyn.

'What next?' said breathless Sally.

'We jump down.'

'Whaat?'

'It's fine. You hang yourself over the edge, and then let go. There's a slight rise here, so it's only a couple of feet drop the other side. Like this.' Gwyneth put her leg over the wall, held on to the parapet, and lowered herself down towards the garden.

'And then let go . . . oumph. Come on. It's safe.' Sally followed suit, felt her fingers slipping on the wall, let go, and dropped easily into the garden.

'Where's my torch? Oh, thanks . . . oh, it *was* my flask, look.'

'Shush, will you? Famous cat burglars don't spend their time moaning about broken flasks, do they? Come on.'

Sally picked up her bag, shivering with cold and excitement as she followed Gwyneth through the abandoned garden. Thickets of brambles still bear thorns, even in winter, and the bare branches of overgrown shrubs loomed out of the darkness like the grasping hands of scarecrows.

'It's much more overgrown than it used to be. Ouch! Stupid twigs! It's this way, I think.'

Gwyn and Sally pushed their way through one final tangle of bushes, and the back of Courtney House stood above them, its boarded-up windows staring blindly towards the church.

'It's round the side,' whispered Gwyn.

'What is?'

'The way in. This way . . .'

Sally followed her friend around the corner of the old house, into an alleyway formed by the wall of the house and the wall surrounding the garden. It smelt of damp and rats. A drip from a leaking gutter sounded loudly in the confined space.

'Oh, I don't know if I like this, Gwyn.'

Gwyneth was shining her torch on the ground.

'We're doing fine . . . here we are.' Gwyn's torch shone on an elaborately cast manhole cover two feet or so in diameter. 'Look. It's rather lovely, isn't it? Courtney Iron Works, 1720.'

'What is it?'

'It's the coal hole. There's a boarded-up gate into the street at the end there, look. They brought the coal through there, and poured it down here. Gimme the screwdriver, and I'll lift it up.'

'We're not going down there, are we?'

'It's the only way me and Andrew found in.'

'But we won't fit, will we?'

'I don't know. We can but try . . . there.' The cover lifted, and Sally shone her torch into the black hole.

'I can't, Gwyn, I really can't.'

'It's cool. Look, I tie one end of the rope around this old gutter and drop the other down the hole, so we can't fall. It takes us into the coal cellar, which is linked to the kitchens.'

'I can't.'

'Well, you stay here and keep look-out then.'

'Oh.' Sally thought again of her Enid Blyton books, and all the times the girls got left behind while the boys climbed down into mysterious smugglers' caverns and secret passages. And she didn't like the alley at all.

'Oh, all right. I'll do it. If I can go first. I don't want to be left here on my own.'

'Grab the rope, and hold on. It's tight, but you'll be fine. You're small-boned.'

'Flatterer,' said Sally as she swung her legs into the opening. 'Well, here goes . . .'

She held her breath, and scraped and bumped her way down the coal hole. Her heart was beating faster and faster. She didn't like small spaces. Her breath came in gasps. Her hands were sore and slipping on the rope. And just when she thought she must scream, her feet touched the ground. She called up, 'I'm down,' and pulled her torch from the pocket of her jacket. She watched Gwyn's feet kicking into view, watched Gwyn's coal-dusted face grinning as they stood together. Sally hugged Gwyn with a laugh.

'So here we are,' said Gwyn. 'Inside Courtney House.'

'Where next?'

'Through there. It takes us into the scullery and the kitchen.'

'And where then?'

'Up the stairs and into the main house, I suppose. We never had the nerve to go any further than this before.'

'Why not? After all that to get in?'

'Well, it's haunted, isn't it?'

'Is it? You didn't tell me.'

'This is Pancester, Sally. Everywhere's haunted. Come on.'

They left the coal hole, and passed through the scullery into the kitchen. The two women shone their torches around.

'Weird, isn't it?' said Gwyn.

'It's like a museum,' said Sally as she shone her torch around, and she had a point. The room was dominated by a huge range hung about with spits and skillets, spindles and screens. A large table in the centre of the room was covered in bottles and jars, blackened with dust and decay. The only concession to modernity was an old electric cooker wired in the cowboy style into a thirteen-amp plug.

'Terry would love this, wouldn't he?' said Sally.

'Yes. Don't think he could squeeze down the hole, though, do you?'

'Unless Juliana told him to.'

'Look, there are the stairs.'

'And there, look, just by them, one of those bell boards that told the servants where they were required. Bedrooms, drawing room, morning room ... and library! That's where we should look first.'

'Well, come on then. Let's see if there's anything left of it.'

Gwyneth led the way up the kitchen stairs, and pushed open the green baize door that led into the hall. Their torches showed a sad sight. Mildew colonised the walls, which dripped with condensation. Gouts of dust kicked up by their feet lifted into the air as they walked from room to room. In each they found a similar story of devastation. The pictures ran with damp. The furniture smelled of rot, and much of it had been broken up. Courtney House was like Miss Havisham's dining room after a trashing by sociopathic slugs, their slime trails sparkling on what remained of the carpets.

'What's through here?' whispered Sally, pointing her torch at a door at the end of the hallway.

'Let's see.' Gwyn pulled at the handle, and entered the room.

'Pay dirt,' said Gwyn triumphantly. 'The library. Let's see what they've got.' Their torches showed a large room lined with leather-bound volumes, smelling like Heavily Foxed in the old days of no sales.

A thump which seemed to come from the floor above sounded through the darkened room. 'What's that?' said Sally.

'Shush. Let's listen.' They stood together silently, holding hands now.

'Nothing,' breathed Gwyn after a while. 'Just some falling plaster, probably. Or a rat.'

'Come on, Gwyn,' said Sally, her voice coming in gasps. 'Let's look at these books and then get out of here. You take that side, I'll start over here ...'

'OK ... oh. These aren't books at all. They're just built into the wall, to look like books.'

'Over here too. Not a book in the place.'

'So what do we do now?'

'Gwyn! I bet some of these dummy books slide out, or something, revealing the entrance to a secret passage, or a priest hole. In the books, they always tap the walls, to see if they sound hollow. Come on!'

At the same moment, both women heard a step behind them, and spun on their heels. Standing in the doorway, a torch in one hand and a pistol in the other, stood Dr Q Sandahl. He smiled at them.

'So. You have not found what you were looking for?' he said. 'What was it, I wonder? Some pathetic scrap of paper which would prove the little bookseller to be a Courtney? You have taken to believing your own deceits, clearly.'

'How did you get in?' asked Gwyn.

'The same way as you. Look, here is your rope. I am an excellent climber, and I did not need it, so I thought I would do you the service of returning it to you. My office is in the castle tower, you know, from where I have a most illuminating view of the churchyard and the back of Courtney House. I saw you both at once. I found it highly enterprising of you to break in in this way, and thought that I would come and have a word. I have a professional interest in the criminal mind, of course. Empty your bag, if you would, Miss Gould.'

'No way. Get lost,' said Sally.

'Ah ha ha, very spunky, Miss Gould. But perhaps you are overlooking this fine fellow?' He lifted his gun. 'He really insists that you do as you are told. The bag, please. On the floor. Thank you. Now, if you would empty it? What do we have? A broken Thermos flask? I will never understand the English. A sodden sheet of newspaper? A wire coathanger? And a Tupperware box. If you would open that for me.' Sally complied, and an overpowering and unearthly stench filled the room.

'Egg sandwiches?' said Gwyneth. 'You made egg sandwiches?'

'I like egg sandwiches.'

'Is that all?' said Q. 'If you would tip your bag upside down? Thank you. Well, at least I haven't caught you with any stolen property. That will count in your favour, if I decide to call the police.'

'You wouldn't dare,' said Gwyneth. 'That piece would get you banged up, or didn't you know handguns were illegal?'

'You are right of course, Miss Gabatini. I'm sure we can come up with something more imaginative than the police. Let's see. Ah, yes. If you would be kind enough to fetch those chairs? That's it. A matching pair, I should say, Sheraton. A shame that they are in such bad condition. And put them back to back? Now, sit in them. Sit!' He gestured at them with the gun.

Sally and Gwyneth did as they were told.

'What else can we do, Sal? He has the gun,' reasoned Gwyn.

Sandahl wound the rope around the two chairs, which bit into the arms of the two helpless women. He tied an expert knot.

'There. And now, since you are so fond of egg sandwiches . . .' Sure that the women were securely tied, he put down his gun. He took the sandwiches from the Tupperware box, and stuffed two by force into Sally's mouth.

'If you hurt her ...' growled Gwyneth.

'Why should I wish to hurt your friend, Miss Gabatini? Whereas you ...' Suddenly, unexpectedly, he slapped Gwyneth around the mouth. Blood trickled out from her lip.

'You see what happens if you hurt my friends? You hit Juliana, I hit you. And now ... your sandwiches. I do hope you like egg too ...'

But before he could force the sandwiches into Gwyneth's mouth, another figure appeared in the darkened room, as if from nowhere, as if from the walls, and before Q had time to react and to pick up his gun, the newcomer biffed him over the back of his head with the flat of a large broadsword. Q dropped the sandwiches, sank to his knees, and keeled over on his side, unconscious.

'Have at thee, varlet,' said the newcomer. It was Edmund, the Pancester tramp. He smiled at Gwyneth, and started to eat one of the discarded sandwiches.

'Tasty,' he said.

Wally Oop

'Yes, Edmund, if it's not too much trouble, when you've finished your sandwich, do you think you could possibly see your way clear to untying us?'

'Oh, of course, Miss Gwyneth. Sorry. Here we go . . . this is a good knot . . . hang on, let me take those sandwiches out of your mouth, Miss Sally . . . there you are.'

Sally was red-faced and choking. She spat out the rest of the sandwich.

'Thanks, Edmund. You were wonderful,' she said.

'Only doin' may duty, ma'am,' said Edmund. 'Hold still while I get this knot . . .' Sally looked down and watched Edmund's strong fingers, blackened with filth, as they struggled with the rope.

'That's got it. There.'

Edmund unwound the rope from around Sally and Gwyneth, and they stood up from the library chairs rubbing their arms. Sally hugged Edmund, and almost wished she hadn't, smelling as he did of regurgitated thousand-year-old cabbage water.

'How did *you* get in, Edmund?' asked Gwyneth.

Edmund smirked.

'Same way I always do. Through the side window. The board is loose. Has been for years.'

'You mean . . . *this* is your drum? Courtney House?'

Edmund nodded.

'Well, I needn't have worried about you. I thought you were

under a bridge or something, but all the time you were in a Grade One listed building. A bit damp, though, isn't it?'

'I have my own darling little room upthtairth,' lisped Edmund. 'I'm comfy ath can be with my dollieth and my teddieth.'

Sandahl groaned and stirred.

'What are we going to do about him?' said Sally.

Gwyn pondered for a moment. 'Call my dad, I think. He'll know what to do. Where's my mobile?'

Taff was still awake, working through his VAT returns.

'Hello, sweetheart. What can I do for you?'

'Dad, we're up shit creek. We need you. Sally'll come and pick you up in the car.'

She raised a questioning eyebrow at Sally, who nodded her head.

'What is it, love?'

'She'll tell you in a minute.'

Sally shot off to get Taff in Terry's Subaru. Gwyneth sat with Edmund in the library; when Sandahl stirred again, Edmund gave him another whack with the sword, which quietened him down.

'What are we going to do with the gun, Edmund?'

'Don't like guns, I don't.'

'No, me neither. I guess we'd better not touch it. It's covered in his dabs. I suppose . . . I suppose we could just leave it here.'

Edmund shook his head.

'Well, perhaps Dad will think of something. I wish they'd hurry up. What's keeping them?'

They heard Sally returning with a grim-looking Taff. Gwyn hurried to meet them.

'Where is the fucker?' he said. 'I'm going to fucking pitch him.'

'Sorry we've been so long. Your dad said he needed something from the garage,' whispered Sally.

Taff's Italian hot blood and adopted Welsh passion catalysed into fuming anger when he saw the blood on Gwyneth's mouth. He came into the library black-faced with rage. Seeing the unconscious figure of Sandahl on the floor, he started to kick him savagely, in the stomach, in the balls, in the head, until Gwyneth and Sally held him back. He was breathing heavily, and tears ran down his cheeks.

'And if you ever touch my fucking daughter again . . .' he growled.

'Dad, Dad, leave it.'

'Are you all right, my love? Are you OK?'

'I'm fine. But what are we going to do with him? And with the gun? Should we call the police?'

'No way, love. I'm gonna pitch him. Leave the gun here for now. No one's touched it but him, have they? Good. Help me get him into the car.'

Edmund helped Gwyn and Taff drag Sandahl through Courtney House to the window that the old tramp used as his entrance. Broken glass still jagged from the frame, and it cut Sandahl's hand as they pushed him through. He groaned as he landed on the ground.

'Right. Let's get him to the car. Sally, you make sure no one's watching.'

They bundled Sandahl on to the back seat, and Taff folded himself in beside him. 'Come on. Sally, you drive,' he said. 'Gwyn, you sit next to her and navigate. Edmund, you get back inside and hide the gun. Use a clean handkerchief to handle it.'

Edmund looked outraged.

'Well, something clean. A piece of newspaper, anything. Come on, Sal, let's go.'

Edmund watched the car pull out of Guildhall Square, and climbed back into the house.

'Where are we going, Dad?' said Gwyn as the car drove through the streets of Pancester.

'The old pontoon bridge. Above the Falls. For a pitching.'

Sally was white and shaking as she drove out into the countryside.

'Down here,' whispered Gwyn. They turned into a narrow lane.

'Stop here,' said Taff. Sally pulled off the road next to an old army bridge, its girders casting a lattice of shadows on the dark river water by the light of the moon. They pulled Sandahl from the car, and Taff pushed him into the ditch, where he lay, sprawled awkwardly.

Taff smiled at Gwyn and Sally. 'There now. We should take off his clothes, reely, but it's the middle of winter, and we don't want the fucker dying of hypothermia, do we? Where's that varnish I got from the garage?'

'What varnish? What are you doing?' said Sally.

'It's another old Pancester tradition. Pitching. In the old days they used to get undesirables and cover them in hot pitch and feathers,' said Gwyn.

'Oh, Taff, you can't,' said Sally.

'I know. I haven't got any pitch or feathers. But I have got this.' He dug out a five-litre can of Ronseal from the boot of the car, unscrewed it, and emptied it over Sandahl's head, his hair, his face and over his clothes. The brown goo coalesced around Sandahl's nose and mouth, covered his eyes. Taff spat into his face.

'There,' he said. 'It does exactly what it says on the tin.'

Gwyneth was still laughing hysterically when she and Sally got back to the flat after dropping Taff off at home.

Whittaker was horrified when Sally and Gwyneth told him the story in the morning, but as soon as he established that they were OK, he began to look on the bright side.

'Kicked him in the balls, you say? Juliana is going to be needing a new boyfriend, isn't she, don't you think? And she'll be much nicer now Sandahl is out of the picture. He'll never show his face here again. That's the point of pitching, isn't it? To drive them away? It was always him goading her on, I bet. And when we get the car park stopped, she'll see that I was right all along, and the veil will lift from her eyes, and she'll be like she was before the Plummeting, and she'll love me again.'

'It puzzles me,' said Gwyneth to Sally, 'how someone like Terry can be as talented, as amusing, as kind-hearted, as successful as he is, and still be a gibbering basket-case when it comes to women.'

'He's a man, isn't he?'

'Yes, I admit that. But he is the worst example I've ever known. Most men faced with attempted murder take the hint, and leave it at that. But not Terry, oh no. He persists in his deluded infatuation. Psychiatrists could write papers about him.'

'Er ... I am still here, you know.'

'Oh, are you? I thought they'd have taken you off to the funny farm by now.'

'Oh, ye of little faith. Juliana shall be mine. The Secretary of State will be granting our appeal any day. And then, it's a one-way ticket to lurve city for me and Juliana. You'll see.'

It will be noted that Whittaker was owning up again to the fact that his feelings for Juliana had not abated simply because she had hospitalised him. It was the fact that he had burnt the box containing his virtual porno lover that gave him new hope. Whittaker was convinced that as long as he stayed away from Zahid's, he would be rewarded by a chance at the real thing. The burning of the box, as a sacrifice to the Gods of Love, meant that Juliana was now even more likely to fall into his arms than before. After all, the universe is a strange place, and love its most remarkable and inexplicable phenomenon. Perhaps superstition makes as much sense as anything else.

Sahdahl's first reaction when he awoke in the icy chill of dawn was that he had gone blind. His head felt as though it had been split in two, his balls as though they were located halfway between his kidneys, and his side as though he had been crushed by a bulldozer; none of it mattered compared to his blindness. His breath came in short gasps as he groped his hand on to his face. The varnish was still tacky, and Sandahl realised that his eyelids were glued shut. He felt water in the ditch where he lay, crackled with cat ice, and he spooned it on to his face and rubbed at his right eye. He felt the varnish dilute, and wash away, and with a painful effort, he peeled his eyelid open. He saw where he was, by the pontoon bridge, a little above the Tickled Trout, and tried to stand. His side was agonising; he pushed his fingers into his ribcage, and felt a worrying give from one of the bones. He couldn't stand fully upright, he was in too much pain, and could only get himself up into a kneeling position. His body was shot through with agonising trembling which he couldn't control, caused by the bitter cold. He started to crawl towards the pub.

He hammered on the door until a very aggrieved-looking landlord appeared at the door in his bathrobe.

'Who is it?'

'Help. I've been attacked. Please call me an ambulance.'

The landlord looked at Sandahl and grinned. 'You've been pitched, my friend. We don't help them as 'ave been pitched here.'

'Please. I can't make it into the city. Please will you call me an ambulance?'

The landlord sighed. 'All right, I'll call you an ambulance. But you can wait there till it comes.'

'Please don't leave me here. The cold is killing me. Please let me wait inside.'

'I told you. We don't help them as 'ave been pitched. I don't know what you've done, but I bet you deserved it. I'll call you an ambulance, but you can't come in my bar.'

The landlord slammed the door, and Sandahl sat shivering in the doorway for twenty minutes, until the ambulance came bumping slowly down the track to pick him up.

Later in the morning, Sandahl phoned Juliana from his hospital bed and told her something of what had happened.

'But, Q, this is terrible. You must call the police at once.'

'My dear, that will not be necessary. Or expedient. But if you could call Mrs Wiseman in my office and ask her to visit me at once. I need to speak to her urgently.'

'I'm coming to see you.'

'After Mrs Wiseman has called. I will get her to phone you and tell you when it is convenient.'

'But Q . . .'

The line clicked dead.

Juliana made the call, and sat in her office, biting her lower lip. Whoever or whatever it was that had done this to Q, she was going to find out, and she was going to hurt them bad, if she could. And when the day finally came that the Secretary of State turned down the anti-car park campaign's appeal, she was going to go in so hard that not one filthy disgusting hippy was going to get away from the Dole Acre with their filthy disgusting vans. She was going to destroy them, smash them, burn the camp to the ground. And then she was going to build the loveliest, sexiest, most innovative visitors' car park the world had ever seen. And the name of Juliana Blezzard would be famous throughout the length and breadth of the heritage industry.

After Mrs Wiseman called, she hurried to the Infirmary. Q's hair had been shaved off. His face was covered in bandages. Another bandage was strapped around his broken rib. A cage had been placed under the bedclothes so that the heavy bedclothes did not rest on his bruised testicles.

'My darling,' she said, reaching for his hand. Q smiled.

'Hello, my dearest,' he said.

'Who did this to you? Who shaved off your lovely hair? I'll kill them.'

'My dear girl, I am so glad to see you. I love you very much, you know.'

'And I love you. But tell me what happened.'

Sandahl told as much of the story as he could remember; of his attempted abduction of Sally and Gwyn, of the blow to his head by an unknown assailant, of waking up in the ditch, blind and battered and half-dead with cold.

'Those dykey bitches? What were they doing in Courtney House? I'll bet Whittaker is something to do with it. I'm going to kill them all.'

Q shook his head. 'No, my dear, you are not. You are going to continue to turn this little corner of the Dark Ages into one of the most successful visitor attractions in the north. Nothing will destroy it more effectively. No. Killing, that's my job.' He smiled. 'And dear, do remember that Mrs Wiseman is one of the most efficient secretaries I've ever had.'

Customers in the 4i's that evening heard the scream of fire trucks out on the ring road, receding into the distance. In the morning, Pancestrians were relieved to read in the *Mail* that no one had been injured in the fire at the Tickled Trout.

There was lots to talk about for the good people of Pancester as January passed, apart from the unexplained fire. The Secretary of State still had to make his pronouncement concerning the car park. Which way would he jump? Did you see in the *Mail* that *Time Gang* were coming to do a dig on the Dole Acre? When are those blessed hippies going to go? And the Wally is coming, the Wally is coming. Wally Oop, the violent Candlemas street-football game that sets the hearts of Pancestrians all a-flutter, was only a few weeks distant. None of this mattered to Sir Oliver Courtney or Taffy Gabatini, not even Wally Oop, which usually filled their heads at this time of year. They had other concerns.

The engagement was announced in the *Mail* between Sir Oliver Halton Courtney, of Courtney House and the Fox Hole, Pancester, and Penelope Pauline Lester, eldest daughter of Mr and Mrs Walter Lester, 27 Oak Drive Way, Purley. Oliver was at once ecstatic and nervous.

His ecstasy came from Penny's acceptance of his proposal, of course. But Sir Oliver was nervous that his application to have the body of his grandmother exhumed would be allowed. And what then? What if the DNA tests showed he wasn't a Courtney? He would die of embarrassment. And what would Penny think? Would she call off the engagement? And what if he *was* a Courtney? That might be almost as bad. Would he be expected to make speeches? He enjoyed the handshaking and smiling, somewhat to his own surprise, but nothing would make him want to give speeches. But as a Courtney, he would be expected to open things and attend things, *noblesse oblige* and all that. Worry made him lose concentration, and the anti-car park website seemed further away than ever.

Taffy, however, was in a state of euphoria. Every day passed in a dreamlike state of wonder. Dawn couldn't do anything with him. His head had been turned by the fact that on 15 January, See For Miles Records had released a compilation CD entitled *Caveman Twang: Thirty-Two English Rock Instrumental Gems,*

1956 to 1963 – and there, at track twenty-six, was The Knight-watchmen's only single, an instrumental version of Cliff's first solo hit, 'Move It', issued unsuccessfully on the Pye label in 1962. He liked to play it over and over again, and had ordered fifty copies of the CD for the shop.

'A brilliant idea, Terry, wasn't it?' ranted Taff one morning over coffee in the Fox Hole, the track playing for the umpteenth time that morning in the background. Dawn had come in to see what Taff wanted for tea, and her smile of greeting for Whittaker looked suspiciously like gritted teeth as she sat through the song again. 'Us doing Shadows numbers, you see, but they hadn't done a version of "Move It", and Pye saw a gap in the market, so we did it, didn't we? We had a great guitarist in them days, George "Hank" Riley, great he was, listen to him, "Da-nang nanga nanga dang-a nanga wanga dang-a!"'

'It wasn't a hit at the time?'

'No. It was like they said at Decca, there just wasn't any call for guitar bands in 1962.'

'Yes, but they said that to Brian Epstein, didn't they? About The Beatles?'

'Bloody Beatles. Ruined rock and roll in this country, they did. Ah, but you see, our day is coming again. "Gems" they call us here. And look at the comprehensive sleevenotes! Look! And there's a photo and everything. I really think this time round The Knightwatchmen are going to be huge, Terry, I really do. I've been teaching the lads "Move It". They're coming on, they really are, and they'd be better yet if only they'd stop listening to gangsta rap or whatever they call it and start listening to some real music. Funny to think, none of them were even born when Cliff sang "Devil Woman", isn't it? Hey! Perhaps I should send Cliff a copy of the CD?'

'Neil says the producer of *Time Gang* is coming up this week. And I hear the Clanghandlers are meeting down on the Tinderbox for a tactical discussion tomorrow night.'

'Yeah, yeah. Da-nang nanga nanga dang-a nanga wanga dang-a!'

'He'll be over it in a week or two, Terry. By the time the Wally comes his belly will be full of fire,' said Dawn.

Gwyn accompanied Whittaker to the session at the Tinderbox, home of Pancester FC, and traditional training ground of the Clanghandlers since 1902. The Tinderbox is so called because it was the site of the burning of the Holy English Martyrs, after whom the cathedral was named. The Ringlers got together at the Gallowtrees, now home to Pancester Cricket Club, but previously the site of the hanging of the Protestant martyrs.

'I didn't know women took part, Gwyn. I thought they just watched,' said Whittaker, when she announced her intention to go with him to the training session.

'Up until this year, Terry, that has been true. But this year, I shall be the first woman to take part. People will moan. But I'd like to see them stop me. There are no rules in the Wally. Women aren't barred. It's just that no one's ever done it before.'

'Er . . . when you say no rules . . . I mean . . . there must be some.'

'Oh, no. Not a one.'

'So, um, it's *very* rough, then?'

Gwyneth grinned. 'You could say that, yes.'

'Oh. And I *have* to take part, do I?'

'No. You don't *have* to. You could be shamed for ever, if you prefer. Ostracised. Mocked. Hounded out of Pancester.'

'Oh. Right. Well . . . I'm, er, looking forward to it, then.'

There is no real organisation of either side in the Wally, but every year, one or two senior players take it upon themselves to call a meeting, where various stratagems and ruses are discussed, only to be subsequently ignored in the day-long, thousands-strong mêlée that is Wally Oop. The real point of these pre-Wally meetings is to get mongered in the pub afterwards. This year, Taff had secured the services of the hippies for the Clanghandlers some months previously.

'They're big buggers, lots of 'em, and hard as nails. And we can use all the help we can find.'

There were at least a couple of hundred Clanghandlers milling around the pitch at the Tinderbox. Ash, Ronnie of the Pink Bus and Phil the Painter sought out Whittaker and Gwyn through the crowd.

'I'm still not quite sure what we have to do,' said Ronnie of the Pink Bus.

'Well, it's quite simple. The mayor throws up the Wally at seven in the morning, and the game ends when one or the other side scores a goal, usually well after midnight,' said Gwyn.

'Yeah, but what is the Wally? And how do you score a goal?' asked Ronnie of the Pink Bus.

'Haven't you read your Dadd?' said Ash, whom Whittaker felt was in danger of going native and staying on in Pancester even after the decision about the car park. 'The Wally is a roll of leather tied with waxed cord. And the Ringlers score a goal if they get the Wally down to the door of the Holly Bush, while we score if we can get it up to the church porch.'

'And that's why the Ringlers almost always win,' said Gwyn. 'Although the porch is bigger than the door of the Holly Bush, they always manage to push us down, while we have to push them up. Well, this year, it's going to be different.'

'Is it?' said Terry.

'Of course. This year, they've got us.'

'It's ironic when you think about it,' said Phil the Painter, leaning on his stick.

'What is, Phil?' said Terry.

'Well, me being one of the tiny handful of travellers with a genuine interest in rugby, and also being the only one of the crew who can't play in the Wally.' He tapped his bad leg thoughtfully.

'Did you play rugby, Phil?' asked Gwyneth.

'Yeah, man. I was good. I played for Taunton until 1968.'

'What, until you got your injury?'

'No, man. Until I took acid. I never played again after that. Couldn't see the point of it any more. But I'd like to do the Wally.'

'You could give us some tips, Philip,' said Ash.

'If you get the chance, bite the fuckers' ears. Never fails, man.'

'Yeah, cheers, Phil,' said Whittaker. 'We'll remember that.'

*

The following week, the producer of *Time Gang* and two of his researchers came to see the site for themselves. Neil Winterburn looked rather lovely in an old Fair Isle sweater, his tight blue jeans tucked into wellingtons, his unruly golden hair rumpled in the breeze. He looked every inch the television archaeologist, and the producer liked him at once. Emma and Gemma had taken the precaution of removing their bras and wearing skimpy vests, February or no, and parading up and down with wheelbarrows in front of the male researcher, so they were in too. Even Tony the Tunneller, as head honcho of the hippy digging party, had made a special effort, and had smeared his face with extra mud. He and his crew would be perfect for a bit of local colour.

'Let's have a look at your geofizz, Neil,' said the producer.

'Sure. We only had a day or so. We'll need some more. But here's what we've got ...'

The producer blanched a little as he saw the outline of the Temple of Priapus. 'That would give you something to think about in the morning, Neil,' he said.

'It makes the Cerne Abbas Giant look like a speed freak getting out of the swimming pool, doesn't it?'

'Certainly does. Well, so what do you have in mind? I know you've told my researchers, but tell me again.'

'Well, interpretation, of course. When was it built, and so on. But in terms of excavation, we'd like to give the shaft a good going over, and then get stuck in on the bell-end. I'm sure we can lick it in the time available. Lick it?' he appealed to the researchers, who smiled politely.

Winterburn took the producer and his researchers to the 4i's for dinner.

'Mmm, this is good,' said the producer, with a mouth full of Candlemas salad. 'Isn't it the guy who used to cook in Rococo? Super. Look, Neil, yeah, smashing, everything looks go. We like you, we like the Temple, we like the hippies ...'

'We like Emma and Gemma,' said the male researcher brightly.

'Especially their nipples. First-rate on the telly. At least we won't mind working in the cold, eh? Oh, another thing. I've contacted the old duck with the snails – Professor Daggers, isn't it? You never quite know what you're going to find on these occasions, so it's as well to have a couple of experts on tap in case we need to fill in a bit of time. He's so old, he probably remembers when the temple was still standing. So, we'll be arriving on thirty-one Jan, to start shooting on Feb one. It's three days' shooting, so that will be Fri, Sat and Sun, pack up and bugger off home on the Mon. Hope that suits? We've booked into the Pancester Riverside, so it had better.'

'No, that's great. No . . . hang on . . . it's the Wally.'

'What is?'

'February the second. Candlemas. The street football game. All able-bodied men are expected to take part, even visitors. Fascinating medieval survival, actually. Have you read Dadd on Pancester? You should. None of the hippies will be available on site, as they'll all be scrapping in the town. Me too, actually. You just get sucked in.'

'Oh. Can't we get them to hold it a week later, or something?'

'Er . . . no. No. It's been held at Candlemas for six hundred years, at least.'

'Well, I tell you what. Our people will keep digging, but we'll give 'em Timmy to play in the game, and film him. Even more local colour. The Tourist Office will love us.'

'Ah. I'm not sure they will, as it goes. Have they been co-operative when you've spoken with them?'

'Not terribly, no. It's this business of the car park. In fact, they told us you were digging illegally.' Neil blushed. 'But we thought, hell, it's too good to miss. And they're not going to want to kick off with us there, are they? Anyway, we're on your side. Who on earth would want to build a bloody car park over something so unique? When do you hear about your appeal?'

'Any day now, apparently. I'm amazed it's taken so long.'

Juliana was also becoming impatient for the result of the appeal. She understood that the thing had to be seen to be done correctly, in order for it to stand, and the memory of what the Secretary of State had managed to do with that funnel in the photographs Q had shown her reassured her that, beyond all doubt, the decision was going to go the council's way. But she itched to unleash her dogs of war: the police and sheriff's men, the 'bailiffs' who were actually heavies from the museum spoiling for a fight with the hippies. Everything stood in readiness, including the warrants for repossession of Dole Acre. She longed to see her enemies' homes smashed and burning. She missed Q, and visited him twice a day in the hospital.

'You burned down the Tickled Trout, didn't you, darling?'

Q smiled.

'Tell me that's just the start, dearest. Tell me we're going to finish off the 4i's too.'

Q held a finger to his cracked lips. 'My dear, they're letting me out tonight. I shall come and stay with you in the flat for a day or so, until I feel stronger. I'll tell you all about the plans then. Do not worry. Vengeance shall be mine. You must rest assured.'

Time Gang brought brilliant winter sunshine with them on their arrival in Pancester, and Day One of the shooting was exciting and fast-moving. Two trenches were started, one halfway up the shaft, where the geophysics showed good evidence of walls, and another by the slit-like entrance to the bell-end. Neil Winterburn was interviewed, and his jeans were so tight, and he swept his hair out of his eyes in such an impressive way, that the producer thought of offering him a contract on the spot for his own TV series. Professor Daggers had come along, just as the producer had promised, but was showing no interest at all in the proceedings; instead he busied himself down by the riverbank looking for another example of Planorbis Pancestrum. Mrs Innes always made sure that he had a cup of tea when she brewed up for the workers.

The cheerfulness of the hippy volunteers and Emma and Gemma's straining efforts with the wheelbarrows fitted in perfectly with the enthusiasm and expertise of *Time Gang*. Timmy Rubenstein was everywhere, between the trenches and the city and the interpretation tent, but he still found time in the late afternoon to interview Taff, to ask him about the Wally. Taff explained all about what was expected of players in Wally Oop, due to be held the next day, and all about how his group, The Knightwatchmen, had just had their single reissued on a compilation CD.

'It's called *Caveman Twang*, Timmy. Look, I've got one for you, bach. Compliments of the band.'

'Yes, but to get back to Wally Oop, what tactics will we be using in the game?'

'Well, Timmy, I'm sure you can come up with a "wizard wheeze". Eh, Timmy? A wizard wheeze? D'yer get it, Timmy? A wizard wheeze? You know, like in the programme you do with that Mr Bean?'

Timmy Rubenstein managed to find a world-weary smile from somewhere deep within his soul, like the professional he was. He gave Taff a signed photo of himself, and hurried off to see another earthenware dildo that one of the Gang had unearthed in Trench Two. Taff walked back to the shop to pin the photo on the wall, next to the one from Terry Dene. Whittaker and Mrs Innes were sitting in the bookshop, drinking coffee. Mrs Innes had been crying, Taff could see at once, and Whittaker looked as though he were going to be sick.

'What's the matter? Look, I've got Timmy Rubenstein's photo. Cheer up.'

Whittaker looked at Taff. 'Brian Carless just phoned. Our appeal has been turned down. Juliana has won, and now she'll never respect me.'

'Turned it down? He can't have.'

'Well, he has. We've lost. I don't think I'll open the restaurant tonight. I think I'll go down and see Ash. Coming, Mrs I?' His voice was flat and colourless.

Mrs Innes visibly shook herself. 'Very well, Mr Whittaker. I'd like to be the one to tell Sandra and Syd and Steve and everybody. And the poor donkeys, too. We'll call a meeting.' She wiped her eyes with the corner of her skirt.

'At least we gave it our best shot, Mr Whittaker. At least we tried.'

*

The Committee Against the Car Park prepared to hold what Mrs Innes and Whittaker thought must be their last meeting, at eight in the evening in the Medlicotts' yurt down on the Dole Acre. Brian Carless had been persuaded to come and address the meeting, after Mrs Innes had given him assurances that the donkeys were safely out of his way on the other side of the dig. Everyone was there: Whittaker and Mrs Innes, Sir Oliver Courtney, his brother, Dexter Halton, his fiancée, Penny Lester, Gwyn and Sally, Taff and Dawn, Steve and Sandra Medlicott, Ash and Phil the Painter, Neil Winterburn and Syd Montague-Forrester, who had been coaxed out of the tunnels to hear the bad news. Professor Daggers had even stopped scouring the banks by torchlight, and was balanced on one of the log benches, his shorts riding up over his ancient hairless knees. The yurt had never been so crowded.

'Whew, it's cold out here. Haven't been on the surface since November. When I get back to Portugal, I'm going to build an underground house,' said Syd.

'Well, I think you can book your ticket, Sydney. The game's up, I'm afraid,' said Mrs Innes.

'How do you mean, Auntie?'

'It's incredible, but true,' said Brian Carless. 'I'm sorry to say the Secretary of State has turned down our appeal.'

'What?'

'He can't have.'

'Well, he has. And we've got nothing left, I'm afraid.'

'What about Oliver?' asked Dexter. 'We should be getting permission to exhume Lady Abigail within the next few weeks. Then we can prove that Oliver is a Courtney, and that no alterations can be made to the Charter without his consent.'

'And what about the missing Charter itself? I know Gwyn and Sally didn't find anything in Courtney House, but surely there must be other places we could look,' said Sandra Medlicott.

'If you could suggest where such places might be, then I'll happily arrange to have them searched. And as for Oliver, it's going to take years to satisfactorily establish his identity as the Courtney claimant,' said Brian.

'And what about the tunnels? This place is like a ruddy Gruyère cheese,' said Syd. 'Any heavy plant moving on to the site is going to cause subsidence on a massive scale. We can still hold the buggers off for weeks.'

'It's ironic, if you think about it,' said Phil the Painter.

'What is, Phil?' said Ash.

'Well . . . oh, no. No, come to think of it, it's not, no. It's sad.'

Steve Medlicott licked his lips. 'The . . . energy . . . is disturbed, unsettled. This is not . . . the end.'

'But it has to be, Mr Medlicott. We have explored every legal avenue, and each one has proved to be a dead end. Nothing remains to be done,' said Mrs Innes.

Tears stood out in Professor Daggers' eyes. 'Will no one save my snail?' he sniffed.

'We will resist,' said Syd.

'We will prove who Oliver really is,' said Dexter.

'We have lost,' said Mrs Innes.

And so the committee was split into three factions. Steve, Sandra and Syd, with the support of the hippies, proposed further resistance. Dexter, Oliver, Taff and Dawn were in favour of delaying tactics while Oliver's claim was proved. Mrs Innes, Brian Carless and Neil Winterburn wanted the committee to face facts.

'I've seen it a hundred times,' said Neil. 'What these people want, they get, and often pretty ruthlessly. But, you know, I've never really thought for a moment that the savages had taken over this country so effectively that they could destroy something like the Temple of Priapus. But I was wrong. How they did it, I mean, got to the Minister, and scuppered such a watertight case, I don't know, but they did. And any day now, they're going to come steaming in here with a repossession order. They are dangerous, if you ask me. And they've tried to kill Terry, and kidnapped Gwyn and Sally, and I think the time has come to look after our own hides, and get out of it.'

'But what about the Temple?' asked Sally.

'Oh, I don't know. Who cares? Certainly not the powers that be. Let Timmy and his lads give it a going over, I guess.

Sociologists have decreed that we are useless. They've cut off our balls. At least we'll have recorded the thing before it gets turned into the apparently much more useful car park.'

For the first time in its brief existence, the Committee Against the Car Park was unable to agree, and the meeting ended without reaching any useful conclusion.

'I think I might stay down here tonight, Mr Whittaker. Just for old times' sake. One last time. I enjoyed the women's camp, you know. It was one of the best things I've ever done,' said Mrs Innes.

Whittaker was too distracted to care. He belonged to a faction of his own, the Unrequited Love Party. He had matched his manhood against that of Q Sandahl, and had proved wanting. Q might have been hospitalised by Taff, but he had still won. Juliana would never go for him now. And none of his friends cared or sympathised. They were all glad that he had lost her, the One Woman He Had Ever Really Loved. All the signs of affection that had seemed so obvious to him were apparently really evidence of Juliana's hostility, after all. Why were they so hard to read? So what if she'd tried to kill him: at least she wasn't indifferent any more. And if he'd misinterpreted her actions, well, he wasn't alone. Meaningful glances that turn out to be meaningless, a snog at the office party that turns out to be a drunken bet – everyone gets it wrong sometimes. How many casual shags have turned out to be casual for one of the parties, and important, or heartbreaking, for the other? Sometimes, you can be with someone for years, only to discover that you'd got it all wrong, and misread the situation, and they didn't really care about you at all. And under these circumstances, it is better not to have loved than to have loved and lost, Whittaker felt. He went back with Ash to his van for a smoke.

The night before Wally Oop is the quietest night in Pancester's calendar. The shopkeepers, from long experience, take care to board up all their windows. The pubs are usually empty, as the men get an early night to build up their strength for the long day ahead. Many of the women sit up a little later than their husbands, praying that they won't be injured in the game. One woman in particular, Gwyneth Gabatini, had prayed that she might not be injured, as she got herself ready to become the first female in history to take part in Wally Oop.

Mist rises from the river, opalescent in the spotlights from the city wall. An owl hoots. Hardly a car passes on the ring road. The camp was silent, expectant. The Pink Bus was darkened, the drummers stilled. Only Terry Whittaker was sleepless. Ash had passed out hours ago, but still Whittaker stayed on in the van, staring at the glow from the wood-burner, and occasionally adding more logs.

He looked at his watch. It was four in the morning. Sleep was somewhere else entirely. He opened the door of the van, picked up Ash's torch and stepped out into the Dole Acre. The cold came as a shock after the overheated van, and his body was shaken by it. He walked shivering across the camp towards the Medlicotts' yurt, where Mrs Innes was staying, hoping that someone might be awake. The yurt was dark, and he could hear Rolly's snoring through the canvas walls. He turned, and walked back towards the van.

He saw something on the ground by the light of the torch, a little pinkish greyish cone, a mushroom with a slight kink in its thin stalk. It must be the very end of the season, so this must be the very last of the legendary Dole Acre mushrooms, thought Whittaker. This time next year, all this will be car park. Whittaker bent and picked the 'shroom, and popped it into the pocket of his fleece.

Back in the van, Whittaker saw Ash's copy of the Reverend Clement Dadd's book beside the sleeping hippy's bed. Whittaker picked it up, and read again the entry on Wally Oop. How on earth was he going to keep it together in that heaving crushing scrum for ten, twelve, fifteen hours? Ten, twelve, fifteen. Ten . . . twelve . . . fifteen . . . He must have nodded, because he was suddenly jerked awake by the sound of someone banging on the panels of the van.

'Wake up, gentlemen! It's almost six o'clock, and the Wally is here!' It was Taff, his belly full of fire just as Dawn had predicted. He had set himself the task of acting as the hippies' alarm clock, and was going round the vans and tepees rousing his new players.

Whittaker rubbed his eyes, as Ash sat up.

'Still here, Terry?'

'Yeah. Didn't feel like being alone. Hope it's OK?'

'Of course. Put the kettle on the burner, we'll have some tea.'

Whittaker made scrambled eggs with bacon as Ash got dressed. They opened the doors of the van, and saw signs of fires being lit all around the campsite, and hippies emerging, blinking, into the pale light of dawn. From high on the city walls the Alarumist sounded the Ramstheng to announce the new day. Syd and Tony the Tunneller crawled out from the entrance to the underground city. The Wally had arrived.

Taff bustled over to Ash's van. 'Good morning, gentlemen. I hope you feel like breaking a few Ringler heads today.'

'I sure do, Taff,' said Ash. Whittaker nodded, but he was not telling the truth. He was exhausted, depressed and hopeless.

'Come on then. Finish your breakfast, and let's get going,' said Taff. 'Look at the bridge!'

Crowds were already streaming over the Pack Bridge, with men from Laikley come to take part in the game, men from the outlying estates and Blackhampton, and tourists eager to participate in the oldest surviving version of football in Europe.

'Come on, come on, come on. Wally up in twenty minutes!' Taff, helped now by Steve Medlicott, was rounding up the hippies, and marshalling them towards the gate. 'See you up there, Terry!'

'Yeah. Sure.'

'You all right, Terry?' asked Ash.

'Yeah, I'll be fine. Didn't get any sleep, that's all. You get on. I'll just grab another cup of tea. They can kick off without me, if it comes to it.'

'OK, guy. I'll see you up there.'

Whittaker watched as the last of the hippies left the site and trailed over the bridge. He was really not feeling up to this, not at all. But not to go was the greatest shame that could befall any

Pancestrian, native or adopted. He had to go, had to get through it. He needed something to energise him, to mask his despair, to stop him thinking about Juliana. He poured himself a mug of tea, and felt in his pocket for his handkerchief.

And found the mushroom. He held it up. It was slimy and wizened, the length of a match, its pointy grey cap the size of a fingernail. Whittaker ran his thumb over the delicate pink gills. Such a tiny thing. Surely it can't have any real effect, not just one. But Whittaker thought of the Second Pancester Free Festival, the non-stop dancing, the sheer energy of the ravers, and he thought what the hey, maybe this'll give me a bit of pep, and he popped it in his mouth and swigged at his mug. He felt the mushroom go down like a miniature oyster.

He finished his tea, and walked away from the van. Mrs Innes came out from the Medlicotts' yurt to put the kettle on the fire, saw Whittaker, and waved urgently at him. He walked across, his legs feeling as though they had been transplanted from one of Juliana's Beanie Babies.

'Still here, Mr Whittaker? Wally was up five minutes ago.'

'Yes, I know. I'm just trying to liven up. Couldn't get to sleep. My limbs have turned to porridge.'

'Your mind wouldn't stop whizzing round, eh? I was just the same.'

'I'm going to walk around, if you'll excuse me, Mrs I. Got to get the old legs working before I can go into town. I'm a chef, you know. This is a bit early for me.'

'Well, don't be too long. The Clanghandlers need every man today.'

'I know, Mrs I. I know.'

Whittaker wandered away from the camp towards the site of the dig. The *Time Gang* archaeologists had just started work, and waved a greeting up at him. Timmy Rubenstein and his cameraman, Whittaker reasoned, would be in the city, trying to film the Wally, if they weren't swept up into the game. On the furthest part of Dole Acre, away from the camp, and roped off by the dig, was the area reserved for the donkeys. Whittaker stood by the side of the Balls and watched the donkeys pull feebly at the salty grass of the ancient meadow. Poor old geezers, he thought. Off to Laikley Children's Zoo for you. It seemed a terrible shame. After everything the campaign had tried to achieve: the preservation of traditions and of archaeological wonders, of rare water snails, of the king and queen of all psychedelic mushrooms (and why wasn't his working?) – with all the high and lofty aims, the poor donkeys were still getting the worst of it. A tear came to Whittaker's eye, and he walked towards the old animals. As he reached the nearest donkey, it raised its head from the ground, and stared at Whittaker with mild grey eyes. Whittaker reached out, and scratched it between the ears.

'Good morning, Mrs Donkey,' said Whittaker.

'Good morning, Mr Whittaker,' said the donkey.

Lions Led by Donkeys

Talking donkeys are fairly rare in literature, and the only examples that spring to mind are Bottom and Eeyore, though doubtless I am showing my lack of scholarship, and there are plenty of others. Aesop, for example, is probably stiff with them. It is fair to assume that Bottom's voice is a kind of generic Shakespearean rustic, while Eeyore, of course, has that gloomy, stoical, almost martyred tone that makes him so funny. The donkeys on Dole Acre, Whittaker found to his surprise, sounded like neither, but more like Margeret Rutherford in *Passport to Pimlico*, at once querulous and commanding.

'It's a lovely morning for the Wally,' said Whittaker.

'Yes, it is. I'm rather surprised to see you lurking about here, young man. You should be in the thick of it.'

'I'm sorry, I don't know your name.'

'Edith. And I'm not married, so I'd prefer it if you didn't call me Mrs Donkey. And this is my friend, Katherine.' A second donkey had walked across to join them.

'Hello, Mr Whittaker. A pleasure to meet you properly at last. I've heard all about you from dear Jocelyn Innes,' said Katherine.

'Don't fawn, Katherine. It doesn't suit you. Mr Whittaker was about to tell me why he's spending his morning down here with us old biddies instead of having it out with Johnny Ringler in the Wally.'

'Oh, I'll go up in a bit. I didn't sleep, you see. Finding it a bit difficult to get going this morning.'

'A young man like you? You should be full of the joys of spring,' said Edith.

'Don't nag the poor fellow, Edith. You know yourself how difficult it is to get off with all that blessed drumming going on.'

'Oh, why do they do it, Mr Whittaker? I like many of the young people who have come to stay on our field very much. They may be filthy dirty . . .'

'And someone should take a curry-comb to their coats . . .' added Katherine.

'Yes. But they are respectful and kind for the most part, and very concerned for the countryside. But they will bang away on those drums. Why do they do it?'

'I've never known, to be honest with you. I think it might be a tribal thing.'

'Well, not for the first time, I'm glad that donkeys are not tribal animals. Tribal my Aunt Fanny! Everything I dislike about humans turns out to be tribal. Sectarianism – tribal. Nationalism – tribal. Hippy drumming – tribal. I sometimes think it's about time you did away with all this silly tribalism,' said Edith.

'Well, actually, they weren't drumming last night. It was worry keeping me awake as much as anything.'

'Worry? What on earth do you have to be worried about?' asked Katherine.

'This place. The Dole Acre. You know they're going to turn it into a car park. We tried to stop them, but . . .' Terry trailed off.

'Yes, Jocelyn Innes told us yesterday. It's most unsettling.'

'Most,' agreed Katherine.

'I know. It just seems crazy, when you think of the true value of this place. There must be some other way to sort out Pancester's parking problems,' said Whittaker.

'You know, the thing that upsets me the most is that Lady Lettice hasn't raised a finger to try and stop them,' said Edith.

'The Courtneys used to care about Pancester,' said Katherine, 'but Lady Lettice seems oblivious to all the recent goings-on.'

'I'm sorry, ladies, but Lady Lettice died a long time ago.'

'Lady Lettice Courtney? Dead? Are you sure?' said Edith.

'I'm sure.'

'When?'

'Nineteen seventy-two.'

'Nineteen seventy-two? Are you mad? She comes to see us every week. Brings us a big bag of carrots,' said Edith.

'But ... it can't be. No one has seen her since ... well, 1972.'

'Well, bless my soul. We see her every week. Tuesday. Or is it Wednesday? And we keep telling her about this car park business, but she just says, "Hello, donkeys", and gives us the carrots.'

'We like the carrots, you know,' said Katherine, 'but she just doesn't seem to understand us when we tell her about not wanting to go to the zoo. She's not a donkey whisperer, like you.'

'But ... where has she been all this time?'

'Well, where do you think? In Courtney House.'

'Oh ... you mean ... my God! Edmund!'

'Who?'

'Edmund. The tramp. He lives in Courtney House too. He must have been scavenging for Letty all these years while she hides up in the New House. That's how he got in in the first place. Letty must have let him in. And now he's a kind of manservant for her, while she stays locked up in that ruined old mansion!'

'Except for when she comes to give us the carrots, obviously,' said Katherine.

'That seems strange to me. Why has no one else seen her?'

'Perhaps she doesn't give anyone else carrots,' said Edith.

'She's always been most particular about who she associates with,' said Katherine.

'Are you sure?'

'Of course we're sure. Don't you think we'd recognise a person of her quality? Dead, indeed,' said Edith.

'Look, I'm sorry, but I have to go. If you'll excuse me?'

'Of course, dear. You should have been in the Wally long ago.'

'I'm not going into the Wally. I'm going to Courtney House to find her, and get her to stop the car park. She clearly doesn't know what's been going on!'

'Well said,' said Edith.

'Bravo!' said Katherine.

'Goodbye,' said Whittaker, starting to run, all feeling now returned to his legs. 'I'll come and tell you how I got on later.'

'Good luck!' shouted Edith.

'What a nice man,' said Katherine, as the two donkeys watched Whittaker lumber across the Dole Acre.

'Let's hope he's in time, dear. Or it's Laikley Children's Zoo for us.'

Mrs Innes spotted Whittaker jogging through the deserted camp, and flagged him down again.

'Still here?'

'Yes,' he puffed. 'I'm just going into the city now. You're still here too?'

'I'm making tea for Professor Daggers and the *Time Gang* people. Emma and Gemma are still here, as well. Nothing will drag them away from their beloved dig. Or the telly cameras.'

'You didn't fancy watching the Wally then?'

'I just want to spend a last few days down here, really, before they clear the site.'

'Look, I've got to go. You'll never believe what the donkeys just told me.'

'No, you're probably right. I don't suppose I would.'

'Must dash, Mrs I! I'll be back, with a big surprise for everyone. See you later.'

Mrs Innes stood open-mouthed as she watched Whittaker's approximation of running, out of the Dole Acre and on to the Pack Bridge. What could he mean? Did he really think he'd been talking to the donkeys? Poor man. Pancester had clearly gone to his head. Perhaps someone had put something in his tea.

While Whittaker was chatting with the donkeys, up in the Guildhall Square Gwyn had been arguing with her father.

'Are you raving, girl? You can't join in the Wally, and you know you can't.'

'Well, tough, Dad, 'cos I am. I'm not going to be another one of the women who've stood and watched and passed drinks and pies to the players over the years. I'm a Pancestrian born and bred, and I'm playing in the Wally.'

'You'll get killed.'

'Do you think so?' asked Gwyn, smiling. Taff looked at his daughter, tall and strong with her swimmer's physique, and smiled back proudly at her.

'No, love. I don't. But don't come crying to me if you break your nose and Sally doesn't fancy you any more.'

'I won't, I promise. Look, here's the Mayor.'

Guildhall Square was packed with thousands of people, the men to take part, the women to watch and pass refreshments and scream encouragement. A line was painted across the square, and the two warring factions, Clanghandler and Ringler, stood eyeball to eyeball along its length. Some of the players were bare-chested and covered with grease; others wore old sweaters and T-shirts – almost all wore steel-capped boots. The snarling and shouting front rows of the two teams, driven by generations of factional hatred, made the All Blacks in their *haaka* look like chorus boys on a picnic in Kensington Gardens.

The last time anybody seriously attempted to count the number of players in Wally Oop, in the late nineties, it was estimated that some fifteen thousand men took part, divided roughly in half. The academic who attempted the count, an anthropologist from the University of Luton, was unable to do more than estimate before he was caught up in the thing, and had ended up playing a very creditable game for the Ringlers.

The carillon sounded seven, and the Alarumist, as is customary, sounded a blast on the Ramstheng. The Mayor, somewhat nervously, walked slowly along the line from the Guildhall to the centre of the square carrying the Wally, a roll of leather, perhaps a foot long and five inches round, tied up in scarlet waxed cord. The Square fell silent as he pushed his way through the crowd. He reached the centre, crossed himself, shouted 'Wally Oop', and threw the Wally high into the air. Immediately the teams surged forwards, and the Mayor was stuck between them, holding on to his hat as the crush began.

Ronnie of the Pink Bus leapt into the air, caught the Wally

before it could hit the ground, dropped to his knees, and crawled back into the body of the Clanghandlers, who charged forwards, fists and boots flailing, into the ranks of the Ringlers. Still crawling, Ronnie clung to the Wally as the Clanghandlers advanced some fifty yards, before the combined weight of seven and a half thousand Ringlers managed to take back control, and stopped the Clanghandlers from gaining any more ground. Ronnie stood up, and threw the Wally along the line, away from the centre of the vast scrum towards the flanks, where he thought that the Ringler pressure might be less formidable. He watched as one of his teammates caught it, watched as the new Wallyman was swamped by Ringler hordes. Some locals clapped him on the back. 'Well done, lad. You've gained us a few yards, there! Keep it up!'

The epicentre of the crush shifted towards the ruck for the Wally. Gwyn and Taff were ten or so rows behind, and they put their heads down and heaved into the backs of the men in front, attempting to push the scrum forwards. Gwyn's heart was racing, but she could not, in all honesty, say that she enjoyed the acrid smell of male sweat or the howling and screaming which started to emanate from the steaming crowds. All she could see was the not entirely clean bum crack of the player in front of her as she heaved him forward. But within several minutes it became obvious that the scrum had stopped, and the first real stalemate of the Wally had been reached, with neither side able to move forward at all. Any relaxation from either of the huge teams might give their opponents a chance to gain some ground. So Gwyn stayed with her nose buried in somebody's fat arse, holding on for dear life, and wondered why she'd ever decided to do this crazy thing.

Juliana and Q watched the Wally go up from the window of his office. She looked at her watch.

'I'll give them till nine,' she said. 'By then, the Wally will be really under way, and no one will know what's hit 'em.' Q nodded his assent and Juliana spoke into her walkie-talkie.

'McCracken? It's Control here.'

'Go ahead, Control.'

'How are you doing?'

'Well, we're all in position, Control, but my men are not happy. They want to be in the Wally themselves.'

'Well, tell them to keep their testosterone bottled up for another hour or so, and then they can go and smash up the hippies' camp. That should get rid of some of their aggression.'

'OK, Control. Are the bulldozers ready?'

'Nearly. They're just being unloaded from their carriers out on the Blackhampton Road. They'll be in position by nine,' said Juliana.

'Good. And ... er ... the "bailiffs"?'

'They're here with us. Don't worry. They'll be with you for zero hour.'

'OK, Control. Over and out.'

Juliana looked around her in Q's office. Q continued to stare at the Wally from the window, his back to the room. The entire staff of the museum, including Mrs Wiseman, stood around wearing black leather jackets. There were at least a hundred of them. Some weighted lead pipes against their palms. Others stood leaning nonchalantly on pickaxe handles, while others still prepared Molotov cocktails. This was going to be fun. Juliana called for attention.

'Ladies and gentlemen. Can I please have your silence? Thank you. As you know, a foul crime was perpetrated against our beloved Director some weeks ago. He would now like to say a few words to you before today's event.'

Sandahl swung round in his chair. The skin on his face still showed signs of where the varnish had been peeled painfully away. His hair and his eyebrows and eyelashes had all been waxed away by the pitching. He had not been into the museum since being released from hospital, and some of the staff gasped in horror when they saw their leader's piebald face.

Q addressed them. 'As you know, I have been in hospital for the last few weeks, thanks to the efforts of our hippy friends. Today is the day when we take our revenge. I, alas, am still not fit enough to join you, and shall be co-ordinating our efforts from here, whilst Ms Blezzard runs things on the ground. Do not feel inhibited when you are destroying their camp, as you have the full protection of the law. You are bailiffs, sheriff's men, and you can do whatever you like. Just go out there, and play your natural game. Enjoy yourselves. And when you are smashing and burning and looting, remember that an insult to me is an insult to all of us! To you! To your wives and lovers! An insult to me is an insult to your old mothers! Do not forget, when you are crushing these useless creatures under foot, that they have insulted your mothers!'

The heavies cheered, and Juliana, smiling, turned again to watch the progress of the Wally.

Neil Winterburn was enjoying himself thoroughly; Timmy Rubenstein less so, especially since he had to try and talk to the camera as well as avoid being crushed to death. 'We've ... been ... playing ... for ... what seems like ... hours,' he shouted, trying to make himself heard above the din of the Wally. 'And nothing really seems to be happening except that we are trying to hold our position. I think we may have surged forwards a few yards at the start ... but for an hour or so, neither side has gained any ground. I have no idea which side has the Wally ... It's like a cross between a rugby scrum and a commuter train into Waterloo in here ... even if I wanted to move ... I don't think I could ...'

'Put that bloody camera down, lad,' gasped Frank Welford, who was behind Timmy and Neil, to the cameraman. 'And start pushing.'

'I can't!' squeaked the cameraman. 'I can't move either way!'

'Fun, isn't it?' yelled Neil Winterburn.

'No,' said Timmy and the cameraman.

This was the situation as Whittaker arrived panting in the Guildhall Square. His way to Courtney House was blocked by a wall of heaving sweaty backsides and a frenzy of screaming, shouting sound. He started to back off, to try and find another way round, when a couple of Pancestrian women standing on the pavement, *tricoteuses* in a previous existence, saw him and started to jeer.

'Yah, where are you going, fat lad?'

'Too pansy for the Wally?'

'I'm trying to find another way round to get up to the church. Then if we could get the Wally and pass it back this way, with some fast runners we could sneak it past them.'

'Oh.'

'Right clever that is.'

'What would be the best way?'

'Oh, let's think. Now then. What way would be best?' said the first hag.

'Bum Alley would be best,' said the second, 'they often make a break for it that way, but they're a bit beyond it this year. Oh, I know. You could go back down West Street, and turn down Fenner Street, and then through Hobson's Passage. That'd take you on to Bum Alley . . .'

'And from there you go round the city walls, and up the Cat's Creep . . .'

'Thanks!' said Whittaker, trotting off. 'I'll be back in a bit, let you know if it works.'

At the corner of West Street and Fenner Street, Whittaker had to pause for breath, doubled up, his hands on his knees. The tumult of Wally Oop filled the city, even away from the action. He would join in as soon as he had winkled Lady Lettice out of Courtney House, he resolved. No one would be able to say then that he was too pansy for the action. Looking up, he thought he saw the greasy, ragged figure of Edmund turn into Hobson's Passage, a hundred metres or so on the right. He shouted, 'Edmund! Wait!' and started to jog breathlessly after the old milestone inspector. On reaching Hobson's Passage, his nose was violated by Edmund's trademark stench, and he hurried through it with his handkerchief over his nose. Whittaker paused again, gulped at the air, then staggered on into Shy Street, across from the boarded-up windows of the 4i's and the Fox Hole. He looked to his right, through the archway, back into the Guildhall Square, where the vast press of bodies wrestled in fruitless combat. Unless

Edmund had gone that way to join battle, Whittaker reasoned, which was unlikely, since even the keenest Wally fan would be reluctant to spend the afternoon with his nose pressed to the seat of Edmund's trousers, then the old boy must also be taking the back way to Courtney House. He half trotted, half walked as fast as he was able, and turning on to the city walls, saw Edmund some way in front of him. He called again, 'Edmund! Wait!' and the tramp turned, saw Whittaker, picked up the tails of his vile old mac, and started to sprint round the corner and out of sight. Whittaker made no attempt to chase after him. He was completely winded. He sat on a bench, and looked over the walls and down on to Dole Acre.

He saw the tiny figures of the archaeologists excavating the Temple of Priapus, and watched the donkeys, ears flopped in front of their eyes as they munched the grass. He saw the camp, largely deserted but for a handful of hippy chicks tending the fires and keeping stoned watch on the children. He saw Mrs Innes with Rolly, walking towards the dig carrying a steaming teapot and half a dozen mugs on a tray. He saw Emma and Gemma, their nipples like blind cobbler's thumbs, pushing their barrows and gurning at the cameras. He saw Planorbis Pancestrum, hiding from Professor Daggers, clinging to the mud banks of the river, saw every pink whorl of its shell by the edge of the foaming water.

He rubbed his eyes, and watched the scene dissolve and change, and now he watched as slaves unloaded stone from Roman barges pulled up to a makeshift quay, watched as workmen erected wooden scaffolding to frame the great Temple building which grew out of the ground as though it had been filmed by a time-lapse camera, and watched as the first worshippers entered into the vast building, the huge bell-end crowned with gold. And now he watched as the worshippers drifted away, watched as the departing Romans stripped the gold from the roof of the Temple, watched the cobbled road past the site sprout grass and bushes, watched as the Saxons arrived, and pulled away the stones from the roof and walls, and started to build their new settlement on the hill above the Athon. And he saw the great longships come up the river, the mouths of their dragon prows carved into fire, shields hung from their sides, watched as the women of Pancester led by the beautiful Lady Wildaburga beat the raiders off, saw a funeral pyre for the dead of both sides lit by the victors, watched the greasy smoke curl into the sky.

And Whittaker watched as more workmen came, and pulled down the last of the Temple walls, and watched as they built the elegant curve of the Pack Bridge over the river. He saw villeins build low walls and sluices and flood the Dole Acre in autumn, collecting the river silt to improve the spring feeding of their cattle. He saw Sir Kenelm, dressed in the height of sixteenth-century fashion, taking the Aoldermen round the old field, and pointing towards the site of the Temple, watched the women of Pancester walk over the field of their ancestors' victory, and light their candles for the Eastering. He saw the sluices fall into disuse, watched the cattle dwindle and vanish, watched as thistles and couch-grass claimed the Dole Acre for their own. He saw the building of the ring road and the arrival of the donkeys. And finally he saw road-layers and mixers spew tarmac and concrete over the ancient water meadow, witnessed the opening of the car park by Dame Margot Prosser, a triumphant Juliana whispering into her hearing aid, watched as the fleet cars of salarymen from mock Georgian estates in Cheshire disgorged their loads of semi-educated children, who sprinkled the barren asphalt with votive offerings of crisp packets and hamburger boxes, which lifted in the breeze and fell into the river like a hard rain. Whittaker watched as the rubbish bobbed on the tide out towards the sea. And he rubbed his eyes again, and the car park was gone, and the camp had returned.

But now he could see vanloads of police waiting by the Laikley turn-off for the bulldozers which made their implacable way along the ring road. Whittaker shook his head and looked again. They were still there. The bastards, he thought, the bastards. They're going in today, during the Wally. I must find Letty. Only Letty can stop this. And he stood up, and started to run again, around the city walls towards Courtney House.

The side of Courtney House overlooks the city walls, and there is a narrow staircase, called the Cat's Creep, which links the path around the walls with the entrance to the New House, and to the large green in front of St Gilbert's. As Terry ran towards the bottom of this alleyway, he could swear that the roar from the Wally was getting louder, closer, coming up behind him even. He stopped and looked around. He couldn't see anything, but it certainly sounded very much nearer. From behind him again, he heard a scratching and rattling sound. He spun around a second time, to see a manhole cover lift, and Syd Montague-Forrester's head come sticking up from the pavement.

'Hello, Terence. Where are we?' said Syd.

'On the city walls. Near the bottom of the Cat's Creep.'

'First class! Hold this, will you?' He handed Whittaker a battered roll of leather and cord, and pulled himself out from the ground. 'Come on, Ronald, Steve. Chop chop. Quick march.' Ronnie of the Pink Bus and Steve Medlicott climbed out from the drain and stood beside Syd.

'What's this?' said Whittaker.

'What do you think it is? It's the bloody Wally. Oh dear. Here come the Bosch. Up the Cat's Creep, lads!' Steve snatched the Wally from Whittaker's hands. A third time, Whittaker looked behind him, and now the source of the noise became evident, as hundreds of angry Ringlers came streaming along the walls. Syd, Steve and Ronnie had already reached the bottom of the steps, and were taking them two at a time, and Whittaker started to pad after them, but the Ringlers were coming up closer and closer behind him, and not for the first occasion on that day, he considered adding some low-fat items to his menu.

He could only manage one step at a time, but had wheezed his way up almost a third of the long stone flight before the foremost of the chasing Ringlers grabbed at his ankle and he came crashing to the ground. They turned him over, to make sure he didn't have the Wally, and then leapt over him and rushed on up the steps. Ringlers, pouring up the alley like toothpaste up a tube, were falling over Whittaker's prone body, so he was yanked to his feet and carried up the steps by the weight of pressure from the pursuing group. He didn't touch the ground, and he popped out on to St Gilbert's Green like a cork from a bottle of mixed metaphors, like a bullet from a pun.

As soon as he regained his senses, Whittaker saw that Syd and his merry men had been caught in a pincer movement in the middle of St Gilbert's Green by two streams of Ringlers, one which had come storming up Church Street, and another that came round the side of the castle. Clanghandlers were on their heels, pressing forward their advantage. Now a third stream from up the Cat's Creep joined the throng. The Ringlers had snatched the Wally from Steve's arms and had gone storming off down Church Street again, turning their retreating players, and forcing them back into the wall of advancing Clanghandlers. The great scrum engaged once more, and the Wally was lost in the ruck, halfway down Church Street. So even though Syd's audacious plan to produce the first Clanghandler win since 1952 had failed, it had moved the action right up into Church Street for the first time since 1976. Things were beginning to look good for the Clanghandlers. The ruck was becoming more bloody now that play was confined to the narrow street, rather than the wide Guildhall Square, and casualties emerged from the rear of the maul on to the green with hankies pressed to bloody noses, as Ringler shouts urged on the attempt to force the Clanghandlers back down the hill and into the Square.

Whittaker pushed open the wrought-iron gates in front of Courtney House, and hurried round to the side window which Gwyn and Sally had told him was Edmund's way in and out. He found the loosened board, pulled it aside, opened the window catch, and climbed into Courtney House. It was much as Gwyn had described it, sea-green dark, the light and noise shuttered out. The women had already explored the ground floor, and had not found any sign of Edmund, so Whittaker looked for the stairs. Portraits of dead members of the Courtney family lined the walls, dripping with damp. Whittaker reached the upstairs landing, and noticed a light coming from underneath one of the doors in the corridor to his right. He pushed it open, and entered a room very different from the rest of the house.

He held his breath.

The boards had been pulled away from the windows so that the room was flooded with light. A fire burned brightly in the grate, with a kettle hanging from a hook in the chimney breast just starting to sing. A bed in the corner was covered with a faded patchwork quilt, and on shelves all around the walls was a large collection of Victorian dolls and battered teddy bears. A figure in an aquamarine ball dress with matching silk elbow-length gloves, her back to the door, stooped in front of the fire preparing the tea. Whittaker gulped.

'Lady Lettice Courtney?'

'Yes?' said the figure, turning. Whittaker gasped as he saw her face.

'Edmund?' he said.

'Also yes. Tea?'

'Edmund?'

'Yes?'

'Are you really Lady Letty?'

'Yes. One lump or two?'

'Two. No, one. Trying to cut down.'

'Milk?'

'Thank you.'

'Do sit down, Terry. Here.' Edmund/Lettice guided Whittaker into an armchair, and handed him a delicate cup and saucer.

'Thank you. Thank you.' Whittaker didn't quite know what to say. His hands were shaking, and he tried to steady his cup. Playing with gender boundaries is almost compulsory for pop musicians, but is very rare amongst tramps, and Whittaker had been put on the back foot.

'Sorry I ran away from you just now. I thought you were trying to get me to be in the Wally, but, as you know, we girls simply don't play rough games,' said Edmund/Lettice.

'Gwyn's in it,' said Whittaker, sipping his tea from a shaking cup.

'Is she? Frightfully modern young woman, that one. I'm not

sure I approve.' Edmund/Lettice sipped her tea, and wiped her beard with the back of her gloved hand.

'Lady Lettice, why have you pretended to be a tramp all these years?'

'Oh, for a spree, I suppose. I got bored with all the responsibility. Of being a Courtney, of looking after the house. And this seemed to suit me for the role.' She stroked her greasy beard.

'It's not false then?'

'Good heavens, no. All my own, every inch of it.'

'So what happened after the Free Festival? After the mushroom tea?'

'I'm not entirely sure. I woke up the morning after on the riverbank, naked as a baby, and covered in hair. I expect the responsible thing to do would have been to go to the doctor, and make myself available to science as a real-life Mr Hyde. But do you know, quite suddenly, I didn't give a fig for responsibility any more, all the bloody stupid forms you have to fill in, and I just mooched back here, and locked myself in for a few weeks until the food ran out. Then I dug out some old things of Daddy's, and a top-coat left by the gardener, and was born again as Edmund the tramp. I enjoy it. I'd much rather root around for grub than cook.' Whittaker noticed that, as Lettice, she did not share Edmund's propensity to change his voice every few minutes, and spoke now in her own languorous aristocratic tone, which sounded uncannily like that of Fenella Fielding.

'Poor old Syd was broken-hearted. He was looking for you for ages,' said Whittaker.

'Was he? Bless him.'

'We've all been looking for you. It's this car park thing, you know.'

'I'm afraid I don't read the papers any more, darling. Can't be fagged, I'm ashamed to say. I just find all the news terribly, terribly dull.'

'But you must have heard us talking about it. What about when you found the Charter in my dustbin? You must have known why it was so important? You were there while we were talking about it, I know you were.'

'I just fancied some of that smoked eel. If I'd wanted to spend my whole life listening to the babblings of tradesmen and kitchen girls, I wouldn't have adopted my current lifestyle, would I?'

'Well, the City Council are trying to prove that you're dead, so that they can get their hands on Dole Acre, so they can build a car park there.'

'Still run by the same bunch of puffed-up little counter-jumpers, is it, the council?'

'It's all been planned by Juliana Blezzard, the Chief Tourism Officer.'

'Oh, I don't like her. Or that smarmy Levantine I whacked with my sword.'

'Well, please can you come and help us stop them? The police and sheriff's men are getting ready to clear the protesters from the Dole Acre.'

Lady Lettice, as I feel we must now call her, made a petulant little moue with her mouth, and scratched her beard. 'Oh, God, can't you sort yourselves out? I really don't know that I can be bothered.'

'Or you could give us the Charter, the real one, if you know where it is.'

Lady Lettice sighed. 'Well, aren't you clever to have found out about that? But it's all the way downstairs, and it's too, too exhausting.'

'What about your son? Don't you want to see him? He'd do anything to stop this car park.'

Lady Lettice sat bolt upright on the bed, and stared at Whittaker. 'My son? What do you mean?'

'You see what you miss by not reading the *Pancester Mail*? Your son, the one who was taken away from you. We found him. His name's Oliver. He's President of our campaign.'

'My son, my little baby? You've found him?'

'Yes. He runs the bookshop.'

'Does he? I've seen him. A devilish handsome man. Courtney

through and through. Where is he? I must go to him at once.'
Lady Letty stood up.

'Yes, good. I'll help you find him.'

'And you say he would want me to stop these dreadful people and their little municipal schemes?'

'Very much so.'

'And the Charter would help him, you say?'

'More than anything.'

'Well, come along then, Terry. What are you waiting for?' And without waiting to change into her Edmund gear, Lady Lettice Courtney picked up her handbag and swept from the room like an old-fashioned dowager. She lifted her skirt and trotted down the stairs. Whittaker followed her into the room full of dummy books, and watched as she pulled down a leather-bound volume of Hansard. A door, hidden in the walls, clicked open.

'Sally said that there would be secret passages,' said Whittaker, following Lady Lettice again, as she led the way down a narrow lightless corridor.

'Of course there are, darling. Courtney House is riddled with 'em. That's how I crept up behind that awful little man. Here we are. Hang on. Just let me light a candle.' Whittaker listened as Lady Lettice scrabbled around for matches, and watched in wonder as her spark illuminated a large room, full of books and rolled-up manuscripts.

'It's the vault from the old house. The fire didn't touch it, so we've always kept our most precious things down here. Let me see . . .' She riffled through a stack of documents. 'Charter, charter, charter, grant of land to Blackhampton Parish Church, 1267, no, establishment of fish weirs on the Athon, 1423, no use, ah! Here we are. This should be it.' She pulled down a roll of vellum tied up with a ribbon, and unfurled it on the reading table.

'Haven't got my reading glasses, darling. Is that what you've been looking for?' Whittaker looked over the document by candlelight, saw the word "Charter", saw the date 1503, found Sir Kenelm's signature, and looked up triumphantly at Lady Lettice.

'Yes, Lady Lettice. This is exactly what we've been looking for.'

'Then come on, Terry. Pick it up. And take me to my son!'

Shenanigans in the Boiler Room

As Whittaker and Lady Lettice left Courtney House to try and find Oliver, and as Gwyn and Taff and Neil and Timmy Rubenstein and the hippies and the rest of the Clanghandlers tried to stem the tide of enraged Ringlers from forcing the Wally back down the steep hill of Church Street and into the Guildhall Square, Mrs Innes was making yet another pot of tea for the *Time Gang* archaeologists. Even here, outside the city walls, the roar from Wally Oop filled the cold air. Mrs Innes looked sadly around her. In a few days, she thought, all this will be gone, all the colourful vans, all the kind-hearted young people who have tried so hard to help with no motive other than a commendable interest in preserving rare mushrooms, all gone. The council will get a warrant to clear the site, and it doesn't really matter if nephew Syd and a few other hotheads try to stop them, because look what happened at the Newbury bypass and Manchester airport and a hundred other places like them. They will just bring in the sheriff's men, and clear them off the site. And then, if the council have any sense at all, they will start construction work promptly, before Oliver can establish his claim. A couple more weeks at the outside, and this place will be gone for ever. It was a shame . . . no, not a shame. A crime. An outrage. Rolly sniffled.

'Yes, I know. It's very sad, old soldier. Very sad.' She dabbed some cream on his sores, and waited for the kettle hanging over the campfire to boil.

Her thoughts were interrupted by shouting and whistling from over towards the entrance from the ring road on to the Dole

Acre. She climbed up on the bench beside the fire, and saw blue vans emptying their loads of riot-ready police, who came charging through the gate and on to the site, shouting and whistling at the handful of hippies who had stayed behind. On the Pack Bridge she could see the column of guides, curators, archivists and conservators from the National Museum of Crime and Punishment marching towards the Acre, their pickaxe handles over their shoulders.

'Oh, my God, Rolly. They're coming in. Today. During Wally Oop. How dare they? How *dare* they? Come on, Rolly! Come on!' She ran as fast as she was able towards the site of the dig, shouting, 'Emma! Gemma! Quick!' Heads popped out from the trenches.

'What is it, Mrs Innes?' shouted Emma. 'What's up?'

'Heh ... theh ... they're coming to clear the site. Look!' She pointed at the advancing line of riot police, their perspex shields held in front of their faces.

'Not during the Wally, Mrs Innes, they can't! It int right!' said Gemma, wide-eyed.

'Well, look at them! Come on, girls,' she said. The archaeologists started to climb from the trenches after Emma and Gemma. 'No, the rest of you stay here, and try and keep them off the dig.'

Mrs Innes, like a latter-day Lady Wildaburga, with Emma and Gemma on either side of her, crunched over the frosty ground and through the camp towards the ring road. She was stopped by police in the dancing space in front of the Pink Bus.

'I'm sorry, Mrs Innes, we're going to have to clear you all from the site. The council has a warrant. If you could move along now please, taking all your belongings with you,' said a young sergeant.

'Billy Welford?' said Mrs Innes. 'You should be ashamed of yourself, coming down here instead of helping your dad in the Wally. Look at him, girls! That's what they used to call a blackleg!' Emma and Gemma screwed up their eyes and stared into Billy Welford's face.

Billy reddened. 'It's nowt to do with me, Mrs Innes. We just do like we're told.'

'Fascist pig!' said Emma.

'Yeah. That's what all fascists say,' said Gemma.

'That's as maybe. But we're still moving everyone off.'

'Mrs Innes! Look at them!' said Emma, pointing across the site.

'What on earth do you think you're doing?' shouted Mrs Innes at two policemen, who were trying to drag a hippy mother by her legs from the door of her home, a converted bus.

'Leave me alone! Leave me alone!' screamed the hippy, holding on to the door frame. Mrs Innes, Emma and Gemma shouted at the policemen, urging them to stop. They let go of the hippy's legs, and she pulled herself inside the bus, bolting the door behind her.

'I'm sorry, madam, we've been told to clear all these people off the site,' said the first policeman.

'But these are their homes! You have to give them time.'

'Well, they haven't got it,' said the second. He banged on the windows of the bus. 'Oi, you! Out of there!'

'Who is in charge here?' said Mrs Innes.

'Deputy sheriff. Over by the gate', said the first policeman.

'Come on, girls! And you, keep your hands off that young woman and her children!'

Nearer and nearer to the gate, the site looked more and more like the 1968 Democratic Convention in Chicago, as policemen wrestled the hippy women and children from their vans and tepees. And now Mrs Innes and her party could hear the sound of smashing glass from the direction of Phil the Painter's caravan as the sheriff's men arrived on the site. A hundred hardened criminals: hitmen, pirates, robbers, murderers, burglars, conmen, forgers, arsonists, cracksmen, fences, pickpockets, embezzlers and shoplifters, swarmed around like outraged hornets. They took their pickaxe handles and lead pipes to the windows of the vans. Ash's forge, left outside his van, was overturned and smashed out of recognition. There was a large explosion as one of the buses was torched, followed by screaming and the hard sound of laughter. Flames licked from the top of the tepee nearest the gate. Mrs Innes was ready to kill by the time she reached the police Range Rover parked by the side of the ring road, where Juliana sat laughing with Inspector McCracken.

'You,' said Mrs Innes. 'I should have known. This is part of the job description for Chief Tourism Officer, is it? Smashing and burning?'

'Deputy sheriff for the day, Mrs Innes,' said Juliana, leaning from the window. 'And I'm here to enforce the order that says these weirdos must be off the site by eleven.'

'But you are destroying their homes! And there's only a few women and children left.'

'Well, they shouldn't have parked here, should they? All they've brought is filth and noise. Percentile visitation is down five on the year. So hard luck to them. My bulldozers are going in the minute we get all the scum off the site.'

Mrs Innes noticed for the first time that three great yellow bulldozers were idling by the side of the ring road.

'And later on they're sending a horsebox over from the zoo to pick up the donkeys. You've lost. It's over. Go home, if you don't want to be hurt.'

'Emma, Gemma, you stay here. Rolly, stay with the girls. Do anything you can to stop them. Fetch Professor Daggers, and get him somewhere safe. I'm going to find Mr Whittaker, and get help.' Juliana climbed from the car, and laughed at Mrs Innes.

'What can a couple of morons from Laikley High do to stop us? And what can Fatty Whittaker do? How can flabby old Cuggles stop all this? Just go home, old woman. Go home.'

'We can cut yer fookin' tits off, yer fookin' cow,' said Emma, pushing her face into Juliana's.

'Yeah,' said Gemma. 'You go on, Mrs Innes. We'll stop the fookin' bitch. Go on! Hurry!'

'Arrest these stupid little tarts, Inspector. Threatening behaviour.'

But Emma and Gemma were Laikley girls, and evading arrest was second nature to them, so they skipped back into the site, followed by Rolly, while Mrs Innes started to run into Pancester to raise the alarm.

She could manage no more than twenty yards before she had to stop, her heart hammering in her ribcage. She clutched her side, and stared despairingly at West Street stretching up the hill in front of her. She tried to catch her breath, and walked as fast as she was able on to the Pack Bridge, and stopped again. 'Slow and steady gets there, Jocelyn,' she said aloud to herself.

And then she heard a braying sound from the gateway to Dole Acre. She paused, and turned to see Edith the donkey trotting up the bridge towards her. 'Oh, what is it now, dear? I really don't have the time.'

Edith lowered her head, and bent her knees.

'What? You want me to ride? Edith, dear, are you up to it?'

Edith put back her ears and gave out a stentorian hee-haw. Mrs Innes looked at West Street rising steeply in front of her, looked into Edith's urgent eyes, shrugged, and climbed on to the donkey's back. Edith stood up, and trotted off with Mrs Innes sitting proud and upright on her back.

Pancester is a small place, and if you wish to see someone, then nine times out of ten, you will be able to find them without any difficulty. Often, just to think about someone is enough to bring them into your presence, and you will suddenly meet them in the street, in the pub, in the Fox Hole, or around the other shops. Under normal circumstances, if Mrs Innes wanted to find Whittaker, she just popped into the 4i's, and there he was. If Whittaker wanted to see Oliver, he could just nip next door and find him. Nothing could be simpler. But when the narrow streets are packed with fifteen thousand howling maniacs battling over a piece of rolled-up leather, and when every available place on the pavements is crammed with a similar number of screaming women urging their menfolk to victory, it is less simple. In fact, it would be best if you could wait till the next day to track down your friend. This luxury was denied both Mrs Innes and Whittaker.

Edith ran faster than she had for at least twenty years, over the

Pack Bridge, through the West Gate, and up West Street. Mrs Innes sat swaying on her back. She must find a committee member, or one of the hippies, or Sydney, or someone, anyone, who would help her muster reinforcements. The council could not be allowed to get away with this. Thank goodness she had always had a good seat.

She and Edith arrived in front of the Guildhall, and saw the main body of the Clanghandlers on the other side of the square at the bottom of Church Street, slowly being forced back down the hill by pressure from the Ringlers. Mrs Innes hopped down from the donkey, rubbed her ears in gratitude, and ran towards the back of the scrum, shouting, 'Mr Whittaker! Mr Gabatini? Sydney! Can you hear me?' But it was hopeless. How could anyone hear her? Her voice was one among thousands of shouting voices; how would anyone be able to distinguish hers from the rest? She reached the Clanghandler rear, as it was inched back into the Square, and despaired. There was no way through. She held her head in her hands, and turned around to see Timmy Rubenstein and his cameraman sitting on the kerbstone, examining the remains of their equipment. Timmy had a black eye, and was not looking in the best of humours.

'Mr Rubenstein,' said Mrs Innes. 'You are needed elsewhere.' Timmy looked up, and recognised her from the day before, when she had brought him tea and biscuits.

'Hello,' he said. 'I don't think we can film any more local colour today.' He poked at the ruined camera with his foot, and laughed bitterly. Mrs Innes sat down beside him.

'Mr Rubenstein, the deputy sheriff is, at this very moment, forcibly evacuating the squatters from the car park camp using the techniques of the totalitarian state. Your colleagues are trying to protect the dig from imminent destruction. You must get down there and try to stop them. Perhaps they will listen to you.'

'You're kidding?' said Timmy.

'I wish I were. Unfortunately, I am not. Please. There's not a moment to lose.'

'What shall I do about this?' said the cameraman, looking at his shattered camera.

'Leave it!' said Timmy, standing up. 'Leave it and come with me! Come on!'

'What about Neil?' said the cameraman. 'Hadn't we better get Neil? If the Temple's in danger?'

'Mr Winterburn?' said Mrs Innes. 'Where is he?'

'He's just there, look, trying to spur on the Clanghandlers from the rear,' said Timmy. Now Mrs Innes could see Winterburn for herself, some ten metres or so away, a grin all over his face, his shirt ripped from his back and blood pouring from his nose as a result of what rugby commentators call 'shenanigans in the boiler room'. He was shouting encouragement and attempting to regroup the Clanghandlers' faltering defence.

'Oh, thank God. You go, Mr Rubenstein, please. I'll need Mr Winterburn. Edith! Edith!' The donkey trotted obediently across.

'Edith, can you take Mr Rubenstein back to the Dole Acre? Perhaps he can do some good? You can? Thank you, dear.'

Timmy Rubenstein looked nervously at the donkey. 'Oh, I'm not sure . . .'

'Don't be silly, dear. Edith has four legs, she'll be much quicker than your two. Come on! Up you get! Now, off with you! Neil! Neil!'

Winterburn turned and waved, in time to see Timmy Rubenstein clinging uncertainly to Edith's neck as she trotted back to the Acre, his cameraman struggling to keep up. Winterburn limped across, and sat next to Mrs Innes on the kerb.

'Hello, Mrs I. Where are they off to? Getting a new camera?'

'No. The barbarians are at the gate. In fact, they're through the gate, and are coming up the garden path with a Betterware catalogue.' And she told Winterburn about the strong-arm techniques which were being used down on the Acre.

Winterburn was white with anger. Mrs Innes could see that he was shaking when he spoke. 'Let's go and stop them,' he said quietly.

'How? How are we going to stop them? I've sent Mr Rubenstein back to the site. He's famous, perhaps he can remonstrate with them, make them see sense. But we must find some decent reinforcements, or stop the Wally, which is going to be difficult, isn't it?' Winterburn looked at the whooping and bawling barrage of bodies as it was forced out into the Square from the bottom of Church Street.

'It's going to be impossible, Mrs I. Nothing can stop the Wally. And how are we going to find anyone, never mind persuade them to come down to the Acre? Let me go down there!'

'No, please, Mr Winterburn, don't leave me here alone. We've got to find Mr Whittaker or Dexter or someone.'

'But Mrs I, how?' said Winterburn desperately. 'Just look at it.'

The Clanghandlers were now in full retreat, forced by the Ringlers across the Guildhall Square, and Mrs Innes and Winterburn were in danger of being swept up in the scrum. Even if Mrs Innes could recognise Whittaker or Taff or Dexter in the middle of that boiling sea of straining humanity, which was unlikely, how was she going to get through to them to let them know what was happening?

'I don't know, Neil. We need a miracle, I'm afraid.'

'Auntie Jocelyn?' called a voice from close by Mrs Innes' feet. 'Is that you?'

'Sydney? Where are you?'

'Down here.' Mrs Innes looked down the storm drain beside her, and saw Syd's face grinning up at her from under the cover.

'Are we back in Guildhall Square?' he asked.

'Sydney, thank God. Get up here at once. Something's happened.' Winterburn lifted the drain cover, and Syd climbed out, followed by Steve Medlicott and Ronnie of the Pink Bus, all dripping with I dread to think what, and smelling of Edmund's armpits on a hot day.

'Ha!' said Syd. 'They thought they had us stuck up on the green, thought they had all the entrances covered, so we exited the same way we got up there. Silly buggers forgot to cover the drains. What's happening? Looks like we've been forced back into the Square.'

'More to the point, we're being forced off the Acre,' said Mrs Innes, and she told her friends about the raid, and how the hippies were being forcibly evicted, and how the bulldozers were ready to roll.

'My old lady's still down there, the mothers. If they've done anything to her or the Pink Bus . . .' said Ronnie. 'Come on!'

'Mr Ronnie, there are hundreds of police down there, together with a highly trained and motivated detachment of professional thugs. The police will stay within the law, just, but the gang from the museum has no such scruples. They are out to hurt people. What good can we do on our own? A few more people won't make the slightest bit of difference. Mr Timmy Rubenstein has gone back, because I think in this day and age, one famous person has more clout than a hundred ordinary folk, more's the pity, and he'll be doing what he can. Our job is to stop the Wally, and take thousands of bodies down there.'

'But, Auntie, how are we going to do that?'

'I'm not sure, but we must find a way. Oh, thank the good lord, here's Mr Whittaker.'

'And he's got old Edmund with him,' said Winterburn.

'Who appears to be wearing a rather fetching ballgown,' said Sydney.

Letty had avoided the Wally by leading Whittaker through alleyways and passages, over back-garden walls and into dark snickets, until they emerged into Shy Street, a little way up from the 4i's. Whittaker was panting with exertion, and his left knee was grazed from wall-climbing. He leant against the door of the Fox Hole to catch his breath.

'Oh, do come on, darling,' drawled Lady Lettice. 'I want to find my son.'

'Just give me a moment, Lady Letty. I'm a chef, not a cat burglar.'

Lady Letty sighed, smoothed down her frock with her greasy hands and ran her fingers through her copious and filthy beard.

'Do I look OK? I want to look my best for my boy.'

'You look smashing, Lady Letty.'

'Do you think my blue suits me? Do you think he'll like it?'

'I'm sure he will.'

'Or do you think I should have put on my pink?'

'No honestly, Lady Letty, the blue is the thing. Come on, let's go and see if we can find him.'

As Whittaker and Letty emerged from the archway which led through to Shy Street, they could see Mrs Innes and her group waving frantically. They hurried across to join them, and arrived at the same time as Dawn, Sally and Penny Lester, pushing Papa Nico between them. They had been watching agitatedly from the pavement. As the three groups joined, everybody started talking at once. For some reason he couldn't quite understand after-wards, Whittaker found that the babble of disjointed, shouted exchanges made perfect sense to him.

'They are destroying the Acre whatta do you think you are doing standing around when you should be in the scrum the police are smashing the vans isn't it exciting Neil what have you done to your nose isn't Oliver brave this is Lady Lettice the tunnels'll keep the beggars out if they've hurt my old lady we've got the Charter the missing Charter where's my boy Mr Whittaker Juliana is clearing the site I know I saw from the walls Auntie says we've got to stop the Wally but how can we stop the Wally are you insane where's my boy where's my boy where's my boy?' said Neil Winterburn, Papa Nico, Ronnie of the Pink Bus, Sally, Syd, Mrs Innes, Penny Lester, Lady Lettice, and a voice which Whittaker recognised as his own, all at the same moment. Whittaker raised his hand, and the group fell silent.

'Papa Nico,' said Whittaker. 'We are not in the Wally at present because dark angels are circling over the Dole Acre, and we must repel them. I know what is happening, I have seen it all, from the walls. And I have found Lady Lettice Courtney. And she has the Charter. We can stop them.'

'Letty?' said Syd, looking round in amazement. 'Where?'

'Oh, Sydney, men are so fickle. Who'd have thought you'd have forgotten our last shag, under the stage at the Free Festival in a thunderstorm?' said Lady Lettice.

'Letty?' said Syd, grabbing her by her hairy upper arms, and looking into her eyes. 'Letty? Is it really you?'

'Of course it is, you daft old sod. Sorry I haven't been in touch for a bit. Got bogged down in the tramp thing, you know.' Syd hugged her, and kissed her on the mouth. She pushed him off.

'No PDAs, Sydney, I beg you.' Syd stood back and looked at her.

'You could do with a wax, old girl,' he said. 'Most extraordinary beard I've ever seen on a woman in my life, and I was posted in Hereford at one time, so I've seen a few.'

'Please, Lettice,' said Mrs Innes, 'we can all catch up on our news later. The problem at the moment is with these thugs who are smashing up the camp and bulldozing the Temple of Priapus, and if that really is the Charter you are holding, then we need you to come at once and stop them.'

'My dear Jocelyn, I couldn't give a fig about some bourgeois little car park,' said Lady Lettice.

'But it's Courtney land, m'lady. Your land. A Courtney never gives up their land without a fight, do they?' said Winterburn.

'Hello, you're rather dolly, aren't you? I've seen you in the kitchen at the 4i's, haven't I?'

'Yes, Lady Lettice. And I'm sure we'd all be terribly grateful if you could see your way clear to helping us.'

'Oh, look here, Edmund, or whatever your name is,' said Sally, 'if you really have got the Charter, hand it over for goodness' sake, and stop mucking about.'

'Ah, Miss Sally,' said Lady Lettice in her Edmund voice. 'Alas, I'm rather afraid that Edmund is no more after this. His cover has been blown. It's back to the cares and woes of the Estate Office for me, darling. And as for the Charter, you can't have it unless my son says you can. I've brought it for him, not for you.'

'But look at them! He's right in the middle of that! How are we going to get him out of that?' said Ronnie of the Pink Bus. He pointed at the crush of the Wally, thousands of shouting grunting howling bodies jammed together across the width of the Guildhall Square, the two sides very nearly back in their original starting position, a great column of steam rising from their straining backs into the wintry air.

'No son, no Charter,' said Lady Lettice. The group groaned. Penny Lester walked forward, and bobbed a diffident curtsy.

Everyone thought she was very brave. It is never easy meeting in-laws for the first time, especially when they are black with filth and stinking to high heaven.

'Hello, Lady Lettice. I'm Penelope Lester. I'm engaged to Oliver. I'm certain that he would want you to let these people have the Charter.'

'Oh, you are, are you? Humph. Well, my dear, it's no go, I'm afraid. You're not married yet, even if you do turn out to be suitable. Bring me my boy, and you can have it. Otherwise, back it goes into the vault.'

Whittaker raised his hand again. 'I know of a way. Steve? Mr Medlicott? Can you do it, do you think? Can you send to him?' he said.

Medlicott stepped forwards and, shading his eyes from the sharp sun, looked towards the Wally. He closed his eyes, and licked his lips.

'The ... energetic patterns are confused. There are ...' he rocked his head back and forth a few times, as if counting, '... fifteen thousand three hundred and seventy-nine men in there. And one woman. The woman is the clearest ... it is Gwyn ... so that must be Taff behind her ... ah ... hang on ... got him. He's four rows in front of Gwyn. No, he's gone again ... he's back ... he's gone. Sorry.' Medlicott opened his eyes.

'Send to Gwyn,' shouted Sally. 'Tell her to get him.'

'What do you think, Steve? Worth a try?'

'I'll have a go, Mr Whittaker.' Steve closed his eyes again, and started to hum. The hum came from deep within his chest, deep and low, quietly at first, but with increasing power, so that those standing nearest to him were forced to cover their ears.

'I wish he'd stop that dreary humming, Syd,' said Lady Lettice.

'You've got a nerve, old girl,' said Syd, trying to run his hand up her leg. 'You hum like billy-o.'

In the middle of the Wally scrum, Gwyn was feeling bruised, battered, and on the edge of exhaustion. She had held the line and held the line, until the Ringler shouts showed that Syd's drain ploy had worked, and then she'd almost fallen over in the mad forwards rush of the Clanghandler pack up Church Street towards St Gilbert's. Her father had held her arm as they chased across the Square to support Syd's audacious attempt on goal, only to find themselves jammed like sardines in Church Street, unable to move forward any further, without the room to scrimmage, feeling themselves forced slowly back down the steep street. Now Gwyn was head down again, her arms wrapped around the waist of the man in front, aching from trying to hold him steady. Her legs were heavy from trying to get some grip on the icy cobbles of the Square, and her spirit was almost broken from the realisation that they were right back where they started, and that it probably wasn't even midday yet.

I must be bloody mad, she thought. Why in God's name did I think it so important to be the first woman in the Wally? What was I trying to prove? This is worse than the main drag at Glastonbury on Saturday night. I need to get out of this and have some rest. Everyone does, every hour or so, it won't be chickening out, I just need a drink, it's the sensible thing, the most tactically aware thing to do. But how do I get out?

And then it came to her as clear as day. Of course. She must find Oliver. He was only a few rows in front of her, she'd seen him re-engage in the scrimmage. He could get her out. He would understand, everyone needs a break from this.

She turned her head as best she could, and screamed at her father, who was holding on to her from behind, 'I've got to go and find Oliver! I'm going to crawl through. Ready?' Taff nodded, and leapt into her place as she dropped to her knees and started to crawl forward through the angry forest of legs.

'Coming through!' she shouted to the men above her. 'Coming through with a message from the rear!' The legs got out of her way as much as possible, but still her hands were covered in blood within a few feet, as honest Pancester boots ground her fingers into the cobbles. After somehow forcing her way through three rows of stamping legs, breathing the fetid air of fifteen thousand sweating feet, she saw what could only be Oliver's socks, one yellow and one black, off to her right. She grabbed his calves and pulled him down. He raised his eyebrows in greeting.

'Oliver, you've got to help me get to the pavement,' screamed Gwyneth. Oliver looked puzzled.

'Why?' he shouted. Gwyn had never heard him speak so loudly before.

'I don't know. I can't stand any more. You've got to help me get to the pavement. Come on, Oliver!'

Oliver shrugged, stood up, and started to shoulder his way through the heaving mass, with Gwyneth gripping him gratefully by the arm.

'Shout "Hospitaller",' said Oliver. 'They'll let us through. They'll think you're injured.'

'Hospitaller!' shouted Gwyn. 'Hospitaller!' The crowd eased a little, and Oliver was able to force a way out of the pack, and on to the pavement.

'Thanks, Oliver,' said Gwyn, with a hug.

'Why me and not your father?'

Gwyn looked puzzled. 'I don't know,' she said. 'Oh, but there's Sally and Mum and everyone. Look, we came out right by them. Wasn't that lucky? Over here, hey, guys!'

'There they are, look,' shouted Sally, and the group around the no-longer-humming Steve Medlicott came running across. To Gwyn's surprise, everyone was much more interested in Oliver than in her, which hardly seemed fair. Penny hugged him. Even Dawn, Gwyneth's own mother, was busy clapping him on the back. Only Sally came over to help her.

'Why's Oliver so bloody popular all of a sudden?' she said. 'Look at my hands!'

'No time to explain, poor sore darling. Watch!'

Whittaker took the bemused Oliver by the elbow and led him towards Lady Letty.

'Lady Lettice Courtney, allow me to introduce you to your son, Oliver. Sir Oliver, your mother, Lady Lettice.' Oliver stood open-mouthed in front of what looked suspiciously like a tramp, in an aquamarine Norman Hartnell ballgown with matching gloves, shoes and evening bag.

Lady Lettice sniffed and wiped her bulging purple nose on her elegant glove. 'Hello there, m'boy. How have you been?' she said, her voice choked with emotion.

'Very well, thank you, Mama,' said Oliver, the light of joy illuminating his eyes.

'Hasn't he been well brought up?' she said, looking around her and smiling. 'Mama! How charming.'

'If you please, Mama.'

'Good man. Well done. Now look here. Sorry about your grandmama farming you out, and all that. She was a real stickler for form was Mummy. I was terribly, terribly upset, but there really was nothing I could do. I'm sure you'll understand, and agree with me that what's done is done and can't be helped. It's the Courtney way. Time to move on, start again. What do you say, old chap?'

'Oh, Mama!' said Oliver, falling into his mother's arms with a whimper. Lady Lettice looked awkward as she embraced her long-lost son. Oliver cradled his head into her beard.

'There, there,' said Lady Lettice. 'Calm down now, m'boy. Dry your eyes. That's it. Now listen here, your friends have been telling me all about this car park the bloody council is trying to build on our land. Is it true?'

'Yes, Mama,' said Oliver, dabbing his eyes with the corner of his handkerchief.

'And is it true that you wish it stopped?'

'Why, yes, Mama.'

'Then it *shall* be stopped. Here's the original Charter of 1503, which has remained with the family all this time. Take it, m'boy, take it. You're going to have to learn all about this sort of thing if you're going to help me pick up the reins of the Estate.' Lady Lettice handed Oliver the Charter, and the committee crowded around.

'Is that it, Mrs Innes?' asked Dawn. 'The missing Charter I found out about?'

'Yes, Dawn, I believe it is. Look, here, Sir Kenelm's signature. And here, the disputed clause. It looks like grazing rights to me.'

'Of course it's grazing rights, darling Jocelyn. The Courtneys don't give away their land, and there were no flies on Sir Kenelm,' said Lady Lettice.

'Yeah, but come on,' said Ronnie of the Pink Bus. 'My bus might be getting trashed, my old dear beat up. What are we going to do with this?'

'Well, I thought about stopping the Wally somehow,' said Mrs Innes, 'but this will prove that what they are doing is illegal. It should be enough.' And she told Oliver and Gwyneth about the sheriff's men moving in to trash the site. Oliver's eyes, his Courtney eyes, lit with the light of battle.

'I still think we'll need some numbers, yeah?' said Ronnie. Oliver nodded forcefully, blushed furiously, and sucked air into his lungs.

'I agree,' he said suddenly. 'I . . . agree. This can't go on. This must be stopped. Terry, if you'd come with me? And you, Mrs Innes, and of course my dear mama, if she'd be so kind, and you, darling Penny. The rest of you, just wait here a moment.'

'Oliver!' said Penny.

'Blood will out, Jocelyn,' said Lady Lettice triumphantly to Mrs Innes, as they followed Oliver, Penny and Whittaker up the Guildhall steps.

Oliver stood at the top with his small band of supporters and surveyed the scene. The huge ruck still filled most of the space, with stragglers emerging from the rear, and newly refreshed players taking their place. Smaller skirmishes, often set up as dummies to move the Wally about, were breaking out all over the Guildhall Square.

Oliver took a great breath, and shouted.

'SILENCE!'

As though turned off by a switch, the Wally stopped. From all over the Square, players looked up from the maul at the figures on the Guildhall steps, scene of so many ceremonies and dramas in the centuries-old history of Pancester. Where moments before there had been cacophonous uproar, there was now a hushed whisper.

'It's the Voice,' said Lady Lettice, proudly. 'The Courtney Voice. The last one of us who had it properly was old General Sir Wyndham Courtney, my great-grandfather. Used it to great effect at the Battle of Omdurman, we were always told.'

'Thank you,' said Sir Oliver. 'Now you men know that I would not have interrupted your festivities lightly, unless I had some vitally important issue to put before you today.' His voice carried clearly across the Square to the great crowd, who all nodded at one another, and said things like, 'Aye, right enough,' and 'Aye, he's not one to stop the Wally lightly is Sir Oliver,' as though they had been used to his little ways all their lives.

'But the fact of the matter is,' continued Sir Oliver, 'that the forces of progress and change are advancing with an army of destruction across that part of my mother's land known as the Dole Acre. Now, I know that one or two of you think this car park idea is a good one. And I agree, it is the very devil to park here. We have never denied that. But my good friend Mr Terry Whittaker here has put forward a programme of environmentally sound transport restructuring which would obviate the need for the new car park altogether!' The crowd cheered, and threw their hats in the air. Dexter stared across at his brother from the middle of the pack, and went running across to join him.

'But even as we speak,' said Oliver, 'the council is using the most brutal methods imaginable to clear our peace-loving travelling community from the Dole Acre. They are burning and smashing people's homes. Their bulldozers stand poised, ready to wipe the Temple of Priapus from the colourful weft and warp of Pancester's tapestry of customs. The donkeys will be put into cattle trucks and shipped away to goodness only knows where. Planorbis Pancestrum, rarest and least assuming of all our watersnails, will be crushed under the hobnailed boots of developers.' Dexter came running up beside his brother, and shook his hand.

'Dear God, who is that?' said Lady Letty. 'He's got a face like a pig's arse drawn on a piece of crumpled-up writing paper.'

'His twin brother, Lettice,' whispered Mrs Innes.

'I can see I've got a great deal of catching up to do,' said Lady Lettice.

'The council has decreed that we shall have this car park. They claimed that they were entitled to build it under the terms of the Charter granted to the City of Pancester by my illustrious ancestor, Sir Kenelm de Courtney. They produced a forged copy of the Charter in support of this claim,' continued Sir Oliver. 'My brother and I have opposed them from the beginning. Now my mother here, returned to the heart of our community from an enforced absence, has given me the original of this document, which establishes beyond all doubt that the council does not have this right at all. Today it is Courtney land under threat. Tomorrow they could insist on building a car park in your back garden! Is that what you want?'

'No!' shouted the crowd.

'I ask you now ... will you come with me to the Dole Acre, to stop this betrayal of our ancient rights?'

'Yes!' screamed the crowd.

'Then follow me!' And Oliver grabbed Penny's hand, jumped down the steps, and started to run towards the top of West Street, which led down to the Pack Bridge, retracing in reverse the route that Edith the donkey and Mrs Innes had taken earlier that day.

And everybody in the square raced after them pell-mell. Lady Lettice and Mrs Innes ran, Whittaker and Dexter ran, Sally and Gwyn and Ronnie and Ash and Phil and all the hippies, Neil Winterburn and Steve Medlicott and Syd Montague-Forrester, Taff and Frank Welford, still in the thick of the pack, all ran as fast as they could. The Mayor and Aoldermen, and the Alarumist and Martha and Dennis from the 4i's, and Trevor Mallinson and his supporters on the council, and Ted Blezzard, his shop closed for the day so that he could compete in the Wally, and Ursula Armistead, holding the hand of her youngest grandson, they all ran. Dawn ran, pushing Papa Nico, who waved his sticks and shouted 'Tally-ho', and all the Wallymen, Clanghandlers and Ringlers alike, and all the watching women and children, and the butchers and bakers and scented ethnic candlestick makers, and the data-input clerks and the hands from the maggot factory, and the IT consultants and the beauty therapists, and the dentists and the solicitors, and the binmen and the part-time lecturers in further education, all ran after Sir Oliver, down through the narrow streets of old Pancester town, joining together to become a great flood of angry Pancestrians, a righteous tide.

And the flood came pouring out of the West Gate, and over the Pack Bridge, with Sir Oliver, bold Sir Oliver, at its head, his fiancée by his side.

And so the whole population of the little city came down to the Dole Acre, and filled it with angry noise.

Juliana did not look terribly pleased to see them.

The Battle for Dole Acre

Emma and Gemma had not been idle in Mrs Innes' absence. After they had eluded the grasp of Inspector McCracken and his men, they dodged back through the site, gathering up as they went the few hippy women and children who had yet to be evicted. They half-dragged, half-carried poor Professor Daggers away from the riverbank, and dropped him protesting into the trench. Added to the handful of archaeologists who were preparing to defend the dig, they had perhaps twenty bodies.

'Right,' said Emma, assuming command, and pointing to several members of her small force. 'I want you all to gather up donkey shit to make bombs. Rolly . . . you stay here, and don't lick yer tumour. You, you and you, go with Gemma, take some of the tape we use for marking out the trenches, and string it between those three buses parked over there. Gemma, you can hold up the filth for a bit? Keep 'em off the dig?'

'I know a good way to make bombs,' said Professor Daggers. The defenders looked at the old gentleman.

'And what's that, Prof?' said Emma.

'Well, you take a little piece of sodium from your bicycle lamp, pop it into an old lemonade bottle, and then you micturate on it, hee hee hee. You've got to be quick though, or it'll blow up in your hand. Has anyone brought their bicycle with them?'

Emma and Gemma looked puzzled.

'They don't have sodium in bicycle lamps any more,' said one of the archaeologists.

'They don't have bicycle lamps any more,' said another.

'Well, how do people see to ride at night?' asked the professor.

'I'm sorry, Prof, we don't have time to go into it now. I've got to run,' said Emma.

'Where are you going, Em?' said Gemma.

'I'm going down int tunnels. See you in a bit.' And Emma ran towards the nearest entrance to Syd and Tony the Tunneller's anti-car park grotto.

'Come on!' Gemma urged her troops, as they spun a web of red and white warning tape around and between the three buses nearest the dig. 'They're coming, look.'

The police were advancing line abreast towards the makeshift barrier, and behind them lurked the sinister figures of the sheriff's men, pickaxe handles at the ready. The bomb-makers hurried towards the web with their donkey grenades.

'Wait till you can see the pinks of their eyes,' growled Gemma. 'Ready? Fire!' A rain of donkey turds splattered on the advancing police as the hippies and archaeologists pelted them with the squelchy bombs. As the police reached the barrier, they tried to force a way through, but were repelled by the shitty fusillade, and it looked as though they might be held off, when a couple of Molotov cocktails from the sheriff's men were lobbed over the heads of the police and on to the roofs of the buses. Flames licked over the hippies' homes.

'Bastards!' screamed the hippies.

'Back off,' shouted Gemma. 'Back to t'dig!'

Emma, streaked with mud, came running across to rejoin them in Trench Two as the police cautiously advanced across the site, towards where the guerrillas were lying in wait to pelt them again.

'Aright Em?' said Gemma.

'Aye. Reckon that should slow 'em down.'

'What yer do?'

'Took out the supports ont tunnel by t'gate. Listen.' There was a crash, and a gunning of engines. 'There,' said Emma. 'That should do it. Fookers.'

Over at the gate, watching columns of smoke rising from the

camp, hearing the screams of mothers dragged from their homes and the cries of frightened children, Juliana had her blood up. Her cheeks were flushed, her eyes shining. This was the best thing ever, better than lying next to Q or Trevor, better than eating at the 4i's. This was it. This was life, this was power, this was success, a one-way ticket out of Pancester for the Big Time. A delicious feeling of warmth, powerful and liberating, passed up through her body, and she felt herself go weak at the knees with pleasure. She had never before experienced such ecstasy, such deep, sensual satisfaction.

She purred into her walkie-talkie. 'Blue seven, this is Control.'

'Blue seven here, Control.'

'Send in the bulldozers.'

'But, Control, we haven't got all the people off the site. There's still a pocket of resistance in the archaeologists' trench.'

'I don't care, it's well past twelve, and they should have been gone an hour ago. They've had plenty of warning. Send in the bulldozers.'

'Very well, Control. Blue seven out.'

She heard the roar from the great engines, and saw billowing blue smoke issue from the exhaust chimneys of the yellow Leviathans. They rumbled across the ring road on massive caterpillar tracks, and stopped as the first of them reached the gate.

Juliana ran across and shouted up to the driver in his cab, 'What's the matter? Why have you stopped?'

'Can't fit through the gateposts, miss.'

'Well, knock them down, you idiot. And then clear all these disgusting vehicles out of the way! Push them into the river!'

'Right, miss.' The driver engaged his gears, and the bulldozer crawled forwards, ripping out the gateposts and part of the wall as it drove on to the Dole Acre.

Syd and Tony had built their tunnels well, and Emma had been careful with her removal of the props, and so it was that the second bulldozer was able to get on to the site, before the first slid sideways into a pit ten feet deep which had suddenly opened up on its right-hand side.

'Jesus!' said the driver of the second machine, and rammed his bulldozer into reverse, only to find himself backing into another of the collapsing tunnels. He tried to drive out forwards, but his angle was too steep. His nose pointed at the sky, while his tracks screamed as they tried and failed to pull the bulldozer out. The driver turned off the engine, and hopped down from his cab. His mate from the first bulldozer joined him. They looked at their beached 'dozers, and grinned at one another.

'Reckon that's it for the day, don't you, George?' said the first driver.

'Aye. Let's go join the Wally,' said the second, and they trotted off together over the bridge.

Juliana shouted instructions into her walkie-talkie to little effect. There was no one left in the cabs to hear them, anyway.

This was the situation as Timmy Rubenstein came trotting on Edith over the Pack Bridge, his ex-cameraman puffing and panting some way behind. They saw the site swarming with police, many hurrying back towards the gate to investigate the noise, and others still trying to get at the dig, where Emma and Gemma were organising a final resistance from their redoubt. They saw smaller numbers of shaven-headed men in leather jackets, smashing up the windows and setting fire to the hippy vehicles. They saw the useless bulldozers trapped by the snares of Syd and Tony the Tunneller.

'Come on, Johnny!' said Rubenstein to his cameraman. He leapt down from Edith's back, and like Boris Yeltsin on the tank in front of the White House, he climbed up on the rearmost of the stranded bulldozers, and started to harangue the police.

'You cannot do this!' he shouted. 'This is the action of neo-Nazis!'

'Arrest that man!' screamed Juliana to McCracken. 'Get him off my lovely bulldozers! And get the bulldozers out of those holes!'

'We can't arrest him, Miss Blezzard,' said McCracken.

'Why not?'

'He's on the telly, miss,' said a constable. 'He's in that . . . what is it? The one where he always has a "wizard wheeze"?'

'Aye, that's right funny, that is. That Mr Bean's in it,' said McCracken.

'Right. If you're not going to stop him, I am!' And she ran towards the bulldozer with Timmy Rubenstein on top, and tried to climb up the caterpillars towards him. But she slipped backwards, and landed on her arse in newly frothed mud, which just about ruined the Armani suit that Q had bought her for her birthday, to match his own.

'Are you OK?' asked Timmy Rubenstein, peering down at her.

And Juliana said, as she lay on her back in the mud, 'I know where you live. I've got friends. You'll never work again,' which just made Timmy Rubenstein laugh.

So it is easy to understand why Juliana was not in the best of moods when, upon dragging herself to her feet, she saw the entire population of Pancester, with Sir Oliver Courtney at their head, come thundering over the Pack Bridge, around the corner and on to the Dole Acre.

'Oh, bollocks and bugger!' she said, stamping her foot. 'Bugger bugger bugger bugger bugger bugger bugger bugger buggerbuggerbuggerbugger. Bugger. Inspector McCraken! Inspector McCraken! Arrest these people!' But McCracken was cowering inside his Range Rover while enraged Pancestrians rocked it to and fro. He looked frightened stiff through the window, and was gibbering into his short-wave radio, little realising that the aerial had been pulled from the roof.

Still the people poured over the bridge, and crowded through the entrance to Dole Acre. Now they divided into several large factions. The largest, led by Ronnie of the Pink Bus and the hippies, started to chase after the sheriff's men from the National Museum of Crime and Punishment. The thugs may have been heavily armed, but they were outnumbered by hundreds to one, and they were quickly rounded up and placed under guard while a bucket chain was formed, to bring water up from the river to put out the fires on the van roofs. And as soon as the fires were extinguished, the jeering crowd pushed the museum guides one by one into the river, and forced them to swim to the other side of the Athon. They climbed out on the opposite mud bank, their leather jackets ruined, and slunk off.

Another party chased the police away from the dig, and liberated the besieged archaeologists. Emma and Gemma stood on the parapet of Trench Two like heroines in a Socialist Realist painting, their dyed hair streaming in the breeze behind them. Professor Daggers was helped out, and he stood smiling toothlessly, his mud-stained bobble hat at a raffish angle. Here and there the policemen had a go at standing on their dignity, and they tried pointing out that Dole Acre was council property as from eleven o'clock and no one had a right to be there without authorisation from the council, but they were jeered at and pelted with donkey turds, and their helmets were knocked off. So the police packed up their things and made their way home sheepishly, like schoolboys with a note from the headmaster in their satchels. Only poor Inspector McCracken remained, trapped in the Range Rover that had now become an impromptu children's adventure playground.

And a third group, led by Sir Oliver Courtney, gathered around Juliana, who was screaming at the thousands of new visitors to the site, 'This is council land! You have no right to be here!'

Ted Blezzard stepped forward, and put his arm around her shoulder. 'Come on now, lass. Don't take on so.'

Trevor Mallinson put his arm around her other shoulder. 'I tried to stop them, darling, I really did. But they were like beasts.'

Juliana shook herself free from her supporters, and stared into the faces of her accusers. 'Well?' she said. 'What do you want?'

Mrs Innes stepped forward, brandishing the Charter. 'Ms Blezzard,' she said, 'I have here a document which proves beyond question that this land remains the property of the Courtney family in perpetuity, and that the City Council only enjoys the right to graze animals on the Dole Acre.'

'It's a forgery,' said Juliana.

'No, my girl, it's yours that's the forgery, and well you know it.

327

Mr Turner? Where's Mr Turner? Just come and have a look at this, will you?'

Mr Turner, the mild-mannered curator of the Lady Abigail Courtney Museum and Art Gallery, stepped nervously forward.

'Mr Turner, what do you make of this?' He peered at the Charter through his spectacles, which had been bent badly out of shape in the Wally.

'It's not my period, you understand,' he said, looking up, 'and I'd have to send it to my friend in Cambridge, of course, but a first glance would support your theory, Mrs Innes. In the light of this exciting new discovery, I'd be quite happy to send our copy for X-ray.'

'Thank you, Mr Turner.'

'But the Courtneys are dead. We're still going to court to prove our right to take over the land,' said Juliana.

'Well, that's where you're wrong, young lady,' said Lady Lettice. 'We're not dead at all. I am Lady Lettice Courtney, and this is my son, Sir Oliver, the twenty-seventh baronet. And this is our land, and I'm afraid it's you that's here without authorisation.'

'You? You're just a filthy old tramp. How can you prove that you're who you say you are?'

Lady Lettice dug about in her evening bag. 'With this. I always keep it in here. One never knows when one might be whisked off by some wonderful man to Deauville or somesuch.' It was her passport, recently renewed, showing a picture of her in a smart twinset, the Courtney pearls worn over her beard.

Then Mrs Innes said, 'Ursula? Is Ursula about?'

'Here I am, Jocelyn,' said Aolderwoman Armistead, still holding her grandson's hand.

'You are both a JP and Letty's oldest friend. Would you confirm her identity for us, please?'

Aolderwoman Armistead looked at the passport, and then looked deep into Lady Letty's face. 'Oh, Letty,' she said. 'I do wish you'd written.'

Tears stood out in Lady Letty's eyes. 'I'm so sorry. It just seemed so much easier to let everything go, the house and the

Estate and everything. It had all become such a bore, you know. But I missed you very much, dear Ursie.' And the two old friends hugged one another.

'Bath salts for your birthday this year, Letty, I think,' I said Aolderwoman Armistead, letting go.

'But we have the Secretary of State's say-so on the millennium car park project. There's nothing you can do to stop us,' said Juliana.

'I'm afraid that's not quite the case, Ms Blezzard,' said Brian Carless, elbowing his way through the crowd and keeping a watch on Edith, who stood surveying the scene with serene eyes. 'With this new evidence, the Secretary of State will be forced to send the thing for judicial review at the very least, no matter what you and Dr Sandahl did to nobble him. Certainly Aolderwoman Armistead, in the light of these recent findings, has the power to order an immediate halt to work on Dole Acre. And ownership reverts to the Courtneys with the positive identification of Lady Lettice.'

'But don't take it too hard, Ms Blezzard,' said Neil Winterburn, stepping forward. 'Sir Oliver has been one of the staunchest supporters of the recovery of the Temple of Priapus, and I'm sure he'd wish to see a new interpretation and visitor facility here on the Acre. Lots more lovely visitors. Could be an award in it, if it's tastefully done.'

'And we'll be happy to report on your progress on the show,' said Timmy Rubenstein, climbing down from the beached bulldozer.

'And the energetic patterns remain . . . intact,' said Medlicott. 'If they had been destabilised . . .' (he sucked air through his moustache) '. . . I would not have liked to answer for the consequences.'

'And we've still got the jolly old snails. Don't forget them,' said Syd Montague-Forrester.

'Hee hee hee. Yes indeed. Ho yes. The snails,' echoed Professor Daggers.

'And your daughters, when you have them, will still be able to come a-Eastering every year,' said Dawn.

'And we will still be able to fight for the honour of the bread rolls,' said Papa Nico.

'And we'll come back every autumn, man, and liven the old place up,' said Ronnie of the Pink Bus.

'Oh, great,' said Juliana. 'Bloody great. Well, you can keep your stupid field. I mean, who cares if visitor numbers fall due to inadequate parking facilities? I don't any more. I wash my hands of the lot of you, you stupid small-minded bunch of fossilised old fogeys. You can't face change, can you? You're scared of anything modern and progressive, aren't you? Well, you might have won here, but your day is over. Over! And you can sort out your own short-stay visitor car-parking, and see how you get on with it. I don't think you'll find it that easy. Because I quit! Do you hear? I quit!' And she turned on her heel and walked away.

'Not so quickly, my dear,' came a sibilant voice.

Juliana turned again with a gasp. A figure with its head in a balaclava came through the throng, his arm around the neck of Penny Lester, a familiar gun held to her head. The crowd fell silent.

'Lady Letty!' whispered Gwyn. 'I thought you were hiding the gun.'

Letty blushed, rather prettily under the circumstances. 'Sorry, darling. I forgot. Never did like 'em. The little greaser must have nipped back and got it.'

'What is it? What do you want with my fiancée?' said cool Sir Oliver.

The figure, still holding the gun to Penny's temple, released her neck, and pulled off his balaclava. The crowd gasped, but Taff could not quite suppress a smile when he saw the state of Q's skin. Sandahl grabbed Penny's neck again.

'Nothing. I want nothing with your fiancée, Mr Halton. You see, I refuse to acknowledge your spurious title. And if you give me the Charter, and allow the duly elected council to reclaim its rightful land, I will gladly return your fiancée to your side.'

'Don't be a fool, man!' said Sir Oliver. 'You'll never get away with it! Let Penny go, and we'll say no more about it.'

'No, Mr Halton. Release the Charter, and we'll say no more

about this brazen occupation of council land.' He pushed the gun harder into Penny's temple.

'Sandahl!' said Whittaker, stepping forward. 'Sandahl! Don't do this. You can't win. Let her go.'

'Why, so you can pore all over *her* underthings? Don't think we don't know about you at the museum, Mr Whittaker, because we do.'

The whole population of Pancester turned and stared at Terry. Whittaker felt himself dying inside. This was the humiliation to end all humiliations. To have his sex life exposed to his friends. He stepped backwards. And his mobile rang.

'Hello?'

'Hello, boy. Hope I didn't catch you with your cock up?'

'Dad, this isn't a great moment.'

'No, son, this is the perfect moment. You need me. What did I teach you? Think!'

'Nothing really, Dad, to be honest.'

'Nothing, boy?'

'Well, except the plumber joke.'

'Then use it, son! Use it!'

'But, Dad . . .'

'Use it, boy! Tell him the joke!'

'OK . . . OK . . . tell Kenny Courtney we found Letty, Dad.'

'I will, son. Good luck. Tell it good.'

The line went dead, and Whittaker found the whole crowd still staring at him. He cleared his throat. 'Dr Sandahl. Wait. Let me tell you something I learned at my father's knee.' He held Sandahl's gaze with his own.

Sandahl sneered. 'Little good will it do without the Charter,' he said.

'No. Wait. It's important. Er . . . there was this bricklayer, you see. Wasn't very bright. Lived with his pet, a parrot. And one evening, just before bed, he noticed that one of the pipes in his bathroom was leaking. So he called his friend the plumber, who said that he would be there at ten the following morning. Well, come the morning, and the bricklayer has completely forgotten about the plumber's visit. So off he goes to work, leaving the parrot in charge. And at ten, of course, the plumber turns up, and knocks on the door.

"'OOIZZIT?" shouts the parrot.

"It's the plumber, come to fix the pipes."

"OOIZZIT?" shouts the parrot.

"It's the plumber, come to fix the pipes."

"OOIZZIT?" shouts the parrot.

"It's the plumber, come to fix the pipes."

"OOIZZIT?" shouts the parrot.

"It's the plumber, come to fix the pipes."

"OOIZZIT?" shouts the parrot.

"It's the plumber, come to fix the pipes."

"OOIZZIT?" shouts the parrot.

"It's the plumber, come to fix the pipes."'

Beads of sweat appeared on Sandahl's forehead, and the gun shook.

"'OOIZZIT?" shouts the parrot.

"It's the plumber, come to fix the pipes."

"OOIZZIT?" shouts the parrot.

"It's the plumber, come to fix the pipes."

"OOIZZIT?" shouts the parrot.

"It's the plumber, come to fix the pipes."

"OOIZZIT?" shouts the parrot.

"It's the plumber, come to fix the pipes."

"OOIZZIT?" shouts the parrot.

"It's the plumber, come to fix the pipes."'

A child started to sob, and was hurried away by his mother.

"'OOIZZIT?" shouts the parrot.

"It's the plumber, come to fix the pipes."

"OOIZZIT?" shouts the parrot.

"It's the plumber, come to fix the pipes."

"OOIZZIT?" shouts the parrot.

"It's the plumber, come to fix the pipes."

"OOIZZIT?" shouts the parrot.

"It's the plumber, come to fix the pipes."'

A woman in the crowd screamed in terror.

"'OOIZZIT?" shouts the parrot.

"It's the plumber, come to fix the pipes."

"OOIZZIT?" shouts the parrot.

"It's the plumber, come to fix the pipes."

"OOIZZIT?" shouts the parrot.

"It's the plumber, come to fix the pipes."

"OOIZZIT?" shouts the parrot.

"It's the plumber, come to fix the pipes."

"OOIZZIT?" shouts the parrot.

"It's the plumber, come to fix the pipes."

"OOIZZIT?" shouts the parrot.

"It's the plumber, come to fix the pipes."'

Sandahl's hand was shaking uncontrollably now, and the sweat dripped down his ruined face.

'Be careful, Terry,' whispered Gwyn.

But Whittaker was remorseless.

'"OOIZZIT?" shouts the parrot.

"It's the plumber, come to fix the pipes."

"OOIZZIT?" shouts the parrot.

"It's the plumber, come to fix the pipes."

"OOIZZIT?" shouts the parrot . . .'

'Oh, Mr Whittaker. You've just signed your death warrant . . .' said Sandahl through clenched teeth.

'No, Q!' screamed Juliana. But it was too late. He pulled the gun away from Penny's head to aim it at Whittaker, which was just long enough for Sir Oliver to lunge at Sandahl, knock the gun from his hand, and wrestle Penny from his grasp. Ronnie of the Pink Bus and Syd Montague-Forrester grabbed Q's arms, and Edith the donkey picked up the gun in her gentle mouth, and carried it to the banks of the river. With a movement of her head, she threw the revolver into the Athon. It disappeared with a plop.

'Fiendish, Mr Whittaker, fiendish,' said Q.

'Could some of you men nip off and release poor Inspector McCracken?' said Sir Oliver.

McCracken was fetched from the ruins of his Range Rover.

'Arrest this man, officer,' said Sir Oliver.

'What for?' said McCracken sulkily.

'For forcible abduction and possession of a firearm,' said Penny, clinging to Oliver's arm and rubbing her neck.

'Any witnesses?' said McCracken, looking sheepishly at Sandahl.

'Oh, don't be ridiculous, man,' said Lady Lettice. 'The whole city saw it. Take him away and put him in charge. My son and I will stop by later to make sure that you've done the thing properly.'

McCracken looked at Lady Letty's beard, and into Sandahl's burning eyes. 'Yes, Lady Lettice,' he said. He pulled out his handcuffs, and he and Sandahl walked away, chained reluctantly together.

'Q!' shouted Juliana. 'Q!!!'

Sandahl turned and looked at her. 'Do not worry, my dear. Many things can happen at a jury trial. I'll be back soon, you'll see!'

Juliana held her hands to her mouth, and started to follow her lover.

'Juliana! Wait!' Terry called to her, and she stopped. As she turned, Whittaker thought she had never looked more beautiful. Her tear-streaked face was still proud and defiant. Whittaker ran after her.

'What is it now?'

'Juliana. Now that we're not fighting any more, I want you to know that you're welcome to come to the 4i's whenever you like. And I was also wondering ... if you'd like to come out for a drink some time? I know lots of other jokes. And now that Q is locked up, and I've stood up to you instead of bothering you all the time, you can surely see, quite clearly, that I am the better man, and worthy of your love. And I did catch your apple, after all.'

Juliana's eyes narrowed, and she spat in Whittaker's face. 'And if you ever come near me again, I really will kill you,' she said.

Whittaker wiped the spittle from his face, and remembered how the animal rights protesters had sprayed Juliana. 'That's a no, then?' he said sadly.

'You really are stupid, aren't you?' said Juliana.

'Am I? All I did was love you.'

'No, you didn't. You don't know me, so how can you love me? I'm just one of your fantasies. Something for your head to wank over, that's all I am. Next time, just buy a porn mag, yeah? Save everyone a lot of shit.' And she turned on her heel after the retreating figures of McCracken and Sandahl.

'I tried that,' said Whittaker sadly, to her back. He thought of the first time he had seen her, helping on the desk in the Tourist Information Office, thought of his obsessive love for her and about how he had stolen a pair of her knickers, of the box with his Juliana lookalike porn. And he realised that she actually had tried to kill him, that she really did hate him, and that she probably had good reason. He shrugged to himself.

So Whittaker finally accepted that he hadn't got the girl, after all. He watched her sadly as she walked back alone over the Pack Bridge into the city, and felt the last of his dreams crumble away to dust.

And that was that.

Oh, well, he thought. Plenty more fish in the sea. Perhaps I'll meet someone who likes me next time. That'll make a change. Mind you, she did have a point.

We really could do with a new car park.

He walked off to find Sir Oliver.

Sir Oliver was looking for the Mayor. 'Ah, Mr Mayor, good afternoon. I wonder if you would be so kind as to lend me the Alarumist for a moment? To attract everyone's attention.'

'Of course, Sir Oliver. Geoffrey, if you would oblige us?' The Alarumist raised the Ramstheng to his lips, and sounded the great note, which rang around the site and silenced the crowds. Sir Oliver climbed up on the bulldozer, and began to speak again.

'Men and women of Pancester,' he said, 'today, we have won a great victory. The car park has been stopped!' And everyone, even those who had supported the project just hours before, started to clap and cheer. Sir Oliver smiled, and raised his hand for quiet.

'Thanks to your courage and forbearance, the people of

Pancester have once again held back the forces of change for change's sake. Most especially, the courage of my future wife, and that of our good friend Mr Terry Whittaker should be commended. Without their level-headedness, things could have been very much worse.' He pulled Penny to his side, and kissed her.

'Very much worse indeed. You will be glad to hear that my mother and I are committed to reopening Courtney House ...'

'Are we?' said Lady Letty. 'Well, he's the baronet, I suppose.' And she smiled proudly.

'... and to repositioning ourselves in the centre of this community, where we rightfully belong. And I pledge to you now that we will not rest in our beds until we have seen through the implementation of Mr Terry Whittaker's plan for a new transport infrastructure!' More clapping, and more cheering, and the Mayor shook Whittaker's hand.

'So, without further ado, let us return to our great annual contest! If anyone knows where the Wally has got to, that is!' Laughter as the crowd started to look on the ground for the roll of leather tied up with scarlet waxed string. No one could find it.

And this was because Gwyneth had found it ten minutes before, by her foot, where some over-excited Ringler must have dropped it to watch Sandahl's moment of madness.

'Sally,' Gwyneth had said quietly, from the corner of her mouth. 'Pick it up. Quickly. But don't let anyone see you. Good. Give it here.' Sally handed Gwyn the Wally, and she stuffed it up her sweatshirt. 'Now, let's just quietly walk away. That's it. Slowly and quietly walk away. Don't do anything that attracts attention.'

Sally and Gwyn stood on the Pack Bridge, and looked down at the Dole Acre. Thousands of people milled around between the smouldering buses, but they could just pick out Timmy Rubenstein and Neil Winterburn walking across to the Temple of Priapus to resume the excavation. They heard the Ramstheng ring out, as it had done every day in Pancester for more than a thousand years, and could just make out Sir Oliver's speech above the slow burble of the brown river.

336

'Look, they're all trying to find the Wally,' said Sally.

'Well, then, here goes nothing,' said Gwyn, and she produced the Wally from inside her jumper, and started to shout and wave it about. Some people near the entrance looked up, and saw her on the bridge.

'HEY! There it is!'

'That lass has got it! HEY!'

'Come on! Quick!' they shouted.

And Gwyneth started to run, and the Dole Acre started to empty as the Wallymen realised what was happening, and for the second time that day everyone in Pancester played follow-my-leader, only this time in reverse, as they raced back over the bridge and up through the city streets.

Gwyneth knew that she was a good runner, and that she had a good start, but it was a long way up West Street and through the Guildhall Square. And the Ringlers had some fast runners, and she could hear them gaining on her, as she entered Church Street and summoned her strength for the run up the steepest part of the hill. And they may well have caught her, but for the fact that the Clanghandlers had some fast runners too, who managed to catch most of the Ringler vanguard and bring them down in crunching tackles. And so, with the noise of battle behind her, and pursuing Ringlers and Clanghandlers almost on her heels, her heart pounding and her lungs fit to burst, Gwyneth Gabatini, the first woman ever to take part in Wally Oop, ran up Church Street, over St Gilbert's Green, and, with a body swerve that took her out of reach of the grasping hands that had almost caught up with her, she planted the Wally in the church porch.

It was over, and the Clanghandlers had won, for the first time since 1952. Gwyneth was hoisted on to her teammates' shoulders, and carried in triumph through the streets down to the Holly Bush, waving at the Clanghandlers and their supporters, who lined the streets and cheered until their throats were sore. Dawn and Sally and Taff held on to one another, and wept with pride as she was carried past them in the Guildhall Square.

'I always knew she'd be brilliant at it,' said Taff. 'It's the Welsh in her, see.'

'I don't follow,' said Sally.

'Rugby! The Welsh national game! Superb, she was. See her running with that Wally? She could play scrum-half for Wales, she could.'

'If she hadn't been born in England,' said Sally.

'To English parents, one of them of Italian extraction,' said Dawn.

'National identity is meaningless unless self-selected, my love,' said Taff with pride. 'You can be English if you like. But I am Welsh by choice, and that makes her eligible. Doesn't it?'

Later that evening, at the traditional post-Wally hog roast on the Guildhall steps, Whittaker was talking with his friends about the events of the last year and the campaign to stop the car park.

'Q worries me,' said Sally. 'I hope he goes down for a very long time indeed.'

'I wouldn't be so sure if I was you, Sal,' said Winterburn. 'He's a slippery customer, that one. We've not seen the last of him here in Pancester, you mark my words.'

'I tell you what worries me,' said Taff. 'It's all very well our Gwyneth winning the Wally, and Dad getting the Pancester Dole and that, but now the Ringlers get to stage the Mummers' play, and I won't be the Doctor next year.'

'Never mind, love,' said Dawn. 'You'll lose the Wally next time. The Clanghandlers haven't won it in successive years since 1902–3.'

Taff smiled. 'Aye, that's right enough, cariad. And the Ringlers are bound to make a pig's ear of the play.'

'What worries me,' said Gwyn, 'is that after all our attempts to get the car park stopped democratically, we had to rely on a couple of loopy old aristos to pull us out of the shit. I mean, I'm glad and that, but it was a bit sick to watch everyone fawning over them, and following them about like sheep. No offence, Lady Letty.'

'None taken, darling,' said Letty, yawning.

'Gwyneth!' said Papa Nico. 'Don't ever let me hear you speak like that again about your betters!'

'Your grandad's right, love,' said Taff. 'Pancester's always better with a Courtney in the New House.'

'Yes, but how come I've known him my whole life, and I've never heard him say more than three words together before today? And now suddenly, he's like this great orator,' said Gwyneth.

'Needs must where the devil drives, my dear,' said Mrs Innes. 'And he is a Courtney, you know.'

Martha and Dennis walked across hand in hand.

'Hello, you two lovebirds. How are you?' said Dawn.

Martha was smiling the smug smile of the sexually satisfied. 'Oh, Dawn,' she said. 'Dennis has asked me to marry him!'

Everyone stood up and shook hands with Dennis, and hugged Martha, who looked as though she was going to explode with joy.

'Of course,' she said, 'Dad's not going to like it. And the cats are going to have to go. But there. Everyone's entitled to a bit of happiness, I always say.'

'I never had you down as a ladies' man, Dennis,' said Whittaker. 'What's the secret?'

'Stand up straight, Mr Whittaker, and ask politely. And don't spare the brilliantine. Ladies can't resist a well-groomed man.'

'I still don't understand about the bicycle lamps,' said Professor Daggers.

'It's joost not cool to 'ave one,' said Gemma.

'But don't people get killed?' asked the old naturalist.

'Aye,' said Emma. 'But at least they die cool.'

'I'll tell you what's been worrying me,' said Syd, Lady Letty nestling into his shoulder. 'What happened with the bloody parrot?'

'Oh,' said Terry. 'The plumber, unable to stand any more, passes out in the porch of the house. And the bricklayer comes home drunk, and it's dark, and he falls over the plumber, and he says, "OOIZZIT?" and the parrot says, "IT'S THE PLUMBER, COME TO FIX THE PIPES."'

Syd whistled, as the friends groaned and held their heads.

'I've a good mind to kill you myself,' said Lady Letty. 'Where's that blessed gun?'

Phil the Painter, leaning on his stick, came over with Ash the Scrap Metal Man and a tall, dark-haired and curvaceous woman in her late thirties wearing leather trousers and a purple puffa jacket.

Whittaker realised with a jolt that he recognised her from somewhere. She was ... she had a certain ... there was something about her that ...

'Hello, all. What a day,' said Ash. 'I don't believe you've met my daughter, Rowena. She's just got off the train to come and stay with me for a few days. Funny time to pick, with the van all smashed up. But we'll manage somehow.'

'Hello,' said Rowena with a West Country burr, smiling around at the friends. 'I've heard all about you.'

'Hello, Rowena,' said Terry brightly, his heart beating with newborn passion. 'Are you married? You can come and stay with us in the flat if you like, while your dad does up the van. We've got plenty of room.'

Rowena went white, and said, 'Terry?'

'Yes?'

'You're Terry?'

'Yes?'

'Don't you recognise my voice? You used to call me on the phone. I recognised yours at once.'

Whittaker thought of his experiments in phone sex, and wondered that the girl could remember him from one call.

'Oh. I'm ... er ... I'm sorry it was so short. But thank you, anyway.'

'Short? We talked for ages. Don't you remember? The Truckers' Helpline? When you said I should write a book? You never phoned me back.'

'Oh, my God! That was you?'

'Yes! I was hoping you'd call for ages. I've left the Helpline now. I've written the book, and I've just got an agent. I owe it all to you, Terry.'

'I love you, Rowena,' said Whittaker.

'Terry!' said Sally sharply. 'Don't go too fast!'

Rowena laughed. 'I don't mind at all,' she said. 'I'm looking forward to getting to know you better, Terry.'

'Now, that's what I call ironic,' said Phil the Painter. Terry blushed.

'It seems to me, Mr Whittaker,' said Mrs Innes, 'that we all owe you a great deal. We couldn't have done any of this without you. You kept our spirits up when our heads were dropping, you paid all the bills, you were marvellous in the meetings with all that stuff about reducing car use in Pancester, and then to top it all you found Lady Lettice, and brought her back to us.'

'And saved my life with that horrible joke,' said Penny.

'Hear, hear,' said Letty. 'And you found my son for me. I will always be grateful to you, Terry.' She hugged Sir Oliver, who smiled happily. Dexter Halton stood up and proposed a toast.

'To Terry Whittaker. Our friend and fellow Pancestrian!'

And the friends all stood, and raised their paper cups full of the hot mulled wine that is always served on Wally Night. 'To Terry. Friend and fellow Pancestrian!'

'Thank you. Thank you very much. But there's one thing that still puzzles me.'

'Oh, and what's that, Terry?' asked Lady Lettice.

'The mushrooms. I took one this morning, and nothing seemed to happen to me. A bit of an anticlimax after the build-up Syd and Steve gave them.'

'Well, that is strange, Terry,' said Lady Lettice. 'Look what happened to me,' and she stroked her beard. 'But you know, as we journey down life's highway together, thank you Ronnie' (this to someone passing her a microphone) 'now and again all sorts of strange things happen that we can't explain.' From behind Whittaker a drum kit started up. He spun round. Taff was there, kicking up a little backbeat on his kit, which had appeared from out of nowhere.

'You see, Terry,' crooned Lady Lettice into the mike, 'life is hard, and when we want everything explained, all we are doing is chaining ourselves to the wheel of birth and death, the wheel of pain.' Whittaker looked around him again, and saw Sir Oliver pick up a bass and start to set up a little groove with Taff.

'In this wonderful universe in which we live,' said Letty, 'some things just can't be explained, however much we might want them to be.' Suddenly Gwyneth and Sally cut through the funky beat with some fat wah-wah guitar chops, and Dexter came in on some congas, and Neil Winterburn cooked a stewing little brew whilst seated at a Hammond organ. Stevie Medlicott, Penny Lester, Syd and Mrs Innes formed a happening horn section, Mrs Innes' hands flashing as she manipulated the slide on her trombone.

'So instead of asking for what we want, we should maybe try finding out what we need,' chanted Lady Lettice. Whittaker swung around again to see Martha and Dennis and Timmy Rubenstein and Dawn and Sandra Medlicott and Papa Nico and Ronnie of the Pink Bus and Phil the Painter and Ash the Scrap Metal Man and his enchanting sexy daughter with beautiful eyes and dark straight hair and a figure to kill for, and Brian Carless and Aolderwoman Armistead and Emma and Gemma and Edith and Katherine the donkeys plucking and bowing at violins and cellos until, with a great whooooosh, Lady Lettice kicked into 'You Can't Always Get What You Want', and everybody else, the whole population of Pancester, who were packed into the Guildhall Square, started swaying and singing the choir part with an overwhelming angelic 'Aaaaah'.

Well, the mushrooms may be overrated, thought Terry, but I love it here anyway. This is my home now. And these are my friends. And that's weird, because I didn't want a new home, or a load of new friends, or I didn't think so, anyway. That wasn't what I was looking for, when I first came here. I just wanted something different, something new to try for a bit, to get away from London and my dad for a few weeks.

That was all I wanted.

But, like the song says, sometimes, if you're lucky, you get what you need.